MURDER AT RAVEN'S HOLLOW

LOUISE MARLEY

Copyright © Louise Marley, 2025

The moral right of the author has been asserted.

To request permissions, contact the publisher at rights@stormpublishing.co

Ebook ISBN: 978-1-80508-396-2
Paperback ISBN: 978-1-80508-398-6

Cover design: Ghost
Cover images: Shutterstock

Published by Storm Publishing.
For further information, visit:
www.stormpublishing.co

ALSO BY LOUISE MARLEY

Murder at Raven's Edge
Murder at Ravenswood House

For my parents,
who would have been thrilled to see this series take shape,
who would have had the very best time suggesting names for the
cafés and animals,
and who would have forced copies of the books onto everyone
they knew...

PROLOGUE

Twenty-five years ago...

The dream always began the same way.

Fish finger sandwiches for tea (slightly charred), while their mother loaded her little car with one large suitcase, two buckets and spades, and a deflated blue dolphin. Mum locked the front door, waved to old Mrs Moore across the square, who knew absolutely everything about everyone, and then they were off, weaving in and out of the rush-hour traffic and singing along to Britney, Christina, and P!nk.

'Are we there?' her little brother asked, as soon as they'd left the city.

She rolled her eyes. She'd seen the map. She knew the trip was going to take at least two and a half hours. She'd already asked.

'Soon, darling, soon,' Mum replied.

'Are we there?' he asked, as they eventually left the motorway and lurched along a series of winding lanes.

Mum laughed. 'Almost.'

'Are we there?' he asked, as the car was swallowed by a deep, dark forest.

Mum turned in her seat, her ponytail swinging. 'Not long now,' she smiled. 'Do you see the river?' She pointed through the passenger window. 'Look down to the bottom of the slope.'

They could see the river glinting silver through the trees, so they nodded, but without enthusiasm. It felt as though they'd been driving for ever.

'That river leads straight to the beach. Keep a close eye on it. You'll see kayaks at first. As the river becomes wider, there'll be dinghies and yachts and pleasure boats. The bigger the boats, the closer you are to the sea.'

Both children stared hard at the river. There were no boats to be seen, only a few bored-looking seagulls. Her brother's eyes began to close.

Mum winked at her in the rear-view mirror.

It was hypnotic watching the river curve leisurely between the trees. The distance to the opposite bank slowly widened. There were still no boats. Maybe it was too late in the day? The fading sunlight bounced off the water, hurting her eyes, so she turned her attention to the other window and the forest.

It was then that she saw the monster.

It flew out of the dark wood and ran alongside the car, its eyes glowing white fire.

She screamed, even though she knew it couldn't really be there.

'Darling,' Mum soothed, turning her head, 'what on earth is the—'

A loud bang rocked the car. The windscreen shattered like a spider's web.

(This was the part where the nightmare began.)

Mum slumped over the steering wheel. Without her to guide it, the car lurched off the road, tilted and began to roll. Over and over. Faster and faster.

Branches scraped the side of the car with an ear-splitting shriek. Her head smacked into something hard. She saw stars, but they weren't real. None of this was real.

She felt it was important to remember that.

'It's only a dream, only a dream, only a dream...'

There was an explosion of white.

The car stopped spinning. Her world shifted into something calmer. The air was thick and hot, sound was muffled.

Her brother was screaming.

Her mother was silent.

'Mum? Mum!'

The front of the car had filled with water. It was lapping at the dashboard and around the gear stick. Her brother still cried, but quietly now, as though he knew no one was coming.

She tried to open the door but it was jammed, even when she swivelled around in her seat and kicked it. She banged her fist on the window... and that's when she saw him.

A man on the edge of the riverbank, staring as though he didn't know what was real either.

She slammed her palm against the window. 'Help us!'

Why didn't he do something?

What was wrong with him?

Was he just going to walk away?

ONE

Present Day

14th December

The village of Raven's Edge glittered prettily with frost, a slight dusting of snow on the thatched roofs, the gaps between the cobblestones glinting with ice. Wreaths of holly hung on every door, and later, when it grew dark, each window would be outlined by fairy lights. Yet beneath the charm of the crooked cottages and narrow alleyways, there was always an impression that something sinister lurked amongst the shadows, something dark yet elusive. An indefinable 'something' that the inhabitants made a very good living from.

Detective Sergeant Harriet March had grown up in Raven's Edge. She knew every story and where the truth met the lie in each one. Now she lived in what had once been the servants' quarters of the largest house on The Square. Five hundred years ago the house would have been occupied by someone important. Now it was home to Foxglove & Hemlock, a florist that specialised in lavish decorations for fashion shoots and film sets, but still found time to sell pretty Gothic posies to the tourists.

The owners, Amelia Locke and Gabriel Fox, lived in the apartment beneath Harriet's. They were quiet, kept to themselves and were never any trouble, which was all Harriet required from her neighbours. It was always an inconvenience to arrest someone she knew.

This morning Harriet was standing at her stove eating scrambled eggs straight from the pan, unable to settle, unable to relax, not quite sure what to do with herself, because today was her first day off since... Well, she couldn't remember. Several high-profile murder cases back-to-back had kept her and the Murder Investigation Team busy throughout the summer and into autumn. An entire day stretched out before her with absolutely nothing to do and, quite frankly, it was terrifying.

As her brother Ryan had once said, 'Harriet, you need a hobby – one that doesn't involve dead bodies.'

She'd laughed, as he'd meant her to, but his words had stung. When did she have *time* to cultivate a hobby? She worked, she ate, she slept. She read two books a week and occasionally went to the pub with her best friend Sam King, also a police officer. And she liked to cook – providing it didn't involve more than five ingredients, one saucepan and thirty minutes. Wasn't that enough 'hobby' for anyone?

Finishing the scrambled egg, she dropped the pan into the sink, where it joined the saucepan and crockery from last night's dinner (she wasn't a great fan of washing-up), before making a barista-grade cappuccino in the fancy machine she'd bought after spotting one exactly like it in the kitchen of a recent murder victim.

OK, maybe she did need a hobby.

The coffee machine caused the kitchen window to steam up, so she wiped the sleeve of her sweater across the glass. The sky was a brilliant cerulean blue and the sun high enough to sparkle on the frost. It was going to be a beautiful day. When had she last enjoyed a sunny day? To go outside and just *be*, rather than sprint down the street after another suspect?

Was it sad that she couldn't remember?

She pulled a pink wool coat over her cable-knit sweater and leggings, scooped up her coffee and newest book, and left the apartment. Even at five foot four she had to duck to step onto the tiny sloping staircase that led to the ground floor and use her shoulder to shove forcefully at the squat but heavy oak door that opened onto the large garden behind the house.

The sunlight had melted the frost on the decking but it glistened on the shaggy, overgrown lawn. She placed her coffee on the wooden table, careful to use a ceramic coaster (Amelia was irritatingly particular about coasters) and sat in one of the Adirondack chairs, which was too low, and too slanted, and would take too much effort to get out of again, but then Amelia had always been more about aesthetics than comfort.

While the pale green decking resembled something out of a lifestyle magazine, with its trailing ivy and terracotta tubs of Christmas roses, the garden beyond was a tangled wilderness that Harriet never dared venture into in case she couldn't find her way out again. She knew little about shrubs and flowers (apart from the obvious ones), and at this time of year everything looked dead anyway, but she couldn't help feeling there was something that had been there before but now... wasn't.

Decking, pot plants, furniture—

Wait...

Where was the *fence*?

Three six-foot panels of feather-edge fence, which bordered the east side of the garden, had been removed overnight, along with the gate, exposing the garden to the lane where they parked their cars. It seemed a strange thing to do, but then Amelia and Gabriel often did things that made no sense and Harriet had long given up trying to work out why.

Not that it was any of her business. She was going to sit here and read her book until her fingers went numb, and then she'd relocate to her sofa. If she was really bored, she'd visit her mother, who'd pretend to be pleased to see her and offer life advice, along the lines of: 'When I was your age I had a business of my own and two children under five, and had already buried one husband and was about to bury a second,' as though it was something to aspire to.

But maybe it wouldn't have to come to that.

Harriet settled back in the chair and took a sip of coffee. Hot, creamy, sugary... *perfect*. That machine had been *such* a good investment. The sun was warm on her face, the garden idyllically quiet, apart from a persistent, irritating beeping, and—

A shadow fell over the decking, blocking the sun and causing a sudden chill. She looked up. Gabriel Fox was standing in front of her. All sharp cheekbones, shiny black hair and a too-wide grin; in his cotton trousers and cable-knit sweater (rather too similar to her own), he looked as though he should be presenting a television programme on gardening, rather than getting his hands dirty actually doing some.

'Hey, Harry!'

She did hate it when people called her 'Harry'.

'Your car is fine,' he said.

That focused her attention. 'Why wouldn't it be fine?'

Anyone that knew her would, at this point, be very careful what they said next.

Gabriel merely grinned. 'Exactly! So there's nothing to worry about.'

Harriet's car was parked in the lane. She couldn't see it from here but, over his shoulder, she *could* see a lorry backing into the space where the fence should have been. The cause of that persistent, irritating 'beep, beep, beep', no doubt.

Wait.

Hold on.

A lorry carrying a skip?

Something must have shown in her expression because Gabriel cleared his throat and said, slightly more guardedly, 'As I said, your car—'

She got up and pushed past him. Any detective who believed everything anyone told her was a fool who deserved to be shifted to Traffic.

'*Harry!*' he called plaintively but she ignored him, squeezing between the lorry and what remained of the fence, and running into the narrow lane.

It had been late when she'd arrived home last night, as always, and very dark because the lane had no lighting. She couldn't quite remember where she'd parked Little Red.

The lorry seemed about to drop the skip carelessly into the gap where the fence had been. Beside the gap was Gabriel's mud-splattered Land Rover, with Amelia's MG next to it. Way, way, *way* down the lane, practically under the trees, thankfully, was Harriet's beloved MX-5.

'I did *try* to tell you!' Gabriel caught up, slightly out of breath. He needed to come out from behind his desk and do more gardening. 'See, nothing to worry about! If the skip was to hit anything, it'd be *my* car.'

He thought that was reassuring?

'Gabriel, next time lead with, "Hi, Harriet, I'm having a skip delivered today, but don't worry because *it'll be nowhere near Little Red*"!'

The confusion was evident on his handsome face. 'Isn't that what I said?'

'No!' She turned back towards the decking. 'Honestly, Gabriel. You know how I feel about my car.'

'Yes, which was why—'

'What do you need a skip for anyway?'

'We're having a clear-out.' He fell into step beside her. 'The glasshouse was full of junk left by the last owner.'

'Glasshouse?' Was that posh for greenhouse? She didn't come into the garden very often but she was sure she would have noticed if Amelia and Gabriel had a greenhouse. 'What glasshouse?'

'Beneath the trees,' – he waved in the direction of the forest that seemed to loom closer every time Harriet looked at it – 'in front of the wall, you know?'

No, she didn't. 'There's a wall?'

He huffed. 'I admit the garden needs work, hence the skip. I've got to supervise delivery but if you want to take a look, follow the stepping stones to the right of the magnolia tree and the statue of Aphrodite.'

It sounded like directions to pirate treasure. Harriet might not be able to distinguish a magnolia tree from any other tree or shrub, but she could see a sorry-looking slab of stone, roughly carved into the shape of a woman, half-hidden beneath the long-dead grass, with stepping stones leading away from it.

Stepping stones had to lead somewhere. That was the rule.

The truck started up again.

'I've got to go.' He thumbed towards the truck. 'Go take a look. Amelia is down there. She'd love to show you around.'

Amelia and Gabriel must have even fewer hobbies than her, if they were this excited over a greenhouse. But, as promised, the paving slabs led between the shrubs and under the trees, emerging onto a small patio in front of a stark, rusting structure that resembled a giant birdcage. Was this the glasshouse?

Brown leather furniture had been piled up beside the door, presumably waiting to be loaded into that skip, along with several boxes of what Ben, Harriet's boss, would have politely described as bric-a-brac and she would have called junk.

'Hi, Harriet. I thought I saw you coming up the path.' Amelia emerged from the skeleton of the glasshouse, wiping filthy hands on equally filthy dungarees. She had nut-brown hair, elegantly swirled up on top of her head, and large hazel eyes that never missed a thing. 'You've picked a lovely day to come into the garden. Has Gabriel sent you to see our glasshouse? He's so proud of it. We had no idea it was here when we took over the business.'

Could it be called a glasshouse if there was no longer any glass?

'Wasn't it shown on the plans?' Harriet asked.

'The boundary is marked but the forest has been taking over the garden for years, so the glasshouse was completely hidden. It's in good condition, minus the glass, so we're going to restore it.'

'That'll be a lot of work.' Harriet stared at the forlorn ruin. She could have sworn she heard the glasshouse creak, which was not reassuring now she was standing right next to it. Large and circular, maybe it *had* been beautiful once – she appreciated the elegantly curving lines that remained – but there wasn't a single pane of glass left and the forest had completely grown around it, entombing it.

It gave her the creeps.

'We're not sure how old the glasshouse is,' Amelia was saying. 'Possibly early Victorian? It might have been an orangery. Gabriel has been in touch with a firm that specialises in this kind of renovation. They're going to make a start after Christmas. I just have to clear it first. It will be a fabulous place to sit and relax next spring. Would you like a look?'

No, I would not like to go inside your creepy old greenhouse, thank you.

'Um... that's very kind of you but—'

Amelia laughed. 'It's perfectly safe! There's no glass and the structure's firmer than it looks. I've been working inside all morning without a single mishap. It has an amazing vibe, almost as though it's alive.'

That was hardly a selling point.

Ten-year-old Harriet would have loved to hide in a derelict glasshouse but as an adult she had a stronger sense of self-preservation, and she should have said so. For when she took too long to answer, Amelia linked an arm through hers and pulled her through the door.

'Come on, it'll be fun!'

It was like walking into a cave. The air was unpleasant: stale, with the sweet scent of rot. It was colder out of the sunlight, and everything was tinged with a strange green light. Harriet glanced up. Growing through the remains of the roof were tree branches and ropes of ivy as thick as her wrist.

It was the perfect setting for a horror movie, but for relaxing with a book on a sunbed? Not so much.

The ground had been paved with red bricks, laid in a pretty starburst pattern around what had once been oval flowerbeds, but the bricks were mossy and the flowerbeds filled with dead weeds, and everything was coated with the glitter of tiny shards of glass. Amelia had lugged most of the rubbish outside, but Harriet could still see the overflowing boxes of someone's once-cherished possessions. She spotted a framed photo in the dirt and picked it up. It was of a toddler sitting on a toy pony on wheels. It could have dated back to the 1990s.

She held it up. 'Doesn't the last owner want these back?'

Amelia shrugged. 'He told me to chuck everything into the skip.'

'Charming.' Harriet put the photo frame into one of the boxes.

'Some of the bricks in the floor are missing. They'll need to be replaced. I might pave over the flower beds at the same time. It would be a shame, but I need the space for my larger arrangements. What do you think? Pave or keep?'

Harriet was more bothered about whether her cappuccino was getting cold, but politely turned towards the flower bed where Amelia had been digging. Whatever had been planted there was now a mountain of dead stuff on the path; only bare earth remained, with a neat pile of tea-coloured sticks beside an ominous hole.

Harriet did a double take.

Damn.

On her day off too.

She pointed to the sticks and said, as casually as she could, 'What's that?'

Amelia grimaced. 'As well as using the glasshouse to store rubbish, I think someone buried their pet dog here.'

Harriet leant over the flower bed for a closer look.

Amelia (being Amelia) had taken each bone out of the ground, carefully knocked off the loose soil and created a well-ordered stack on one side. There were lots of little disarticulated bones and one long, distinctive one. Had she really not got a clue?

Harriet dug her phone from her pocket and switched on the torch, shining it directly onto the bones. 'I don't think that was a dog, Amelia.'

'A horse? Some of the bones are quite big. How long do you think it's been here?'

'No idea.' But not over one hundred years, unfortunately, which would have conveniently made it someone else's problem.

She took a few photos, close-up and long-range, and sent them to Ben.

Amelia peered over her shoulder. 'What are you doing?'

'Taking photos to send to my boss.'

'Detective Inspector Taylor? Why would he be interested?'

Did Amelia really have no idea what she'd dug up? Had she never watched a TV murder mystery or a true-crime show?

Harriet straightened to deliver the bad news.

'I'm sorry, Amelia. I've got to call it in.'

'Call what in? What are you talking about?'

Harriet's phone beeped a response from Ben: *Are you trying to find us extra work?*

She tucked her phone back into her pocket. 'They're not animal bones.'

Amelia continued to regard her blankly.

'They're *human*.'

TWO

Detective Inspector Ben Taylor had often bought flowers from Foxglove & Hemlock, usually for his girlfriend Milla, but like most of the shops in Raven's Edge, he'd never bothered looking beyond the elegant storefront. The house was larger than he would have thought, a mellow stone building three storeys high – taller than most of the dwellings in the village and treble the width.

As it was coming up to Christmas, there were red-potted spruce trees on either side of the entrance steps. A large wreath of holly and fir, decorated with cones and cinnamon sticks, hung on the door. In this, at least, Foxglove & Hemlock's decorations were traditional.

Other wreaths had been propped against a slatted wooden table beneath the window, ready for the Christmas Market, with thick bunches of holly, mistletoe and fir piled along the top.

It was a beautifully festive display and Ben's fingers itched to buy something to decorate his cottage, but he already had a wreath for his door courtesy of Gloria Lancaster, the little old lady next door to him who'd been a great friend of his late grandmother. Even though Mrs Lancaster didn't really approve of him since his divorce, he still found the occasional gift from her garden left on his doorstep, and she was always offering to babysit his daughter.

Sophie was probably the only reason Mrs Lancaster still deigned to talk to him.

Putting down the spray of holly he'd picked up (he could hardly turn up to a crime scene with it), Ben walked up the short flight of stone steps to the shop, only to be faced with a large cardboard sign taped on the door that said:

POLICE

with an arrow underneath, pointing left.

In other words, no shortcuts through the shop.

He sighed and dropped back to the pavement.

A muddy lane ran between the florist and the gift shop beside it, petering out as it met the encroaching forest. He recognised Harriet's beloved MX-5 parked at the end, a black MG behind it, along with a Land Rover so filthy it was hard to determine what colour it was.

Between the three cars and the high street was a line of small white vans used by the Force's Crime Scene Investigators, as well as the distinctive blue BMW driven by Lucia Serrano, a forensic archaeologist invited to attend whenever bones were discovered where they shouldn't be. The forensic anthropologist would have been contacted too but he usually said 'Send me a photo' to confirm the bones were human and just waited for them to turn up in his lab.

The garden behind the florist was a jungle of overgrown and mostly dead shrubs. Ben showed his warrant card to the officer on the cordon and collected a sealed pack containing a scene suit from a box on the ground. The owners had built wooden decking along the length of the house. There was no roof, so it could hardly be called a veranda, but it was prettily painted in pale green with little lights wound around the banister and edging the steps. There were dozens of pots of white heather, Christmas roses and green skimmia, under-planted with bulbs that were beginning to poke through the frosty soil.

A few feet from the back door was a low wooden table with two Adirondack chairs pulled up beside it. Harriet was sitting in one, the sunlight glinting on her blonde curls. She was sipping something from a mug that was undoubtedly coffee, a fat hardback book on the table beside her. Outwardly she seemed relaxed, but from the way one finger was tapping on the edge of her mug, he could tell she was desperate to be on the other side of the police tape stretching across the lawn.

It was strange to see her wearing a pink coat and black leggings instead of a trouser suit but then he never usually saw her outside of work.

He never saw any of the Murder Investigation Team outside of work.

'Good morning, DS March.' He climbed the two steps onto the decking. 'Isn't this taking working from home a little too far?'

'No coffee for *you*,' she grinned back.

He leant one hip against the banister to pull on the scene suit. Harriet tactfully looked in the opposite direction, having witnessed him struggle before. He liked to believe it was his height that made him so unsteady on one leg. Harriet had already told him his sense of balance was rubbish.

'Will you cancel your day off?' he asked, carefully tucking his blond hair into the hood.

That brought her attention right back.

'What for?' It was as though he'd suggested abseiling down the church steeple. 'When was the last time *I* had a day off?'

'I'm sorry, that wasn't meant the way it came out.' He

pointed to the hardback book, which featured an illustration of swords and flowers on its cover. 'You don't appear to be doing anything else...'

'I was reading that while I waited for *you*. I have my day completely planned out. Loads of stuff to do. Super busy.' She put her mug down rather too heavily. It hit the table with a thud and foam splashed over the edge. 'I wanted to hear what Lucia had to say. It will save you having to repeat everything tomorrow.'

That was the excuse she was going with?

'You could have asked her?'

'Lucia wanted to wait for the Senior Investigating Officer. She was expecting to brief you and had to make do with me. She's now in a mood.'

'You were the first officer on the scene.'

'*I'm* only a detective sergeant.'

'That makes no difference—'

'Tell that to Lucia. Both of us know that,' – she paused to smirk – 'but when it comes down to it, I don't think rank *really* matters to her.'

'Then why—'

'Basically, Lucia likes you better than me – and she's heard on the grapevine that you're single...'

Ben kept his expression neutral but inwardly groaned. 'Then she heard wrong.'

'You and Milla are still together?'

Did she *have* to sound so sceptical?

'Yes!'

Mostly...

After a row six weeks ago, causing an almost irrevocable split, it had been Milla's idea to go back to the beginning and get to know each other as friends before resuming their relationship. She was right but it didn't make the time they spent apart any easier.

'If you want to enter the inner cordon with me, you'll have to suit up.' His words came out sharper than he'd intended.

'Too late. My hair, clothing fibres, everything, are already all over it.'

'Did you touch anything?'

Her eyes narrowed. 'Do I look like a rookie?'

'That's not the point, Harriet. You're on the database, like everyone else. We can exclude you. But humour me, please? Put on a suit.'

There was a great deal of huffing as she went to collect one, then took off the pink coat and pulled the scene suit over her sweater and leggings.

'What do we know?' he asked, as she ducked under the tape and led the way across the lawn, following a series of stepping stones into the most overgrown part of the garden.

'Nothing about the body so far. He, or she, is completely skeletonised. The remains were found by Amelia Locke – my landlady – who owns the house, the garden and the floristry business with her partner, Gabriel Fox.'

'Business or romantic partner?'

'Business – as to the other, I've never liked to ask! I know they met at college, and they live together on the floor beneath me, but I don't know if they share a bedroom. They're friendly towards each other, and obviously affection-ate, but not necessarily in a romantic way. It could be because they're typically British and not demonstrative in public, or maybe they've been together so long some of the magic has gone.'

The 'magic' has gone? He watched Harriet stride out along the stepping stones. Was that how she saw romantic relation-ships? That after a few months, or even years, the 'magic' disap-peared? Then again, she was five years younger than him and he didn't think she'd dated in the entire year he'd known her.

Why was that?

It was hardly a question he could ask, so instead, 'How long have Amelia and Gabriel owned Foxglove & Hemlock?'

'About two years. Before that, the florist was owned by the Kinsella family, although Gabriel's mother, Hestia Fox, was the manager here until five years ago. When the opportunity came up for Gabriel and Amelia to buy the business, they jumped at it. They've made a real success of the shop, adapting it to the vibe and personality of the village.'

The locals did like to play up the quirky folklore of Raven's Edge.

'Do Amelia and Gabriel own the house too?' he asked.

'I assume so, but I can ask Dakota to check?'

DC Dakota Lawrence was the member of their team who usually had anything involving more than a basic internet search shoved in her direction.

'Could you also ask Dakota to check the names of all the previous owners and occupiers?'

'Dakota's already on it.' Harriet's tone flattened into a familiar 'don't tell me how to do my job' voice.

Back to a less contentious topic: 'You said Amelia found the remains?'

'They've recently discovered a greenhouse they didn't know they had – I know, right? – and they've been clearing it out ready for a firm who specialise in renovations to begin work in January.'

'How do you "find" a greenhouse in your own garden?'

Harriet glanced back and grinned. 'Have you seen the state of the garden? I don't think anyone's been beyond the decking in years. Amelia and Gabriel are far too busy with work, although Amelia did say the greenhouse wasn't marked on any plans.'

'The plan would be with the deeds,' he said. 'Every time the house changed hands, a plan with clear boundaries would have been drawn up. Hopefully this won't be our problem, if the remains are over a hundred years old.'

'Yes... About that. As the CSIs tracked back and forth past my chair, I got the distinct impression they believe the remains aren't that old.'

'Damn, I was hoping to have a peaceful lead-up to Christmas...'

'Then you're in the wrong job.'

Before he could think up a comeback, Harriet had vanished between two huge bay trees that might have once been clipped into spheres, but were now so overgrown they met across the path.

Gritting his teeth, Ben turned sideways and forced his way through, falling out onto a small paved area. The stones were old, perhaps re-purposed from the house, and formed a base for the rusted dome in front of him. He'd never seen such a thing. It was like a giant birdcage, perfectly round, with a stone base and what were once elegantly arched windows and a curving roof. Several large trees had grown up around it and through it, their branches weaving in and out of the flaking metalwork, which creaked in a disconcerting way.

Whatever it was, it looked as though it was missing a horror film.

'Bloody hell!'

'I *know!*' was Harriet's gleeful response. 'Isn't it *horrible*? If it were mine, I'd pull it down and sell it for scrap metal, but Amelia's called in fancy renovation specialists.'

If Amelia and Gabriel did have money to burn – in which case, their business must be doing very well – the glasshouse would be stunning when it was finished. Now, however...

There was more police tape barring a gap that was possibly an entrance, but no sign of anyone inside or out. With no one to stop him, Ben lifted the tape and ducked beneath it, coming face-to-face with the forensic archaeologist, who looked as though she'd been about to come out. Her look of surprise quickly rearranged into one of warm pleasure.

'Ben! How lovely to see you again!'

'Hello, Lucia.' He held up the tape to allow Harriet to follow him. As usual, she nipped in behind him, keen not to miss a thing.

Lucia's bobbed black hair and light-brown skin were almost completely hidden by the forensic suit and mask she wore, but her dark eyes crinkled at the corners as she beamed delightedly at him.

He attempted a polite smile in return.

Behind him, Harriet turned a strange choking sound into a cough.

'What do you have for us, Lucia?' he asked.

'Well, your victim is definitely dead!'

Why did those who worked with the deceased have such a peculiar sense of humour?

'Human?'

'Oh yes. Unusual though. We don't get many skeletons in the King's Forest District. Not fresh ones, anyway.'

Fresh?

'Quite a few Saxon burials have popped up over the years, and then there was that skeleton in Calahurst last year, which caused a bit of a stir as you can imagine, until someone spotted its top hat had "Happy Halloween" written on it!'

His lips quirked.

He shouldn't have shown weakness. She took a step closer.

He took a step back, pretending to take a look around the interior. It was a shame, because Lucia came across as a kind-hearted, bubbly person, but for some reason she'd become fixated on him – something that had not gone unnoticed by his team.

The luscious tropical plants the glasshouse had once been stocked with were now dried and withered. Amelia had begun yanking them out and piling them into a wheelbarrow, next to a cluster of cardboard boxes overflowing with bric-a-brac. Had the glasshouse – open to the elements – been used for storage? No wonder the boxes were disintegrating.

'Any clue as to how the remains ended up here?'

Hopefully *not* in one of those cardboard boxes.

'Nope,' she said cheerfully. 'Come this way and I'll give you a tour.'

When he hesitated, Harriet prodded him in the back.

Lucia led them to one of the central flower beds, which were laid out in a circular pattern, almost like petals. As she'd carefully removed the soil to expose the bones, she'd created a long rectangular trench. It looked exactly like an open grave.

The glasshouse was such a strange place to bury a body. Why not use the forest? It was big enough for the remains to have never been found – if they were buried deep enough. Perhaps that was the problem? Unless the murder had been premeditated, who carried around a shovel ready to dig a six-foot grave?

Burying the remains here, however, meant suspicion would automatically fall on the owner of the property – or their immediate neighbour. This made his investigation easier – unless someone had deliberately intended it that way?

'The remains are completely skeletonised, as you can see.' Lucia pointed to the top of the trench, where she'd carefully brushed away the soil covering the upper half of a skeleton, including a grinning skull. 'They've been in situ for several years, most likely over ten, possibly even longer. We'll send some samples away for carbon-14 testing, but I suspect that won't give you the more precise answer you're looking for.'

'It could take weeks to get the results back.'

'Yes, I know. I'm sorry. You might have more luck using DNA to aid identification, especially if the victim was local.'

That would also take many weeks, Ben thought. They

weren't going to have this investigation concluded before Christmas.

'As you can see, it was quite a shallow grave, and at some point animals may have discovered the remains. The Crime Scene Manager will update you on what they've found and her team will be going over the site again to be certain, but many of the smaller bones appear to be missing.'

There was an image he didn't want in his head.

'Do you have any good news?'

'A grave was deliberately dug for the body. It was placed neatly inside, the grave was refilled with the original soil, and a large tropical plant placed on top. I've found a twenty-pence coin, dated 1984, in the soil just below the bones. This would imply that the remains have been there for less than forty years...'

Harriet sighed. 'Our case then.'

'Unless the body was moved from elsewhere,' Lucia said gently.

Harriet wasn't going to let that go. 'Or the murderer deliberately planted the coin.'

In Ben's experience, murderers weren't usually that forward-thinking, particularly those acting in the heat of the moment, but there was always a first time.

'Once we remove the skeleton, we may find more evidence relating to the tools used to dig the grave,' Lucia said, 'but at the moment there's little trace evidence, which will make your work extra tricky. As you can see, the body was buried naked, with all its teeth pulled out. Either they had really bad dental hygiene...'

'Or someone did it to conceal the identity,' Harriet said.

'Exactly!'

Terrific.

'Murder,' Ben said, not that he'd suspected any different.

'He'd hardly bury himself,' Harriet muttered.

Lucia winked. 'You'd be surprised.'

Ben thought about that for far too long.

'*Is* the victim male?' Harriet asked.

'From the shape of the skull, the jawbone, eye cavities and so on, yes, I believe the remains to be male. He'll be reassembled and you'll be officially informed as to his estimated height, race, age and sex, which will help you with the identification, and possible cause of death, of course.'

Ta da, Ben thought. If only it were that easy. He might not often see eye-to-eye with his ex-wife Caroline, who was the Force's forensic pathologist, but at times like this, he missed her blunt pessimism.

Harriet leant closer to the trench. 'He has a hole in the back of his head. Wouldn't that do it?'

Lucia's cheery demeanour cracked slightly. 'I'm sure the forensic anthropologist will check for any signs of trauma, and clues as to whether they're ante-mortem, peri-mortem or post-mortem. He'll also carry out a full examination of the bones back at his lab.'

If they'd been looking at a fresh corpse rather than an old skeleton, and Caroline had been present, Harriet would have been given an icy put-down.

Ben quickly said his thanks and his goodbyes, ignoring Lucia's look of disappointment, and shepherded Harriet outside.

It was good to be back in the sunshine again, even if the temperature wasn't much above freezing. The greenhouse had a foul rotting smell. In a few more years, the structure would have collapsed in on itself and the remains might never have been discovered. Part of him resented the extra work, especially before Christmas, but he owed it to the victim to seek justice on his behalf.

Who was this mystery man and why had he been buried in a derelict glasshouse?

Presumably it hadn't been derelict at the time?

'I'll introduce you to the owners,' Harriet said, as they followed the stepping stones back to the decking. 'They've only lived here for two years, so hopefully they won't be high on our suspect list.'

'Why "hopefully"? Are they friends of yours?'

She shot him a look of disbelief. 'Not particularly but I do have to live here and it would be awkward.'

'Point taken,' Ben said and, reaching the decking, began to strip off his scene suit. This was a small village where everyone was either related to or knew each other. The odds were they were already acquainted with the killer.

It was not a reassuring thought.

TWENTY-SIX YEARS AGO...

Tia scowled at her reflection in the old mirror. How was she supposed to see what she looked like with all those brown spots and the silver peeling away?

Honestly, her fiancé was impossible!

He'd bought her the mirror as a surprise early wedding present. She wished he'd asked for her opinion first. It had come from a sale at the local castle and it should have stayed there.

Unless it turned out to be valuable, and then she was sure she'd become very fond of it.

She turned from side to side, letting the petticoats of her wedding dress swish back and forth. There were so many of them she could hardly get through the door. Now this had certainly been worth the money. She didn't need the mirror to tell her she looked like a fairy-tale princess. It was lucky they'd be firmly married by the time he saw the invoice. He could have bought three antique mirrors for the price of this dress, and think what a waste that would have been. Really, she was doing him a favour.

Talk of the devil... The man himself came into their bedroom and stood behind her, sliding the gown from her shoulder to drop a kiss onto one tanned shoulder.

'Mirror, mirror,' he teased. 'You don't need that, or me, to tell you you're beautiful.'

She pouted. 'But it would be nice...'

He laughed and kissed her other shoulder. 'You're beautiful!'

She didn't smile. 'It's bad luck for the groom to see the bride before the ceremony, darling.'

'I came to tell you our friends and relations are already in the church.'

Her friends and relations. His were likely to be conspicuous by their absence.

Let them judge her. She didn't care.

'I'll be five more minutes,' she said.

(More like twenty.)

She turned to put her arms around his neck and sweeten him with a kiss and caught a movement behind him.

A small child was lurking in the doorway, obviously uncomfortable in the formal clothes she'd chosen for him.

Too bad.

'Will he be all right?' she asked politely. Privately, she thought the child was far too young to take part in the ceremony.

'He's looking forward to it. Aren't you, chum?' He pulled the child forward and ruffled his blond hair. 'But we're all getting a little bit impatient.'

Hence the bag of chocolate sweets the child was holding.

'I'll be right down,' Tia said, because that was what he wanted to hear.

It was only as they left, and she did the swishy-swishy thing in front of the mirror again, that she realised some of the spots she could see in the mirror were moving with her – reflections of marks on her snow-white gown.

Five little brown ovals clustered around one much larger one.

Tia tilted her head and frowned. How had they got there?

It was almost like one small but perfectly formed chocolate handprint...

THREE

Just outside the village, beyond the famous humpback bridge, was a narrow, overgrown lane that no one had bothered to record on a map. It meandered lazily through the forest, between ancient trees and long-forgotten signs of human habitation, into a natural hollow, where a surprisingly large sunlit garden had been mostly set to lawn, as if the owner hadn't cared for the distraction of flowers.

In the centre of this garden was a house of dark-grey stone. It had long slender windows and sharp spiked gables, creating a curiously stretched appearance. The roof tiles were of grey slate, the chimneys high and twisted and, directly over the door, a little tower had been added, almost as an afterthought.

The house would have been stunning on a windswept moor or perched on the edge of a granite cliff. In the centre of a sunny circular lawn, surrounded by a ring of red-berried rowan trees, it looked sadly out of place.

Also out of place was the green Porsche that had been parked neatly parallel to the front of the house and the woman standing beside it. In deference to the weather, she wore a black jersey dress, knee-high boots and a long wool coat in exactly the same shade as the car.

Iris Evergreen removed her sunglasses. The surrounding forest was deathly quiet. Was that normal? No birds tweeting, no woodland creatures scampering – or whatever woodland creatures did. It was winter and very cold; she hoped they were hibernating. She *could* hear the faint rumble of the River Thunor somewhere deep in the forest, although the sound was blended with a louder rumble from what she guessed was the removal lorry as it tried to navigate the narrow lane. But it would be nice to keep the house to herself for a little bit longer, so she hurried up the stone steps to unlock the door.

It swung open quietly. On the other side, beneath the tower, was a large round entrance hall with an unusual vaulted ceiling – the kind more usually seen in an underground crypt. Although the stone had been painted pale grey, each rib was highlighted in silver, which also ornamented the spaces between – sharp, spiked patterns that echoed the stark, frosted branches of the trees outside. It was clever and incredibly beautiful.

According to the floor plan she'd received from the solicitor, there'd be a sitting room on the left. She pushed the door and peeped inside. The room was unfurnished and two storeys high, but she could easily imagine her 'thinking sofa' in front of that gloriously tall window, and a cluster of squashy chairs around the black granite fireplace. Like the exterior, there was a deliciously eerie vibe running through the house, although it was the room behind her which she was most excited about.

She stepped back into the hall and opened the opposite door.

The library!

Daylight flooded through two tall windows with stained-glass panels at the top. One window faced south, the other east, which was fortunate because the wallpaper was a very dark green and the shelving cabinets were black with intricately carved tops. Like the hall it also boasted a high, vaulted ceiling and, wedged into the corner, a spiral staircase leading into the tower.

It took 'book nook' to a whole other level but it was the library's fireplace that really took her breath away. The black granite surround had been carved into the shape of a snarling dragon.

The most curious thing was why her mother had never mentioned owning this amazing house. The solicitor had told her that Cressida Wainwright had inherited it on the death of her father, Walter Wainwright, five years ago. Iris hadn't even known he was alive. For the past fifteen years it had been just her and her mother, living in that draughty house in Primrose Hill as it fell to bits around them. The two of them against the world.

The other mystery had to be why Cressida hadn't sold this house after inheriting it. Judging from the size, the general maintenance must have consumed a big chunk of her monthly budget. It didn't make sense – especially if Cressida and Walter had been estranged and the house held unhappy memories for her...

It was all very odd.

Still, their family hardly fit the parameters of normal.

Iris almost missed the dark and dingy oil painting beside the fireplace, practically invisible against the forest-green wallpaper. She stood on tiptoe for a better look, then gave up and used her phone torch, running the beam around the gold frame until it hit an inscription: *Clement Wainwright*.

Wainwright had been her mother's name, so he must be a relative. A great-grandfather? Great-*great*-grandfather? Whoever he was, he'd been elderly at the time of his portrait – in his sixties, at least – but wore the kind of tweedy jacket that could date from any time period, from late Victorian to early twentieth century. Had he been responsible for designing this very peculiar house? He looked far too staid.

A loud knock echoed mournfully around the hall.

Iris grinned. How wonderfully Gothic. She was going to *love* living here.

When she opened the door a bear of a man stood outside. 'Is this...' – he studied the worksheet in front of him and said the name of the house carefully and, for the most part, accurately – 'Álfheimr?'

They both turned to the slate sign nailed into the stone beside the door.

ÁLFHEIMR

'Yes, that's right,' although that would have to go. Home of the Elves? *Really?*

'Are you Ms Iris Evergreen?'

She could almost read his mind: *Green clothes, green car, green name...*

The colour had always been lucky for her. That was why she'd chosen 'Evergreen' for her pen name. Now it was her legal name too. Not Wainwright, or her stepfather's name, Hemsworth, but hers and hers alone.

'That's me.'

'We have a truckload of stuff for you,' he said.

Considering the amount she'd paid them to carefully pack and transport all her worldly goods from the old house in Primrose Hill, she sincerely hoped they did.

'I'm pleased to hear it,' she said, smiling in case he thought she was being sarcastic. Her literary agent was always telling her off for being too blunt. 'And stop *joking*. No one expects you to make *jokes*. Your deadpan delivery confuses people. You're a writer, not a comedian!'

Her agent did love to suck all the fun from life, but he was very good at what he did, meaning she would soon be financially secure. It was a lovely position to be in, after having to scrimp and save for much of her adult life.

'Most of what we've packed appears to be books,' the man frowned, as though that was a bad thing, 'and we were instructed to take special care of this.' He stepped aside to reveal a long glass box, encased in bubble wrap and resting on the veranda behind him.

'Excellent.' She'd worried it wouldn't survive the journey.

'It's a *coffin*,' he said, eyes narrowing.

She really ought to remember she wasn't in Primrose Hill anymore.

'Not quite,' she said. 'It's a—'

'It's a glass *coffin*.'

'It's a *film prop*,' she said firmly. 'My publishers bought it to celebrate my book sales hitting the five-million mark.'

His expression remained carefully blank. It was as though his opinion of her had flown past 'odd', completely bypassed 'eccentric' and was now edging towards 'might be dangerous'.

She got that a lot.

'Why don't you bring it into the library, along with my writing desk?' she suggested. 'There's an alcove between the bookshelves.' It would stop anyone tripping over it and would do until she could buy some kind of display table. 'The writing desk can go in front of the window. In the meantime, I'll make us all a cup of tea!'

He regarded her suspiciously once more, before he and his colleague picked up the writing desk and heaved it into the house, although there was a slight delay when they spotted the hall's vaulted ceiling and its pattern of silver trees, and abruptly stopped, mouths falling open in synch.

'Great, isn't it?' Iris said. 'Now, would it help if I put a sticky note on each door, so you and your colleague will know where to put the furniture and boxes? You don't need to unpack. As you've mentioned, most of the boxes contain books and I can put those onto the shelves myself. I'm sure you'll want to be off as soon as possible?' She certainly hoped so. She wanted to be left alone to explore this beautiful house. 'It's a long way back to London...'

They didn't take their gaze from the ceiling. 'Uh huh...' said the bear-like one.

Had he even heard what she'd said?

She walked into the library in the hope that they'd follow, which they did.

'Bloody hell!' The bear-like removal man was now staring at the snarling dragon over the fireplace. 'That's...'

'Unusual?' Iris suggested. Her tolerance was wearing thin. Surely, in their line of work, they saw all sorts of things? 'Beautiful? Amazing?'

'*Weird*,' he said. Shaking his head, he stomped back outside for the coffin, closely followed by his colleague, who apparently didn't want to be left alone with Iris, or even be inside the house at all.

Was she the only one to see the beauty of the place? Sure, she *could* have stayed in her old home, so terribly empty after the death of her mother, staring at those identical white walls, going slowly crazy talking to herself and never seeing anyone – unless she went to a festival or a book signing, which she usually found too overwhelming.

With the money she'd made from her writing, she could have bought a large modern house months ago – *if* Erik hadn't been bleeding her dry. But now he was gone and she finally had control over her money.

As the men began unloading boxes from the lorry, Iris wandered over to the window and stared out at the strange circle of rowan trees that bordered the garden, as though keeping the forest at bay. They were attractive, yet, like everything else, decidedly odd.

As she turned away, a flash of movement caught her eye.

Paranoia immediately kicked in and she stepped away from the window.

Had someone been standing there, watching her? She knew she hadn't imagined it but it still didn't make sense. Why would anyone be wandering about the forest in the middle of winter? She'd seen the map. The River Thunor enclosed her land on the south and west boundary, with the road to the north. No one could wander through the forest and end up in her garden by accident – that had been another part of its appeal.

Could someone be *spying* on her? Perhaps the press? How would they have found her? The only people she'd told about her move from London had been her publishers, her agent and the family solicitors. Thanks to Erik, she no longer had any friends left to tell. Everyone else contacted her online. They didn't need to know where she lived and that suited her fine.

It wouldn't be the first time she'd attracted unwanted attention from journalists. It had been another reason she'd been so keen to leave London – before anyone else could make the connection between Iris Evergreen and Iris Hemsworth.

That was the trouble with becoming unexpectedly rich and famous. There was always someone digging about in your past, hoping to make money from a juicy scandal, no matter who they hurt in the process.

And if anyone looked past 'Iris Evergreen', and went beyond 'Iris Wainwright' to 'Iris Hemsworth'?

They'd certainly hit the jackpot.

FOUR

Harriet led Ben around to the front of Foxglove & Hemlock, through the main entrance and up a wide staircase directly into a reception room on the first floor. Sunlight filtered through lattice windows, catching on coloured-glass 'witch' balls suspended in front of them, creating pretty patterns on the dark oak floors. The doors that presumably led to other rooms were firmly shut. Ben wondered what the rest of the house was like but it was unlikely he was about to receive a tour.

Flames crackled in a stone fireplace. Amelia perched on the edge of an ancient blue sofa in front of it, twisting long reddened fingers. Gabriel had taken occupancy of an easy chair directly beside the fireplace, one ankle resting on the other knee, exposing a good few centimetres of tanned skin between trousers and sock.

A tan he was unlikely to have acquired in Raven's Edge.

Ben turned his attention back to Amelia who, in her current nervous state, would be easier to obtain information from. She was much as Ben would expect a florist to look, wearing cotton dungarees over a blue sweater. Her nut-brown hair was swirled up on top of her head, with no discernible clips or grips – a skill he could appreciate after hours spent trying to tame Sophie's curls for school – and eyes that were a warm hazel. She had a sprinkle of freckles over her nose, a tan to match Gabriel's and a streak of dirt on one cheek – presumably from the garden. Her hands were clean, although red and chapped.

As soon as he'd appeared, Amelia had begun apologising for interfering with his crime scene by removing the bones from the soil. Her hands, when she stopped twisting them, were shaking. He realised they were so red because she'd been scrubbing and scrubbing at them.

'I'll make us a nice pot of tea,' Harriet said soothingly. 'You've both had a horrible shock. No need to show me the kitchen. I'm sure I can work it out.'

A perfect opportunity for her to have a quick snoop around, in other words.

Ben glanced at Gabriel. He'd be most likely to protest. Perhaps he'd offer to make the tea himself – it was his house, after all.

Gabriel, however, was giving every indication that he was used to having other people do things for him. A large house, foreign holidays out of season, an expensive car... A flourishing business or inherited wealth?

He could almost hear Harriet's voice in his head: 'Judging much?'

Could two florists be capable of murder?

Oh yes. Anyone, given the right opportunity and circumstances, could be a killer.

Pushing those thoughts to the back of his mind, he adopted what he hoped was a soothing tone. 'If you hadn't "interfered", Ms Locke, we might never have found the remains. Now their family will have closure, we'll be able to discover who did this, and the victim will have justice.'

If he had a family.

Ben didn't miss the worried glance Amelia exchanged with Gabriel though.

Interesting...

'I thought they were *animal* bones,' she said. 'I *touched* them. With my *hands!*'

'You had no idea the remains were there?'

'Obviously,' Gabriel said, before she could answer.

Perhaps he should have split them up and questioned them separately but, in theory, they weren't suspects – yet.

'I thought it was a grave for a dog,' Amelia continued. 'We used to do that when I was a child – bury the cat or rabbit in the garden somewhere where it'd remain undisturbed.'

Yet this was a glasshouse, with flower beds that would be regularly weeded and dug over – although not recently, judging by the state of the rest of the garden.

That led neatly to his next question.

'How long have you lived here?'

Gabriel answered. Amelia was too busy blowing her nose.

'Two years. It was a dream of ours to have our own floristry business. The first attempt was in Norchester, but the rent was too high and the footfall too low. We couldn't believe our luck when this place became available. It was already a florist, you see, and had been for years, so we didn't need to do more than some minor renovations and change the name. "Foxglove & Hemlock": Gabriel Fox and Amelia Locke. We thought the new name fitted the rest of Raven's Edge: The Crooked Broomstick, The Witch's Brew, The Secret Grimoire...'

'You named a florist after two extremely poisonous plants?'

'Yes, but not many realise it. Hemlock has associations with witchcraft, but some assume foxglove is nothing more than a harmless wild flower.'

More fool them. Ben's grandmother had taught him at an early age that practically everything growing in a garden would poison him if ingested, and foxgloves were the worst of all.

Every part was lethal, including the leaves, which people often mistook for borage.

Ben turned to Amelia. 'Who did you buy the business from?'

Again she glanced towards Gabriel, waiting for him to answer. She hadn't struck him as the kind of woman who would easily defer to a man, so why was she so reluctant to speak for herself? Was it important that she didn't say the wrong thing?

'Niall Kinsella,' Gabriel said, without even looking at his partner. 'The man ran the business into the ground. He hadn't a clue. He inherited it from his father – Eoin Kinsella – who owned the business for over thirty years. Instead of selling the place on to someone who knew what they were doing, or putting in a manager, he tried to run it himself and went bust within a couple of years. We got it cheap.'

Ben scribbled the names down in his notebook, adding an arrow to Gabriel's name, and a question mark.

'We're still receiving letters from companies he owed money to,' Amelia said.

'Do either of you have an address for Mr Kinsella?'

Amelia glanced at Gabriel, who nodded.

Permission given, Amelia jumped up. 'It's in my address book. I'll fetch it.'

Which left him alone with Gabriel.

'This is a lovely house,' Ben said. It was one of his standard lines. Always say something nice about a person's house/garden/pet/child to encourage them to relax. 'How old is it?'

Gabriel seemed a little too relaxed, leaning further back into the chair, smiling at Ben as though they were friends having a catch-up over a drink. How old was he? Late twenties? Perhaps a little too young to be their murderer but the sooner they had a date on that skeleton, the better.

'The house was built in 1504,' Gabriel said, 'but it's had several alterations over the years. The front facade has been changed. The bow windows were added in Victorian times. We believe the house was originally built in the shape of an "E" but now only the main part of the house remains.'

So the skeleton *could* have been buried beneath the floor of the house?

Then he remembered Lucia saying the remains weren't that old.

Another theory hit the deck.

'Do you know who owned the house before Eoin Kinsella?' That would save Dakota a bit of research. 'Was there any information with the deeds?'

'Possibly,' Gabriel shrugged, 'I didn't bother to look that closely. History's not my thing. I'm more about the here and now.'

Yet he'd known the exact date the house had been built.

'Where are the deeds?'

'With my solicitor.'

Not a bank?

'You own the house outright?'

'Yes.' Gabriel's defences went up again.

'The solicitor in the village? Greenwich & Byrne?'

'Yes, that's right.'

'Would there be a problem if we asked to view the deeds?'

'N... no. Not at all.'

'Thank you,' Ben said. 'You've been very helpful. If we do need to access the deeds, we'll let you know.'

It all depended how old the skeleton was, but Land Registry would probably be their first port of call.

Harriet returned with a tray of teas and coffees. Ben took his gratefully. He still hadn't warmed up from the cold outside, despite the fire.

Amelia followed behind, Kinsella's address written out for him on a slip of paper.

He thanked her and slipped the note into his pocket.

'If we have any further questions we'll be in touch,' he said, draining his cup and placing it back on the tray. Ironically, the picture on the tray was of a typical English country garden, bearing no resemblance to the one outside. 'If we could ask you to stay out of the garden for the time being? We might need to make further searches.'

Amelia was horrified. 'Not go into the garden at all?'

'Just stay this side of the tape,' Harriet said kindly. 'You can still use the decking.'

It wasn't the answer Amelia wanted. 'But the glasshouse?' She exchanged glances with Gabriel, as though expecting him to argue the case for her. He merely shrugged. 'We need to clear it ready for the renovation.'

Gabriel was quicker to catch on. 'Will you be searching for more bodies?'

Amelia squeaked and her cup rattled in its saucer. 'You think there are *more*? That there could be a *serial killer*?'

How had they gone from a few old bones to serial killer?

'We need to be thorough,' Ben said, hoping he sounded reassuring. He glanced towards Harriet, who caught the hint and quickly drank her coffee, placing the mug back onto the tray. 'Thank you for all your help,' he said, standing up. 'If you think of anything else that you feel is relevant, please let us know.' He dropped a business card onto the coffee table. 'If you could stay out of the garden until we've had the opportunity to thoroughly search it, that would be great.'

'Of course,' Gabriel said, immediately jumping up to see them out – hoping to get them off the premises as soon as possible, presumably. 'We'll do everything we can to help.'

Ben waited until they'd walked out of the shop and the door had safely closed behind them.

'What do you think?' he asked Harriet.

'Guilty as hell.'

'Me too,' Ben sighed. 'Not murder, but—'

'Definitely *something*. Did you see the way Amelia kept looking at Gabriel, as though waiting for permission to speak? That is *so* unlike her. Usually she's bossing *him* around.'

'Still want to stick to your day off?'

'Of course!'

He was surprised but didn't push it. 'OK, I'll see you tomorrow at the briefing. And Harriet? Don't be late.'

'When am I ever—' She broke off as his eyebrows rose. 'OK, fine, whatever. What are you going to do now?'

'See a man about a cadaver dog.'

'Cheery.'

'How about you?'

She held up her phone, showing a dozen missed calls and messages.

'I've been summoned to visit my mother.'

Marriage was not the fairy-tale ending Tia had expected it to be. Her new husband was thirty, which seemed like a great age to Tia, but he behaved like someone twice that. He had no desire to go on holiday and thought pubs and restaurants were an expensive rip-off. Although extremely popular, he didn't appear to have any close friends apart from the people he worked with, and Tia had no desire to ask any of them to dinner.

She continued working at the florist, even though her husband would have preferred her to give it up. She joined the tennis club, and went diving and sailing in Port Rell. She went to the hairdresser, the manicurist and the beautician. At no time did she ever appear less than stunning, but her husband didn't seem to care what she did or what she looked like or what she wore. He collapsed into bed at 10.00 pm every evening without fail, completely exhausted and no good for anything.

Meanwhile, her old friends from university were going clubbing, had holidays abroad, fabulous careers – they had lives.

After less than six months' of 'wedded bliss', Tia lay in bed beside her husband (who was snoring loudly and wearing old-man pyjamas buttoned up to his neck), clenched her fists and made a very dangerous wish.

'Please God, send me a little excitement...'

FIVE

People always assumed Harriet's parents were dead.

Everyone knew her father had died while saving the lives of two young children, when Harriet was only a few months old. In those days there had been no fancy medal to commemorate police officers who'd died on duty, but a collection had been organised and a gold medal awarded; a medal which now lay in a small blue box tucked into Harriet's underwear drawer because she couldn't bear to look at it.

No one ever asked about her mother.

Mostly Harriet tried to forget she existed.

This would have worked brilliantly except Anya March occasionally remembered she had a daughter. This usually happened after Anya (or a friend) had been given a speeding or parking ticket – 'Don't worry, my daughter will sort that out for you' – even though Harriet had tried to explain, *multiple* times, that (a) she was a detective sergeant for the Murder Investigation Team, *not* Traffic, which was a whole other department, and (b) (more pertinently) *it would be bloody illegal*.

As Harriet walked up the drive leading to her mother's house, the immaculately raked shingle crunching beneath her boots, the cold nipping at her cheeks (the top of her ears *and* her nose), anxiety churned in her gut.

Except it wasn't *proper* anxiety because Detective Sergeant Harriet March, who regularly brought down and disarmed men twice – no, *three* times her size – would *never* feel anxious about meeting her own mother. That would be ridiculous.

Her pace slowed as she rounded the large clumps of rhododendrons and saw Anya's house in front of her. In her head, it always reminded her of one of those scratchy black and white horror films her friend Sam liked to watch. In reality, it was a perfectly nice red-brick Victorian villa with well-scrubbed steps, an obligatory Christmas tree standing sentry and a large wreath on the door, which was far too conventional to have been made by Foxglove & Hemlock.

The door opened before Harriet had the chance to change her mind and walk briskly in the opposite direction. On the other side stood a woman with grey hair to match her grey dress – *not* Harriet's mother but the housekeeper, Mrs Nore, glowering down at her.

Despite the usual less than warm welcome, Harriet always felt sorry for Mrs Nore. It couldn't be much fun working for Anya. Why did her mother make the poor woman wear a uniform, for goodness' sake? The super-rich Graham family had a housekeeper *and* a butler, and Harriet had only ever seen them wear normal clothes.

'It's a form of insecurity', Grandma Belle had told Harriet once. 'Anya believes people look down on her, so, to her, everything is about ensuring they're envious instead.'

This could explain why Anya felt the need to have a housekeeper, a maid *and* a gardener, as well as a manager to oversee her three shops. She also served on the parish council and various committees, gave regular parties throughout the year, was second only to Brianna Graham in the village hierarchy, and yet she still lived in this museum of a house, when surely she'd have been happier in a modern apartment in Norchester?

(And – *bonus!* – Harriet would have seen her even less.)

'Good afternoon, Miss March,' the housekeeper said coolly, despite Harriet having told her, *many times*, to use her first name. 'Mrs March has asked for luncheon to be served in the conservatory.'

At least it would be warm.

After the death of her second husband, Anya had reverted to the name of her first. The widow of a hero apparently had more prestige than the widow of an antiques dealer.

Harriet was quite capable of finding the conservatory on her own but Mrs Nore had one job to do and was determined to do it. Harriet refused to part with her coat in case a quick getaway was required. There was a short, inelegant tug-of-war; Harriet won and followed Mrs Nore through a series of large, museum-like rooms painted in 'heritage' colours and crammed with fussy furniture and ugly things. Anya's second husband had dealt mainly in Victorian antiquities and the house was full of arte-facts once looted by someone's great-great-great-grandfather before being sold on for profit.

Harriet thought they should be given back.

'To whom?' Anya had enquired coldly, when Harriet had pointed this out. 'The original owners would be long dead, even if we could track them down.'

'Then give them to a museum in their country of origin.'

'Who'd promptly stuff them in a box in a backroom and forget about them. Such a waste when we can enjoy them every day, right here.' Anya had all but patted Harriet's head, which would have been difficult because Harriet was four inches taller. 'You do have some strange ideas, sweetie.'

Mrs Nore, surprisingly speedy for a middle-aged lady, was now almost a room ahead. Pointedly she stopped and waited in the corridor, as if she thought Harriet coveted these horrible things and was just waiting for an opportunity to slide one into her bag.

The corridor led into a modern conservatory which housed the indoor swimming pool. Conscious of her boots dropping snow, mud and goodness knows what else onto the gleaming tiles (where others would walk with bare feet), Harriet slunk around to the seating bay as quickly as possible. The view was onto the garden but the windows were closed and the heating was on high. The unpleasantly stale, humid air reminded Harriet of Amelia's glasshouse. She could almost imagine tendrils of ivy curling around and through the panes of glass and shuddered. Was it worth telling her mother about the skeleton they'd found? No, better to wait for the formal announcement. Anya was not great at keeping secrets and the story would be all around the village soon enough.

Currently, there was no sign of her mother or anyone else. The pool was smooth and unrippled, and there were no puddles of water around the edge. Harriet shoved one of the windows open a crack and was rewarded by a blast of frozen air. Already she'd forgotten how cold it was outside.

The housekeeper wheeled over a hostess trolley filled with enough food for twenty people: tiny vegetarian sandwiches and iced cakes that would disappear in one bite, all arranged on tiered stands.

Ben would have been impressed. He loved the green stuff that resembled dandelion leaves and was always nagging her to eat more vegetables and salad.

Right now, Harriet would kill for a bacon and cheese panini from The Witch's Brew.

Seriously, there wasn't even ketchup.

She had peeled back one of the sandwiches to investigate further – hummus, avocado and cucumber? Ugh! Was there nothing on this trolley suitable for carnivores? – when something growled.

She looked around before remembering to look down.

Crouched by her feet was a fluffy white gremlin with spindly legs, an oversized head, bug-eyes and floppy ears, like something out of a cartoon. It was a wonder she hadn't trod on him.

Caesar. Her mother's white chihuahua.

'Are you coming between me and my lunch?' she asked the dog, attempting to gently push him away with the toe of her boot. 'Not recommended.'

Caesar dug his needle-sharp teeth into the leather.

'Caesar!' She tried to gently shake him off. 'Remember who's ahead of you in the pack, you daft dog.'

Evidently the dog didn't agree because the decibel level went up, along with the pressure on her boot.

A tinkling laugh echoed down the pool, followed by a familiar sing-song voice that always gave Harriet the chills.

'Will you two ever be friends?'

The dog immediately released her, flying towards the diminutive blonde at the other end of the pool who bent to scoop him up, revealing a hot pink swimsuit beneath a white towelling robe.

'Caesar, you naughty boy,' she said, cuddling him close as she walked towards Harriet. 'Are you terrifying my poor daughter?'

My daughter. As though she were a possession. Another of those looted antiques, never to be handed back.

'It would take more than a tiny dog to terrify me,' Harriet said, quite truthfully.

'Hear that?' Anya stage-whispered to Caesar. 'She believes you're harmless but we know better, don't we?'

Caesar yapped happily, more proof that he had no sense whatsoever. Anya laughed again and took a tiny sandwich from the trolley, holding it out for the dog to take from her hand.

Harriet had to hide her smile when the dog promptly spat it out.

'How's Mummy's little baby?'

(That was addressed to Caesar.)

Maybe the dog *had* got it right with his place in the pack.

Anya nuzzled the dog's nose and Caesar licked her in return, then she put him firmly on the floor. The dog danced about a bit, barking excitedly, but soon got the idea he was no longer the centre of attention and lay on the floor instead, his bug-eyes watching Anya adoringly.

Anya gave the trolley a dismissive glance, then picked up the bottle of prosecco cooling in an ice bucket and made herself a buck's fizz with barely a centimetre of freshly squeezed orange juice. As she pushed her sleeves back, a diamond bracelet dangled from her wrist, catching the light. Was business really that good or had it been bought for her by an attentive lover?

The answer presented itself when a large man, also wearing a white towelling robe, walked up behind Anya, pulled back the edge of her robe and kissed her shoulder, all while looking Harriet up and down in the same way Harriet would have regarded a bacon sandwich, had one been there.

Well, *yuck.*

Now *she* felt as though she needed a cleansing dip in the pool.

'Dean, this is my daughter, Harriet,' Anya said, laughing again as he showered kisses along her neck and tried to bat him away, forgetting she had a glass in her hand. Her buck's fizz sloshed over the edge and dripped onto Caesar, who sneezed and shook his head in confusion.

Poor little thing.

'Harriet, this is Dean Hunter, my new friend.'

Friend, eh?

The man reached over Anya's shoulder and helped himself

to a handful of sandwiches, shoving them all into his mouth at the same time.

Nice.

He winked at Harriet, discarded his robe on a sun lounger and strode off towards the pool.

Should she warn him of the dangers of swimming after eating?

Nah.

He dived into the water, barely creating a ripple.

Harriet turned her attention back to her mother, who was arranging herself on the other sun lounger. 'Why did you ask me here?'

At least Anya always came straight to the point. 'The man who owns the shop next to mine in the village keeps parking his lorry right where it blocks the view of my boutique. Not only does it reduce daylight for my staff and customers, no one can see us if they're driving past. I'm losing business.'

'Why would he do that?' Harriet asked, already having quite a good idea.

'How should I know?' Anya tipped the remaining buck's fizz into her mouth. 'I've always been as nice as nice can be.'

Yeah, right.

'You must have done something to upset him?'

'Why must it always be *my* fault? Maybe the guy is an arse? Have you considered that?'

Harriet sighed. 'There are yellow lines on the high street. Your neighbour can't park there unless he's loading or unloading.'

'Exactly my point! And he has a perfectly good loading bay around the back like the rest of us.'

'If he's not breaking the law, there's not a lot I can do about it.'

Anya's blue eyes turned steely. 'You could arrest him?'

'Not if he hasn't broken the law.'

'What's the point of having a daughter who's a policewoman—'

'Police *officer*.'

'Whatever – if you can't arrest anyone?'

'If I arrested him for no reason, *I'd* be breaking the law.'

Anya stared at her. 'You're serious, aren't you? My goodness, if someone had told me that my own daughter would ever speak to me the way you do...' She broke off to shake her head, her long blonde hair rippling about her shoulders. 'Well, really!'

What could Harriet say to that? 'Sorry?' She wasn't sorry! If anything, she was *angry*. Angry that her mother made her feel this way, angry that her mother *saw* her this way – a tool to be used – if and when she remembered Harriet's existence.

Why was she even here?

'I have to go,' she lied. 'I need to get back to work.'

At least that was one excuse no one ever questioned.

She remembered to step over the dog lying beside Anya's feet, so forlorn he forgot to growl, and exited via the conservatory doors to avoid going back through the house.

As she walked down the drive, she reflected that if one of her friends was in a relationship that made them feel like this, she'd tell them to bail out the first chance they got.

SIX

The removal men had left Álfheimr by mid-afternoon, as if they couldn't wait to escape. What remained of Iris's lonely life in Primrose Hill was now carefully, if sparsely, arranged throughout the house. Each room had a pile of cardboard boxes waiting to be unpacked but her stomach was rumbling and it was well past time to explore the village.

The temperature hadn't got much above freezing, but as she walked down the driveway, snowdrops were emerging beneath the trees and cyclamen bloomed in the patches of sunlight. The lane was longer than she'd remembered but eventually emerged beside a quaint medieval pub, all whitewash and blackened beams, with troughs of winter pansies and heather outside and some kind of deciduous creeper growing up over the door and around the windows.

She fished a photo out of her bag. It showed a young woman with straight black hair and a pale complexion proudly holding a baby wrapped in a blue shawl, although not much could be seen of the baby other than a tuft of black hair. Blurred into the background was a whitewashed house with purple wisteria tumbling around the door and windows.

Iris held the photo up, comparing it to the view in front of her.

The pub had been recently repainted. The name – The Drop – was now over the door and the rotting eighties windows had been replaced with something smarter and more sympathetic to the sixteenth century. Despite all that, it wasn't hard to see the two buildings were the same.

She turned the photo over, even though she knew what was written there.

Cressida & Iris
1994

Here was proof she'd visited Raven's Edge before, albeit as a baby.

Who'd taken the photo? Her grandparents? Her *father*? She'd found it in an album after her mother had died, hidden away in her mother's 'treasures' box. Iris hadn't even known the album existed.

Carefully, she slid the photo back into her bag and walked over the bridge and into the village, past thatched cottages with pretty gardens and colourful half-timbered houses clustered around a square. There was a florist, a bookstore, boutiques and gift shops. A café named Spellbound offered fortune-telling with every pot of tea. Another café, in the narrowest, most crooked house Iris had ever seen, had a queue trailing right out the door, along with the most delicious scent of freshly baked cookies.

Where should she go first?

The bookshop, *obviously*.

Painted a warm, orangey pink, The Secret Grimoire leant slightly to the left, as though cuddling up to its neighbours, yet the windows were all perfectly straight – emphasising the lopsidedness of the rest. Two stone steps, hollowed by centuries of use, led up to the door and, on either side, a tiny Christmas tree sat in a terracotta pot wrapped in a gold bow.

Iris peeked through the window. Expecting potion bottles and crystal balls, it was a shock to see copies of her own book, *The Ivy Crown*, expertly arranged against a backdrop of winter evergreens.

With the move to Raven's Edge, she hadn't yet unpacked the box containing her author copies. This was the first time she'd seen the book in real life, and the cover was *gorgeous* – white, with a silver crown tangled with ivy.

She took a photo to send to her agent and then hurried up the steps, remembering to duck beneath the low beams, only to trip over a little table just inside the door. The display – ironically her entire backlist – teetered ominously.

She caught them before they crashed to the floor.

So much for sneaking in unobtrusively.

Sliding the armful of books back onto the table, she attempted to pile them up the way they were before, then took one back, flicking through the pages to find the first chapter. Two months it had taken to perfect that opening paragraph. Two panic-stricken months after her mother had died, her deadline approaching like an express train, when she thought she'd lost her ability to write.

How her mother would have loved to have seen her success.

Damn, she missed her.

'It's selling well,' a voice intruded on her thoughts.

She promptly dropped the book.

It was deftly caught by the man behind her. His russet hair curled messily over dark-brown eyes and he looked far too healthy for someone who spent all his time in a bookshop. And she knew that because his name badge said:

Whittaker Smith

Manager

'I didn't mean to startle you,' he said. 'I recognised you from
your photo.' He pointed to the back cover. Her own face stared
back like a stranger, far more glamorous than she'd ever
appeared in real life. 'Because your books are set in the village,
they're incredibly popular with our customers. Incorporating
our folklore was genius.'

He paused, presumably expecting her thanks or at least for
her to say *something*, but all she could do was stare at him.

That was the trouble with living on her own and never
seeing or speaking with anyone. Her social skills were zero.

'Aren't they?' he prompted. 'Inspired by Raven's Edge?'

How to put this?

'I've never been here before...' Judging from the photo in her
bag, that wasn't strictly true. 'And I know nothing about any
folklore.'

'But your description of the forest surrounding the village,
the crooked cottages and humpback bridge, they're so recognisable. Even your main character, Meg, has the same name as our
witch.' His brown eyes turned rueful. 'Damn, it's what I've been
telling everyone. I'm going to be in so much trouble for false
advertising.'

Her conscience pricked sharply. She wouldn't want him to
get into trouble.

'My mother grew up here,' she said, 'in a house on the other
side of the bridge. When I was a child, she'd tell me fairy tales
about an enchanted forest and a shapeshifting raven queen.
They stuck in my mind and inspired my stories. Are you telling
me her stories were real?'

He grinned. 'Real-*ish*.'

Returning the book to the pile, she attempted to drape the
fake ivy around it.

Bemused, he watched her struggle for a moment, before

gently batting her hand away and restoring the ruined display in seconds.

'Your mother's fairy tales sound like the stories we tell the tourists,' he said. 'Our Raven Queen was known as Magik Meg. She was a real person, a healer, tried as a witch in 1696 and thrown from the humpback bridge.'

The bridge she'd just walked over?

Iris shuddered. 'That's horrible!'

'Plot twist: Meg turned herself into one hundred ravens and flew away. It's why she was given the nickname "the Raven Queen".'

'So it *is* a true story?' Realising what she'd said, she grimaced. 'I mean, *obviously* it's not a true story... Oh, that poor woman...'

'Much like every other legend in Raven's Edge, there's always a tiny grain of truth. The consensus is that her friends helped her escape and faked the whole raven thing.'

How could anyone fake turning into one hundred ravens?

'In my book, Meg's stolen away to the Underworld by an evil fae prince. Do you have a portal to the Underworld here too?'

She half-expected him to say, 'Sure, check out the second aisle in the grocery store but watch out for Cerberus, he slobbers.'

He thought for a moment. 'There's the Gateway to the Dead? Outside the village, on the road to the moors, you'll find an ancient stone arch. Follow the track on the other side and you'll come to a wide clearing. A big battle was fought here during the Civil War. The casualties from both sides were buried where they fell. Hence the name: Gateway to the Dead. We're very literal here in Raven's Edge.'

'I had no idea...'

'If you want to find out more about the village, speak to Ellie at the museum. She knows this stuff inside out. So... *Can* I tell the tourists that Iris Evergreen based her series of bestselling fantasy books on the legends of Raven's Edge?'

That wasn't a bad idea. If people linked 'Iris Evergreen' with Raven's Edge, there would be less likelihood of her being linked to somewhere else – or *someone* else.

'OK,' she said. 'If you like.'

He beamed and held out his hand. 'I didn't introduce myself. I'm Whit Smith. I own the bookshop. It's great to meet you in person. I love it when authors pay us a visit. Are you staying locally?'

'I've recently moved into the old family home on the other side of the bridge.'

'Cool, and, if you can forgive me for being crass, could you possibly sign our stock before you go?'

Was he serious? 'The last time I offered to do that, the store owner was horrified. Mind you, I had walked in off the street.'

Much like now...

It was fortunate her agent wasn't here. She could almost hear him yelling into her ear: 'For goodness' sake, woman! Sign everything!'

'I'm not going to lie,' he said, 'signed copies are extremely popular. You'd be doing me a huge favour. Usually it's the big-name bookshops that have first dibs on the special editions, sprayed edges and the like. We don't get a look in.'

'I'd love to sign them for you.'

'You are my *favourite* author. Come into the kitchen at the back. I'll make you a tea – or a coffee, whatever you prefer – and bring in the stock for you to sign. My assistant, Carmen Serrano, will put the "signed by the author" stickers on for you. Ignore the screaming and jumping up and down. She's a huge fan of your work and will probably explode.'

Iris followed him through a succession of more dimly lit rooms. How did anyone *find* anything? The shop was crammed with books, from the classics to the latest bestsellers. The shelves were double stacked, right up to the ceiling. Books were even piled on the floor.

Whit apparently had no difficulty, casually plucking a slim hardback from a shelf as they passed and handing it to her. 'Here you go. *A Complete History of Raven's Edge*. A gift from us to you, in return for signing your books.'

The cover showed a pretty thatched cottage, covered in scarlet Virginia creeper.

'Thank you!'

He glanced back and grinned. 'You haven't seen how many of your books we ordered!'

The kitchen was a snug little room overlooking a courtyard at the back, a strange mix of old and new, an inglenook fireplace next to a modern stove and a television mounted on the wall between the beams.

While Whit busily made three mugs of tea – the third presumably for Carmen – and arranged a packet of chocolate biscuits on a floral plate, Iris flipped to the index of the book he'd given her and searched for her mother's surname: Wainwright.

There were several mentions of *Clement* Wainwright – the man in the portrait on her library wall. She turned to the relevant page. Clement had a chapter to himself. From what she could gather, skim-reading while Whit went to collect the stock, Clement Wainwright had been an Oxford professor whose career had nosedived after he became obsessed with the occult.

The *occult?*

And she thought *she* was the black sheep of the family!

'This is only the first batch,' Whit said, appearing out of nowhere and dropping a stack of books beside her. 'Carmen will be along in a moment with some more. Are you sure you don't mind doing this? I feel I'm taking advantage.'

'There is one thing you could help me with.' She took a photo from her bag. Not the one of her mother by the bridge, but a man in a navy-blue suit standing outside a church. 'Is this the local church and do you recognise him?'

Whit took the photo and frowned. 'Yes, that's St Francis's Church, but I've no idea who the man is. Is it an old photo? I've not lived in the village for long. I'm originally from Norchester, and Carmen and her sister are from Madrid.' He handed the photo back.

'I believe he's a relation and that he used to live here about thirty years ago. I found the photo amongst my mother's things after she died.' Iris returned the photo to her bag. 'Do you know of anyone else who could help me identify him?'

'It might be worth going to the local museum and speaking with Ellie Garlick, the curator? She knows everything about the history of the village and might be able to put you in touch with someone who could help you, maybe one of the older villagers?'

'Where's the museum?'

'It's in the centre of the village, in what used to be the old manor house, with a stone gateway outside. It looms over everything else.'

'It sounds spooky!'

He laughed. 'Welcome to Raven's Edge!'

The social event of the year was the summer party given by Patrick and Rosemary Graham at their mansion, King's Rest. Patrick Graham was a wealthy publisher. His wife, Rosemary, a talented artist.

As Tia walked through the elegant rooms, she reflected that she and her husband were probably the poorest, most unimportant people there. How on earth had he wrangled an invitation? How did he even know these people?

It transpired that he worked regularly with Patrick's mother, Brianna Graham, who was chairperson of the parish council. So while everyone else danced and drank, and had a wonderful time, he'd spent the entire evening discussing potholes and speed limits in a little huddle with the other council members.

Tia despaired of him, she really did. Did he even know how to have a good time?

Bored out of her mind, she left him to it, heading out into the garden, hoping to find at least one person under thirty. She didn't – but a live band was playing classical music on the terrace and there were paper lanterns hanging from the trees, creating a magical atmosphere. It was a fairy tale come to life.

All that was missing was Prince Charming.

SEVEN

Desperate to see a friendly face, Harriet headed off to visit her grandmother. On the way she phoned her brother, who, judging from the laughter and music in the background, was having a much better day.

She launched into a five-minute rant about how awful their mother was before remembering to ask, 'How are you?'

Ryan laughed. 'Don't hate me but I'm having a brilliant time with Luca and his family in Sorrento. It's unseasonably warm at eighteen degrees and we're eating pizza by the pool.' Luca was Ryan's best friend and bandmate. 'Why don't you fly over and join us? Spend Christmas. I'll pay for your ticket.'

Christmas in Sorrento with the eccentric Corbellini family, at their beautiful old villa surrounded by lemon groves? It was *so* tempting.

'I promised Grandma I'd spend Christmas with her.' Since Grandpa Reynald had died, Belle didn't have any family other than her and Ryan.

'Bring Grandma Belle too!'

She was touched he'd offered but, 'You know Grandma is

all about celebrating a traditional English Christmas. We'll be fine. Maybe next time? It'll give me a year to talk her round.'

He sighed. 'Only if you promise not to let Anya get to you.' Ryan never referred to Anya as 'Mum', but then she was his stepmother. 'You know she only calls when she wants something. Block her. I did, years ago.'

But Anya was her *mother*.

'If I don't speak with you before, enjoy Christmas with Grandma Belle,' he added. 'Me and the guys will video call you after lunch.'

What would Belle think when she received a drunken phone call on Christmas Day from a bunch of exuberant musicians?

She'd love it.

In the meantime, Anya would expect Harriet to attend her annual Christmas party next week as though nothing had happened.

Meet my daughter, the detective sergeant.

And Harriet's only excuse for getting out of that would be if someone else got themselves murdered.

In the summer, Isabelle March's thatched cottage, with its exquisite country-style garden of hollyhocks, roses and lupins, was one of the most photographed in the village. It even featured on the postcards sold in the gift shops – something that had completely confused Grandma Belle when she'd spotted one. 'Why would anyone want *my* old cottage on a postcard?'

Thankfully, there were no tourists taking selfies today. Harriet pushed open the little blue gate and walked up the path, the door opening before she could knock.

She was enveloped in a warm, floury hug. 'Harriet! How lovely to see you!'

Here was someone who loved her *without* strings.

She sniffed the air. What was that tantalising scent? Cinnamon? Oranges?

'Are you making mince pies?'

'Could you smell them all the way to the police station? Is that why you're here?'

'Busted,' Harriet agreed, toeing off her boots to leave in the hall, and slinging her coat on the end of the banister as she passed the tiny, crooked staircase.

The main hub of the house was the kitchen. It was also the largest room, dominated by a massive wooden table in the centre. A table that Grandpa Reynald had always sworn was as old as the cottage. He was probably right. Harriet couldn't see how else it had got through the door, even if it had been dismantled.

Grandma Belle put the kettle on. 'Do you have a day off? That's unusual, isn't it? Are things quiet up at the station?'

'Yes, yes and no.' Harriet took her usual place at the table, immediately feeling as though she were a teenager again, watching her grandmother cook while she struggled with her maths homework, and Ryan and Grandpa tinkered with an old motorbike out in the backyard.

Life had seemed so much simpler then.

'Oh dear. Well, you probably need a break from all those murders.'

'Just the one murder,' Harriet said, hoping she wasn't speaking too soon. She didn't want Grandma Belle to worry that the village had turned into crime central. 'Amelia Locke dug up a very old skeleton in the back garden of Foxglove & Hemlock.'

'The poor woman! What a horrible shock for her!'

'Uh huh.'

Best not mention the part where Amelia and Gabriel were high on their list of suspects.

'Do you remember any of the previous owners?' she asked

her grandmother. Dakota was currently researching this, but it was hard to beat local knowledge.

'Hmm... Well, the florist opened around thirty years ago. Some man called Kinsella. I can't remember his first name. He wasn't very hands on; he left it in charge of a manager – Hester? Hestia? Strange woman. Always thought she was better than everyone else. I didn't have much to do with her. She died about five or six years ago and it was taken on by one of the family.'

'Thanks! That's a big help.' Harriet quickly scribbled it down in her notebook. When she looked up, a large mug of coffee had arrived on the table. It was accompanied by a sandwich of thick granary bread containing ham and cheese, along with a plate of mince pies, fresh from the oven.

'This is amazing, thank you!' Harriet bit hungrily into the sandwich. 'I've just come from visiting Mum and I'm starving.'

Her grandmother frowned. 'Didn't Anya offer you lunch?'

'Her housekeeper did make some pretty sandwiches.'

(For Dean and the dog.)

Harriet could see Grandma Belle trying hard not to judge. '*Pretty?*'

'*Vegetarian,*' Harriet stage-whispered.

Her grandmother rolled her eyes. 'Eating a vegetable won't kill you, Harriet March.'

'Best not to take the chance though, eh?'

Grandma Belle sighed and, pulling off her apron, took the seat opposite. 'Have you and Anya fallen out again?'

That would depend on whether they'd ever fallen 'in'.

How had Grandma Belle come to that conclusion from a joke about sandwiches?

Harriet helped herself to a mince pie but put it onto her plate rather than straight into her mouth because her grandmother was making it obvious she expected a reply.

'My mother is a hard person to like.'

'Anya hasn't had it easy. She lost two husbands in a very

short space of time and couldn't cope living on her own with two small children. She was deprived of the joy of raising you and Ryan while building up her business, and I expect she feels guilty about that.'

'Did Anya actually *want* to raise me and Ryan?' Because Harriet hadn't seen any evidence of it.

'Don't be too hard on her. She's missed out on all the usual things you young people get to do and now she's... making up for it.'

'You heard about the new boyfriend too, huh?' Harriet bit into the mince pie – warm and fresh from the oven. 'Grandma Belle? These are *heaven!*'

Her grandmother sighed. 'I'll put the rest in a tin for you to take into work,' she said. 'Consider it my Christmas gift to the Murder Investigation Team.'

'That will make you *very* popular,' Harriet said.

Watching her grandmother counting out the mince pies – two for everyone and an extra one for Sam – it was interesting how she knew exactly which department Harriet worked for and all the names of the people she worked with.

Why did her mother find that so difficult?

After lunch, Harriet fixed a dripping tap in the downstairs cloakroom and brought a box of books down from the attic. While she waited for her grandmother to sort through them, ready for Harriet to deliver to the charity shop, she couldn't resist taking a peep into her childhood bedroom, complete with a curling Rihanna poster still stuck on the wardrobe door, and her precious Leigh Bardugo collection in the bookcase. At some point she'd have to sort through everything, but right now it was comforting to know that it was here just as she'd left it, if she wanted to come back – which she didn't, but if she did.

The room on the other side of the little passageway had

belonged to Ryan but he'd left home at eighteen and all his possessions had been boxed up and shipped to his London house. Now it was a guest bedroom, even though their grand-mother never had any guests.

As she opened the door to take a look, it occurred to Harriet that this must have been her father's bedroom as a child because it was much bigger than hers.

The bookcase here was a twin to Harriet's but had photos on it rather than books, since Ryan would take strumming on his guitar over reading any day. There was an old photo of her father as a teenager, propped up beside one of the (now tarnished) silver trophies he'd won at school for sport. Harriet slipped the trophy into her bag. She'd take it home, clean it and bring it back on her next visit.

The photo slithered onto the floor. She picked it up. Her father was grinning sheepishly at the camera, his shoulders rounded; even at that age he stooped slightly because he was conscious of his height. A motorbike wheel was visible in one corner. The same motorbike Ryan and Grandpa had tinkered with, almost forty years later?

George March had died when she'd only been a few months old. She'd never known him and only had Belle's and Ryan's memories to fill in the blanks.

Her mother, despite enjoying her status as a hero's widow, never spoke of him.

Harriet sighed and put the photograph back. It was spooky how much Ryan now resembled him, but no matter how many times she stared at photos of her father, she'd never been able to feel a connection.

He could have been anyone.

EIGHT

It was growing dark by the time Iris arrived at the village museum, even though it was only mid-afternoon. A raven, its feathers ruffled up for warmth, was perched on one of the gateway pillars, watching as she approached. On the left pillar was carved the word 'Buckley'. On the right, 'Manor'. And beneath the 'Manor' bit, someone had added a rusted metal sign that said: 'Museum'.

The house had been built of mellow stone with dark-brown roof tiles. There was no garden, only a few desultory slabs of stone between the house and the road, barely enough to be considered a courtyard. The door was open, accompanied by the lure of heat, so Iris walked through it, stepping into a large square entrance hall, dark with gloomy panelling, brightened only by a ferocious display of weaponry – muskets and swords arranged into circles and swirls. But the swords were rusted and the muskets looped with cobwebs, and everything was furred with grey dust.

'It's a fiver.'

In the shadowy light, it took a moment for Iris to locate the speaker. A woman, either the same age or slightly younger than her, was sitting behind a battered old desk that had been tucked beside the door. With her bright yellow suit and clashing conker-coloured hair, Iris wasn't quite sure how she could have missed her.

Was this Ellie? The curator?

Hunched possessively over a heavy old book, the woman could have been cosplaying a librarian specialising in demons. *Had* she been the one to speak? There wasn't anyone else here. The museum gave off distinct undisturbed-tomb vibes: dusty display cabinets with bits of rusty armour, pyramids of cannon balls waiting to trip up the unwary, family portraits with varnish so grubby they could have been of anyone.

Could one of them be a Wainwright?

Eagerly, Iris moved forward.

'Hey, you! That'll be a fiver!' The woman scowled over the top of black-framed spectacles.

Iris tried to coax her half-frozen face into a smile. 'Hello, I'm Iris... Wainwright. Could I speak with the curator please?'

The woman retrieved a little wooden sign, partially hidden beneath a cascading pile of paperwork, and slapped it onto the desk, front and centre.

Ellie Garlick
Curator

'*You're* the curator?'

'Manager, curator, event-organiser, receptionist, cleaner and child minder.'

Child minder?

Because she worked in a museum?

Iris's lips twitched. 'I'm trying to identify a man in a photograph—'

'Are you coming in or going out?' Ellie asked. She had a strong Yorkshire accent. 'Make your mind up. I'm very busy.'

'In,' Iris said. 'About this photograph—'

Ellie held out her hand. 'That will be five pounds.'

Iris dug the required amount from her purse and was given a yellowing raffle ticket with '7' written on it. Evidently they didn't receive many visitors.

She started again. 'I've just moved into the village—'

'Good for you.' Ellie went back to her book. It appeared incredibly old. The paper was thick and ragged at the edges, the print heavy and curling...

'And?' Ellie had glanced up again.

'What?'

'You've just moved into the village *and*...?'

'Yes, into a house called Álfheimr. It's on the other side of the bridge—'

'You mean Raven's Hollow.'

'*No*, the Gothic revival house.'

'Raven's Hollow,' Ellie repeated. 'Also known as the Wainwright house. It was called Raven's Hollow for almost a century until that idiot Clement Wainwright got his hands on it. I don't know why his descendants didn't change it back again. They did everything else to disassociate themselves from him.'

'You know about the Wainwright family?'

Ellie regarded her suspiciously. 'Don't you? They're *your* family.'

'It's... complicated.'

'Families always are.' Ellie returned to her book. 'Go through that door. The route is laid out in a circle, with arrows. Upstairs is out of bounds. There are security cameras, so don't think of sneaking over any ropes because I'll know.'

This was hard work. 'Do you have anything about the Wainwrights?'

'No.'

'Then why...'

Ellie leant forward, placing both palms on the desk. 'You're in the *museum*. I assumed you wanted to see *around* the museum, so I'm telling you the best way to go about that.'

'But I—'

'Have a nice day.'

Iris leant over the desk and flipped the book shut. It was larger and heavier than she was expecting. The table shook and a small cloud of dust floated into the air.

'Could you please just listen to me? I want to know about the Wainwright family, particularly Cressida and Walter. I want to know about Raven's Hollow and I want to know about Clement Wainwright. Most of all, I want to know about the man in this photo!' She waved it in front of Ellie's nose. 'Can you help?'

Ellie tilted her head. 'You seem tense. Would a cup of tea help?'

'Will that be another fiver?'

'Free, from my kitchen. We don't have a café. No point when the village is full of them.' She shrugged. 'Whatever. Your choice.'

Even though she was pretty much awash with tea, Iris said, 'I would love a cup, thank you.'

'Then follow me.' Ellie strode off between the tall glass cabinets.

Iris hurried after her. 'Aren't you going to lock the door?'

'Why?' Sly grin. 'No one ever comes here.'

In a tiny kitchen that might once have been a scullery, Ellie made two strong teas in bright-red mugs. She didn't use a teapot but bashed the teabags against the side of the mugs (Iris tried not to wince), half-heartedly splashed in some milk, then handed a mug to Iris with a careless, 'Follow me. I have something to show you.'

That sounded promising.

Walking in the opposite direction to the arrows, they entered a much brighter, white-panelled room with a carved plaster ceiling and large windows onto the street. At first glance it seemed to hold a collection of doll-houses, but then Iris realised she was looking at the village in miniature. The detail was incredible. She recognised all the shops she'd walked past earlier, including The Secret Grimoire, and on the very far side of the room was Álfheimr – no, Raven's Hollow – all spiky gables and stained-glass windows. Written on a peeling plastic panel was a short paragraph about its origin, above a sketch of a Victorian gentleman with ginger hair and impressive whiskers.

'Raven's Hollow was designed by Alistair Harrow,' Ellie pointed to the sketch, 'for a wealthy tea merchant, who gave it to one of his daughters as a wedding present. I don't think she liked it much because as soon as she and her husband moved in Strange Things Happened.'

'What sort of strange things?' Iris bent to touch one of the stained-glass windows – they were so incredibly realistic; they even opened – only to have her hand slapped away.

'The usual childish pranks if you want to stage a haunting. Paintings turned to the wall, doors that wouldn't open, doors that wouldn't stay closed, precious items disappearing and then reappearing as if by magic. A subsequent explanation was that either the bride or the groom had no desire to live there but didn't want to antagonise the father. Another is that the family upset the servants or local people in some way, so the pranks were played to get rid of them. The house was rented out for the next eighty years without any complaints, until Professor Clement Wainwright bought it in 1920, purely because of all the stories attached to it. Instead of a poltergeist, he said it was "the fair folk" who were to blame. He then went all out trying to prove fairies were real. The newspapers of the time completely savaged him. His reputation was ruined. No one took him seriously after that. So he walked into the forest one day and never came back.'

Iris knew exactly what it felt like to draw the wrong kind of attention from the press.

'How awful for him!'

Ellie tilted her head, as though she couldn't work out if Iris was joking. 'He brought it on himself. He came from a wealthy family. He never had to do a proper day's work in his life. There was no one to rein him in or tell him to get a grip. He'd racked up huge debts. By "disappearing", his wife could have him declared legally dead.'

'Yet he'd be forced to live the rest of his life in hiding. Don't you find that sad?'

Ellie waved a dismissive hand. 'That's what happens when you're given too much wealth and privilege. He was carried away by his own cleverness.'

Iris wondered if she should stand up for an ancestor she hadn't known existed until that morning. 'Do you have anything else about the Wainwrights?'

'No, they weren't a local family. Clement was born in Manchester. I'm not sure where his wife was from but she didn't return there after his disappearance. Just remained in that strange house with their only son.' Ellie abruptly downed her tea. 'Are you done? Because I have to get back to work. Feel free to wander about – well, not free, because you've just paid five pounds – and don't go up the stairs either.'

'Wait!' Iris quickly tugged the photograph out of her bag. She'd almost forgotten what she was here for. 'Before you go, there was one other thing. Do you know who this man is?'

Ellie barely glanced at the photo. 'I've never seen him before in my life.'

Tia glanced back into the drawing room. Her Prince Charming was now discussing dog waste bins, of all things. Did he know there was a party going on around him? He certainly hadn't noticed she'd left his side. The man was infuriating!

Spinning away, she collided with a waiter, knocking the tray of drinks from his hand.

The resulting crash was as spectacular as one might expect.

They both stared at the mess.

He swore under his breath.

Here was someone having a worse evening than her.

'I'm sorry,' she said.

He shrugged, kicking the broken glass into a flower bed and tossing the tray in after it.

'No problem,' he shrugged. 'I'm about to be fired anyway.'

'How do you – Ah...'

Stepping through the French doors and onto the terrace were her husband and Brianna, wearing identical expressions of disapproval.

'Damn,' Tia said. 'That's my evening over.'

The waiter followed the direction of her gaze, then looked her up and down and smiled.

'Would you like me to take you away from all this?' he said, holding out his hand.

'What?' Surely he hadn't meant—

He rolled his eyes. 'Yes, I am asking you to run away with me. Well, to a nice little wine bar I know.'

Now it was her turn to look him over. Not much taller than her, he had blond hair cut very short, and a wicked gleam in the bluest eyes she'd ever seen.

Did she really have to think twice?

'Yes, please!'

'Then come on.' He grabbed her hand and pulled her between the dancing guests, down some steps and around to the front of the house, where a line of cars had been parked all the way down the drive. He picked a sleek black sports car and held the door open for her.

Was the car his? Tia was shocked to realise she didn't care, just slid inside, feeling the kind of thrill she hadn't experienced in months.

Would her husband be furious with her?

Oh, yes.

Did she care?

Not in the slightest.

Maybe it would teach him to appreciate her.

NINE

Iris made her way home. The weather hadn't improved and it had begun to snow – tiny bitter flakes that sliced her cheeks and blew over the cobblestones, as if some invisible creature were creating a path especially for her.

Led astray by the scent of freshly baked cookies, she called into The Crooked Broomstick and was served by a man with white-blond hair wearing an apron with broomsticks printed on it.

But when she turned into the single-track lane that led to Álfheimr – Raven's Hollow? – another person with white-blond hair was walking ahead of her.

A visitor?

She didn't know anyone.

And then she remembered all the people she'd spoken to today, and the stories she'd told about who she was, why she was here and what she was looking for.

Was someone looking for her?

'Hello!' The wind stole her voice away.

She walked faster, sliding a little on the snow as she tried to catch up.

The flakes had fallen in the gaps between the trees, frosting the lane and prettifying the frozen mud in the potholes. No footprints had been left in front of her but something white was weaving between the rowan trees ahead of her.

Ignoring the way the lane curved left towards her house, Iris stepped into the woods, where the lane narrowed to a track and then a path. Had there once been other houses here, centuries ago? She could see recognisable shapes – a wall, part of a doorway, a window – the outlines blurred by ivy. How long ago had they been abandoned?

The path led through a clearing, up an incline and then back down again, before twisting away between the trees. Iris was no longer sure in which direction she was headed. All the trees appeared the same. Did this path lead into her garden? She hoped—

Her feet slipped from under her and suddenly she was out of the trees, blinking at the light and sliding rapidly down a muddy slope towards the edge of the gorge.

She didn't have time to scream. She flung out her arms, hoping to grab something – a tree trunk, a branch, even brambles – at this point she didn't care. If she went over the edge, that would be the end of her.

Her hand smacked a concrete post. She bit off an oath but hooked her arm around it, abruptly sliding sideways instead, her shoulder wrenching as she was jerked to a stop.

For a moment she lay there, the snow fluttering into her eyes.

Then reality hit.

Bloody hell!

Her new coat would be ruined.

Better the coat than you.

Was this what had happened to Clement? One unwary step and a deadly plunge into the gorge? Then why all the rubbish about the fairies taking him?

Fairies made for a better story.

Iris dug her heels into the loose soil and shoved backwards, trying not to dwell on the fact that her left boot was mostly dangling in mid-air.

Once she reached the post, she flung both arms around it and pulled herself back onto her feet. Only then did she dare look behind her.

A narrow chasm of nothing but air, and below, great lumps of rocks with the River Thunor crashing over them.

The drop wasn't huge but she would have been killed like that poor witch, except she didn't have the ability to turn herself into ravens.

It was no consolation to realise the stone post she was hanging onto was part of a boundary fence – a line of similar posts clinging onto the rocky cliff like broken teeth. Stepping around the post, she launched herself at the nearest tree, grabbing onto that, and then the one beyond it, until the ground was firm beneath her and she could see her own footprints on the path.

By the time she staggered out from the forest and onto the lane, the snow had stopped completely, otherwise she might never have seen the white-furred creature hunched on a branch at eye level.

Was that what she'd been following through the trees?

A cat?

It mewed, somewhat pathetically, its fur wet and bedraggled.

'How did you get out here?' She took a step towards it and it cringed away. Noting the mud streaking its fur, the way its ears were flattened against its head and its drooping tail, she softened her tone. 'What are you doing out here, sweetheart? This is no place for you.'

'Meow!' it said again.

When she held out her hand it sniffed her fingertips cautiously.

'Aren't you beautiful?' She gently stroked its head, fondling behind its ears.

It arched into her touch and she picked it up, holding it against her coat, hoping it wasn't going to stick its claws into her as a thank-you. But it snuggled against her as she walked up the drive and went into the house.

TEN

When Harriet returned home to Foxglove & Hemlock, the garden behind the house was empty and quiet. With all the foot traffic, the long grass had been flattened and the stepping stones were easier to see. She itched to duck beneath the tape and follow them through the shrubbery to the glasshouse, but knew better than to trample all over a crime scene, even if the CSIs had finished their work. She turned away and stepped up onto the decking.

The back door was locked, which wasn't surprising considering the fence was down and so many strangers had been traipsing in and out of the garden. Gabriel's skip was still empty. The boxes of junk had been taken to Calahurst Police Station to be searched and logged as potential evidence.

Harriet unlocked the back door and headed up to her flat, dropping her coat onto the sofa and switching on her coffee machine. The little kitchen window soon steamed up. She pushed it open, then heard the creak of the garden door below and footsteps going out onto the decking.

Amelia seemed to be grumbling about cancelling the renovation until the New Year.

'The work will be quicker to complete when the weather turns warmer,' Gabriel replied. From the tension in his voice, he'd had this conversation several times already today. 'Look on the bright side, the police took all the crap away with them.'

'They'll soon bring it back when they realise it's a load of old rubbish.'

Harriet leant closer to the window. Now that *was* interesting, because it implied Amelia had always known what was inside those cardboard boxes. Had she also removed any potentially incriminating evidence?

Harriet grabbed a notebook and pen and scribbled that down.

Amelia spoke again. 'It gives me the creeps to think of that skeleton buried there for all those years, without anyone knowing. I touched those bones!'

'You were wearing gardening gloves,' Gabriel said, 'and you were fine when you thought the bones belonged to a dog!'

'Yes, a much-loved pet that had died peacefully of old age – not a *person*, who'd once walked and breathed, and was somebody's son – or daughter. Did Harriet say anything more about it to you? Was the skeleton a man or a woman? Were they *murdered*?'

'One of the forensic guys said it was a man, young to middle-aged, and that he had been there for a few decades.'

'Do you think Harriet knows any more details?'

'Of course – but she's hardly going to tell us!'

'I suppose she's not allowed to. Do you think she'd know when we'd be allowed back into the glasshouse?'

Gabriel's sigh was loud enough for Harriet to hear from the attic. 'Does it matter? We've missed our slot. The workmen won't be able to start until January now, maybe not until March if the weather doesn't perk up.'

'Can you arrange for the skip to be collected and the fence

put back? I hate the idea that anyone can walk in and out of the garden.' Silence. 'Do you think that's how the murderer got in?'

'Unless he lived here...'

Amelia squealed. 'Thank you for putting that idea in my head. Now I won't be able to sleep tonight.'

Gabriel chuckled. 'Maybe we could do... something else?'

Harriet quickly moved to close the window, having no wish to hear any of *that* conversation, but then heard her name mentioned and froze.

'Can you have a chat with Harriet, to see if things can be speeded up? It's ridiculous not being allowed into our own garden.'

'It might sound better coming from you,' Gabriel said. 'Harriet thinks I'm an idiot.'

Harriet winced and firmly closed the window. She really needed to work on her poker face. And, in the meantime, she'd get up super-early tomorrow, so she wouldn't have to speak to either of them.

15th December

The cadaver dog (a super-friendly black Labrador called Jasper), along with his handler, Reg, were booked to attend Foxglove & Hemlock the following morning. Ben checked everyone had what they needed to proceed, then left Ash in charge of the scene while he and Harriet drove to Norchester to interview the former owner, Niall Kinsella. They couldn't spare the time to hang around waiting for the dog to find (or not find) something.

'I should have booked today off too,' Harriet grumbled, as she drove out of the village. 'I bet that would have been fun.'

'*Fun?* Watching a dog hunt for a dead body? Harriet March, I worry about you.'

'I meant the dog was cute!'

'Would you rather I'd left you there and brought Ash with me? It's not too late to turn back.'

She side-eyed him.

'Thought not,' he said, and settled back in the seat to read the case notes.

Norchester should have been a thirty-minute drive away but took less time because of the way Harriet swerved in and out of the traffic. As usual, the city was full of tourists and last-minute Christmas shoppers, but Harriet managed to squeeze the car into a tiny parking space down a little side street.

Niall Kinsella lived in a house at the end of a smart Georgian terrace, tucked in beside the city walls. It had been built from the same stone and each house had been recently renovated, the attics transformed into open-plan living spaces with glass-walled balconies overlooking the top of the wall.

On the inside, the house had been thoroughly modernised and decorated in neutral colours – a bit too neutral, Ben decided, unable to see much evidence of the occupant's personality.

He took a seat on a stone-coloured sofa, directly opposite an incredible view of the forest, but it didn't take him long to realise that anyone walking along the top of the city walls (they were a huge tourist attraction) could see straight into this room and, if they were brave enough, step off the wall, over the glass panel and onto the balcony.

Niall Kinsella had prepared a tray of coffee and biscuits on pretty shell-coloured plates with matching mugs, and seemed pleased to see them, giving them as friendly a grin as Jasper the cadaver dog had when they'd first met him. Did Kinsella never have visitors? On the way up the stairs, they'd passed a small, sterile room with a laptop and three monitors, along with every sign that Kinsella worked from home and lived alone, without even a pet for company.

Kinsella was an attractive man in his mid-thirties with dark-blond hair and pale skin, and the kind of fine lines fanning out from his eyes that were caused by squinting at a computer screen all day. He was wearing jeans with a blue and white open-necked shirt, despite the bitter cold outside, but the heating was on high and Ben was soon sweltering in his suit.

'This view is *amazing*,' Harriet said, dropping onto the sofa beside Ben as he was about to take a sip of coffee. She helped herself to two shortbread biscuits. 'But isn't it weird to have people staring in at you all the time from the wall?'

Harriet could always be relied upon to ask the one question anyone else would be too polite to mention.

Kinsella's friendly grin didn't diminish. 'I'm used to it after living in Raven's Edge. Tourists would walk past my sitting room every day and try to see inside – the oak beams and inglenook fireplace would fascinate them. If I forgot to lock the door, they'd come right inside, as though they thought it was open to the public!'

Ben tried to remember what the interior of the florist had been like. 'Do you mean Foxglove & Hemlock?'

'No. When I left home I rented a cottage in Church Lane. It was a pretty little place. Only one room per floor, no good for a family, but it suited me fine.'

It sounded like the kind of house Ben's girlfriend, Milla, lived in.

'Your father used to own Foxglove & Hemlock,' Ben said. 'Wasn't that the family house?'

Dakota had already researched ownership of the house as far back as the early twentieth century, but he wanted to hear Kinsella confirm it.

'That's right.' Kinsella took the chair to one side of the coffee table. 'The house originally belonged to my grandfather, who was the village doctor. When he died, my father started the floristry business, calling it "Kinsella's". That was in the nineties. In those days, people would come from miles around to buy flowers from there.' He sighed and stared sadly into his coffee.

Ben waited for Harriet to say, 'They still do,' but fortunately she kept quiet. It helped that she'd taken another biscuit.

'These are great,' she said, biting into it.

Kinsella perked up. 'Do you think so? Thank you! I made them myself. I was trialling a new recipe.'

Despite himself, Ben reached for one of the biscuits. They did taste good. Dense and buttery.

'Are you a chef, Mr Kinsella?'

'Me?' He seemed surprised to be asked. 'No, it's only a hobby. I bake to de-stress and, as it turned out, I'm better at it then I ever was at floristry; but I have a proper job now. I'm a financial advisor.'

Somehow Ben managed not to choke on the biscuit. Hadn't Gabriel said that Kinsella had run the floristry business into the ground? What if that wasn't true? (Something else for Dakota to investigate.) Was Ben guilty of what he was always telling Harriet not to do – believing someone's testimony without the evidence to back it up?

'As DC Dakota Lawrence would have explained on the phone to you yesterday, we've found human remains in the glasshouse behind Foxglove & Hemlock.'

'That old thing? Is it still standing? It was derelict when I was a child.'

'You don't seem surprised to hear about the human remains though?'

'Well,' Niall said, colouring slightly, 'it *is* a very old house. I assume the body was too? It's close to the church. Could the land have once been part of the graveyard?'

Ben sincerely hoped not. They hadn't the time, the manpower or the budget to start digging up medieval remains on the off-chance a modern corpse was among them.

'The forensic anthropologist is running tests,' he said,

'which are in no way conclusive, but we believe the remains are less than fifty years old.'

'Less than fifty, eh? I wonder if...' He trailed off, before starting again, his voice sounding strained. 'This is going to sound odd, but my father disappeared one day. I saw him at breakfast, I didn't even bother to say goodbye when I went to school, and that was the last I saw of him. I never did find out where he'd gone. My stepmother wouldn't say, my brother couldn't care less – there was a big age gap between us and we weren't really a close family. Occasionally I did wonder if my stepmother had...' He stopped abruptly, just as it was getting interesting. 'Um, I probably shouldn't say stuff like this without a lawyer present...'

'Are you suggesting that the remains might be your father?'

He was quiet for a moment. 'Do you honestly believe there's a chance they may be? My stepmother had him declared legally dead but I'd rather think of him gallivanting around Europe with a bunch of mates. He always wanted to travel but Hestia would never leave the flower shop. She loved it more than she loved him.' Kinsella sighed heavily. 'I didn't go abroad myself until I was seventeen. A college trip to Italy. I've never forgotten it. Those were the days. Ironic, really. Now I can afford to travel, I don't have the time.'

Ben was at a loss what to say.

Thankfully, Harriet jumped into the breach. 'When did you last see your father?'

'I was about ten, so this would have been... twenty-five years ago? I can't remember the exact date. It might have been summer, but I'm guessing now. Sorry.'

At least it was a lead. Plausible, if slightly fantastic, and it would depend on the age of the skeleton.

Wouldn't that be convenient though? Everything neatly concluded in time for Christmas.

'Did anyone else live in the house with you at that time?' Ben asked.

'No, only my father, stepmother, younger brother and myself.'

'Do you remember anyone else going missing in the village at that time?'

'People are always going missing in Raven's Edge! They usually turn up in the end – unless they don't want to be found.'

'When you owned the business, did anyone live in the house with you?'

'It was far too big for me. I turned the rooms above the shop into two apartments, which I rented out, and I lived in the terraced house in Church Lane that I told you about. Gorgeous little place. I regret giving it up, but it wasn't practical after I started this job. I needed a reliable phone and internet connection for a start.'

'Were you aware that your stepmother left several boxes of possessions in the glasshouse, along with some miscellaneous furniture? The current owners say you instructed them to throw everything into a skip.'

Niall nodded cheerfully. 'That's right. No point in hanging onto the past.'

'Those are personal belongings, Mr Kinsella. Photographs, school reports, correspondence... Are you sure you don't want anything?'

DC Freddie Kuang from Calahurst was currently sifting through everything in the chance it might be evidence but, after that, they'd like to hand it back. There was nowhere to store it in Raven's Edge. The evidence cupboard was exactly that: a small room in what had once been the attic. The one at Calahurst Police Station wasn't much better.

'I'm sure.' Kinsella sounded rather definite. 'There's nothing of my father's – Hestia threw everything out when he left.

When she had him declared legally dead, everything went to her – held in trust for me.'

'You don't feel that you might want your own belongings back? That you might regret us disposing of them on your behalf?'

'I can see I'll have to be blunt. My childhood was an unhappy time for me. I don't want to be reminded of it. I was confused about who I was and what I wanted to be, and how I wanted to spend my life and who I wanted to spend it with. My stepmother and I didn't agree on a lot of things – anything, really. Later (after much counselling), I wondered if Hestia took the opposing view just to spite me. It was my counsellor's advice to cut her out of my life (after giving her a final warning), because it was too upsetting to deal with her. When she died, about five years ago, the house and business came to me – but there was no money to go with it – she'd spent it all. She finally had her revenge on my father for leaving her.'

'But you still tried to make a go of the business?'

'I felt I owed it to my father, but what do I know about flowers? I can barely tell a daffodil from a tulip – I admit it! I didn't want to let anyone down – the staff and so forth – but, in the end, I was forced to sell the house and business to my brother and I started afresh, in another town, doing something I was better suited to. Ironically, my father would probably have approved.'

Ben glanced down at his notes. Turned back a page...

'Your brother?' Had the *brother* sold the property to Gabriel?

Now it was Kinsella's turn to appear confused. 'Yes, after my father married Hestia, they had my brother – half-brother, I suppose you'd call him. My father left the house and business to be shared equally between us after my stepmother died. Because I'd been to business school and had worked in finance, I was supposed to take care of the day-to-day running of the shop and share half the profits with him, but I never *made* any profits. It was a great weight, dragging me under. I nearly had a breakdown over the thing. So I sold up.'

'Does your brother still own a fifty per cent share in Foxglove & Hemlock?'

'Yes, that's why it was easier for Gabriel to buy me out. He only had to come up with half the money.'

Ben tried to get his head around this. 'So your brother *still* owns a fifty per cent share?'

Kinsella stared at them as though he thought them a pair of idiots.

'No, Gabriel owns everything, because Gabriel *is* my brother.'

The stranger's name was Aaron Cooper and he did own the black sports car, along with a rather nice apartment overlooking Calahurst Marina. He'd been serving drinks to help his sister, whose company had been hired to do the catering for Brianna Graham. It might take a while for his sister to forgive him for running out on her, but he was sure she would... eventually.

'So what is it you do?' Tia asked, as they sipped negronis at a little bar overlooking the water.

'I'm a detective constable,' was his somewhat sheepish reply.

'Here, in Calahurst?'

'Recently posted to Raven's Edge.'

Just a few doors down from where she lived!

'How about you?' he asked.

'I work in the florist, Kinsella's.'

'I know it,' he nodded his head. 'So why were you at the party with that bunch of boring old—'

Laughing, she quickly cut him off. 'I was with my husband!'

Aaron promptly choked on his drink.

But by the end of the evening, he'd asked to see her again.

ELEVEN

Iris woke up because the cat was licking her nose.

When she tried to pull away, she found it was sitting on her hair.

Iris eased herself free. 'There are easier ways to tell me you're hungry.'

The cat blinked pale-green eyes. With all the excitement yesterday, Iris had forgotten to sponge it down and the poor thing still had streaks of mud in its white fur. She certainly won the prize for most irresponsible cat owner. Not that it *was* her cat. She ran her fingers over its neck, checking for a collar, but there was nothing. Had it been microchipped? She needed to find a local vet.

But in the meantime...

Iris scooped up the cat and took it into the bathroom. The cat, which turned out to be female, was furious at the impromptu sponge bath, yowling loudly and scratching Iris's hand as a thank-you, before going off to sulk in a corner.

Iris grinned. 'There you go! You're now sparkling!'

When Iris ran herself a bath, the cat became brave enough to walk around the old-fashioned roll-top, occasionally batting at the bubbles with a paw and nearly sliding in several times, despite Iris firmly putting her back on the floor.

By the time Iris had pulled on another of her identical black jersey dresses (super-comfy and it was one less decision to make in the morning), her food order from the local grocery store had been left on the doorstep in several large paper bags. Another trick she'd learnt to avoid leaving the house. She'd ordered proper cat food as well as a litter tray. She tipped dry food into a bowl for the cat to sniff at disparagingly, while she cooked herself a full English breakfast, only for the cat to run away with a rasher of bacon when her back was turned.

Iris tried to encourage the cat to return home by leaving the front door open, but it took one glance at the snow, tail twitching, and stalked off into the library. She found it later, curled up in a puddle of sunlight on the windowsill, which was, coincidentally, directly over a cast-iron radiator.

It must be lovely to be a cat, Iris thought, settling down at her desk in the library, just as someone knocked on the front door. It echoed hollowly around the hall. On the other side of the library window, an attractive blonde forty-something impatiently stepped from foot to foot on the drive. She was holding a floral tin. Was she selling something?

The woman glanced sideways, saw Iris and waggled her fingers.

Was it too late to hide beneath her desk?

Probably.

Sighing, Iris hit 'save' and went to open the door.

'Hi,' the woman beamed. She was tiny, barely above five foot, with long pale-blonde hair, parted in the middle. 'I'm Anya March. I live next door.'

Iris tried to remember what was next door other than trees and more trees. 'At the pub?'

'I wish! No, The Laurels. It's a big old Victorian house, somewhere over there.' Anya squinted at the surrounding trees.

'I think. It's hard to tell with this forest. If I didn't know better, I'd swear those trees move, but don't let me put you off living here!' She giggled, the high-pitched sound at odds with her sophisticated appearance. '*Anyway*, I've brought you a cake! Welcome to the neighbourhood!' She shoved the tin she'd been holding at Iris.

Iris stared at it. Anya had brought her a *cake*? Wasn't that some kind of code that meant she had to invite the woman inside?

'My housekeeper made it,' Anya said, leaning forward as though they might be overheard. 'Golden rum cake with walnuts on top. You wouldn't want to eat any cake *I* made, trust me!' She giggled again, high and girlish, as though someone had once told her it sounded charming, and now she couldn't laugh any other way.

'I'm sure it's lovely,' Iris said. 'Thank you very much.'

Please go away and leave me alone.

'This is a very unusual house.' Anya peered past into the hall. 'Quite something, with the tower and all the stained glass. I don't believe I knew it was here until you moved in. Well, I knew it was *here* but not that anyone lived in it or that it looked like *this*.'

Iris was insulted on behalf of the house. 'It's a Gothic revival.'

Anya laughed again. 'I didn't even know Gothic was dead.'

Give me strength.

Was there no way to get out of it?

Iris took a deep breath and tried not to sound as though she was speaking between clenched teeth.

'Would you like to come inside and have a look around?'

Please say no...

But Anya had already squealed, 'Oh my goodness! Would I?' and shoved past.

Iris sighed and closed the door while Anya 'ooh-ed' and

'aah-ed' her way through the hall, only pausing to stroke the silver paintwork ('Does this represent that sinister ring of trees outside? How strange!') before marching into the library.

Why had she left her laptop switched on with her work-in-progress open on the screen?

If a blank screen could be called a work-in-progress?

She hurried after Anya, still carrying the cake tin, but Anya had stopped dead in front of the fireplace.

'Is that a *dragon*?' She rapped on its snout with her knuckles, something Iris had not dared to do in case it broke and fell off. The fireplace must be nearly two hundred years old; it was a miracle it had lasted this long without cracking or someone ripping it out. 'Made out of *stone*?'

'Granite, I think.'

'Where did you buy it?'

'It came with the house.'

'Oh.' Anya wrinkled her nose. 'Well, if you want to get rid of it, I can recommend someone to chisel it out for you. He's fabulous with his hands, if you know what I mean?' She winked.

What? *What*? Who *was* this woman?

How to politely say, 'Not a chance in hell'?

Anya's attention flitted over the bookshelves. 'Why do you have so many books?'

Iris always tried to avoid telling people what she did for a living, but she didn't like lying either. 'I use them for my work and I love reading.'

'Just like my daughter! She always has her nose in a book. No wonder she doesn't have a boyfriend. I keep telling her that she'll never meet anyone if all she does is read and go to work.'

That sounded pretty much like heaven to Iris.

'What work does your daughter do?' she asked.

Anya shrugged. 'She's in the police. Some kind of special squad. Such a shame. She always had a good eye for colour; I thought she'd work for me. I work in fashion – perhaps you've been in one of my exclusive boutiques? But no, Harriet *had* to join the police force like her father. He was a detective superintendent, you know? Killed on duty. A true hero, God rest his soul.' Anya cast her eyes down, holding her hands in front of her as though she were praying.

'How awful,' Iris said. 'I'm so sorry.'

Anya shrugged. 'It was years ago. I've been married and widowed again since then. You can't let these things define you.'

Iris opened her mouth and closed it again. What could she say to that?

Now it was her turn to fidget from foot to foot. Her arms were aching. The cake and its tin were surprisingly heavy. Yet Anya showed every sign of wanting to continue her 'tour', having a lovely time verbally tearing the house to shreds, and Iris couldn't bear it.

'Why don't I put the kettle on?' she suggested, somewhat desperately. 'We could have a cup of tea and a slice of cake? What do you think?'

'Sure, if you want? Coffee for me, no cream, no sugar.'

Cream? All Iris had was semi-skimmed milk!

'But you will have a slice of cake?'

'Goodness, no! All the sugar that went into that? Very bad for me.'

But fine for me?

Her fingers tightening around the cake tin, Iris headed in the direction of the kitchen, hoping Anya would follow. She did, merrily chatting all the way.

The cat reappeared as they entered the kitchen, weaving between Iris's legs and mewing hopefully.

'Oh, what a beautiful kitty.' Anya bent to give the cat a downward pat. The cat squirmed away, taking refuge beneath the bar stools. 'What's it called?'

'She's called... Sparkle,' Iris said, remembering all the mud and how hard it had been to get it off, and how much fuss the cat had made.

'Is it just you and the cat? No husband, no children?'

Iris toyed with the idea of inventing a husband and six children, all with names beginning with 'A': Alfred, Albert, Anastacia, Aloysius...

'Just me.' No need to mention the late, unlamented fiancé. Although, now that Anya was here... 'This was my mother's family home. Maybe you knew her? Her name was Cressida Wainwright?'

'No, I can't say that I did.' Anya ran her fingers over the cabinets. 'I do like the sage green. Such a fresh, clean colour. The rest of the house is a bit gloomy, isn't it?' She opened a cupboard and then a couple of drawers, and peered inside. 'Not much storage space. How do you get on with that?'

'Absolutely fine.' Iris slid the cake tin onto the counter before she was tempted to crown Anya with it. 'Because there's only me.'

'Meow,' the cat said pointedly.

'And Sparkle.'

'Oh yes,' Anya repeated. 'Just you.'

There was something in the way Anya spoke that made her feel uneasy. *Should* she be broadcasting the fact that she lived alone?

'My brother Justin will be moving in any day now,' she lied. 'He's currently working in America. He's an economics professor.'

'Lovely,' Anya said, turning over the wine bottles in the rack to check the labels.

This woman was a piece of *work*.

Although she'd far rather shove Anya out into the snow, Iris switched on the kettle and set a cafetière on the counter.

'What kind of coffee would you like? Do you prefer

Ethiopian? Colombian? Java...?' Anya did *not* look like the kind of person who'd drink instant.

'Colombian,' Anya said. She was stroking the bar stools, perhaps to check if they were real leather. Iris had bought them online, shortly before the move, purely because she thought they were practical and pretty.

Iris made the coffee and cut two large slices of cake and slid them onto plates. If Anya didn't want hers, Iris would eat it herself. It was turning into that kind of day.

Anya happily chatted away, telling Iris all about her life in Raven's Edge, which, from what Iris could gather, mostly revolved around going to the tennis club.

'You must join!' Anya beamed.

Over my dead body, Iris thought.

'I'll nominate you for membership. You'll be sure to make lots of friends.'

Who said she needed friends?

Did she *look* like someone who needed friends?

'I'm having a party in a few days' time. You absolutely must come to that! Bring your brother! The more men, the merrier! I'll introduce you to everyone.' Anya tucked into the cake, waving her fork as she carried on talking about herself, inadvertently scattering crumbs onto the tiled floor, which Sparkle immediately hoovered up before slinking back beneath the stools.

It was hard not to zone out, but when Anya mentioned that she was thinking of opening a menswear shop to complement her existing boutiques, Iris suddenly remembered the photo of the man in the suit.

'That's absolutely *fascinating*,' she said, interrupting a surprised Anya mid-story. 'But you've reminded me of something I'd like your opinion on. I'll fetch it from my bag.' Her bag was in the sitting room, and Iris half-expected Anya to follow her, but when she returned to the kitchen she was right where she'd left her, trying unsuccessfully to tempt Sparkle out from beneath the stools. 'I know this is an old photo, but have you any idea who this man is?'

Anya took the photo and her easy smile vanished, as though someone had hit 'reset'. She stared at the photo for a surprisingly long time before abruptly handing it back.

'No.' Her tone was cold and clipped. 'He doesn't seem familiar and I've lived in Raven's Edge all my life.'

Why did 'doesn't seem familiar' feel like code for: 'Hell, yeah! But I'm certainly not telling *you*.'

Then Anya asked the question that no one else had thought to.

'Why do you want to know?'

There was no reason not to tell her the truth.

'He's my father,' Iris said. 'I'm trying to find out what happened to him.'

TWELVE

Norchester had been built on the site of an old Roman fort. Many of the roads followed the traditional grid pattern and some of the shops and cafés still had traces of the original Roman buildings in their basements. Ben and Harriet chose a café a few doors down from Kinsella's house, which turned out to have thick glass tiles in the floor revealing the Roman foundations below.

Ben would have preferred a table in a dark corner, so they could talk about the case without being overheard, but Harriet was fascinated by the glass tiles and wanted to sit right next to one, much to the amusement of their waiter.

Ben ordered Portobello mushrooms on sourdough toast, Harriet asked for a sausage and caramelised onion sandwich on granary bread, and then covered it in ketchup as usual.

Ben watched in disbelief. 'How can you *eat* that?'

'Easy,' Harriet said. 'I open my mouth and shove it in.'

She proceeded to do exactly that, making a point of licking her fingers afterwards.

By the time their coffee arrived, the café was less busy. Ben felt more confident of speaking without being overheard.

'So, what do we think?'

'Could have done with more onion,' Harriet said.

Someone had had too much coffee. 'About *Kinsella*.'

She grinned unrepentantly. 'Let's say I'm glad you booked the cadaver dog if there's likely to be an entire village buried in that garden. Do we have Jasper for the whole day?'

'As long as it takes.' With that overgrown garden it could take forever.

'Does Niall Kinsella really believe his mum might have done away with his dad and buried him under the decking?' Harriet shook her head. 'What a family!'

'I'll see if Dakota can trace any record of him. No one completely disappears; they usually leave a trail of financial transactions. I'm more interested in why Gabriel lied about his relationship to Kinsella.'

'He didn't exactly lie but surely he'd know we'd find out the truth sooner or later. Does he think we're a bunch of idiots?'

'I received the distinct impression Gabriel Fox believes he's smarter than us, smarter than anyone, and I'm hoping that will trip him up. He's too young to have been involved with killing our skeleton, but perhaps he knew it was there? It was his family home. Adults talk in front of children, not realising how much they hear or understand.'

'Maybe, but anyone he wanted to protect, like his mother, is long dead.'

'What about his family's reputation?' he said.

Perhaps she wouldn't understand. Harriet's father had been a hero whereas his own relations were criminals – and that wasn't an easy thing to admit to. People were quick to judge. It was why he'd moved away eight years ago.

'I suppose so,' she said.

'We agree they're hiding something?'

'I've always thought they were strange.' Then, when Ben raised an eyebrow, 'What?'

'We'll have to interview them again.'

She grimaced. 'Can't we save that until we're really bored?'

'There are other avenues of investigation.'

'Such as? Most of our witnesses are likely to be dead too!'

Trust Harriet to point that out.

He drained his coffee and went to the counter to pay.

When he returned, she waved her work phone and said, 'The forensic anthropologist has the skeleton reassembled in his lab.'

All those little bones...

'That was quick work.'

'I expect he has lots of assistants to help. Maybe it's like doing a giant jigsaw puzzle? Wouldn't that be weird?'

He'd rather not think about it. It always surprised him that Harriet, despite her angelic appearance, could be quite ghoulish.

'Our victim is definitely male, about five foot eight, probably white,' she said. 'The head injury appears increasingly likely to be the cause of death – blunt instrument, nothing specific, too early to tell, blah, blah, blah. The anthropologist estimates he died about twenty to thirty years ago. Again, too early in the process for specifics.

'Meanwhile, Dakota has sent us all a list of missing persons for the relevant time period, but she's narrowed it down to three possibles. Sam has gone to check out two of them but the one who's top of her list has a next-of-kin who lives here in Norchester, outside the city walls in the posh bit. Should we pay a visit, seeing as we're here?'

It was convenient but, 'Were we supposed to be doing anything else this afternoon?'

She grinned. 'Probably, but who cares about that?'

.   .   .

As Harriet drove, Ben read through the extensive notes Dakota
had sent them, along with a poor-quality photo of the possible
victim; it was the size of a passport photo but turned out to have
been taken from a warrant card.

Ben read that again.

A *warrant* card?

He'd been a police officer?

Detective Constable Aaron Cooper (no middle name), aged
twenty-five, had been deployed to CID at Raven's Edge for less
than twelve months before he'd failed to come into work one
day. His attendance record had always been abysmal, so no one
paid much attention. By the time his supervisor had thought to
officially inquire as to the reason for his absence, Cooper had
been missing for over a week.

Yet his apartment gave every impression he'd intended to
return. He had a well-stocked refrigerator (albeit with the food
going off), dirty crockery left in the sink, and a half-drunk mug
of coffee in the sitting room. His DVD player had been set to
record his favourite shows, several windows had been left ajar,
and the latest Jack Reacher novel, the spine cracked open, lay
on his nightstand.

His friends had suggested that he might have fallen into the
marina while drunk. But the marina was busy and the river was
tidal. Anyone that fell into it would eventually wash up in Port
Rell, on Fisherman's Beach.

No body was ever found.

Ben had worked at Raven's Edge Police Station for exactly a
year, in what had once been the CID offices but which were
now assigned to the Murder Investigation Team. Why had he
never heard of DC Cooper? Why wasn't there a memorial
plaque or framed photo on the wall, as there was for other officers who had died on duty – such as Harriet's father?

Because the official line was that Cooper had vanished
deliberately: no body, no death. Ergo, he was still alive.

Even though his bank account and credit cards hadn't been touched?

And there was no record of him leaving the country?

And his car had been left in the car park at Raven's Edge Police Station?

(Apparently no one had noticed that for a week either.)

Who the *hell* had been in charge of this case?

To add to that, as Ben worked his way through the notes Dakota had sent him, he built up a concerning impression of the man: work-shy, lazy, arrogant. Refused to work as part of a team. Problems with authority.

It wasn't a great testimonial.

As no body had been found, and because Cooper had the reputation for going AWOL to meet various women when he should have been working, the investigating officer's eventual conclusion was that Cooper had planned his disappearance deliberately – probably with one of the aforementioned women.

Ben's opinion was that a man with Cooper's temperament would have been a prime target for murder by someone he'd thoroughly annoyed – but that was an easy conclusion to draw with hindsight.

So *was* it Cooper's body in the glasshouse, deliberately desecrated to hide its identity?

It was a lot of trouble to go to, when a simple whack over the head and shove into the marina would have been much more convenient – and far easier to blame on an accident.

But if he turned this on its head...

What kind of person would think to strip a body of clothing and any ID – including its teeth?

Someone who made a habit of this kind of thing?

Or someone who knew how to hide a murder and disappear before they could be incriminated?

Which led to the obvious question...

Had DC Aaron Cooper been the victim – or the murderer?

'I want to be with you,' Aaron told Tia, three months later. 'Sneaking around, stolen moments – it's not enough for me.'

'What are you suggesting? A weekend break in Paris? That would be lovely!' She hugged him. 'Although I'm not sure how I'd explain my absence to my husband? Actually, he might not even notice I'd gone...'

Aaron laughed and took her hands in his. 'I don't think you understand, baby. I'm asking you to marry me! I don't have a ring yet. I thought you could choose one that you liked, but—'

'Oh, but I can't! How disappointing. I'm already married!'

He flinched, his smile fading. 'Thank you for reminding me. Let me put it more plainly. Leave him and marry me. We can live in my apartment and then choose somewhere together.'

That tiny little apartment overlooking the marina? He had to be joking!

He was being a little slow with the punchline though.

'Why?' she asked eventually.

'Why what?'

'Why do you want to marry me?'

'Because I love you!'

'Oh...'

He was adorable when he scowled like that.

'Tia? What's the matter? Don't... don't you love me?'

'Of course I do!' she lied. 'What a silly question!'

She threw her arms around him and kissed him, and that seemed to distract him very nicely, but it had got her thinking.

How much did he love her?

Would he die for her?

Or, more to the point, would he kill for her?

THIRTEEN

Harriet drove into a small, exclusive estate of large, modern houses, one step down from a gated community. Big gardens, triple garages, the occasional swimming pool and *very* quiet.

What would it be like to live here instead of Raven's Edge?

Boring. You wouldn't even know you *had* neighbours behind those immaculately trimmed hedges.

On the other hand, you could get up to all sorts of mischief and no one would ever know...

Like murder?

'It's this house,' Ben said, indicating one of the largest. 'Number fourteen. There doesn't seem to be a number thirteen though...'

'Did you know living at a number thirteen can knock £5,000 off the value of your house? Although I don't feel that would trouble the kind of people who can afford to live here.'

'£5,000 is £5,000, however well-off you might be,' Ben said.

That sum wouldn't bother a member of the wealthy Graham family, but Harriet knew better than to say so, because of his relationship with Milla Graham.

Deep in thought, she misjudged the dip in the pavement,

bumped the car up the kerb and onto a curving, paved drive, and parked directly in front of a cherry-red front door. Instead of Christmas trees, bay trees were planted either side of it, their glossy red pots matching a bay wreath on the door.

She beat Ben into knocking. She always preferred to knock, rather than ring a bell. You could never be sure a bell had worked if you couldn't hear it yourself.

There was never any mistaking *her* knock.

'Remind me again,' she muttered, as the outline of someone approaching could be seen through the frosted-glass panel, 'who have we come to see?'

'DC Aaron Cooper's last surviving relative,' Ben said. 'His sister, Mrs Janie Ware – née Arnott, née Cooper. Sole owner of Cooper Event Organising, formerly Cooper Catering. They've been established for over twenty-five years.'

'And are very successful.' Harriet pointed to a line of expensive cars she'd spotted in the garage.

There was a shadowy movement and the electric garage door began to sweep down. Ben and Harriet had been spotted.

Guiltily, they turned as the front door was opened by a blonde forty-something woman, whom Harriet thought seemed familiar. Hopefully she hadn't arrested Mrs Ware in the past.

'Hello,' Mrs Ware said. 'You must be the police. DC Dakota Lawrence explained you'd be on your way. She didn't tell me why, but I can work it out. It's about Aaron, right? You've finally found him.'

Was that scorn in the way she said 'finally'? That didn't bode well.

Managing not to exchange a wary glance with Ben, Harriet said, 'I'm DS Harriet March and this is Detective Inspector Ben Taylor.'

'An *inspector*, eh? I *am* honoured.'

Working with DCI Cameron meant Harriet was fluent in

sarcasm, confirmed when the woman gave Harriet a sharp glance before turning and walking into the house.

Harriet lingered on the doorstep feeling like an old-school vampire. Well, Mrs Ware hadn't actually *said* 'Please come in.' As she wasn't a suspect, they couldn't force their way inside. What were they supposed to do?

Ben nudged her. 'She left the door open,' he pointed out, stepping around Harriet and heading into the house. 'That's considered a subtle hint.'

Grumpily, Harriet followed him inside and closed the door behind her. 'You know I don't do "subtle".'

The chilly reception was hardly surprising. Janie Ware thought they were here to inform her they'd found her brother's remains. It would be an extremely traumatic experience for her. Of course she wasn't going to be pleased to see them – and it didn't help that every indication was that Aaron Cooper's disappearance had been badly handled by their colleagues at the time.

Janie led them into a sunny sitting room overlooking a well-tended garden at the back of the house, and politely offered hot drinks.

After all the coffee Harriet had knocked back this morning, it might be more prudent to decline, like Ben, but she nodded. Once Janie was out of the room, she could have a good snoop.

'That would be lovely,' she said, and Janie withdrew to make it.

Harriet immediately headed over to one of two floor-to-ceiling bookcases, filled with the latest hardbacks, as well as many framed photos of the Ware family, who all seemed to be tanned, sporty, blond and blue-eyed. Amongst them were older photos, perhaps from the nineties, of two teenagers grinning at the camera, so alike they could have been twins.

Janie and Aaron?

Harriet turned to make a comment to Ben, only to find Janie standing directly behind her, holding a mug of coffee.

Damn, that was quick!

'Lovely photos!' she said, taking the coffee.

Behind Janie, Ben rolled his eyes and gave her an ironic thumbs-up.

Janie was frowning. '*What* did you say your name was?'

'Harriet March.' Why was *that* important?

Again, Harriet spotted an expression of distaste on Janie's face before she turned away to place her own mug on a coffee table and sit on the sofa.

Maybe she *had* arrested this woman in the past.

Harriet exchanged a worried glance with Ben but he shrugged and picked up another photo from a collection on top of a piano. It was a professional portrait of Aaron Cooper, wearing a suit, perhaps in celebration of something?

'Would it be possible to have a copy of this?'

Janie's gaze softened. 'That was his twenty-first birthday. I have a matching one but it's in a box somewhere. I still had acne but Aaron was always incredibly photogenic. He never bothered to pose, just looked at the camera and grinned.' She took the photo from Ben, her hand lightly stroking the glass, and Harriet wondered if she was about to tell them she couldn't bear to part with it. But then she said, 'I'll scan it for you now, if you like.'

Harriet waited for her to leave the room before whispering to Ben, 'She definitely doesn't like us.'

'Whoever originally investigated Aaron's disappearance handled it very badly *and* we've never found his body. Not a sterling performance.'

'We don't know it's him for sure,' Harriet felt obliged to say.

'You think? Have you seen all these photos? The Cooper family are very, very close. There's no way he would have disappeared without letting them know where he was.'

'Exactly!' Again, Janie had returned silently. 'I explained and explained until I was blue in the face but none of you would take any notice.'

What could they say to that?

It was safer to remain silent.

'My husband is scanning and printing off the photo for you,' Janie said. Was that who'd closed the garage doors? 'He has more patience for that kind of thing and I want to ensure it's the best quality for you. I know you'll be taking copies and sharing them back and forth and so on, so they have to be high resolution.'

'Thank you,' Ben said. 'That's very kind of you.'

'I *want* to help! I need to have Aaron's disappearance thoroughly investigated – for me and my family. My parents died a few years ago sadly. I'm sure the worry didn't help.'

'I'm so sorry,' Harriet said. 'It must have been horrible for you.'

'Yes,' Janie said, glancing at her sharply. 'It was.'

Even if the skeleton wasn't Aaron, Harriet knew Ben couldn't make any promises about reopening the investigation into Aaron's disappearance unless more evidence came to light.

There was an awkward silence.

Janie seemed to thaw slightly. 'I know everyone thought Aaron ran off with a woman, and there was one particular woman he was keen on. He kept telling me "she's the one". Up to that point, he'd dated lots of women, but no one special.'

Harriet snuck out her notebook. 'What was her name?'

'No idea. I'm not sure if it was because he didn't want to jinx the relationship by talking about it – although he was normally quite a practical person who didn't believe in that kind of thing – or if there was some reason their relationship had to remain secret.'

'Could she have been married?' Ben suggested.

'Possibly. He'd know I wouldn't approve – I divorced my

first husband due to infidelity on his part – but for Aaron to disappear like that? It would have been very, very unlikely. We were close: only a year between us. People often mistook us for twins. Even after my first marriage we went sailing together every weekend, the way we'd done as children, and he'd help out if I was short-staffed.' She laughed. 'He'd hate every minute and spend all his time grumbling. He was a terrible waiter, always dropping things, spilling things, never missing the chance to chat up a pretty woman. He was a terrible flirt but never meant anything by it. He never brought anyone home. There was no one special – not until her.' Janie paused and blinked quickly. 'I miss him so much.'

Tactfully, Ben waited a moment and then asked, 'Was it you who reported him missing?'

'No, his work colleagues. I never worried if I hadn't heard from him for a few days, because he always had a good reason and he always got in touch – eventually. But this time... This time I knew something was wrong.'

Ben exchanged a glance with Harriet.

'So,' Janie said, in the kind of no-nonsense tone she probably used on her staff, 'I assume you *have* found a body and that's why you're here?'

'We've found remains but we're yet to confirm the identity.' Ben went on to explain that once it had been confirmed, they'd let Janie know the result as soon as possible and, hopefully, find the person responsible. Justice for the victim. Justice for the family.

It was why the Murder Investigation Team had been set up. It would be horrible, *unbearable*, for someone you loved to disappear and never know what had happened to them. Harriet couldn't imagine it.

'Anything you want, anything you need, I'll let you have it,' Janie said. 'You can have more photos. If you want my DNA, it's yours. Dental records – would they help? The dentist we

used sold the practice to someone else. I assume they would
have been passed on to some kind of head office?'

After this length of time, they were likely to have been
destroyed.

'Thank you,' Ben said, 'we'll let you know if we do.' He
could hardly mention the skeleton's lack of teeth.

'Anything you want,' Janie said. She glanced at Harriet
again. 'I don't want revenge on whoever did it. I only want
closure.'

Janie's husband entered the room at that point, with what
Harriet assumed was Aaron's photograph inside an A4 enve-
lope. He handed it to Janie with an enquiring expression. She
gave a brief nod and he put his arm around her shoulder and
hugged her.

'I always believed Aaron had been murdered,' Janie's voice
trembled. 'Whatever anyone said. He was my brother and I
loved him very much, but he had a habit of rubbing people up
the wrong way. He could be thoughtless, even blunt, and didn't
take well to authority figures. I was surprised when he
announced that he wanted to be a police officer. I'd assumed
he'd do something in hospitality or the tourist industry. He
loved sailing and windsurfing, and always took the time to chat
to people. He was so friendly.' She sighed. 'Your colleagues
wouldn't believe me. They'd worked out their own scenario,
without any proof. That he'd run off abroad somewhere.
Without using his passport or credit cards? I don't think so! I
never liked the man they put in charge of the investigation.
There was something about him. He automatically assumed the
worst of Aaron. It made me wonder if they'd had some kind of
confrontation in the past.'

Harriet was not surprised to hear Ben ask, 'What was his
name? Do you remember?'

It was a long time ago but could the investigating officer still
be alive? They could interview him; find out why he'd been so

certain Aaron had left the country. There must have been *some* evidence for that.

'It's not something I'd forget,' Janie scowled. 'He died himself a few months later, trying to rescue some children who'd fallen into the river.'

Harriet's blood ran cold. Surely it couldn't be—

Janie looked at her directly, a sneer to her lips. 'His name was Detective Superintendent George March.' She paused to hammer it home. 'Was he a relation of yours?'

FOURTEEN

Harriet was far too quiet on the drive back to Raven's Edge.

For someone who had an opinion on everything, it was unsettling.

Ben had expected her to explode in defence of her father the minute they were back in the car.

Yet she hadn't.

Why was that?

For the first ten minutes he allowed her to process what Janie Ware had said about George March; once they were clear of the city and heading back through the forest on a relatively straight part of the dual carriageway, he said gently, 'It must have been hard for you, hearing your father spoken about in that way?'

Harriet shrugged carelessly but her fingers tightened around the steering wheel. 'It didn't bother me. The woman obviously didn't know what she was talking about. When Dad looked into the disappearance of her brother, he would have done his job, the same way he would have done for anyone else. It wouldn't have mattered to him whether he liked the guy or not. My dad was a professional police officer. He would have behaved accordingly. How else could he have made it to detective superintendent?'

'Cooper and your father were two completely different personality types who couldn't be expected to get on—'

'What does *that* have to do with anything? *Everyone* liked my father. He doesn't need validation from someone who never knew him.'

Hopefully she meant Janie Ware, not him.

'Dad was a *hero*,' she went on to say. 'He gave his *life* to save those children. If you want to go around the village and ask other people what he was like, to get an unbiased view? Fine! You have my permission. I don't care. As I've already said, what Dad thought about Aaron Cooper would have been irrelevant to his investigation. Like us, he would have got on with his job.'

'Detective Superintendent March's ability to do his job is not in question,' Ben said. 'I was asking you how you *feel* about Mrs Ware's comments. They were hurtful. I wanted to check you were OK.'

'How do you *think* I feel? How would you like it if someone slagged off your... mum?'

Well caught, Ben thought, because everyone in Raven's Edge knew what his good-for-nothing father had done, but he was saved from replying by the interruption of his phone.

He slid it from his pocket. 'Taylor.'

It was DC Ash Chopra, sounding remarkably cheerful, which was always a sign of bad news.

'Hi, boss. You remember you asked me to call you if the dog found anything?'

Oh, great...

'Go on...'

Don't say it, don't say it—

'The dog *didn't* find anything and neither did any of the officers involved in the search, although some of the guys did find a couple of dead squirrels – but Jasper ignored those – he's a *sweetheart* – and a whole bunch of junk: a shopping trolley, what seems to be the oil sump from a car, and a few things we're not certain about, which look *disgusting*, but definitely no more skeletons or bodies.'

Thank goodness for that. Finally they'd caught a lucky break.

'Thanks for keeping me updated, Ash,' he said. 'I'll see you back at the station.'

After terminating the call, he relayed the conversation to Harriet, assuming she'd be pleased by the result, or at least relieved that she wouldn't have to move out of her apartment.

Instead she said, 'I want to call into headquarters and pick up the file about Aaron Cooper's disappearance.'

'Dakota's already requested HQ scan all the relevant paperwork and send it on to her. I have it here on my phone. She'd have sent you a copy too. You'll be able to read through it when we get back to Raven's Edge.'

'But who gets to decide what the relevant stuff is?' At the approaching roundabout, Harriet signalled to return to Norchester. 'I want to read everything – *especially* the irrelevant stuff.'

Ben didn't bother to ask why. He knew why.

'Harriet, I don't think this is a good idea, but if you want me to, I'll go through the paperwork and—'

'No,' she said. 'I want to do it.'

He'd worked with Harriet for over a year now and knew she was a good officer. If she needed to do this for some kind of closure, how could he deny her?

'Fine,' he said. 'But while we're in the archives, we'll see if we can pick up anything relative to the other missing persons. We don't have a positive ID on the victim. We shouldn't assume it's DC Cooper from just one interview.'

Unless they managed to match the skeleton's DNA profile with anyone on the system, it was unlikely they'd ever identify it.

He didn't say that to Harriet, but tried to distract her with, 'If our skeleton turns out to be one of the three missing persons, it still doesn't explain why Gabriel Fox and Amelia Locke behaved so suspiciously when we interviewed them.'

For that he was treated to a side-eye. 'Have you not been paying attention? Because I thought it was obvious.'

He allowed her her moment of triumph.

'Amelia and Gabriel might not have been aware the skeleton was buried in the glasshouse but Gabriel must have more than just suspected that his dear old mum murdered his dad – because *that's* why they've never cleared the garden!'

When they returned to Raven's Edge, Harriet took all three files to her desk so that no one could accuse her of obsessing over Janie Ware's accusations against her father. Ben had obviously briefed Sam and Dakota as soon as he'd returned to the MIT office, because they both sidled up to her desk at different times without comment and handed over the intelligence they'd already collected – although Sam's report was accompanied by a cappuccino and a chocolate chip cookie in a bag from The Crooked Broomstick, and a sympathetic pat on the shoulder.

According to Dakota's notes, the skeleton's description (basically only the sex, height, race and possible age) fitted three men who'd gone missing in the relevant time period. (1) DC Aaron Cooper, who'd either fallen into Calahurst Marina while drunk or run off with his latest conquest. (2) Rick Dyson, the village postman, who'd been new to the area. No one could decide whether he'd had enough of the full-on quirkiness and jumped on the first yacht out of Calahurst Marina – or got lost in the forest like so many before him. (A sack of mail had also gone missing; something his bosses seemed more bothered about.) Finally, (3) Miles Leitch, who owed a great deal of money to a great many people – some of them not very nice.

Sam's conclusion had been that Miles *had* jumped on the first yacht out of Calahurst Marina, because there'd been various sightings of him working as a deckhand at ports all around the Mediterranean.

Harriet closed Miles's file and shoved it to one side. So, Aaron, Rick... or possibly even Eoin Kinsella.

Rick's disappearance had been looked into by a detective sergeant who was now the Assistant Chief Constable for Operations. It wouldn't be in Harriet's best interest, career-wise, to find anything wrong with *his* investigation, which centred on the missing bag of mail as a reason for Rick's disappearance. Fortunately, the investigation had been thorough and entirely by the book, and she couldn't find any fault with it.

Poor Rick *must* have got lost in the forest.

She pushed his file away.

Her coffee was now cold but she drank it anyway. Sam was a *treasure*. Her stomach was rumbling so she ate the biscuit and ungratefully wished he'd bought two.

What time was it? The sky outside had darkened to navy-blue and the lights in the station car park below had flickered on. The MIT office was quiet, with only Dakota (as usual) still intently tapping away on her laptop, scowling at the screen. Both Sam and Ash's desks were empty. Ben's office door was shut but his light was on, so he was still working. Wasn't he supposed to be meeting Milla for one of their 'date nights' later?

Harriet glanced at her watch. 4.00 pm.

She'd better get a move on if she wanted to run her findings past Ben before he left.

She opened Aaron's file, not for the first time wishing it had been digitalised. It was fat, smelt musty, and there was a squashed money spider on the first page. She flicked it into the bin. At least the file had an index. She ran her finger down it, hoping something obvious would stand out. Potentially of most interest was the list of the people who'd given statements at the time – Aaron's friends, his landlord, his work colleagues, ex-girl-friends. There was nothing from any current girlfriend – but maybe she was the one he'd run off with?

Assuming he'd run off with her.

Harriet sighed and flipped through a few more pages.

After so many years, most of these people would be dead themselves – and wasn't that a cheery thought – but she began putting together a list, putting an asterisk beside those names she thought might be worth interviewing again – *if* the skeleton turned out to be Aaron – she could hardly justify doing it unless they had a valid suspicion that it might be.

Finally she reached her father's report, recommending that the case be closed with the assumption that DC Aaron Cooper had woken up one day and decided to abandon his flat, his job and his entire life to elope with this mysterious girlfriend.

Leaving everything behind? Including – she double-checked the statement from the detective constable who'd broken into the apartment at the request of the landlord – the food in his fridge, a half-drunk mug of coffee, and his DVD set up to record his favourite TV shows?

She was beginning to understand why Janie Ware had been so furious.

If she and Ben had been investigating Aaron's disappear-ance, there would have been a lot more investigating – and that didn't sit well with her.

She studied the report again, making so many notes she had to start a new page. Surely a more logical conclusion would have been that Aaron had fallen into the river from the marina at Calahurst. It wouldn't be the first time this had happened – the tourists, in particular, were always doing it – despite the rail-ings. But the marina was crammed with all kinds of yachts and boats and dinghies. Whenever anyone fell in, there was usually someone right there to haul them out again, whatever the hour, and shove them back onto the quay along with a stern 'Don't do it again'.

Aaron running off with his girlfriend was beginning to sound more logical.

So who *was* his girlfriend?

And why hadn't anyone reported *her* missing?

Tia allowed Aaron to buy her a ring. It was an insignificant little thing, with a diamond the size of a pinhead, and set in such a way to make it appear... well, slightly larger than a pinhead. It was embarrassing. She wouldn't even be seen dead with it around her neck and shoved it into a drawer the first chance she got.

If Aaron was hurt by the disappearance of the ring he never said so, apparently happy to continue with their 'stolen moments'.

He even failed to pick up on her hints about divorce not being their only option.

Honestly, did she have to do everything herself?

FIFTEEN

Harriet wrote her report, along with a list of witnesses she wanted to re-interview, and handed it over to Ben. She then had to stand there while he read it, tapping his fingers against the desk. He agreed that the skeleton was unlikely to be Miles Leitch, but that Sam would chase up the sightings of him tomorrow. That left Rick Dyson and Aaron Cooper – but Eoin Kinsella (the original owner of Foxglove & Hemlock) as the most logical candidate to be their victim.

Ben also agreed that she could conduct her own inquiries. He kept her report but handed her list back with a terse 'Remember who the victim is here', before heading off to a meeting with his own boss, DCI Doug Cameron.

What was *that* supposed to mean? That she'd become so obsessed with Janie Ware's condemnation of her father's investigation that she'd started to see *him* as the victim, instead of the skeleton? That was hardly fair. Janie Ware had made some horrible accusations and—

Maybe it *was* a good thing she was going home. Falling out with the boss was never going to be a good idea and it was clear that Ben seemed to share some of Janie's concerns that her father's investigation of Aaron's disappearance hadn't been as thorough as it could have been.

Yet it was here in black and white. Aaron had been work-shy, argumentative and chased anything in a skirt. If anyone was likely to hop onto an ocean-going yacht out of Calahurst in search of wild adventure, it would be DC Aaron Cooper – and he must have taken his girlfriend along too. That, or she'd spent the last thirty years being very, very quiet about their relationship.

By default (she winced), the skeleton must be Eoin Kinsella – poor guy. Like his son Niall, Harriet preferred to imagine Eoin touring Europe with his friends, well away from rainy old England and his mean-spirited wife Hestia.

And it was lucky she hadn't put any of *that* in her report to Ben, because she would have found herself suffering a long lecture about the Dangers of Making Assumptions.

But she still shoved the (now even fatter) file relating to Aaron's disappearance into her bag before heading home.

The forensic inspection and search of the garden at Foxglove & Hemlock might have concluded but it was still marked out in a grid, with police tape stretched across the lawn, curling and twisting in the wind – as a reminder to Amelia and Gabriel to keep out.

Thankfully there was no sign of them sitting at the table on the decking – hardly surprising, because it was starting to snow – and there were no lights on this side of the house either. Perhaps they'd shut up early and gone out?

Before Harriet could have second thoughts about what she was about to do (with the dark and the snow, it wasn't the smartest idea she'd had), she ducked beneath the tape and ran across the lawn, waiting until she was hidden behind the tangle of shrubs before switching on her phone torch.

It was easier to follow the little stepping stones now the grass had been flattened, and soon she was standing in front of the distinctively round bay trees that marked the entrance to the patio. Someone had cut large chunks out of them since yesterday, *not* expertly, but now there was space to pass between them without snagging her hair or clothing.

And *there* was the glasshouse, looking exactly like a giant cage, looming out of the dark, creaking gently.

It gave her the creeps.

As Ben had said, it was a strange place to hide a murder victim. Why not the forest? Although, if the victim had been killed during winter, it would have been almost impossible to dig a grave outside, especially one deep enough to completely conceal the body. Presumably the earth inside the glasshouse would have been softer.

And who else would have known that?

She stepped forward, holding up her phone to illuminate the interior. It was odd the way the trees had grown over and around the framework, almost completely enclosing it, as though the forest was claiming the glasshouse for its own. No longer visible to the house behind her or those on either side, its existence had been entirely forgotten.

Actually, it was the *perfect* place to hide a body. It would be guaranteed to remain undiscovered for years, if not decades.

So who *had* known the glasshouse was here?

Someone with local knowledge.

Someone... local.

Harriet glanced back at Foxglove & Hemlock, to reassure herself that she could find her way back, but she could barely see the rooftop.

The only entry into this garden was through the house and onto the decking, or via the gate from the side lane.

The obvious candidate to be their victim was Eoin Kinsella.

And the obvious suspect his wife, Hestia Fox – conveniently deceased for the past five years. Case closed, everything finished in time for Christmas.

But...

Harriet slowly turned, peering into the dark, holding up her torch, illuminating the sharp little snowflakes as they tumbled and twisted through the beam, creating lacy patterns on the flagstones beneath her feet. If she wanted to work through her theory, she didn't have much time – unless she waited until tomorrow. But by then, the garden might be under several centimetres of snow.

Carefully she stepped off the patio, trying to keep a map of the garden in her head. It would be far too easy – not to mention seriously embarrassing – for her to get lost in her 'own' garden. Sam would never let her hear the end of it.

Behind her was the house. To the right, the stepping-stone path leading through the bay trees and into the shrubbery. *Could* there be another path through the garden, leading somewhere else? *More* stepping stones weaving between the trees?

She dug her heel into the rotting leaves and scraped around the edge of the patio until her boot hit something hard.

Another stepping stone – and, potentially, another path, heading south.

She was right.

More scratching amongst the rotting leaves revealed a second pale round stone, partially hidden beneath a large rhododendron. She ducked beneath its branches, into the hollow interior. The ground here was softer and she found a third stepping stone, presumably placed before the rhododendron had been planted, and then a fourth, a long-forgotten trail leading further into the garden. Harriet followed it eagerly – and then the footpath disappeared.

That was odd...

She shone the torch around, turning slowly, careful to remember which direction she'd come from.

The beam caught on a pile of rubble – a heap of pale golden stone, the same colour as the house.

Gabriel had mentioned a wall. Was this what remained of it?

A tree had fallen, resting on another pile of debris. The cause of the wall's destruction? She kicked at the leaves with her boot, revealing a line of broken stones. This was where the boundary wall *had* been, a long time ago. When had it fallen? More than three decades ago? In which case, *anyone* could have gained access to the garden from the forest – blowing any list of suspects wide open.

She carried on until she was standing on a wide path that would have been a road maybe a century or so ago, that seemed to lead into the village. Glancing back, she could see the boundaries of her neighbours – clipped hedges, modern red-brick walls and tall fences. In the distance she heard the River Thunor, crashing over the rocks at the bottom of the gorge.

The snow was falling faster, pinpricks of ice, stinging her face. She flipped up her hood and picked her way back into the garden, trying not to shiver as she passed the glasshouse, still creaking and groaning to itself.

That poor man, murdered and buried in secret, with no one to mourn him.

'You'll have your justice,' she muttered, her words stolen by the wind. 'I promise.'

SIXTEEN

Milla Graham had booked a table at The Drop for dinner, beside the window that overlooked the gorge. The bridge and surrounding trees were decorated with thousands of tiny white sparkling fairy lights. It was beautiful and would have been incredibly romantic – if she hadn't been sitting there on her own.

Where was Ben?

Although the pub was super-busy, Sorcha, the manager, came over and asked Milla if she'd like a drink while she waited.

Milla was not sure she liked the implication. Did Sorcha believe she was going to be waiting a long time?

She chose a fruity mocktail with grenadine and orange juice but Sorcha had been right. Forty-five minutes later Ben still hadn't arrived, and by then she was on her third mocktail and Sorcha had come over twice to ask if everything was OK. Milla's smile became tighter each time, particularly when Sorcha reminded her that the table was only hers for two hours.

As Sorcha walked away, Milla tapped her finger against the stem of her glass.

There was no point phoning Ben. If he was too busy to

meet her at the pub, he was too busy to answer his phone, and the signal in the village was terrible anyway.

After almost an hour of imagining everyone in the pub was watching her, speculating that she'd been stood up and feeling sorry for her – something she *especially* hated – she was about to call for the bill when Ben shoved open the door and almost fell into the pub, accompanied by a blast of frozen air and a whirl of fat snowflakes. He was wearing the wool coat she'd bought him over his navy suit, with a navy scarf wound carelessly around his neck. He looked cold and cross, and his nose and cheeks were pink from the cold. He looked adorable.

She nearly ran over to hug him in relief that he was OK, before realising that *would* give everyone something to talk about, but she was sure she had a silly grin on her face all the same.

When Ben caught sight of her across the crowded pub, his grin was just as big.

Why were they continuing with this stupid non-date date thing? *Why* didn't they get over themselves and jump back into bed? They'd certainly get to see each other more – and without the rest of the village watching and speculating.

He hurried over and bent to kiss her cheek before unwrapping his scarf and shrugging off his coat, dropping them half onto a chair and half on the floor. She stood up to rearrange them before they created a trip hazard, and then he kissed her again and she laughed.

'Sorry I'm late,' he said, waving to Nina, the ethereal blonde waitress, and ordering an orange juice, which she brought over almost immediately.

Milla handed over a menu. 'Work?'

'Work,' he agreed, barely glancing at the menu and setting it aside. She'd done the same thing. They'd been here practically every week since early November and now they knew it by heart.

'This late? Is it to do with the skeleton you found?'

He paused, his drink halfway to his mouth. 'How do you know about that?'

She rolled her eyes. 'Nothing stays secret in Raven's Edge. We've all seen the CSI vans parked down the side of Foxglove & Hemlock, and we've had a lovely time speculating about it.'

'Have you? I can imagine.' He knocked back the orange juice as though he wished it was beer. 'Quite precise, knowing it was a skeleton. I'm impressed.'

'It's a big garden,' she said, 'bigger than most around here, but you do seem to be spending a lot of time in there. Have you found *another* body? Are we looking at a serial killer?'

He almost choked on the drink. '*Serial killer?* I hope not!'

'I suppose your team do need to search the garden thoroughly, and it's completely overgrown, which would make things difficult for you—'

'Stop fishing,' he said. 'You know I can't tell you anything.'

'I saw the dog arrive. The black Labrador. He was so sweet, so keen to start work.'

Ben grimaced.

OK, *wrong* approach. 'What's the dog's name?'

'Jasper,' Ben said, after a slight pause – evidently internally reviewing whether he should tell her, and how much he should tell her. 'He's a cadaver dog – a *working* dog.'

'Trained to find bodies?' Cadaver meant corpse, right?

'Dead ones, yes, and traces where they've been. It's incredible what those dogs can pick up on.'

What *had* Jasper found? But, before she could ask,

'When you invited me to dinner,' he said, 'I'd assumed our conversation would be a little more...'

She grinned and waved towards the fairy lights outside. 'Romantic?'

'Yes!' He was smiling though.

'I'm sorry but your work is so interesting.'

'You'd get on well with Harriet. She finds all the morbid forensic stuff fascinating.'

'You don't?'

'It's not my favourite part of the job.'

'What is?'

'Catching the bad guy, obtaining justice for the victim and closure for their family.' Now it was Ben's turn to sigh. 'The skeleton we found has been there for over a quarter of a century. We're making inquiries as to the identity, which will help with finding out who killed him—'

'He was murdered?'

Ben hesitated. Presumably he hadn't meant to say that last bit, a sure sign that he was tired.

'And that he's a "he"?' she prompted.

'Milla,' he warned, 'you know I can't talk about this.'

If he'd been about to expand on that, the chance was lost when Nina returned to take their food order.

Ben asked for his favourite trout almondine with green beans, Milla decided to have the mushroom risotto.

'That's the third time in a row you've chosen risotto,' he said, as they handed the menus back.

'It's my favourite!'

'I thought burger was your favourite?'

'It's my new favourite.'

Before she could find some way to return to the subject of the skeleton, he said, 'How are you getting on working for Kieran Drake?'

Almost two months ago, Milla had begun working for the local private investigator. Mainly for something to do, but she did enjoy the work. Unfortunately Ben and Drake didn't get on, even though Drake had once been a detective sergeant who'd been invalided out of the Force after an injury sustained on duty.

'*With* Kieran Drake, not *for*.' She'd never been great at

working *for* anyone and had much preferred being self-employed (those entrepreneurial Graham genes winning out again). Now she was rich, after recently reuniting with her long-lost family, she didn't have to work for anyone, but instead of making her feel secure, remembering exactly how much her family was worth sent her into a panic. What was a person supposed to *do* with that much money? And the stuff kept coming in.

She'd tried discussing it with Ben once, and received an 'Isn't that a nice problem to have?' response.

'What sort of work are you doing for Drake?' Ben asked. 'Unfaithful spouses? Corporate espionage?'

Was that a dig? 'Corporate espionage sounds like fun but at the moment it's mostly surveillance work for Drake's favourite client.'

They both knew who *he* was. Drew Elliott: Ben's cousin and the kind of arrogant wealthy businessman who liked to know and interfere in everything that went on in the King's Forest District.

Much like her father.

What was it with rich, powerful men? Didn't they have anything better to do then meddle in other people's lives?

'Be careful,' Ben said.

Sweet.

'I don't know what kind of trouble you think I'm going to get into,' she said. 'The work I do for Drake isn't remotely dangerous.'

More was the pity.

'Have you forgotten what he was doing the first time you met him? He was planting stolen jewellery in your apartment! That man has the morals of... Well, he doesn't have any morals.'

'You don't like him.'

'Too right I don't – and I don't for one minute believe he

operates within the law, as he's always trying to convince me. I worry he'll get you into trouble.'

'There's that word again. "Trouble." Sounds like fun. I'd like to get into some trouble so that I don't die of boredom locked up in my little-old-lady cottage.'

'Be serious, Milla. I'm looking out for your best interests here.'

Best interests? Had he really said *that*?

She gave him a second chance. 'Next you'll be telling me to "Calm down".'

That went over his head.

'I'd be happier if you were working for someone else. Anyone other than him.'

If she didn't know him better, she'd think he was jealous. But why would a detective inspector be jealous of a private investigator?

'I don't know if you've noticed,' she said, 'but the only available jobs here in Raven's Edge are in one of the cafés or the gift shops.'

'You used to be a journalist.'

'You're too kind. We both know my "journalism" consisted of writing up reviews for gigs and interviewing musicians no one else had heard of. Plus, the magazine went bust some time ago.' Had he forgotten? 'Any jobs now go to journalists with actual qualifications.'

'There must be a ton of work you can do from home?'

'And never leave my house? How exciting.'

'It's not as though you need to work.'

Ouch. She supposed it was only a matter of time before he said *that*.

'Because I'm so rich, not only do I not need to work, I could own ten of my own detective agencies?'

'I wouldn't have said ten...' Ben began. 'But—'

'Seriously?' she muttered. 'Please let it go.'

Unfortunately, he struggled on. 'Why don't you do charity work, like your grandmother?'

'I'm sure any charity would far prefer a donation than any help from me. I can see there's no point arguing with you about it though. You don't care what I do. You just want me "out of harm's way", and by that you mean out of *your* way, because, who knows, I might make a *good* private investigator.'

'I want to keep you safe, Milla. I still have nightmares about the time a man held a knife to your throat. With your family's wealth, you'd be a prime target for a kidnapper.'

'Keep me "safe"? Never leave the house in case something bad happens? Give you a list of all my appointments, so you can keep track of me? Have an app on your phone that allows you to see where I am at any given moment?' Her father had tried that once. She'd never let him forget it. 'Have you vet the people I meet at work, the people I make friends with, the people I casually exchange a "hello" with on the street?'

'Well...' he made the mistake of saying, as though he was actually considering it.

'Because that would kill me.'

When he showed every sign of continuing to argue, she shoved her chair back and walked out before both of them said something they might regret.

Ben should have run after her and apologised. Now it was too late. Wasn't it?

The tables around him quietened; then, almost as one, everyone began talking again.

The peril of living in a tiny village. By tomorrow, everyone would know he and Milla had had another row. They were probably running a sweepstake at the station as to how long it would take them to split for good.

He sighed and pushed his chair back. As his grandmother

would have said, it was never too late for a man to admit to being an arse.

Before he could get up, Sorcha sauntered over to the table carrying two plates of food.

'You sure made a muck-up of that,' she said, nodding towards the door.

Did she have to sound so cheerful about it?

'Yes, I did.' Sorcha could make what she liked out of that. 'Could you box up the fish please? I'll have it as a takeaway.' He'd lost his appetite but he was sure Binx would enjoy the trout.

He finished his drink while Sorcha returned the food to the kitchen. A few minutes later, Nina returned with the card reader and a box with the leftovers.

He paid and drove home, absolutely shattered. As usual, the house was in darkness. This morning he'd imagined coming back from the pub and spending the evening with Milla, snuggled up on the sofa watching TV.

Or not watching TV.

He'd send Milla some flowers along with a grovelling apology.

Hopefully they wouldn't be returned to him with the heads chopped off.

He was such an *idiot*. Why did he always manage to say the wrong thing?

As he pushed open his front door, he almost tripped over Binx, whose peridot eyes were gleaming in the dark. At least Binx was pleased to see him, especially when Ben tipped the trout onto a plate and set it down for him. Binx made short work of it, purring ecstatically and fussing around Ben, tail swishing in excitement, although he spat out the almonds one by one, slightly chewed, leaving them in a neat circle around the edge of the plate.

It was oddly indicative of his life – and he only had himself to blame.

Two weeks later Aaron received a message from Tia to say her husband would be away overnight at a conference in Kent.

He cancelled all his other plans and called round as soon as his shift ended, careful to walk through the forest and into the back garden, rather than risk entering the house from the high street where anyone could have seen him.

Tia was standing by the back door, waiting to let him in.

He was so happy to see her, he didn't notice the broken window behind her, or the way his shoes crunched over tiny shards of glass.

She took hold of his hand, led him up the narrow stairs and into the bedroom, drawing him over to the window overlooking the garden.

'If I didn't know you better, I'd think you were trying to take advantage of me,' he laughed, bending to kiss her.

The kiss coincided with a faint rattle downstairs, but he didn't notice.

Tia shifted slightly, so that her back was to the door and the moonlight illuminated them.

As the bedroom door swung silently open, Tia lifted his hands and placed them around her neck.

He broke the kiss. 'Tia? What are you up to?'

She screamed, drowning out his words, and shoved him away.

She couldn't have timed it more perfectly.

Aaron stumbled, placing a palm on the window pane to steady himself, only to be yanked upright.

Her husband was standing in front of him, utterly furious...

SEVENTEEN

Iris spent the day working on her new novel and then drove around to the council office before it closed to fill out a form requesting permission to change the name of the house from Álfheimr to Raven's Hollow – only to be told she needn't have bothered: the house already had a number and she could call it whatever she liked. Straightaway she ordered a new sign from the local hardware store to be engraved with:

RAVEN'S HOLLOW

along with the silhouette of a bird.

The next stop on her to-do list was the local vet. The receptionist could find no evidence that Sparkle had ever been microchipped but took a photo of the cat for their noticeboard and promised to email all the pet owners registered with the practice in the hope someone might recognise her.

On the way home, Iris called into the bookstore with the pretence of checking how her sales were coming along – brilliantly, thanks to her signing the stock – but it was really an excuse to see Whit again. She'd never met anyone else who loved books as much as she did.

With Carmen smirking in the background, Whit ultra-casually asked Iris if she'd like to go to The Witch's Brew for tea and cake but, as Sparkle was sulking in a cardboard box in her car parked outside the shop, she had to decline. It was only when Iris drove up the lane to her house that she realised she could have arranged to meet Whit at The Witch's Brew *after* she'd taken Sparkle home. Now it was too late.

'You,' she told the cat affectionately, 'are starting to come between me and my love life.'

Sparkle, lying in the bottom of the box in a pose that could have been captioned 'abject misery', refused to look at her.

Up until this moment, Iris had assumed the little cat was lost. What if someone had deliberately abandoned the poor thing in the woods – *during a snowstorm*? Now Iris had put her into a box and driven her around the King's Forest District for over an hour. Sparkle must think she was being abandoned again.

'Poor baby.' Iris stroked Sparkle's cheek with her finger. 'You'll always have a home with me. I'm halfway to being a cat lady already.'

As soon as her box was set on the floor in the hall, Sparkle bounded happily towards the kitchen.

That cat was going to be so disappointed when she discovered her bowl was empty.

'Give me five minutes,' Iris called, shrugging off her coat and slinging it over the end of the banister. She'd feed Sparkle and then make herself a sandwich.

First though, she peeped into the library, for no other reason than she loved seeing all those bookshelves, even if she hadn't got round to filling them yet. But instead of the neat stack of cardboard boxes she'd left there two hours earlier, they were now tossed around the room and ripped open, the contents scattered across the floor.

What the...?

Then she saw a man standing in the middle of it all, big and muscular, like a heavyweight boxer.

Was she hallucinating?

'Hello,' he said. 'I wondered when you'd turn up.'

She backed away. Her phone was in her bag, slung on the newel post at the bottom of the stairs, over the top of her coat. If she could grab that and get out of the house...

What about Sparkle?

One stride and he'd caught hold of her arm, yanking her towards him. 'No you don't.'

Her panic spiralled. Was this a robbery?

But she'd caught him in the act. She'd seen his face. She could identify him.

Iris began to struggle.

He scooped up a reel of parcel-tape from one of the empty shelves, held it to his mouth and pulled out the end with his teeth.

She swung a punch at his face but he dodged it easily and laughed.

She couldn't knee him, because he was smart enough to keep that part of him well out of reach, and the parts she did manage to smack with her fist felt like rock.

But his humour was fading with every blow she landed. When her knuckles finally cracked against his chin, he cursed and swung her around, shoving her against the wall. Holding her there with the weight of his body, he wrapped the parcel-tape around one of her wrists and then the other, strapping them together.

How could this be happening to her?

Hemsworth...

The library slid sideways as she was tipped onto the floor and the tape wrapped around her ankles. She got in a good kick to his leg – he cursed loudly – but she missed his knee, which would have sent him crashing to the floor beside her.

Damn.

'Are you one of Hemsworth's friends?' She remembered their jeering faces when she'd come out of court. More than one of them had sworn revenge. 'Is that why you're here?'

She'd changed her name. Twice. How had they *found* her?

He shrugged. 'Who's Hemsworth?'

Someone *else?*

Or was this a robbery gone wrong?

Breathe...

There was a way out of this. There had to be.

'I'll give you whatever you want,' she said, aware she sounded desperate but not caring – and maybe that would help persuade him? 'I have lots of money, not here in the house, but I can get it for you. I promise.'

'That's not how I work.'

He'd done this before?

'Did someone *hire* you? I'll pay double – triple!'

'Tempting, but this is a favour for a friend.' He winked and tapped his nose. 'And that's all I'm saying.'

'But—'

He tore off another strip of tape and stuck it over her mouth with 'You talk too much,' and left her struggling on the floor while he walked over to the glass coffin. 'I saw this earlier,' he said, pulling up the lid. 'I thought how cool it was and wondered what kind of woman would have a glass coffin in her house.' He looked her up and down and smirked. 'Now I know!'

She twisted her hands, trying to pull them through the tape, but he scooped her up and dropped her roughly into the coffin, kicking the lid shut with his boot as soon as she tried to sit up.

He crouched, grinning at her struggles. 'That'll confuse the cops,' he said, knocking on the glass, 'but it seems a shame. Asphyxiation is a horrible way to go.'

Furiously, she banged her bound fists against the lid. He jumped back, perhaps expecting the glass to shatter. When it didn't, he blew her a kiss and walked out.

Iris slumped back in the coffin.

Happy thoughts, happy thoughts.

She couldn't let the panic take over. She was using too much oxygen and she had to think clearly.

Ironically, he'd done her a favour. The thing about her glass coffin, as she had repeatedly told everyone, was that it was a film prop. Props had safety measures built into them and – in theory – there were air holes drilled into each end, hidden amongst the swirling engraving.

She'd never had a reason to test that, and the glass was swiftly steaming up, not helped by her damp clothes.

It was terrifying to admit it, but it was getting harder to breathe.

Iris closed her eyes and forced her breathing to slow.

Happy thoughts, happy thoughts...

She could do this.

Unfortunately, once her panic began to recede, her writer's brain was free to imagine every worst-case scenario, starting with:

Had someone *really* instructed him to kill her?

She hadn't *done* anything.

Not recently, anyway.

Not anything that anyone knew about.

A crash from another room forced her attention back. Was that the front door? Had he gone? Was it safe to get out?

If she could.

According to the instructions, she had two choices. Push

against the top and bottom sections, which were designed to pop out of the metal frame with pressure. The simplest method, however, was that the lock on the lid could be opened from inside.

In *theory*.

She had to find the mechanism first though.

Lifting her bound hands, Iris slid her thumbs along the edge of the lid until she found a metal latch – presumably the twin of the one on top. He'd gone the extra mile and fastened it – the bastard – but she pressed hard against the latch, flicking it over and sliding it back until it clicked. Ignoring her heart thudding hard in her chest, and all the 'what ifs' her brain was throwing out, she gently pushed up the lid until gravity took over and it fell back against the wall with a far-too-loud thud.

Had he heard?

Sparkle, who must have come looking for her, immediately put her head into the open coffin, sniffing cautiously.

Iris peeled the tape from her mouth, cursing as it took what felt like a layer of skin with it.

The cat sprung back.

'I'm sorry sweetheart! Did I frighten you?'

By wriggling and twisting her wrists, Iris was able to loosen the tape and slide one hand out, before ripping the tape from the other wrist. It helped that her skin was sweaty. While the cat paced anxiously, swishing her tail, Iris tore the tape from her ankles – easier, because the tape had been wrapped over her thick black tights.

By now, Sparkle had retreated to shiver behind one of the upturned boxes. Iris crawled over, keeping low so as not to intimidate her. 'Did the nasty man frighten you?' she asked, bumping noses with the cat. 'Me too. We really need to have those locks changed.'

'You certainly do.'

It was him again, his big hands resting on either side of the doorframe as he watched her, his expression of disbelief almost comical.

'How the hell...?' He trailed off, glancing over at the coffin and then back to her. 'That was *impressive*. Tell me, darlin'. Have you done this before?'

Iris staggered to her feet. On top of the nearest box of books was a slab of black slate with a miniature metal sword sticking out of it – her Starlight & Sorcery Society award for best romantic fantasy. She'd been wondering what to do with it, and now she had the perfect opportunity to put it to good use.

Only not in quite the way the judges had intended.

She brandished it in front of her. 'Get the hell out of my house!'

He laughed. 'What do you plan to do with that, little girl?'

Little? She was almost as tall as him, but half his width, and OK, he was far stronger than her, but this time she intended to put up a really good fight.

She swung the award, intending to whack him with it, but the movement sent Sparkle out from behind the boxes in a flash of white, distracting her.

The man stepped back out of reach, still laughing, unable to take her seriously.

And tripped over the cat.

Sparkle yowled and shot through the door.

'Sparkle!' Iris dropped the award, letting it crash onto the floor, leaving a significant dent, and ran after the cat, but Sparkle was streaking off to the kitchen, apparently unharmed.

Unlike the man, who overbalanced and smashed the back of his head on the protruding snout of the dragon fireplace.

There was an audible crack.

Later, Iris was ashamed to realise her first thought had been for the fireplace.

Her second had been to grab Sparkle and get the hell out of

there. Maybe run to the pub for help? But as she stepped over the man's crumpled body, she saw a thin trickle of blood coming from one ear, his eyes staring sightlessly at the ceiling.

She hesitated, before poking him with her toe.

He didn't move.

'Bugger,' Iris said. 'Not again.'

EIGHTEEN

Iris had a body in her library.

How very Agatha Christie.

This could *not* be happening.

She sat on the floor of the library with her back against the wall, her knees tucked under her chin and stared at the dead body.

How had her life changed so quickly?

She'd walked into the house, a perfectly normal day, and first this idiot had tried to kill her, then he'd accidently killed himself.

She should phone for an ambulance but he looked dead enough to her.

There was no way she was going to call the police if he was already dead and couldn't be helped. They'd check her past and she'd be right back in prison. She knew how it went. Charge the most obvious suspect. She was practically standing over the corpse with a bloody knife in her hand.

The police would want to know who she was and why she was here – the best way to determine why this man was in her house – but if they delved too deeply they'd find out about Hemsworth and take another look at Erik, and that would be the end of her liberty. This time she'd be sent to prison for life.

If she didn't call the police, what was she going to do with this man's body?

Bury him in the garden? What kind of cold-hearted person did that?

Drag him outside, put him in her car and dump his body somewhere else?

Ugh! No! How could she even *think* of such a thing?

Anyway (as her inner voice helpfully chipped in), if she did that, his clothing fibres and blood would be all over her car, and *her* clothing fibres would be all over him. She watched television. She knew how this worked.

Which took her back to: How *did* one dispose of a body?

Well... there *was* a handy cliff at the bottom of the garden. She could drop him off that?

Basically throwing him away like rubbish? *Lovely.*

And what if he didn't end up in the river? It would be obvious where he'd fallen from – again drawing the attention back to her.

After what had happened last time, she did *not* want the attention on her.

OK. Essential: move the body.

How? Drag him through the house, gathering and shedding forensic evidence? Not a good idea.

Wrap him in a carpet.

She didn't have any carpets!

Wrap him in a shower curtain?

She didn't have a shower curtain; she didn't even have a shower, only an antique roll-top Victorian bath.

Iris looked around the library for inspiration.

There was one thing she did have a lot of...

Cardboard boxes.

What if she taped a bunch of flattened boxes together and dragged him... somewhere?

She could work with that.

Iris had been so deep in thought, Sparkle had come to nuzzle against her and she hadn't even noticed. She stroked the top of the cat's head. Sparkle's eyes were shut and she was purring. Iris wished she felt as chilled. She got up off the floor and went to the nearest window. Snow was falling heavily. If she dragged the man out of the house and down the lane, she could leave him by the side of the road. Everyone would assume that he'd been hit by a car. The authorities would be notified, along with his relatives and friends, and he'd get a decent funeral. She might not owe him much but she owed him that.

She turned to look back at him, slumped against the dragon fireplace.

If he hadn't broken in, if he hadn't stayed in the house after he'd shut her in the coffin, if he hadn't come back into the library...

He'd still be alive.

There was no point wishing it had never happened. When the snow stopped, she'd lose her cover. She had to be practical – or end up back in prison.

So she got busy. She flattened the cardboard boxes and taped them together. She found a skipping rope – bought to help improve her fitness and then never used – to create a handle. She strengthened the holes with more tape. Would it be strong enough? Hopefully. He was a big man and probably very heavy.

Surreally, this reminded her of the times she and her little brother Justin had gone sledging in the park as children. In those days they couldn't afford proper sledges, so they'd used tea trays and cardboard boxes flattened out, just like this.

As she worked, she kept one eye on the falling snow. The

whole plan depended on that to hide her tracks. If it stopped, she'd be stuck.

When the makeshift sledge was complete, she placed it beside the body and rolled the man over and onto it. This was harder than she'd thought. He was so *heavy*. There was a small patch of blood on the stone surround where he'd fallen; it should be easy to clean, but first she had to remove him from the house.

It was tough dragging him out of the library and into the hall, but far easier going outside and down the steps of the veranda than it would have been pulling him up them.

The cold meant her fingers were soon numb. The cord was thick and soft but it still cut into her skin. When she reached the lane, the sledge occasionally hit the top of a rock and got stuck; then he fell off the cardboard and she had to roll him back on again.

'You know, it's a pity you're not still alive,' she grumbled, shoving him back onto the sledge, 'because you *totally* deserve this.'

It wasn't until she was in sight of the main road that she happened to glance behind and spotted Sparkle daintily picking her way through the snow, as though they were going for a country walk on a beautiful summer's day – not hauling the corpse of a would-be murderer down a dark, snowy lane in the middle of the night.

Whatever had scared the cat back at the house, she'd got over it now. Her pristine white fur made her almost invisible against the snow.

'You do realise this makes you an accessory to murder?' Iris told the cat.

Sparkle didn't reply. The snow was getting quite deep but she was determined to keep up. Perhaps she thought Iris might leave her behind?

'I'm not abandoning you, you silly cat. I'm coming back to the house, just as soon as I've got rid of *him*.'

The cat plodded on.

With any luck, the snow was hiding the wide groove she was making, but she'd kick the tracks about a bit on the return journey, to make sure.

When she reached the road, she hesitated.

It wasn't too late to call the police and confess everything.

And then she remembered the last time she'd done that, and how no one had believed her story – understandable; it *had* been a lie – and what had happened afterwards.

Raven's Edge was eerily silent. Perhaps people were staying at home because of the heavy snow?

She dragged the makeshift sledge onto the pavement and in the opposite direction from the village (keeping it away from the lane that led to her house and thus any inquiries the police might want to make), stopping just before a wide gateway with 'The Laurels' written on a low wall. This must be where Anya March lived, and while Iris wouldn't want anyone to get into trouble for something she'd done, Anya had mentioned that her daughter was a police detective. Surely Anya would be the last person the police would suspect of murder?

Iris turned the sledge around so it would look like the man had been walking to the pub, and tipped him off the sledge.

Belatedly, it occurred to her that there should be tyre tracks and so forth if he were to look like a convincing hit-and-run victim, but the snow was still coming down and covering everything.

She folded up the makeshift sledge and tucked it under her arm.

'This used to be easier,' she told the cat, who stared up at her and blinked.

Iris scooped her up with the other arm. 'I'm cold,' she said.

'Let's go home and have a nice hot chocolate, made from scratch, with marshmallows. What do you say?'

'Meow.'

'I thought you would.' Iris walked up the road and into the lane that led to Raven's Hollow, kicking away the tracks she'd made, the snow helpfully erasing everything else.

It took a split second but Tia's husband recognised the intruder. Blond hair cut short, his tan making his eyes bluer than ever: Detective Constable Aaron Cooper...

In his bedroom?

With his wife?

What possible reason...

There could be only one and he didn't need to be a detective to work it out.

He turned his attention to his wife. Everyone – every single person – had warned him that she was too young and too immature, and that the ten years between them was too big a gap. He'd been too blinded by love to take notice.

He'd given her everything – and now he'd been dumped – for this clown?

He waited for her to burst into tears. He waited for her to tell him she'd been unable to help herself. He waited to hear that Aaron was the love of her life, that she couldn't live without him.

He waited for the fatal words: 'I want a divorce.'

On cue, the tears began to flow down her cheeks, but her words took him by surprise.

'Darling! Thank goodness you're here! I thought he was going to kill me!'

What was she saying?

'He must have broken in,' she added.

He frowned. He'd seen no sign of a break-in when he'd walked through the front door, and why would a detective constable be house-breaking?

Her speech also came as a shock to DC Cooper. 'Tia? Why would you say that? You invited me here! You called me!'

If Cooper had remained silent, the evening might have ended another way, but the words caused something inside him to splinter and shatter and burn.

What was that expression? Light the touch paper and stand well back?

'You bastard!' he roared.

His wife jumped. Didn't she know he had a temper?

DC Cooper, who must have heard rumours, took a wary step back.

Had he never thought about what might happen if he was caught with another man's wife? Had he assumed they were going to sit around a table and discuss this like civilised adults? That he'd meekly hand over his wife?

Stuff that.

Cooper's blue eyes widened in surprise right before he punched him.

NINETEEN

16th December

Harriet received a call the following morning about the body discovered by the road leading into the village. A member of the public had called an ambulance. The paramedic who'd arrived at the scene confirmed life had been extinct for some time, and a uniformed officer from Calahurst Police Station had been summoned to allow the paramedic to resume call-outs. The constable had decided that the death appeared suspicious and had contacted Harriet, who would normally have attended the scene with Sam or Ash but, as Ben was standing right behind her in the queue for a coffee and cookie at The Crooked Broomstick (which meant she couldn't flirt with Misha, the barista), he came along too.

Didn't Ben have anything better to do?

Anyone would think he didn't *like* being a detective inspector.

It should have been a five-minute walk but took longer due to the amount of snow that had fallen overnight – at least ten centimetres, which was *not* usual for the south of England.

Unlike countries that regularly experienced heavy snowfall, two flakes of the stuff were enough to send this part of the world into a panic. Schools closed, bus and train services were cancelled, and this was already the third traffic-related incident the paramedic had been called out to.

By the time Ben and Harriet arrived at the scene the ambulance had driven away, and the PC had done his best to preserve the scene by closing off the pavement and one lane of the road with cones. The Crime Scene Investigators and Caroline Warner, the Home Office forensic pathologist, were in attendance. A small tent had been erected to protect the body, preserve the scene and ensure Caroline could work undisturbed.

Harriet spoke to the Crime Scene Manager first, who explained that there was no evidence a vehicle had been involved – although the snow was hindering their investigation somewhat.

This was confirmed by Caroline. 'Death was unlikely to have been caused by a simple hit and run,' she said. 'There is one wound, small and round, on the back of his head. If something had been applied there with force, it would have caused a skull fracture and/or bleeding on the brain, enough to kill him quickly, even if medical treatment had been available. There are no traces of tarmac or gravel or mud or paint or glass, which I would expect to find on a hit-and-run victim, along with other bruising or broken bones. I'll need to do a full PM, as you know,' – here she shot a scathing glance towards Harriet – 'but I believe the victim was hit by an unidentified blunt instrument.'

'Thank you,' Ben said, before turning to Harriet. 'Any theories?'

Harriet was staring at the victim, lying on his side on the pavement, a black anorak hiding his muscular build, dark hair frozen in tendrils over his forehead, and remembered a vibrant but arrogant man in a white towelling robe, winking at her while he kissed her mother.

Dean Hunter? Her mother's latest boyfriend?

It wasn't *possible...*

What the hell was *he* doing here? Could it really be him? She'd only caught a quick glimpse of him, but—

'*Harriet?*'

'Um, could he have been walking home from the pub?' she suggested. Even though there were very few houses between here and Calahurst. 'Or murdered somewhere else and dumped here? Perhaps the murderer wanted the body to be found, otherwise they'd have taken greater care to hide it? Although, with the snow partially concealing the body, perhaps the victim ended up being left here longer than the murderer expected?'

Ben frowned. He knew her too well not to realise something was up.

'Do you recognise him?' he asked brusquely.

That was the thing about living in a small village. In theory, she should recognise anyone from around here. Dean must have come from further afield, Calahurst or Port Rell, even Norchester. Her mother would know, wouldn't she?

Her mother...

Harriet's attention shifted from the body, and was about to search out the familiar sign to her mother's house, when she remembered she was standing next to a detective inspector whose entire attention was on her. She raised her eyes and met his far too astute gaze as innocently as she could manage.

'I'm not sure,' she said. 'Possibly?'

'He might not be local if he's been deliberately dumped here.' Ben stated the obvious.

'But why *here*?' she said. 'If he's not local, is his death meant as a message to someone who is?'

'It's certainly one idea.' Ben was regarding her curiously now. 'Let's get back to the station and set everything in motion.'

'OK,' she said, but didn't move.

He sighed. 'Harriet? Is there a problem?'

'Can you give me twenty minutes? My mother lives right there.' She pointed to the sign: a block of pale stone set in a low red-brick wall. 'I should check she's OK and I can ask her about our victim at the same time.'

That made it sound as though Anya was in her eighties rather than forty-five, but no doubt it would be a shock when she learnt her lover had been murdered and dumped on her doorstep.

This was bad, on so many levels.

'You see, I think – I *believe* – my mother... might know him.'

Ben raised an eyebrow. 'In the biblical sense?'

Of all the things she expected to be doing today, discussing her mother's sex life with her boss wasn't one of them.

'Ye-es. His name is – was – Dean Hunter. I met him for the first time yesterday. Very briefly, which is why I'm not one hundred per cent sure. Can you leave it with me? I'll go and talk to her, break the news...'

'Someone else will have to take her statement.'

'Understood.'

There was a pause before Ben said, 'No problem. I'll go back to the station and begin the briefing.'

As he walked away, Harriet knew he wasn't pleased.

Harriet walked up the drive to her mother's house. She could recall exactly what Dean Hunter had looked like: broad, muscular – a boxer's build, complete with the obligatory break in his hawk-like nose. His eyes had been a deep, dark brown, almost black. Her mother had *always* liked men with brown eyes. His dark hair had been unusual though, because her mother had a definite type, and that type was someone who looked just like Harriet's father.

How the hell had Dean ended up dead at the bottom of Anya's drive?

Obviously her mother hadn't killed him. It was hard to admit, but Anya had a certain amount of ruthlessness (something she shared with Harriet); she'd probably make a very *good* murderer, but from Anya's point of view, killing Dean and dragging him to the end of the drive would have been far too much like hard work. Plus, the man had been almost six foot tall, and her mother barely five.

No, thankfully the murderer couldn't be anyone close to home, but Harriet needed to inform Anya of Dean's death and gauge her reaction before Sam or Ash turned up to take her statement. *This* was why she was tramping up the drive through ten centimetres of slushy snow. *Not* because she cared about Anya (why should she care about someone who'd always made it plain they'd never cared much about her. That would be bloody tragic) or whether she was guilty, but because Harriet cared about her own career.

It was hardly the kind of thing one wanted on a CV:

Father: Detective Superintendent.

Mother: Murderer.

It must be the cold weather that was making her eyes water. She rubbed the sleeve of her coat over her face and then banged forcibly on the door, in far too much of a foul mood to tone down the volume.

Mrs Nore opened the door. If she was surprised to see who was on the other side, she didn't show it. Her expression was as supercilious as always.

'Mrs March isn't at home,' she said, almost sounding pleased.

'You mean Mrs March still has her lazy arse in bed.' Harriet pushed past and entered the hall, surprising both Mrs Nore and herself.

'Mrs March...' Mrs Nore began, determined to assert her authority.

'Oh, for goodness' sake! Go make some coffee or something! I can show myself to her bedroom.'

It was a small consolation that Harriet knew she wouldn't surprise Anya in bed with her boyfriend, seeing as the boyfriend in question currently had a bashed-in head and was lying dead at the bottom of the drive.

Quite a coincidence – except no decent detective believed in coincidences. Had Dean been on his way *to* the house? *Away* from the house?

How the *hell* had he ended up by the *road*?

Leaving Mrs Nore muttering thinly veiled insults at her back, Harriet ran up the central staircase, two steps at a time, until she reached the landing – and then couldn't remember which was her mother's room. The biggest and best, obviously, but each room looked the same from this side of the row of pristine white doors.

A querulous voice called, 'Mrs Nore? Did someone call?'

Gotcha!

Harriet yanked open the nearest door. 'Good morning, Mum!'

Smirking at the indignant squeal from the bed, Harriet strode over to the window and jerked back the curtains.

As bright sunlight flooded the room, Anya shrieked again, falling back against a stack of white pillows, one perfectly toned arm hiding her face from the light. She didn't quite hiss or begin smouldering, vampire style, but it was close.

Harriet's smirk broadened into a grin.

Anya has no power over you, her brother's voice echoed in her head. *Only the power you give her.*

An easy thing for *him* to say. In real life, it didn't work like that.

Plus, Anya wasn't *his* mother.

'What are you doing here?' Anya muttered plaintively. 'Did someone die?'

A natural thing to assume when disturbed this early in the morning.

To her mother, 11.00 am was practically dawn.

'Has something happened to Grandma Belle?'

Was that a hopeful note in her mother's voice? The antagonism between the two women was mutual.

'Grandma Belle is fine, thank you for asking. She sends her love.'

'That's a downright lie.' Anya rolled over and snuggled back beneath the bedclothes. 'Where's Mrs Nore? I haven't had my morning coffee. I'm no good for anything until I've had my coffee. You know that.'

It was one of the few things she and her mother had in common.

'I have some bad news,' Harriet said. 'Your friend Dean has been found dead.'

'Dead?' Her mother sat up, a little blonde head amongst a froth of white lace. '*Dead?*'

Could her mother fake that surprise?

'That's not possible,' Anya said firmly. 'He was here yesterday, perfectly fine, doing his lengths in the pool. You saw him yourself. Are you sure you've not mistaken him for someone else? Hand me my phone. I'll call him now and prove it to you. You'll see.'

The slim, silver phone was perfectly within reach on Anya's nightstand, but Harriet stepped forward and handed it to her all the same.

'Does Dean have any next-of-kin that you might know of?'

'Don't be silly,' Anya snapped. 'We had far more interesting things to do than talk about *that*.'

Could he have been *married*? With *children*?

Revulsion made her speak more plainly than she would have done otherwise. 'If he doesn't have any next-of-kin, you might be required to officially identify his body.'

Anya ignored that, tapping on her contacts and then the number she wanted. It rang four times and then went to voicemail.

She terminated the call. 'He's not answering.'

'When did you last see him?'

Anya was still staring at the phone screen, a tiny frown marring her perfectly smooth forehead. 'Dean always answers his phone,' she said softly, as though talking to herself. 'He's one of those irritating people who constantly has it with them. He even takes it into the bathroom. I'm forever teasing him about it. Why isn't he answering?'

Her mother was in shock and who wouldn't be – woken with the news that a friend had died unexpectedly.

'When did you last see him?' Harriet repeated, more gently this time.

'Yesterday, the same as you. He used the pool, had lunch and then popped out to do some errand or other. He didn't come back. I didn't mind. I have plenty to do and I assumed he'd met up with some friends and that I'd see him today.' There was a pause, presumably while Anya thought this through, and then she swung her legs out of the bed and stood up. She was wearing some delicate, floaty, lacy thing that Harriet didn't care to examine too closely because it appeared to be completely transparent.

Anya went over to the window and looked out. The house was entirely surrounded by snow-covered trees. Even in winter, it had always been impossible to see the road or any of the neighbours. They could have been in the middle of the forest, miles from anywhere.

'It's very odd,' Anya said. 'How can he be dead? He was

very healthy. He worked out; lifted heavy weights. I met him at the gym. A man like him wouldn't be easy to kill. I don't understand how this could have happened.'

Why had her mother automatically assumed Dean had been murdered? Was he the kind of man someone would *want* to kill?

'Neither do we,' she said out loud, 'which is why one of my colleagues will call on you later today, to formally take your statement and ask whether you heard anything last night. A car accident, people shouting, anything out of the ordinary. I suggest you tell them the truth.'

Anya gave her a sharp look. 'Why wouldn't I do that?'

'Even if it's something minor, that doesn't seem important to you, please tell them. In the meantime,' – Harriet took out her notebook and clicked her pen – 'what can you tell me about Dean Hunter?'

'I've told you everything I know. What else do you need?'

What did she think?

'You must know *something* about him? For goodness' sake, didn't you ever *talk* to each other?'

Her mother pouted mutinously, 'Not much, which is not something I should be discussing with *you*.'

'Better me than my boss, so let's start with the basics. Dean's address, his next-of-kin, his job...' Her mother continued to regard her blankly. 'Did he have any friends, any enemies...?'

'*Enemies*? So he *was* killed deliberately?'

Harriet remembered the way Dean had been lying at an angle on the pavement, half covered in snow, as though he'd been callously shoved out of a car and left there.

'Yes, but I'm not allowed to give you the details yet.'

Again, Anya glanced anxiously out of the window.

What was she afraid of? Did she think the murderer was likely to come for her next?

Harriet moved to stand beside her mother. What was it that had caught her attention?

But there was nothing to see through the window except trees in every direction.

TWENTY

As the sun came up, the snow began to melt, turning grey and slushy on the road. Ben's daughter Sophie, who was six, would be bitterly disappointed. She'd already eyed up his old wooden sledge on her last visit. At least, he assumed *she'd* dug it out from the back of the shed. The thing must be at least fifty years old, probably built by his grandfather for his mother when she was a child.

As Ben walked back to the police station, he stumbled as the pavement disappeared beneath his feet. Had he stepped off the kerb? Damn this snow. It was impossible to see what he was walking on – or, indeed, in.

Striking that thought, he took a look around. He was standing on the edge of a narrow lane leading into the forest. He frowned. Not something he recalled seeing before and he'd lived here for most of his life, apart from the eight years he'd spent working in the Met. Where did it lead? Was there a house behind all those trees? He should ask Sam to check it out as part of his house-to-house enquiries, but it would take time to organise a team and set up a questionnaire, and they were supposed to have a briefing first, as well as an update on the skeleton in the glasshouse. Meanwhile, the lane was here, waiting...

He could almost hear Milla's voice in his head, tempting him astray.

But he was a detective inspector, as DCI Cameron liked to remind him. He shouldn't be bothering himself with routine enquiries and routine interviews and routine arrests. His job was to sit in an office all day – and end up like Cameron? Going stir-crazy from the lack of day-to-day policing?

When Ben had first joined the police, fresh out of university, it had *not* been his dream to sit in an office and devise investigative strategy.

He'd wanted to make a *difference*.

He glanced towards the village. If he stepped out into the road, he'd be able to see the sagging tiled roof of the police station, formerly a seventeenth-century courthouse. He was less than five minutes' walk from a mug of hot coffee (even if it was out of the machine), the temperamental twentieth-century central heating system and an even more temperamental boss.

But, as Milla would have said, where would the fun be in that?

He walked down the lane.

It was single track. The ancient trees grew thickly on either side, desperately reaching towards the light. Like the woodland around The Witch's Brew, this must be a particularly old part of the forest, although the undergrowth had been severely and recently cut back. The exposed edges of the cut branches were ragged and raw. Beneath the trees, where the snow hadn't reached, were patches of tiny wild cyclamen, pale pink and white, and incredibly pretty.

He could hear the river at the bottom of the gorge, louder now he was away from the road and the chatter of the CSIs. A memory was coming back to him, of walking down this very lane with his grandmother. They'd been calling on someone she knew but didn't particularly like. An elderly couple who, as it transpired, lived in a tall narrow house with stained-glass windows. It had a Scandinavian-sounding name, something to do with elves, which his grandmother had mocked. She'd explained that, until a hundred years ago, the house had a name that was far more sensible.

Raven's... something?

Pretty much like every other house in the village.

As Ben walked, he noticed the snow in front of him had been churned up, as though many people had walked through it. The fresh snow that had fallen on top was now melting, revealing the frozen layer beneath. Had there been a party here last night? Had the murdered man been a guest? Had he staggered down this lane himself – or had someone helped him – or had they killed him and then dragged him along to the road?

He shook his head. The trouble with his job was that soon you started to see murders everywhere.

A far more realistic theory: wasn't it bin day? He couldn't remember seeing a wheelie bin on the edge of the road but, for all he knew, some little old lady might have staggered down to the road in the early hours, dragging it behind her.

When had it started snowing?

Last night, around about the time he'd met Milla at the pub.

When had it stopped?

He had no idea but he would ask Dakota to check.

He slid his phone from his jacket pocket and took a series of photos, but there was nothing distinct enough to be used as evidence.

Meanwhile, he'd arrived at a fork in the lane. The left side was a driveway, leading between two large rowan trees. Ahead, the lane continued into the forest until it petered out completely. Perhaps there had been other houses here, centuries ago, but he could see no trace of them now, only a few lumps of ivy-covered stone that could have been anything.

He turned in what he assumed was the direction of the house.

The drive sloped into a wide, basin-shaped garden, surrounded by more rowan trees. In the centre was the house he remembered. Stained-glass windows, spiky gables and a narrow turret tower stuck over the entrance. All the woodwork had been painted glossy black. Very out of place was the green Porsche 911 parked beside the front door.

Presumably *that* didn't belong to the elderly couple he remembered.

Had the woman given him a bag of sweets? He couldn't recall, but her husband had been intimidating – the kind of crotchety old man who would never throw a football back if it landed in his garden – more likely to stab it with a garden fork in front of you.

Ben pressed the doorbell but couldn't hear it ring inside, so he knocked hard as well.

Milla called it his 'waking-the-dead knock'.

The woman who answered the door was not old or grumpy. Smiling tentatively, she was almost as tall as he was. Her eyes were cornflower blue, long black hair fell in perfect waves around her shoulders and her flawless skin was the texture of a magnolia petal.

Where had *that* come from?

It sounded like one of those fairy stories he'd read to Sophie...

Hair as black as ebony, lips as red as blood, skin as white as snow.

She lifted one slim dark brow enquiringly, her smile fading uncertainly, and he realised he'd been staring as though in a daze.

'Can I help you?' she asked. 'Are you lost? I'm new here but I know a bit of the village layout.'

He took out his warrant card and held it up like they did in the films – like a conman would.

'I'm Detective Inspector Ben Taylor. And you are?'

Was he imagining it, or had a glimmer of fear just flickered over her face?

Nothing unusual about that: even the completely innocent became twitchy when a police officer turned up on their doorstep unannounced.

Still...

'I'm Iris Evergreen.' She said her name as though he ought to recognise it. Was she an actress or someone famous?

'I'm investigating a suspicious death,' he said, 'and I wondered if you heard anything unusual last night? Did you have visitors? Notice anything strange or out of the ordinary?'

He should leave this to Sam and Ash. He was out of practice.

Iris didn't seem to notice. 'No, I'm sorry. I was working until late and when I do that, I play music quite loudly. The floor-boards practically vibrate beneath my feet.'

She didn't seem the type to disturb the neighbours with loud rock music – although this house was too far away for any neighbour to be bothered what noise she made – but she did have dark circles beneath her eyes, and why would she lie?

'You didn't hear anything?' he clarified.

She was rubbing her hands together, massaging her palm with her thumb. DCI Cameron would have said that was a sure sign of guilt, but Ben, who didn't set much store by body language (it was too easy to fake), decided she was probably cold.

'No,' she replied, 'but we're quite isolated here, aren't we, Sparkle?'

Belatedly, he spotted a cat rubbing against her legs. It was small, not much more than a kitten and an unusual pure white.

The cat sniffed at his legs. Could it scent Binx? Perhaps not. He was wearing wellingtons and his coat was soaked through.

Now there was an idea...

He pretended to shiver.

Milla (a consummate liar) would have been impressed.

'May I come inside?' he asked.

It was obvious that she didn't want to let him in but that could be the quite natural fear of giving a stranger access to her house. Should he brandish his warrant card again?

'OK...' Reluctantly, she stepped aside to let him enter.

'Thank you.' He stamped off the worst of the snow from his boots before taking them off, but there were no carpets for him to muddy, only polished floorboards. He had a vague impression of a curiously round entrance hall, painted pale grey and over-laid with a silver twiggy pattern, before Iris led him further inside, into a more traditional hallway with a staircase in the centre and various rooms leading off it.

Iris obviously wanted him to go into the room on the left.

So he stepped around her and went into the room on the right, which turned out to be... a *library*?

He almost forgot why he was there.

Floor to ceiling bookcases with ornately carved tops and as for that fireplace... He felt his mouth drop open. Was that a... *dragon*?

Who the hell was Iris Evergreen?

'This is...'

Iris sighed. 'Weird?'

'Amazing!'

'Oh!' Her mouth curved into a genuine smile. 'Do you think so?'

'Yes! The house, the library, this fireplace... It's incredible.

I've never seen anything like it.' He took a step forward, intending to gently stroke the dragon's snout, to see how it had been created. 'A beautiful work of—'

'No!' Iris dashed between him and the fireplace, holding up her hand to prevent him moving any closer. 'Don't touch it! It... it's... fragile...'

She was a terrible liar but he did as she asked, taking his time to look the fireplace up and down, including the surrounding floor. There was nothing untoward. No blood splatter patterns, even in the hard-to-clean areas. Only a slight dent in the floorboards, towards the centre of the room, as if she'd dropped something heavy. Nothing that would justify obtaining a warrant, unfortunately.

And now he was seeing murderers everywhere too?

He certainly needed that holiday.

'I'm sorry,' she said. 'I over-reacted. It's just—'

'It's old and fragile,' he agreed.

'Would you like to come into the sitting room? It's far cosier and has lovely views.'

What of? Trees? He saw rather too many of them, living in Raven's Edge. But he followed her into the sitting room and took another good look around. The only furniture was a green three-piece suite grouped around an enormous black granite fireplace – uncarved – and a green chaise-longue set in front of a window overlooking the garden.

'Would you like a cup of tea?' she asked, far too brightly. 'Coffee?'

He turned, finding her blue eyes almost on a level with his, although she wasn't wearing heels, or even slippers.

He was tempted to call her bluff, to see how she'd react, but instead, 'I'd better not, thank you. I just happened to be passing...' Inwardly he cringed. How many times had Harriet used *that* excuse? 'And I wondered if—'

'I'd heard anything suspicious,' she finished for him.

She was regaining her confidence.

So there *had* been something in the library... Would it be worth coming back with Harriet?

Perhaps.

But he didn't want to put Iris on her guard just yet. More evidence was needed if he was going to come barging in here with a warrant.

'I came to this house once,' he said. 'Years ago. With my grandmother. She was friends with the people who lived here. They were an elderly couple?'

'My grandparents,' she nodded. 'Walter and Beatrice Wainwright. I don't know much about them. I never met them. They were estranged from my mother. I have no idea why.'

'How sad.'

She shrugged. 'Families, eh?'

He sighed. Ms Iris Evergreen was certainly guilty of something, but she'd keep until they'd done a little more investigation – into her *and* Dean Hunter – and whether there was a connection between them.

He dug one of his cards from his inside pocket and handed it over. 'If you remember anything unusual about last night – a disturbance, shouting, that kind of thing – could you contact me?'

'Of course.' She took the card carefully, almost as though she thought it might bite. 'There was one thing though...'

He said 'Yes?' a little too quickly.

'Nothing to do with the case, but you mentioned coming here with your grandmother? You grew up in the village? You know everybody?'

'I suppose so.' Although not as well as Harriet and the rest of his team. 'Why?'

Iris went over to the granite mantelpiece and came back with a photograph.

'I've been asking all around the village to see if anyone

recognises the man in this photo.' She handed it over. 'Would you know who this is?'

He took the photo without looking at it. 'Why is it important to you?'

'Before she died, my mother told me that this man was my father. I was hoping to make contact with him – if he's still alive.'

'Yet you don't know his name?'

'No. My mother was always very cagey about that. He left her when she was pregnant, so she wanted nothing to do with him.'

He glanced down at the photo, at a handsome blond-haired man smiling happily at the camera. His first thought was that the man didn't look anything like her but he could hardly tell her that. Finding her father was obviously important to her but... He checked the man's features again. Low, narrow forehead, thick blond hair, dark eyes, possibly brown...

'You're going to say he looks nothing like me,' she sighed. 'I've worked that out for myself, but some children favour one parent or the other, rather than being a mix of the two, wouldn't you say? And I've always been told I'm the image of my mother.'

Whereas Ben was the spitting image of his late father, whom he'd despised.

He looked down at the photo again, treating it as evidence, treating it as a job.

What could he see?

'He's standing outside St Francis's Church – it's the one in the village. He's dressed smartly, either for work or some kind of important occasion. That could be a flower in his buttonhole, it's very small and the photo's bent just there...'

'Really? I never spotted that! I suppose I was too busy staring at his face.'

'Men usually wear flowers in their buttonhole because

they're attending a wedding or another occasion requiring formal dress.'

'A wedding?' Her face fell. 'My mother was never married to my father. It says "spinster" on the certificate for her wedding to my stepfather.'

'That's the trouble when you dig into family history,' he said, handing back the photo. 'You don't know what you're going to find.'

'There's something else you've spotted, isn't there?'

'I ought to be going.'

'Tell me! I need to know! I don't care what it is, if there's something you've seen in this photo that gives away his identity...'

Against his better judgement, Ben tapped the side of the photo. 'That curving white stripe, which could be a car or anything really, but outside a church? Next to a man with a flower in his buttonhole? I believe it's part of a white dress.'

'A bride,' she said sadly. 'He was marrying someone else.'

A statement, rather than a question. She must have suspected...

'The photograph isn't standard size. It's too narrow. If you hold it up, you can see the edge has been cut – with some skill, perhaps with a guillotine? – but ever so slightly crooked.'

'His wife has been deliberately cut out of the photo.' Her voice was light but he could see the devastation in her eyes. 'Damn. That doesn't look good.'

'Only two people would cut the bride out of a photo in that way. The groom – but in that case, why not throw the photo away? Why be reminded of the event? Or perhaps it was someone who cared for the groom but not the bride. I'm sorry it's not better news.'

'It's the most information I've discovered since I began my research. I sometimes felt the locals knew who he was but didn't want to tell me.'

That would fit in with an unfaithful spouse scenario, but he could hardly tell her that.

It did bother him though, that the man seemed familiar. Where had he seen him before?

But the last thing he needed was yet another mystery to solve, so he made his excuses, put his boots back on and left.

He was a big man who'd boxed as a teenager. Aaron Cooper was slight and had probably never even seen a boxing match. The force of the punch was enough to knock Cooper off his feet and send him crashing against one of the nightstands.

He flexed his fist. He hadn't even broken the skin on his knuckles.

Yet the other man wasn't moving...

His anger dissipated. He prodded Cooper with his foot.

'Get up, Cooper,' he said. 'And get out the hell out of my house.'

Cooper didn't move. Had he knocked him out? Was he going to suffer the irony of calling for a cab to ensure the bastard got home safely?

'Cooper?'

He crouched beside the younger man – and saw the blood trickling down the nightstand.

Hell...

'Cooper? Stop messing about!'

Should he call for an ambulance?

He felt for a pulse. At the neck, at the wrist, at the neck once again.

He put his cheek close to the man's mouth, waiting for breath to warm his skin.

'Come on, Cooper!'

He searched for a pulse once more but knew he was wasting his time.

Aaron Cooper was dead.

TWENTY-ONE

Harriet sent a message to Ben, confirming that her mother had identified the body on the roadside as Dean Hunter from Norchester, but Anya didn't know any more than that because they were only 'acquaintances'. Harriet added that she was going to take her meal break and would see him back at the station in an hour, but he didn't reply.

She crossed the road and went into the village church, making her way to the front, where a small, square marble plaque was set into the whitewashed wall on the left. Directly opposite was a window dedicated to St Francis and, as the sunlight streamed through the coloured glass, it created a pretty mosaic across the plaque, which read:

Dedicated to the Memory of
Detective Superintendent
George March
Raven's Edge Police Station
Who selflessly gave his life so that others might live

Beside the plaque was a narrow glass vase wedged into a

metal ring. Harriet refreshed the single white rosebud in it every week, while telling the plaque what she'd been up to.

Today, she couldn't think of anything to say.

For a few minutes she watched the coloured lights play over the surface of the plaque, and then she sighed and whispered, 'Sorry, Dad. I'll be back on Sunday,' and left, feeling a failure as a police officer *and* a daughter.

She stepped out of the church into the chilly sunshine and walked towards the lych-gate.

A man had been placing pretty posies of Christmas roses on a row of graves beside the boundary wall; he was now holding one hand over his eyes as if in prayer. She recognised him as Mal Graham, a member of the super-wealthy family who lived on the other side of the village, in a modern mansion called Hartfell. Harriet had been there once, but on duty rather than as a guest. Would he remember her? They'd met a couple of times since, neither of which had ended well – their personalities grated against each other.

She kept her head down and tried to walk faster, but he glanced up as she passed and soon fell into step beside her.

Bother.

'Good morning, Detective Sergeant March.'

She heard the note of amusement in his voice and knew what was coming next.

Sure enough, 'Tasered any villains lately?'

He *had* to bring that up.

'One time,' she said. '*One* time.'

As Harriet had been obliged to write a lengthy report about it, she didn't intend doing it again any time soon.

She didn't need to ask why he was here. The four identical black marble graves beside that boundary wall belonged to his mother, his twin baby brothers and his cousin, all of whom died when their previous home, King's Rest, had caught fire eighteen years ago.

How terrible to lose almost your entire family in such a brutal way.

Instead of snapping a comeback, he glanced back at the church and then down at her. 'You're upset.'

Yes, but not for the reason he was assuming.

It was hard to get that picture out of her head.

Four identical graves, with four identical posies.

Horrible, horrible, horrible.

She'd only been a few months old when her father had died. There was a hole in her life where he should have been, but she'd had her grandparents and her brother to help fill the space. She'd never known her father as a person, relying on other people's memories to fill in the blanks. She hadn't really missed him, until recently, when it had dawned on her that she'd never meet him or know what he was really like.

How much worse must it have been to lose almost an entire family when you were old enough to truly remember them?

'I'm fine,' she said.

He didn't argue this blatant lie but slowed his pace, allowing her to go through the lych-gate first.

On the other side, she stopped. The Square was in front of her and if she continued walking around it and turned left, she'd end up at the police station. She could even call into The Crooked Broomstick first, for a bag of cookies, but for some reason her feet refused to carry her that way.

Mal was forced to step around her, before turning to regard her curiously. 'Can I give you a lift anywhere?'

'No, thank you,' she said, but didn't move.

'OK, I guess I'll see you around.'

He went over to a gleaming silver Audi parked at an angle beside the church wall, and then glanced back. 'How about lunch at The Drop?'

'I'm supposed to be at work.'

She'd told Ben she was taking a meal break.

'Surely you're allowed to stop for lunch?'

'Not necessarily.' In theory, the Murder Investigation Team worked a regular shift pattern, but in practice that rarely happened. As Sam was fond of saying, 'If only the bad guys worked from eight until eight...'

'My treat?' he added.

If he hadn't said that she'd have walked away.

'I'm quite capable of paying for my own lunch!'

'Whatever you like,' he said, but held open the passenger door.

His likeness to his sister Milla was extraordinary. They had the same lithe build, brown skin and silky black hair. Mal's hair was not as long as Milla's, barely enough to tie back in that half-hearted style he favoured, with a good portion falling around his face. They had the same silver-grey eyes as their father—

As Mal slammed the car door, Harriet realised she'd got into the car without noticing.

Fabulous.

Harriet March: seduced by a pretty face. A disgrace to feminists everywhere.

Mal started the engine, crunched the gears and sent the wheels into a spin.

'Not The Drop,' she said, before he reversed onto the high street. The CSIs would be long gone, but she didn't want to talk about the murder.

'The Witch's Brew?' Mal suggested.

'Ooh, yes please! I'd love a bacon and cheese panini.'

Mal slammed his foot on the accelerator and shot off down the high street.

'Slow down,' she grumbled. 'I *am* a police officer.'

'Detective,' he said, not reducing his speed. 'Not Traffic.'

'It makes no difference,' she said. 'I can still arrest you.'

'That *does* sound like fun but, to spare any awkwardness

later, I feel obliged to inform you that I'm currently driving below the speed limit.'

She glanced over at the dashboard. He was right, damn it.

Within minutes he'd turned into the car park beside The Witch's Brew, jumped out and was opening the passenger door before she'd undone her seatbelt.

'Thanks,' she muttered.

If Kat, the owner, was surprised to see Harriet walk in with Mal Graham rather than Ben, she hid it well. She even brought menus over, which Harriet and Ben never usually bothered with.

Harriet made a show of reading it and then ordered a bacon and cheese panini as she always did.

So did Mal.

Both rejected the coleslaw.

'I hate coleslaw,' Mal said, as Kat walked away.

Harriet stared at him in disbelief. 'Me too!'

That sly smile made a reappearance. 'Does that mean we have something in common after all, DS March?'

'Don't push it.'

He filled what might have been an awkward silence by chatting about a music magazine his father's company had taken over. Both he and Dermot thought that with the right investment and a change of management, it would do well covering the type of quirky news and interviews not readily found online.

'The kind of thing I used to read as a kid,' he said. 'They had such tiny budgets they had to work harder to find unique angles and would often spot new talent before anyone else.'

'You'd have to increase the budget or you'll have trouble finding anyone to run it.'

He smiled. 'We already have someone in mind.'

'If you're planning on offering your sister Milla the job,

you'll have to be more subtle than that. She seems to like working with Drake.'

That erased his good humour. 'Well, we don't.'

By 'we', he presumably meant the rest of the Graham family.

'Surely it's up to Milla what she does with her life?'

'Absolutely! We only want to present her with a range of options.'

Options? *Really?*

Fortunately their food arrived before Harriet found herself in the unlikely position of taking Milla's side – and she didn't even *like* Kieran Drake.

Without thinking, Harriet offered Mal her salad, as she always did with Ben.

He grimaced. 'No thank you. I'm not a fan of salad.'

Something else they had in common. Although when she asked him to pass the ketchup, he swapped it for the bottle of mayonnaise next to her.

She pulled a face. 'Mayonnaise with *bacon?*'

'Mayonnaise with *chips,*' he said, as Kat returned with a small bowl of spicy potato wedges and set it between them. 'Help yourself!'

Harriet waited until Kat was halfway back to the kitchen before grumbling, 'How did you get free chips? I *never* get chips and I've been coming here forever!'

'Don't you?' He widened his eyes in a parody of innocence. 'Maybe they like me better than you.'

That was probably true and not only because he was rich. She couldn't deny Mal Graham had an easy charm – when he decided to use it.

For some reason he'd decided to use it on her.

More fool him.

She lifted the top of the panini and covered her bacon in

ketchup, waving the bottle across it in her usual zig-zag pattern, with a quick swirl around the edge to finish.

'*What?*' she snapped, when she saw him watching her perform this little ritual.

'You like ketchup?'

'I do.'

'Here, have a chip,' he said, pushing the bowl towards her. 'Chips go well with ketchup too.'

She frowned. 'That's not going to make me a nicer person.'

He held up his hands. 'I thought you might like a chip! No strings!'

She felt a flash of guilt. Had visiting her father's grave left her bad-tempered? Or was it the worry that her mother might be a murderer? Whatever, she was in no mood to play games.

'Pick someone else to flirt with,' she suggested, picking up her panini.

He thought about that for far too long. 'Is that what we're doing?'

'Well, *I'm* not.' Harriet took a too-large bite of her panini, which was her tried and tested technique to avoid conversation.

Unfortunately, Fliss Merriweather, the co-owner of Practically Magic, the New Age shop in the village (and local busybody), dropped into the seat between them and made Harriet's day complete.

'Hi, Harriet!' the elderly woman beamed. 'I'm so glad to see you!'

'Lovely to see you too, Fliss,' Mal answered for her. 'Sadly, DS March can't stop to chat because she's in a hurry to get back to work.'

Fliss's sister, Elvira, took the fourth seat at the table, waving aside any objection Mal might have made. 'Trust me, Harriet will want to hear *this*.'

'It really can't wait,' Fliss said. 'We'd be on our way to the police station if you hadn't turned up for lunch.'

Harriet nearly groaned out loud. Had they found a skeleton in their garden too?

'But we thought you wouldn't want your private business broadcast to everyone,' Elvira chimed in.

Private business?

That didn't usually stop anyone in Raven's Edge.

Harriet dipped one of Mal's potato wedges into the dollop of mayonnaise on his plate. Surprisingly, it wasn't bad.

'What's happened?' she asked.

'Shall I leave?' Mal made to get to his feet.

'Bless you, love.' Fliss patted his arm. 'It's no secret.'

Private but not secret? That made no sense at all!

But Harriet took another potato wedge and let it play out.

'There was a woman in here yesterday,' Elvira said. 'She said she's new to the village. Her name is Iris Wainwright – one of the Wainwrights of Álfheimr – Raven's Hollow, as it used to be called.'

Harriet shook her head. 'I'm afraid I have no idea what you're talking about.'

'That funny Gothic revival house between The Drop and your mother's?'

'Oh, *that* house! Yes, I remember it.' To Mal she said, 'It was owned by an elderly couple, Walter and Beatrice Wainwright. Walter didn't like kids. He made me and Ryan do a lucky dip in a bowl of red jelly once when we went trick or treating. I think the "prize" was a glass eye. I was only six. I still have nightmares.'

'How mean,' Mal said.

'I *know*.' She took another potato wedge and again dunked it into Mal's mayonnaise. They really were very good.

Fliss looked between them, and down at the bowl of chips, and unexpectedly smiled. 'Well,' she confided, 'Iris Wainwright writes fairy tales under the name of Iris Evergreen.'

'I've heard of Iris Evergreen,' Harriet said. 'I've read her books.'

They all stared at her.

'They were good. I liked them.'

'Me too,' Mal said.

That conjured up an image she hadn't expected. The suave Mal Graham, reading romantic fantasy?

As usual, the thought must have shown on her face because he pointed to his chest and said, 'Publisher? Famous for collections of fairy tales?'

'I forgot. Sorry!'

'One of our editors put in a bid for Iris's first book,' he said, 'but we didn't offer enough and it sold to a competitor.'

'Blimey!'

'Not *quite* what I said when I watched it hit the number-one position on the *Sunday Times* bestseller chart for eight weeks in a row. Iris's connection to Raven's Edge makes a lot of sense now. The stories feature a witch named Meg who can shapeshift into a raven but she's kidnapped by a fae prince and taken to the Other World.'

'Kidnapped by a fae prince?' Fliss clapped her hands. 'Ooh, how lovely! I'll have to buy it. Do you think Whit would have it in stock?'

Elvira's response was rather drier. 'Very Hades and Persephone.'

'Greek myth,' Mal explained to a confused Harriet.

'I'm embarrassed to admit it,' she said, 'but the shapeshifting into a raven and any fancy myth references went right over my head. I just liked the book!'

'Nevertheless,' Elvira said, 'we thought you ought to know that—'

'Iris had a photograph of your *dad*!' Fliss interrupted. 'She was showing it to everyone in the café and asking if anyone knew who he was. There's a photo of him right there on the wall,' – she gestured towards the fireplace – 'with his name written beneath it, which Iris didn't spot, even though she was standing right next to it.'

Had she heard this correctly? 'Iris had a photo of my *dad*? But why?'

'That's what *we* wanted to know,' Elvira said, 'but we didn't like to ask.'

Harriet raised an eyebrow.

'Elvira wouldn't let me,' Fliss put in. 'I would have certainly asked if I'd been on my own.'

'We told Iris we had no idea who the man in her photo was,' Elvira said. 'We wouldn't pass on that kind of information without speaking to you first.'

Harriet couldn't get her head round it. 'Why would a random woman – even if she is a famous author – have a photograph of my father?'

'Exactly!' chorused the sisters.

'Anyway,' Fliss said cheerfully, 'we thought you'd like to know.'

TWENTY-TWO

Somehow, Harriet was able to finish her lunch and pay for it, and would have walked back through the village had Mal not insisted on giving her a lift.

He wasn't so keen on driving her to Raven's Hollow however.

'Are you sure about this?' he said.

'Yes! I can't let this woman walk around the village waving a photo of my father about. Who knows what people will think?'

The worst, probably.

'And if she tells you something you don't want to hear?'

Harriet didn't reply.

He didn't argue the point further although she knew he wanted to. He also wanted to drive up the little lane that led to Raven's Hollow, but she made him drop her off in the pub car park. The last thing she wanted was Mal Graham becoming involved in her personal business.

'Wait,' he said, as she unbuckled her seatbelt and made to get out of the car. 'Take this.'

'This' turned out to be a plain white business card with only his name and a phone number set out in an elegant black font. No email address, no company name, no job title.

Presumably he expected everyone to already know who he was.

It was a kind thought though.

'Thank you.' She slipped it into her pocket. Should she give him hers in return?

No, he knew who she was and how to find her if he wanted to, but why would he? A lowly detective sergeant (not that *she* ever thought of herself as 'lowly') would have nothing in common with the super-wealthy managing director of one of the most successful publishers in the country. And it would be better for everyone if it stayed that way.

Harriet walked away without giving a polite wave or even glancing back (Grandma Belle would *not* have been impressed), although she did listen hard for the soft purr of his Audi as it left the car park. Would she ever see him again?

Of course she'd see him again! They lived in the same village!

Ahead of her, on the main road leading from Raven's Edge to Calahurst, there was no trace of this morning's crime scene, not even a flutter of tape. Most of the snow had melted, leaving the occasional island of dirt-tipped slush amidst lots of puddles.

Harriet remembered to send Ben a message, telling him she'd had lunch and was following up on a lead, and that she'd explain properly when she saw him again.

He didn't answer. Either he wasn't bothered what she got up to – she was a sergeant, after all – or he was too busy, or wherever he was there was no signal – which encompassed much of the King's Forest District.

The lane leading to Raven's Hollow was now awash with slush. The trees bent over her head, creating a gloomy tunnel and a Gothic background for the house beyond. Had it always been this creepy? The house was as eccentric as she remembered – vaguely church-like, with its two-storey stained-glass windows and little turret tower.

As usual, she didn't bother with the doorbell, just slammed her fist on the glossy black door.

The response was immediate. A curvy brunette, much taller than Harriet, opened the door followed by a curious white cat.

The woman regarded her nervously. 'Hello.'

Harriet automatically bent to pet the cat, which shed white fur all over her suit as it rubbed itself against her leg. She'd practised what to say in her head, but between The Witch's Brew and here, her fancy speech had deserted her.

'Hi, I'm Harriet March. Elvira and Fliss from Practically Magic told me you have a photo of a man that you want identified? They thought I'd be able to help.'

'Oh, how kind!' The other woman's face lit up. 'That would be lovely! I was so convinced he was local, but no one seemed to know who he was. Do come in. I'm Iris.'

Harriet stepped over the threshold into the entrance hall, which was set into the base of the tower. Any other day she'd have fallen in love with the pretty silvery streaks that ran through the grey paint, mimicking the silhouettes of the bare winter trees outside, but her thought processes had turned to mush, much like the snow on the lane.

She needed to get her head straight.

Iris led her into a sitting room that was strangely devoid of furniture, apart from a green three-piece suite clustered around a black granite fireplace, and a kind of bench thing directly in front of the window. The lack of furniture made Iris's voice echo when she offered Harriet a hot drink. Was she waiting for more furniture to be delivered, or was this it?

Harriet declined the drink. She didn't want to be here for longer than she had to.

Perhaps aware of this, Iris fetched the photograph, which she'd propped up on the otherwise empty mantelpiece. It was in colour but faded and creased, perhaps twenty or thirty years old? The kind of photo that used to be developed at a chemist rather than stored and forgotten about on a cloud, which was where all Harriet's photos went.

She felt a shiver of foreboding.

'This is him.' Iris handed the photo over. 'Everyone I spoke to said he seemed familiar, and then they all denied that they knew him!'

Harriet hid a smile. The villagers did like to protect their own. There were enough pictures of her father around Raven's Edge for most people to have recognised him, newcomers or not. He was their very own hero.

She couldn't quite bring herself to look at the photo though.

'Why do you want to know?' Harriet asked instead.

Iris hesitated, as though not wanting to part with the information.

Harriet gave her a gentle nudge. 'I can see it's important to you.'

'I think he might be my father.' Her words slipped out in a rush.

So did Harriet's. 'You look nothing like him!'

Iris frowned. 'You haven't looked at the photo yet. How would you know?'

Harriet didn't *want* to know. Elvira and Fliss had unwittingly given her the bad news already. She knew she didn't have to see the photo. Its edges seemed to be burning her fingertips.

Iris waited hopefully. Harriet forced herself to glance down.

Damn. It *was* her father. There was no doubt about it. The neat corn-coloured hair, the movie-star tan, the broad white smile. She couldn't see the colour of his eyes, but they'd be brown, like Ryan's. It looked a lot like the wedding photo her mother kept beside her bed – only with Anya cut off. What would her father have looked like now? He'd be in his mid-fifties, perhaps already retired from the police. Would he have been proud of her for joining, or, like her mother, think her an idiot?

She blinked as the photo began to blur. This was the part where she handed it back, but somehow she couldn't. It would be like giving a piece of him to Iris. He was *her* father. Why should she have to share?

'I resemble my mother,' Iris said, stepping into the silence. 'Her name was Cressida Wainwright. This was her house.'

Harriet dragged herself back into the present. She didn't remember ever hearing about a *Cressida* Wainwright but it would be easy to check if Walter and Beatrice had had a daughter.

'How old are you?' she asked Iris.

The other woman grimaced. 'Thirty.'

Thirty years ago, her father would have been married to his first wife – Ryan's mother – the ink barely dry on their wedding certificate.

'Where were you born?'

Iris must have expected some kind of interrogation because she replied without hesitation. 'On my birth certificate it says Norchester, which is a city a few miles north of here. I drove past it on my way here from London.'

It wasn't outside the realm of possibility.

'Here's my problem,' Harriet said. 'This photo?' She carelessly flipped it with her finger, as though it didn't mean anything, as though it didn't count. 'This is *my* father.'

It was as if she'd given Iris the biggest Christmas present of her life. Her beautiful face positively lit up with excitement. Harriet half expected her to squeal.

'*Really?* You're my *sister*? That's brilliant!'

Brilliant for whom?

Harriet bit her lip hard, knowing what was likely to come out of her mouth. Tact, as both Ben and Ryan (and everyone really) liked to remind her, was *not* her forte.

'Is he still alive?' Iris asked. 'I mean, I wouldn't want to force myself into your family, to cause any arguments or upset anyone. I know this must come as a huge shock for you.'

She had *no* idea.

It would take time for her and Ryan to come to terms with the idea that their perfect father had been flawed, but Anya would *not* be happy knowing that the name and reputation of the man she'd told everyone was a hero would be forever tarnished by the sudden appearance of a long-lost, illegitimate daughter.

Maybe they didn't need to tell Anya yet.

'I'm sorry to tell you this,' Harriet said, 'but my father is dead. We've never heard anything about any other woman or any secret child. He wasn't that kind of man. It doesn't...'

Sound like him.

Seem *real*.

Make sense.

Was this woman her sister?

No.

Harriet wouldn't believe it.

She *couldn't* believe it.

She needed *evidence*.

'I'm sorry to ask you,' Iris filled the silence, unaware of the struggle inside Harriet's head. 'I know you've already told me, but what's your name again?'

She couldn't *remember*?

Harriet was sure she'd recall every word of this conversation for the next fifty years *and* be able to quote it back verbatim.

'Harriet March,' she returned flatly.

'Are you any relation to Anya March who lives next door?'

Oh, *great*. They'd already met?

'Anya's my mother. I have an older brother; his mother died in childbirth, along with his baby sister.'

'How awful! I'm so sorry.'

Harriet didn't reply.

'This must be a huge shock for you,' Iris said, again.

Harriet sighed. 'Do you have any other evidence, other than the photo?'

That immediately put Iris on the defensive. 'Why else would my mother have a photograph of him?'

Harriet could think of a variety of reasons, starting with coincidence and ending with obsessed stalker. 'How do you know he's your father? Did your mother physically point to this photo and say, "Iris, this is your father"?'

'Of course not.' Iris blinked rapidly, as tears welled up in her eyes.

She'd made the woman cry. Harriet's anger began to dissipate. She'd handled this badly. She'd arrived without making an appointment, without someone like Ben or Sam to keep her calm. She couldn't have made more of a mess of it.

'My mother would never tell me the name of my father,' Iris said, rubbing her sleeve over her eyes. 'He abandoned her while she was pregnant and she never forgave him. But when she lay dying in a hospice, she had a change of heart and told me everything I needed to know was in a box in her study. I found the engagement ring he must have given her, still in its box, and an album of photographs and some letters from her parents.'

It certainly seemed conclusive enough.

Harriet turned the photo over but saw only a four-digit number stamped on the back. Presumably the photographer's reference.

She still didn't believe it.

'What was your father's name?' Iris asked quietly.

'George March. He was a detective superintendent. Worked right here in Raven's Edge.'

'What was he like?'

Harriet took a deep breath, but found she couldn't speak.

What had her father been like?

'He had blond hair and brown eyes...'

That wasn't what Iris meant.

'He was tall. He had a good sense of humour.'

Now she sounded like a dating app.

'He was popular. Everyone liked him. He won trophies at sport. My grandmother still has them. She said he always wanted to join the police. He wanted to help people. He did a lot for charity. He always thought of others before himself...'

He cheated on his wife.

He had an illegitimate child and never told anyone.

No, she couldn't believe it. She *wouldn't* believe it.

Iris was soaking up every word, hardly aware Harriet had paused.

If Iris *was* her sister, it wasn't *her* fault. Harriet knew she didn't have to be so mean about it. She could be kinder. A whole chorus of voices inside her head were now berating her. Voices that sounded exactly like Ryan, Ben, even Grandma Belle. *Especially* Grandma Belle. If Iris was her sister... Well, wouldn't it be nice to have a sister?

'I don't know any more,' Harriet said. 'Dad died a few months after I was born. Apparently two kids fell into the River Hurst and he jumped in to save them. They survived. He didn't.'

'How awful for you, having him taken away from you like that.'

Iris took a step forward.

Uh oh. Was she a hugger?

Harriet took a hasty step back.

For a moment neither of them knew what to say, so Harriet took one of her business cards from her pocket, scribbled out the front and wrote her personal phone number on the back.

'I'll need time to process this.' *Investigate this.* 'In the meantime, if you discover anything else, let me know.'

Iris took the card and stared at the number, then slowly

turned it over and examined the front, with Harriet's job description and all her work contact details.

'You became a police officer too?'

In his memory.

Anya called it 'throwing your life away'. Grandma Belle had seemed sad but unsurprised.

Unable to continue with the conversation, Harriet nodded and turned towards the door. She was running away, she knew that, but she couldn't stay here any longer.

'Goodbye,' Iris said, as the door closed behind her. 'Thank you for coming round.'

Harriet could imagine her still standing in the hall, staring at the photo.

Harriet had grown up without a father, but it must be horrible to not even know who he was or anything else about him.

She could have been kinder.

She *could* have.

Harriet walked slowly down the lane. Should she tell her mother about this latest development? What if it turned out to be nothing and she ended up hurting Anya for no reason?

Although, as Ryan would have said, Anya had never worried about hurting her.

He sobered up quickly. What the hell had he done?

Aaron Cooper had been alive less than two minutes ago. Now he was dead? It didn't feel real.

He sank onto the bed. Nothing felt real.

He glanced at his wife. He wasn't sure he'd cope if she chose now to have one of her tantrums, but she was staring at the dead man with no emotion whatsoever, any tears long since dry.

Why wasn't she more upset?

A man had died in front of her – her lover had been killed – he didn't believe any of that nonsense about a break-in – yet she was... displaying polite interest?

Delayed shock. It must be. Any minute now, she'd collapse into a heap on the floor, sobbing and wailing and—

'What are you going to do with the body?' Her voice was cold. 'You can't leave him here.'

'You' not 'we'.

What did she think he was going to do? Call for an ambulance of course, and try to explain what had happened.

How Cooper had died after only one punch.

A tragic accident.

One of those things.

Who was he kidding? The best he could hope for was to be charged with manslaughter. The worst? Murder. He'd have to go to court. It would be in all the newspapers. Whatever the verdict, he was ruined.

If he went to prison, who would look after his son?

He glanced up. His wife would be on to her next romantic conquest before the prison gates had clanged shut behind him.

He was a fool.

And a bigger fool for considering the alternative.

Pretend Cooper had never entered the house. There'd been no punch and no death. A complete reset. His life back on track. Everything as it had been before.

It could work... couldn't it?

So when she asked again, slightly louder this time, 'What are you going to do with the body?' his reply was just as cold.

'What do you suggest?'

TWENTY-THREE

22nd December

Iris unpacked the last of her boxes and finally felt as though she'd moved into Raven's Hollow. The new sign, with a cute little raven next to the name of the house, had arrived in the post. She took down the one that said Álfheimr and, using the same nails, hung up the new one, watched by Sparkle.

'I name this house "Raven's Hollow",' she said, solemnly tapping a half bottle of sparkling wine against one corner.

The air seemed to ripple around her.

How strange.

Shrugging, she popped the cork and took a swig. Actually, it would be more unusual if something strange *didn't* happen.

She held up the bottle of wine as though to toast the garden – or whatever lay behind the rowan trees in the woods. 'I'm glad you approve,' she said – and then felt silly.

Was *she* now talking to fairies?

She'd spent far too long on her own. Talking to imaginary people who *weren't* characters in her book? *Not* a good sign.

'You know what we need, Sparkle?'

The cat ignored her, staring across the lawn at something beyond the ring of rowans, her tail twitching.

'A Christmas tree!'

And she knew just where to find one...

Sparkle was most put out at being pushed back into the house with Iris obviously going off on an adventure without her. As she locked up, the cat jumped up onto the library windowsill and glared through the glass.

Iris chuckled and walked down the lane and into the village, which looked magical with fairy lights around the doors and windows, everything covered in a faint dusting of snow. How quickly Raven's Edge was beginning to feel like home.

Most of the shops were clustered around The Square. In the centre was a beautifully decorated Nordmann fir, with a market set up around it selling everything to create the perfect Christmas.

Earlier this week, Iris had spotted a stall outside the florist, Foxglove & Hemlock. As well as wreaths and festive garlands, it had been selling real Christmas trees, all lined up against the wall. Now, unfortunately, they weren't there. When she asked the man behind the stall if he had any more, he laughed in her face.

'You're too late, love. They sold out days ago!'

Her cheeks glowed with embarrassment. Did he *have* to imply she was an idiot? Not everyone did their Christmas shopping in August.

'I've been busy.' Wasn't that the truth? She worked so hard that she barely knew what day it was. 'Do you have *any* trees left?'

His smile turned shrewd and he stepped to one side. 'Two, if you're desperate.' He indicated the wall behind him. 'The little one was on its way to the dump but you can have it for free.'

Iris stepped around the counter and onto the pavement, to check the trees more closely.

One was small, not even four foot, and had lost most of its needles. The other, however... She leant back to take it all in. It was beautiful! An enormous Colorado blue spruce, and perfectly symmetrical. How tall was it? Ten foot? It would look perfect in the library. She had to have it!

'How much?' she asked.

He mentioned an eye-watering sum; now it was her turn to laugh. She offered half. He wasn't happy but they agreed on somewhere in the middle. He put his hand out to shake on it.

She hesitated. 'Does that include free delivery?'

His eyes narrowed. 'Where do you live?'

'Just down the road, beside The Drop. A little lane leads to a house called Raven's Hollow.'

'The Wainwright house?'

'Yes, that's the one.'

He shrugged. 'OK.'

They shook on it.

Somehow Iris managed to not squeal with glee, but after she'd paid him and turned away, she walked into a red-headed man who'd run up behind her.

'I thought it was you,' Whit said. He was wearing an outdoor coat and carrying a bundle of shopping bags, but was flushed and out of breath. 'I'm so glad I caught you!'

'Hi, Whit. Is there a problem?'

'No problem.' He dropped the bags and bent over, resting his hands on his thighs. 'Damn, I'm unfit. I suppose it's a drawback from spending all my free time reading books.'

All his free time?

The man on the Foxglove & Hemlock stall made a scoffing sound.

Iris deliberately turned her back on *him* and asked Whit, 'Are you OK?'

He grinned sheepishly. 'Give me a moment. Talk about the weather or something.'

Talk about the weather?

'Well... It's not snowing...' For once.

'Which is a shame,' he said, 'because then I'd have the perfect excuse to sit beside my fire and read even more books.' He straightened, his floppy hair falling perfectly into place over his forehead. 'Whew, that's better. Note to self: Join a gym.'

'That seems a little extreme...'

He laughed. 'I used to belong to one but they politely asked me not to go anymore. I found that I could balance a book on the cardiovascular equipment while I worked out. Apparently it wasn't the sort of image they wanted to project.'

'If you listened to an audio book on your phone, they'd never have known.'

'I tried that but people *would* keep talking to me.'

As his dark-brown eyes continued to regard her amiably, Iris felt her cheeks grow pinker than anything that could be blamed on the cold weather.

I like you. You're funny.

The stallholder groaned. 'Can you two take your meet-cute elsewhere? Some of us have to work.'

Whit's grin broadened. 'Don't get your garlands in a twist, Gabriel.' But he didn't take his gaze from Iris. 'Iris Evergreen, may I invite you to Spellbound for a cinnamon latte?'

'Can you get the time off work?'

'I *am* the boss, plus...' – he lifted his bags – 'I gave myself the afternoon off to do my Christmas shopping.'

Someone else who left things until the last minute.

'Then, thank you. I'd love to.'

She was aware of Gabriel's amusement as Whit took hold of her hand and placed it on his forearm like a Victorian gentleman, walking her around The Square to the furthest corner, where a tiny café called Spellbound was squashed in between a chocolate shop (Something Wicked) and a store that sold herbal remedies (Potions at Number 9). Unlike some of the other houses clustered around The Square, the steps into this building went down rather than up. Combined with the tiny medieval windows, this made the interior gloomy, but it was a quaint little place, with the ubiquitous oak beams and an inglenook fireplace.

Unlike The Witch's Brew and The Crooked Broomstick, Spellbound was deserted, but the cakes displayed on the counter were as mouth-watering as any to be found in Raven's Edge. It was a shame – and rather odd.

A solitary barista was slumped on a stool behind the counter, her head on one hand as she tapped away on her phone with the other. As soon as she saw them enter, she summoned what was presumably intended as a welcoming smile. Younger than Iris, she wore black jeans and a black scoop-necked T-shirt, with a tangle of silver chains around her neck and more wound around both wrists. Her hair was dark blonde and tied back from her face in a stubby ponytail, but two chunks had escaped on either side to brush against her cheekbones. Although she gave every impression of being half asleep, Iris had the idea those watchful golden-brown eyes didn't miss a thing.

'Hi, Whit.' The barista slid off her stool and casually flipped her phone over so they couldn't see the screen. 'You want your usual?'

'Thanks, Phyllis. I'm gasping.'

'I can see. You really need to get out of that bookshop and exercise more.'

'I'm here, aren't I?'

'Not sure Christmas shopping counts.'

Whit held up his collection of bags and grinned. 'What gave me away?'

'Show-off. I haven't even sent cards. I thought I'd wait to see if anyone sent me one first. They didn't. Saved myself a whole bunch of cash.' Curiously, this seemed to please Phyllis. She glanced over at Iris. 'Who's your friend?'

'This is Iris Evergreen. She writes books. Iris, meet Phyllis Halfpenny. She only pretends to be mean.'

'Go ahead, slander my reputation all over the village.' Phyllis leaned one hip on the counter as though standing had worn her out. 'Hi, Iris. What can I get for you?'

Iris studied the board above Phyllis's head, which detailed every known hot drink. 'Can you really make all of those?'

'Ha! Not me!' Phyllis patted the gleaming chrome machine behind her. 'Vlad does the hard work; I merely shovel in the beans.'

'Could I have a pot of breakfast tea, please?' Did that make her sound boring? 'With a slice of ginger cake?' The cake in question looked dark and sticky, and had a thick layer of white icing on top.

'Good choice,' Phyllis said, 'and entitles you to a free fortune-telling. I'll bring the drinks over and do it then – unless we have a sudden rush on.'

From her tone, it didn't sound as though a sudden rush would have ever been imminent.

'Fortune-telling?'

'Uh huh. Your choice. Tea leaves are the most popular but I can do a simple tarot reading or hold your hand and pick up on your vibes.'

Was she serious?

'We'll think about it,' Whit said, gently encouraging Iris towards a seat in the little bay window, where it wasn't quite so dark and they could people-watch.

'I'm not sure I want my fortune told,' Iris muttered, as he pulled out a chair for her. Not that she believed in that kind of thing, but she had so many secrets in her past. Would Phyllis 'read' her mannerisms and gestures and the way she presented herself to gain an insight into her character? Wasn't that how these 'psychics' operated? It was all about picking up on clues.

'That's fine. We'll tell Phyllis when she brings the drinks over.'

'Won't her feelings be hurt?'

'Does Phyllis look as though she could give a damn? Her boss hired her to read tea leaves to bring in the customers, but she knows it isn't everyone's... er, cup of tea.'

Iris smiled. 'I see what you did there.'

Whit grinned back and then they were back to doing the staring into each other's eyes thing until a very unsubtle throat-clearing dragged them to the present. Phyllis casually dropped a tray onto the table, causing everything on it to clink and rattle. It was such a shock that when Phyllis dragged another chair across to their table and sat between them, they were too taken aback to object.

Phyllis rotated her shoulders, stretched her neck from side to side, then waggled her fingers as though playing an imaginary piano.

'OK, let's do this.' She took Iris's hand in both of hers before Iris was aware what was happening.

For a moment there was silence, apart from the low hum of the shoppers in the Christmas market. Then,

'I see dead people,' Phyllis said.

Iris's stomach dropped and she yanked her hand from the other woman's grip. 'Is that a *joke*?'

The barista stared at Iris, but her yellowy eyes were strangely unfocused.

Whit, presumably used to this, snapped his fingers in front of her face. 'Phyllis, cut the theatrics. This is Iris, your new friend. She's local, not a gullible tourist.'

Phyllis shrugged, wholly unconcerned. 'I'm only telling you what I see. Admittedly it's fuzzy around the edges. Maybe I'm distracted due to Christmas coming up. I had a woman with six-

year-old twins before you. They screamed and screamed and
screamed. My head's still ringing. I gave them a bag of apple
doughnuts and sent them off to the museum. Ellie will sort
them out. She terrifies *me*.'

'What kind of dead people?' Iris couldn't help asking.
Could Phyllis really see *ghosts*? She seemed so casual about it.

Phyllis gave her a dismissive glance before taking her hand
again, closing her eyes and tilting her head on one side, as
though listening for something neither of them could hear.

The hairs on the back of Iris's neck began to prickle. It was
incredibly creepy. *Was* the woman genuine?

'A couple of men. They're... wandering about,' Phyllis
murmured. 'As though they're lost or have nowhere to go. No
detail, nothing specific...' She opened her eyes and glared at Iris
as though this was her fault. 'Do you live near the churchyard?
You get a lot of dead people there.'

Iris glanced out of the window, at the church and graveyard
directly opposite the café. Should she state the obvious?

'No, but—'

'Not that then.' Phyllis closed her eyes again. 'How about a
hill? I'm definitely seeing a hill... and an old man in a suit. He
seems frustrated about something... He's pacing... It's dark... He
feels trapped.'

As that didn't sound like anyone Iris knew, she relaxed.
'No.' Raven's Hollow was in a hollow, not on a hill, hence the
name. 'Could they be some other supernatural being?' She
remembered the strange atmosphere that surrounded the house.
'Like... fairies?'

Phyllis's eyes flew open and she burst out laughing, a rough
croaky sound, as though she didn't do it very often. 'Seriously,
girl! There are no such things as fairies!'

'Some people don't believe in spirits either,' Whit said.

'They're idiots,' Phyllis shrugged. 'I've got to get back to
work, in case the boss pops in.' She released Iris's hand and got

up from the table, before turning back. '*Fairies*, you say? Does that mean you live at the old Wainwright house?'

'Yes.' Iris was still unnerved. 'What of it?' *Was* the house haunted?

'That could explain it. The original Raven's Edge settlement was believed to have been located in a clearing in the forest, hundreds of years ago, before they built the humpback bridge and moved over to this side. Probably loads of dead people there.'

'Please don't tell Iris her house was built on an ancient burial ground,' Whit said. 'I saw that movie and it didn't end well for anyone.'

Phyllis merely laughed. '*You* said it! Not me! I only tell it as I see it.'

Iris remembered the little piles of stone amongst the trees, which she'd thought might have once been cottages several hundred years ago. *Could* she be living on an ancient burial ground? It wasn't a pleasant thought!

As Phyllis walked away, Whit sighed and pushed the slice of ginger cake towards Iris.

'Next time,' he said, 'I'm taking you to The Witch's Brew.'

'I heard that!' Phyllis called.

'Actually,' Iris said, leaning towards Whit and lowering her voice, 'I've been invited to a party tonight. Would you like to come?'

'A party?' His brown eyes lit up. 'That sounds like fun.'

After all, what could go wrong at a party?

TWENTY-FOUR

'I have news.'

Harriet, who'd almost nodded off over the Aaron Cooper file, head propped on one hand, realised Dakota was standing beside her desk.

Guiltily, she slammed the file shut. 'Uh?'

Dakota nudged Harriet's coffee a little closer. 'We've found Eoin Kinsella.'

'*Alive?*'

'Yes. He owns a gelateria in Rome. We had an illuminating conversation. He's confused that we think he's dead.'

Harriet took a swig of coffee, luckily still warm. '*He's* confused.'

'It turns out his wife told their kids he was dead but told *him* they wanted no contact. There was no declaration of him as legally dead, either. She made it all up.'

'What a witch!'

'Meanwhile, Sam made contact with Miles Leitch, who is "wintering" in Morocco, working on some millionaire's yacht, meaning our skeleton is either Rick Dyson or Aaron Cooper.'

'It's Aaron,' Harriet said.

'There was no mailbag with the body, but someone could have stolen it?'

'No, because it's Aaron. I'm sure of it. Have you informed DI Taylor?'

'Yes. He said you could start on your list.'

As though she needed permission?

Harriet downed her coffee and stood up. 'Then I'm out of here.'

Dakota moved to stand in front of her. 'Take me with you.'

'No, I'd be taking you from... whatever it was you were doing.'

'I've finished. Please? I never go anywhere. I'm always stuck doing tech. I'm the guy in the white van – except we don't have a white van and I hardly ever leave the station.'

Sometimes Dakota made *no* sense at all.

Harriet had always struggled to get along with her; she was a good officer but completely away with the fairies, and often came up with some truly bizarre theories. However, her lateral thinking occasionally triggered flashes of pure genius.

Harriet would never tell her that though.

'Fine,' – Harriet reached for her bag – 'whatever, but I'm leaving in two minutes.'

The name at the top of Harriet's very short list was former Detective Constable Mitchell Pavey, a local man who'd joined the Force at the age of twenty-one at the same time as Aaron Cooper. They'd been stationed in Raven's Edge and, according to her father's report, had been great friends, right from school. Mitchell had stayed on for a few more years after Aaron's disappearance but, after an eclectic variety of occupations, he now owned an art gallery on Calahurst Marina, where he made a good living selling his own work and that of other local artists.

The gallery was easy to find, so they were early for their

appointment. There were lots of nautically-themed paintings in the window and entranceway, but as Harriet and Dakota moved further inside, the cheerful vibe changed to something more sombre, with large canvases of clustering storm clouds painted in ominous shades of black, purple and green – not *quite* a traditional holiday souvenir. They were signed 'M. Pavey'.

'May I help you?' The woman behind the reception desk regarded them hopefully. 'Do you see anything you like?'

Harriet fumbled for her warrant card, but Dakota beat her to it. 'Hi, I'm DC Dakota Lawrence and this is DS Harriet March. I phoned a moment ago? We have an appointment to see Mr Pavey.'

'I'll let him know you've arrived.'

Leaving Dakota studying a collection of sketches, Harriet returned to the window and stared out at the marina. This was Aaron Cooper's old neighbourhood. With the cobblestone streets and smart Georgian housing right on the edge of the water, the marina was popular with tourists and yachties alike. Mitchell Pavey's target market was right on his doorstep.

It was an interesting career path for an ex-detective constable. Most ex-coppers went into civilian roles at police headquarters, some went into private security. She'd never heard of one becoming an artist before.

'Sergeant March,' a smooth voice said in her ear. 'What can I do for you?'

Harriet turned.

Apparently neither was what the other had envisaged, because his eyes widened in shock. Had he expected someone older, taller... maler?

From her perspective, Mitchell Pavey was younger than she'd thought he'd be – mid- to late forties, and neither did he look like an ex-police officer.

His blond hair was down to his shoulders, threaded with grey and very unkempt, as though he spent a lot of his time carelessly shoving his hand through it. There were lines and shadows beneath his blue eyes and he had the weathered complexion of someone who spent most of his free time outdoors. The jeans he wore, though once expensive, had faded to almost white, their style horribly out-of-date. And he wore them with flip-flops and a white shirt with the sleeves rolled up – in December.

He certainly ticked all the 'artist' boxes – but she'd been expecting an ex-copper.

'*You're* Harriet March?' he said, after an awkward pause.

'*Detective Sergeant* Harriet March.'

A wry smile quirked his mouth. 'George March's daughter?'

Why was he making such a big deal out of it?

'It's not *your* fault, I suppose,' he muttered.

He turned abruptly and Harriet thought that meant their interview was at an end, but he then said, 'Come upstairs. We'll need to talk where we can't be disturbed. Three coffees please, Sonia.'

Dakota lifted her hand, as though she were at school. 'May I have tea please?'

'If you must.' Mitchell headed to the back of the gallery, where a little wooden staircase curled up and out of sight. A thick blue cord blocked it off. Mitchell stepped over it with one long stride.

Harriet, being a foot shorter, had to unclip the cord to allow her and Dakota to follow him to the floor above.

She'd expected a wide studio, full of light, with huge canvases stacked against the wall. Instead, she emerged into a small, rather messy office, crammed (bizarrely) with sailing paraphernalia, art magazines, unopened post and half-drunk mugs of coffee. Mitchell's laptop was decorated with sailing stickers, like a teenager's, but his pot plants were healthy to the point of taking over.

He cleared two chairs to enable them to sit down, but took

the small, squashy sofa for himself, stretching out his legs and contributing to the trip hazards.

It took a moment for Harriet to notice he was grinning at her.

'Studio's upstairs,' he said, pointing to the ceiling. 'Bedroom, sitting room, kitchen – that way.' He thumbed to the door at the back of the office.

How had he known what she'd been thinking? She hadn't said anything!

His grin grew broader.

Ex-detective.

On edge, she took him through the basics: confirming his name, address, years of police service, current employment, and then let him read his original statement to see if there was anything he wanted to add or clarify.

'That's about it,' he said, handing it back.

Had this been a complete waste of everyone's time?

Although she did have three more people on her list...

Mitchell's receptionist brought in three squat mugs of differing colours but each decorated with the same white-sailed dinghy with a red and black hull.

He held his mug up, pointing to it. 'New range,' he said. 'What do you think?'

'Cool.' Dakota turned her mug around to admire it better. 'Is that a wayfarer?'

Harriet, whose nautical knowledge was limited to the difference between a big boat and a small boat, eyed her in astonishment.

'Yeah.' Mitchell's good humour vanished and he put his mug down. 'Me and my mate raced them as teenagers, like other kids raced cars. He died. The mugs are... Well, I guess you'd call them a memorial.'

Had his friend died recently?

The truth hit when Dakota said softly, 'Aaron Cooper?'

Mitchell pushed himself off the sofa and went over to the window. 'It's strange, you re-opening his case. Like... I don't know... A sign? If you believe in that rot.' He turned, regarding Harriet speculatively. 'What brought it on? You found a body? Finally believe someone did him in?'

Finally believe?

Again, Dakota jumped in before Harriet could do likewise – with her big mouth and both her feet.

'We recently found human remains. However, several men of a similar age and build went missing in the area at the same time. We're trying to narrow it down.'

'Where was he found?'

'We can't divulge—'

Mitchell glared at Harriet. '*Where?*'

There was no reason *not* to tell him. Everyone in the village already knew.

'Foxglove & Hemlock,' she said. Then, when he continued to look blank, 'the florist? Big building, just off The Square in Raven's Edge.'

That meant something to him. There was a flicker of recognition; the tiniest spark, but it was there all right.

'Did Aaron know someone who worked or lived at the florist?' she asked him.

Such as his mysterious girlfriend?

'The florist was about three doors down from the police station, but it was called something else in those days.'

'Do you know of any connection with Aaron?'

He shrugged, disinterested.

But they were jumping ahead.

'You were a friend of Aaron's?'

He rolled his eyes.

'You worked together?'

'Is that the best you can do? You know all this. Why repeat

yourself? No wonder it's taken you twenty-five years to find his bloody body.'

If it had been anyone else in charge of the original investigation she might have apologised, but the words stuck in her throat.

Instead, as coolly and calmly as she could manage, 'Perhaps if you told us about the last time you saw Aaron?'

Mitchell sighed. 'It was a Friday. We'd worked together on a job – some dodgy deals going down on one of the boats moored at Port Rell. It's so long ago, I can't remember the details. It didn't go well. Aaron was knocked on the head and I ended up overboard. Anyway, once we'd got the villains cuffed and in the van, he received a text that cheered him up no end. I teased him about it, joked that it was his mysterious new girlfriend.'

'Did you know who she was?'

'Nope. He kept the information close to his chest, so we assumed she was married, possibly to someone we knew.'

Married?

'Could she have worked at the florist? How about Eoin's wife, Hestia?'

'Nah, not his type. Nasty bit of work *she* was.'

'Did you see the text?'

'No but we assumed it was a booty call, judging from his expression, and we gave him no end of grief. That was the last time I saw him. He said something like, "See you on Monday," then caught a cab back to Raven's Edge – he didn't even want to wait to get his injury checked over. He was so happy – the poor sod. Had no idea he was going to his death.'

'You seem very certain he's dead?'

'I'd known him since we were kids. He'd never have abandoned his family without sending word, particularly his sister. Bloody ridiculous suggesting it.'

It took all her self-control not to defend her father.

There'd been nothing in Mitchell's original statement about

a summons via text though. Had he forgotten to mention it – or had it been deliberately omitted?

Harriet turned to Dakota. 'Can you...?'

'No,' Dakota said, quite firmly. 'It depends on the carrier but there's no way that text message would have been saved for a quarter of a century. They're only kept for a matter of months at the most.'

'Bother.'

'Sorry,' Mitchell said. 'I want this guy caught as much as you do. Aaron was only twenty-five, far too young to... Damn!' He broke off and stared out of the window again.

Was this his way of hiding his emotions from them?

'What was Aaron like?' she asked. 'He was a close friend; your colleague. You spent a huge amount of time together. Is there anything else that might be relevant to our investigation?'

'He was a great guy.' Mitchell didn't turn round. 'He cared about people; he cared about justice. That's why he became a detective. He always tried to help. He didn't care who you were. You could rely on him for anything. I don't know what Detective Superintendent March said in his report because it wasn't made public, but there were a lot of cruel rumours floating around.'

'Rumours?'

'That Aaron would skive off work to see his harem of women. *Not* true. He was always professional and, while he liked to laugh and joke with the women he did meet, he went out with very few of them. They said he was a raging drunk – also not true. Sure, he liked a pint or two, but not enough for him to fall into the marina. If I ever find out who spread that one...' He flicked a glance in Harriet's direction. 'The super had it in for him and I've no idea why. I was convinced Aaron would turn up one day, with a cheerful "Had you going!" but he never did.' Mitchell sighed heavily. 'You're going to get this guy, right? The guy that did it?'

'We're yet to formally identify—' Harriet began but was interrupted by Dakota.

'Yes,' she said simply. 'We will.'

'I'll hold you to that.'

Which is *exactly* why Harriet hadn't volunteered—

Mitchell's attention landed back on her, with that same, speculative look. 'Your father?' he said. 'You look just like him. It's uncanny.'

Harriet smiled tightly, decided it was well past time they left and wrapped the interview up.

Dakota bought a mug on the way out.

'You know,' she began, as they emerged onto the marina and began the trek back to the car, 'if Aaron Cooper's dead and Eoin Kinsella's alive...'

It threw a whole new light on their investigation.

How did one dispose of a dead body?

In films, they made it look easy. Kill your victim on a shower curtain – it kept the body, the blood and any stray forensic evidence all in one place. Wrap the body up and seal said shower curtain with duct tape. Voilà! Your body is now grave-ready.

He had a shower curtain and duct tape. The nightstand and carpet would have to be cleaned but ultimately burned or dumped. Blood was impossible to get rid of forensically.

Obviously they couldn't take the body out the front door. They lived on the main street leading through Raven's Edge, right on The Square. Someone would see them, even at this late hour; it was that kind of place.

If they did get the body into the boot of his car, what next? Drop it off the harbour at Port Rell? Without being seen? He wasn't a sailing man; he knew nothing about tides and currents. The body was likely to wash straight back in again.

Wherever he left it, how long would it be before it was found and traced back to them? He might be able to remove as much forensic evidence as possible – ironically, it was what he'd trained for – but who had Aaron told about his affair and where he'd planned on spending his evening? That would put his wife straight onto the 'persons of interest' list.

He put his head in his hands. This was surreal. Would he be responsible for investigating a murder he'd committed? A man could go crazy just thinking about it.

He was crazy for thinking about it.

'Talk to me!' his wife demanded.

He'd almost forgotten she was there.

He wished she wasn't. He wished she'd run off with Aaron into the sunset and never come back. He'd have been devastated – but it would have been better than this.

Aaron was dead because of him. Poor sod.

'Hey!'

'I'm thinking!' he snapped back.

The forest would be the obvious choice. People got lost or went missing there all the time. Their own garden backed right onto it. But at this time of year the ground would be too hard to dig, and leaving the body in a shallow grave would result in it being dug up by animals and found by a dog walker – or, worse still, a tourist.

He was running out of options but what choice did they have?

They could hardly bury the body in their own garden!

That was it...

They couldn't bury the body in their garden... but what if they buried it in someone else's...?

TWENTY-FIVE

Unfortunately, Ben wouldn't authorise a request to DCI Cameron for Harriet to fly to Rome and interview Eoin Kinsella about the skeleton found in his old garden, and the Murder Investigation Team were no closer to finding out who'd killed Dean Hunter either. They *had* discovered that no one seemed bothered Dean was dead. He had no single address but lived at a variety of homes throughout the King's Forest District. He had a flat in Norchester that he never visited; ditto a houseboat in Port Rell. He'd been living with a woman in a penthouse apartment at Calahurst Marina, but when she suspected he'd met someone new, she'd bagged up his belongings for the dump.

Sam brought the bin bags back to the police station to be checked, but it was Ash Chopra, surprisingly, who discovered that Dean Hunter worked casually as an 'enforcer' for a local villain – *not* Drew Elliott – and that the villain in question had been considering 'terminating' his employment due to his unreliability. The implied threat was enough to make Ash nervous about pursuing this line of investigation and he'd returned to the station as quickly as possible, checking over his shoulder all the way.

The head of the MIT, Detective Chief Inspector Doug Cameron, had theorised that Dean must have upset someone important for him to be murdered and his body casually dumped, but he couldn't see the point in wasting more man-hours on it, and was considering closing the case.

What a sad little life Dean Hunter must have led, Harriet thought, as she wrote up her report. No friends, no family – even his girlfriend didn't care if he was alive or dead. Her mother, once the news had fully sunk in, seemed more inconvenienced by Dean's death than anything else.

'Who will be my escort for my party now?' she grumbled on the phone to Harriet later. 'What will my friends think if I don't have a boyfriend?'

'That you have a perfectly full and happy life without one?' Harriet suggested.

'Cute,' Anya mocked. 'Obviously they're not going to think *that*. They'll think I'm past it!'

At forty-five?

'And that I can't hold on to a man.'

Well, she had buried two...

'And that *nobody* cares about *me*.' Anya burst into tears. 'Not even *you*!'

Harriet had never been so pleased to be stuck at work, with the perfect excuse *not* to go rushing over to The Laurels to comfort her mother.

Anya slammed down the phone in disgust – but not before reminding Harriet about tonight's party, as though, like going to the dentist, it was something she'd be likely to forget.

Harriet sighed and stared at her phone. In some way, prob-ably very soon, she'd pay for not driving to her mother's aid the moment she was summoned, but she still couldn't get over the fact that her mother was going ahead with her annual Christmas party when her boyfriend was barely cold in the mortuary.

Anya, apparently, was as keen as everyone else to distance herself from Dean Hunter.

Thanks to her brother being well-known in the music industry, and often needing someone to accompany him to award ceremonies, Harriet had a *lot* of beautiful dresses. As it was coming up to Christmas, she chose a sleek, dark-red gown that had a fine mesh section around the entire middle, but was draped with dangling red beads, sequins and crystals so the minimum of skin was revealed. There were red satin heels to match, but (as usual) she spurned those for a pair of comfy red trainers. She had no intention of driving the short distance to her mother's house and getting stuck in the chaos of cars parked outside.

She fluffed up the mass of blonde curls that drove her mother crazy ('They invented hair straighteners for a reason, Harriet March'), applied a bright red lipstick and a tiny hint of mascara, threw on her old black parka and headed for the door.

The weather was cold but it wasn't snowing. The sky was clear with a huge full moon hanging low in the sky, causing frost to glitter on the roofs of the thatched cottages between the village and her mother's house. By the time Harriet passed The Drop, several other guests were walking in the same direction.

She was halfway down the drive when she spotted Whittaker Smith and, beside him... Was that *Iris*? How long had *they* been friends? They entered the house in front of her and, as Iris handed over her long wool coat to Mrs Nore, Harriet recognised her beautiful asymmetrical green gown as Vivienne Westwood.

When Harriet arrived on the doorstep, she and Mrs Nore glared at each other.

After a pause, when it became apparent that Harriet had no

intention of parting with her scruffy black parka, Mrs Nore stepped aside to allow her through.

'You'll be very hot,' the other woman said, obviously pleased at the thought.

Harriet gave her a leisurely wink. 'I'm *always* hot.'

But as she walked through the entrance hall, crammed with display cases of dead people's things, she unzipped the parka and dropped it casually behind a chair. No one would see it, and she'd be able to collect it on her way out.

In the meantime, she really needed a drink...

Anya March was holding court at the entrance to the marquee. It was a receiving line, Harriet realised belatedly, with everyone forced to queue to greet Anya, as though she were some kind of queen.

In Anya's eyes, she probably was.

'How lovely to see you!' *Kiss kiss.*

'I'm so pleased you could come!' *Kiss kiss.*

'I hope you have a wonderful time!' *Kiss kiss.*

Anya probably hoped no such thing, Harriet thought, as the queue pulled her closer to her mother and she caught a glimpse into the marquee beyond. It had been turned into a winter wonderland, with icicle chandeliers sparkling overhead, white Christmas trees and little tables set with Christmas roses, white poinsettia and trailing ivy.

Whit Smith was standing just inside the marquee, Iris at his side in her gorgeous green gown as they laughed at something another man was saying. Someone Harriet couldn't quite see for all the people between them, but hopefully it would be someone she knew so she'd have someone else to talk to.

All she could see of him was that he had black hair, almost touching his shoulders, and he was carrying two glasses of champagne.

Harriet stood on tiptoe. If she could just see who it was...

'Hello, darling!' Anya was regarding her quizzically.

The queue had moved forward without Harriet noticing. Was she going to get the 'How lovely to see you' *kiss kiss* too?

Anya regarded her with a slight frown. 'You shouldn't wear red, darling. It's a very draining colour and your skin isn't white enough to pull off the contrast. And you're too short to wear clothes that divide you in half.' She poked Harriet's tummy through the mesh and spangles. 'It creates a dumpy effect. Haven't I taught you anything about fashion?'

Dumpy? OK, so she was five foot four but never, *in her entire life*, had anyone said she was *dumpy*. And what if she was? She could wear what the hell she liked. This dress was fabulous on her, she knew that. She'd checked the mirror before she'd come out and this wasn't the first time she'd worn it. Admittedly the last time it had been accessorised with a rock star on her arm – her brother Ryan – but their photograph had appeared all over the press and everyone had said how great she looked!

She rather thought she'd taught herself about fashion!

Before Harriet could say so, the man she'd seen talking to Iris and Whit walked over to Anya and handed her one of the glasses he'd been holding.

'As promised,' he said, dipping his head to talk to her because he was at least a foot taller.

'Thank you, Mal darling!' Anya casually patted his cheek. 'That's so kind of you.'

He jerked back, obviously discomforted by her touch, but as he straightened he glanced over at Harriet – and froze.

Ugh! Was Mal Graham her mother's new crush? Well, she certainly wasn't going to hang around to see how that panned out.

Somehow she scraped up enough confidence to smile at her

mother. 'Thank you for inviting me, Mum. I've had a lovely time but now I've got to get back to work.'

Kiss kiss.

'You've only just arrived!'

'No, I've been here quite a while.'

(The great thing about being a police officer was that everyone automatically assumed she was telling the truth.)

'But darling...'

Harriet didn't feel she could hold her smile for much longer and she certainly didn't trust her voice to continue the conversation. Ignoring her mother's protests, she fought her way back down the queue and into the pool area. From there it was a short walk along the corridor to the entrance hall.

Why was she upset? After twenty-five years she should be used to her mother's criticisms, and she *knew* she looked good tonight.

As for Mal waiting on her mother, what the hell had that been about?

Although, judging from his reaction, if her mother had him earmarked as her new crush, she was going to be disappointed. The feeling was not mutual.

Harriet really shouldn't feel pleased about that.

She dragged her parka from behind the chair in the hall and pulled it on, only to glance up and see Mal in front of her, with the rear brought up by Mrs Nore.

Wonderful.

'Mr Graham!' Mrs Nore exclaimed loudly, making Mal jump. 'How may I help you?' She paused to glare at Harriet. 'Has Harriet been rude to you? I'll ensure Mrs March deals with her in an appropriate manner.'

Harriet snorted. 'Appropriate manner? Like I'm six?'

Mal, meanwhile, stared at Mrs Nore in astonishment. 'Why would anything Harriet says to me be of any business of Anya's?'

Harriet didn't need Mal to defend her. She could fight her own battles. But right now all she wanted was to go home and snuggle up in front of the fire with a good book and a hot chocolate, so she left them to it.

She'd barely got outside before Mal fell comfortably into step beside her.

Again.

'Wow,' he said, as they walked along the drive, 'that woman *really* doesn't like you.'

Harriet abruptly stopped. 'Why are you following me?'

'I wanted to ensure you were all right.'

'But *why*? What difference does it make to you?'

For the first time she saw Mal Graham hesitate before speaking. 'I thought we were friends?'

She remembered the first time they'd met, about six weeks ago, when he'd helped her arrest a murderer.

'If you need rescuing again, Sergeant March, do me a favour? Call someone else.'

'We're not friends.' She turned back towards the road.

'Well,' he said, 'that stings.'

Harriet walked a few more paces, expecting him to follow.

He didn't.

He didn't return to the house either.

She rolled her eyes. *Now* what?

He was where she'd left him, in the centre of the long, sweeping driveway, expensive cars parked on either side, with the Victorian house forming a pretty backdrop behind him. There was no snow, but everything glittered with a hard frost. With him, handsome but shivering, in his formal dinner jacket and bow tie, and her in her long crimson dress (albeit with a tatty old parka on top), they could have wandered out of an old movie.

'Why?' she asked again.

Hearing her own voice, sad and defeated, made her pause. Was that what she sounded like? All the time?

Mal grimaced. 'You keep saying that but I'm not entirely sure what you're asking. I mean, I expect it makes perfect sense to you, but I need some help here.'

She hitched up her dress with one hand and strode back to him, prodding his chest with her finger in much the same way her mother had prodded her a few minutes earlier.

'You don't *like* me,' she said.

He seemed surprised. 'I've never said so.'

'You've always made it perfectly clear every time we've met.'

'I'm sorry. It was unintentional. Perhaps you caught me on a bad day?'

'Four times?' *Not* that she was counting. What had changed his opinion of her? He must want something. That was the only reason anyone outside of work wanted to be friends with DS Harriet March. Even her own mother: *You have a speeding ticket? Don't worry, my daughter will sort that out for you.*

Didn't anyone like her for *herself*?

'Harriet?'

'Why are you being nice to me?'

'I would hope that I'm always nice.'

Someone had a short memory. 'No, you're not.'

'Something I evidently need to work on.'

'Don't feel you need to practise on me,' she said.

'But—'

'I have plenty of friends and I'm sure you do too.'

'Why do you believe I don't like you?'

'*Believe?* I know! Look, what is it you want? Spit it out and let's get it over with. I'm cold and I want to go home.'

He tilted his head on one side, regarding her far too perceptively. 'I've never met anyone quite like you.'

He *had* to ruin it.

'I'm "not like other girls"?' She raised her eyes heavenwards and continued on her way. 'You're a walking cliché, *Mr Graham*.'

He hurried after her. 'Perhaps I should have turned the question around. Why don't you like *me*, Harriet?'

Because he was rich, because he was good-looking, because he was charming, he thought everyone should automatically like him? Because people such as him thought they could do, say and have anything they wanted, and frequently did?

Then she realised that was the third time he'd called her by her first name, rather than his usual sardonic 'Sergeant March'.

'I don't dislike you,' she said. 'I never think of you at all.'

(That was a barefaced lie.)

(She thought of him quite often.)

He sighed. 'Have I been unkind or said something cruel in the past? I apologise. Please, tell me what I can do to change your perception of me.'

The promise that there could be something more between them was there, tangible, sparkling, so close she could touch it. All she had to do was—

No. As Anya would have said, someone like Mal Graham wasn't for the likes of Harriet March.

'Stop. Following. Me.' Confident that she'd had the last word, she stomped off. When she didn't hear a snappy come-back, she glanced back.

She'd wished for it, so she could hardly complain when it had come true.

Mal Graham had gone.

TWENTY-SIX

Iris had not thought much of Anya when she'd visited Raven's Hollow, and she thought even less of her now. The cruel way she'd spoken to Harriet, who was her own *daughter*, and in front of strangers? What a horrible woman.

Whit must have noticed Iris had gone quiet. 'Are you OK?'

She dropped her voice so they wouldn't be overheard. 'I was so looking forward to this party, but it isn't as much fun as I thought it would be. I know Anya is my host and my neighbour, and I shouldn't say nasty things about people I don't know, but she doesn't seem to be a very nice person.'

'I've not had much to do with her, but you'll notice there aren't many local people here.' He handed his glass of champagne to a waiter and then, taking Iris's from her, handed that over too. 'If you're not having fun, why don't we leave?'

'We were having such a nice talk about books.'

'We can have a nice talk about books anywhere. Would you like to call into The Drop for a drink?' His dark eyes turned mischievous. 'Or I could take you to The Secret Grimoire? Lots of books there to talk about.'

Iris raised an eyebrow. 'So we can *talk*... about *books*?'

'You saw right through that?' His mouth twitched. 'OK, I have champagne in the fridge – it was for a book launch in the New Year, but I can buy another – and we can play festive music over the speaker system and yes, talk about books. I'd suggest dancing but—'

Was he serious? 'We'd trip over the books!'

His smile turned wry. 'I need to put up more shelving.'

'*Where?* Where would you put up more shelving? Whit, your shop is overflowing, practically into the street.'

'I can never resist new books.'

'Come on then.' She took his hand and tugged him towards the exit. 'Let's go and see your books.'

But as they passed Anya March, at the head of her receiving line, they both ducked out of view, far too cowardly to admit they were leaving.

After opening hours, The Secret Grimoire was another world. Silent and still – brooding, almost – with none of the buzz Iris had experienced on her previous visits. For a moment it seemed as though the magic had gone, but then she walked through the store and saw all those wonderful books that she'd never have the time to read, even if she lived to be a hundred...

Whit winked and flicked a switch... and thousands of tiny lights flickered into life, cascading up and down the wooden shelving, winding around the oak beams overhead, and even up the banister to the next floor. Without the usual bustle of people, Iris had the space to admire the handmade bookshelves, their edges carved with leaves and acorns, and the tiny wooden mice that unexpectedly peeped around corners and were so easy to overlook. Real holly had been placed on the shelves and occasionally amongst the books, and long ribbons of ivy trailed from the display tables.

Iris had assumed there was no Christmas tree inside the

store. She only appreciated that the twisting pile of green books on the centre table *was* a Christmas tree when she was standing right beside it.

'That is *amazing!*' She stared up at the carefully constructed spiral of books. 'It must have taken you ages.'

He stood beside her. 'I can't take credit, that's Carmen's handiwork. She had to temporarily stick the covers together. People would keep walking into the table and knocking the whole thing over.' He lowered his voice to a whisper. 'Some of them might have done it deliberately.'

'That's incredibly mean-spirited.'

'They'll get a lump of coal in their Christmas stocking for sure.'

'Oh, Whit! Everything is so beautiful...'

'Carmen arranged the evergreens and created the book tree. I was entrusted with the fairy lights, because apparently I couldn't "go wrong" with those, but we've decided to keep them in place all year round. Well, *I* have. Can you imagine having to do this every year? My uncle carved the bookshelf ends and the mice – woodwork's a hobby of his. The holly's a bit of a prickle hazard but no one's sued us yet, and it's only for a few weeks over the holiday season. We just need some music...'

He slid his phone from his pocket and Judy Garland's 'Have Yourself a Merry Little Christmas' softly flooded the store.

Iris's smile faltered. It was a lovely song but so, so sad, and reminded her of everyone she'd lost. Her mother especially, because it had been around this time of year, but also—

No!

If she didn't think about it, it never happened.

'I'm sorry,' Whit said, quickly tapping at his phone. He was far too good at picking up on her feelings. 'Let's try something else.' He scrolled down, frowning in concentration.

Happy thoughts, happy thoughts...

She was aware of him muttering, 'How about Michael Bublé? Everyone loves Michael Bublé.'

She took a deep breath. 'My brother Justin would love this place.' She even sounded normal.

He slid his phone back into his pocket as 'It's Beginning to Look a Lot Like Christmas' filled the store.

'You have a brother?' he said. 'Does he live here too?'

'No, he's an economics professor in America.'

Confusion was evident on Whit's face as he did the maths.

How many people got to be a professor at twenty-seven?

Perhaps she shouldn't have said 'professor' but she'd always thought Justin deserved it.

Iris sighed. Whit had tried so hard this evening, and his bookshop was *enchanting*, yet she'd ruined everything again by being weird.

Perhaps she should accept that they weren't meant to be.

Why was he holding out his hand?

What did that mean? Was she supposed to shake it as they said their goodbyes? To show they were still good friends and that there were no hurt feelings, and all the rest?

Whit smiled. 'May I have this dance, Miss Evergreen?'

The evening passed in a blur. They danced (carefully) between the book stacks, and only twice became hooked up on a holly twig or yanked a curling frond of ivy from a table. And only one pile of books was knocked over, but they were sport biographies so they didn't count.

Whit found a selection of cheese and crackers in his fridge – 'I have no idea why I bought those. I hope it's not Carmen's lunch or we're going to be in *so* much trouble' – along with a punnet of grapes. They flopped down on a pile of beanbags to eat, although Iris had to open the bottle of champagne, because Whit didn't have a clue how to go about it. 'The stuff I drink usually comes out of cans from the supermarket.'

They raised their plastic cups and toasted the shop. They toasted the books, they toasted *Iris's* book, and then they toasted themselves.

'Isn't that supposed to be unlucky though?' Iris said. 'Toasting yourself?'

'Who cares?'

She put the cup down on the floor and flopped back against the bean bag, her head almost touching Whit's. 'I've had a lovely evening,' she said. 'Thank you so much for inviting me.'

'I think *you* invited *me*,' Whit said, 'but why don't we do it again? Maybe in the New Year? I expect you'll be seeing your family and friends over Christmas.'

What family and friends?

'Erm, no. Just me and Sparkle, having a quiet few days, reading our new books.'

'What kind of books does Sparkle like?'

'I know you wouldn't think it to look at her, but she's a huge Austen fan.'

'Does she have a favourite?'

'It's a toss-up between *Purride and Purrejudice* and *Purrsuasion...*'

He laughed. 'Of course it is! OK, why don't I stop trying to be subtle and ask you if you'd like to go to Brianna Graham's party on Christmas Eve?'

He wanted to see her again?

He wanted to see her again!

But that meant she'd have to tell him the truth.

About everything?

She couldn't date him under false pretences.

The light in his eyes dimmed. 'There's a "but". I can see it.'

'I'd love to go out with you, but I need to tell you something first, in case you change your mind about me.'

'You're married?' he said flatly.

'No, I'm not married, but a year ago I was engaged to a man called Erik Hansen.'

For a moment he seemed confused. 'Why does that name ring a bell? Oh... the thriller writer?' The confusion turned to horror. 'Didn't he... die recently? I'm so sorry. Of course, I understand. It's far too soon for you. I should never have—'

'No,' she said, far more bluntly than she had intended. 'Nothing like that. I need to explain though, about what happened between us. And then...' – she swallowed – 'you can decide if you'd rather not see me anymore.'

'Of course I'd want to see you! But please don't feel you have to tell me anything you don't want to.'

How should she start?

The accident? Or way back to the day they met? Maybe that would make more sense.

'I met Erik shortly after I signed my first book contract,' she said, keeping her voice low, which was silly because they were the only ones in the shop. 'Our publisher held an event at a swish country hotel to introduce their new authors to the press. Erik was already a huge star – he didn't need an introduction. Everyone knew him and he was already laughing and joking with the press. Meanwhile, I was completely out of my depth. He was very kind and took me under his wing and, after the event, we started seeing each other. He gave me lots of help and advice, and my books took off massively, but curiously his didn't and the publisher dropped him. I never did understand why.

'Anyway, last year I was invited to a big party in the grounds of an old manor house on the banks of the River Thames. The family that owned it also own the largest independent publishing company in the UK, so there were lots of publishers, agents and authors. Everyone knew each other. It was all very friendly.

'I thought a party would be fun and it would be a chance for

Erik to network and maybe relaunch his career with another publisher, but as soon as we arrived I realised my mistake. He was furious at being my "plus one", although it hadn't prevented him from accepting the invitation in the first place, but he did cheer up when he met some friends. For an hour or so, everything was OK. We followed his friends into the garden – and then I made the mistake of mentioning that I'd visited the house before. My mother had worked in publishing since before I was born and knew everyone, including the family who owned the house. As soon as I mentioned that, Erik's mood crashed.

'I tried to lighten the atmosphere by pointing out an ancient stone dovecote built into a corner of the garden wall and telling everyone that the last time I'd visited, as a child of eight or nine, I'd climbed to the top. It hadn't been hard. There was wisteria growing around the sides, which gave me a foothold. The sloping roof had been the trickiest part, but I'd been so triumphant when I scrambled to the top – only to be yelled at by the gardener and sent back to my mother in disgrace.

'Everyone laughed at my story, except for Erik. He said, quite bluntly – and I can hear him now – "I don't believe you." Perhaps he thought I'd cave in and admit it was a tall tale, but then I thought, "Why should I?"

'It was an epiphany. Erik had got into the habit of putting me down, and I'd got into the habit of agreeing with him for a quiet life. I was enabling him. So I handed him my bag and my drink, strode over to the wall and began to climb it.

'At first everyone was too stunned to do anything other than watch. Then they cheered me on. It was harder than I'd thought it would be – I was older and heavier and the wisteria didn't hold my weight as it had done before, but there were little gaps in the stonework and I was able to get a toehold or a handhold and pull myself up that way.'

Whit smiled. 'How did that make you feel?'

'It was exhilarating! Freedom from being too frightened to

do or say anything that would upset Erik. The further I climbed, it was as though the ties binding me to him stretched and then broke, and I could see him for what he really was. A small man who took professional advice to be unfair criticism; he was prepared to blame everyone around him for his lack of success, rather than being prepared to make changes or try something different.

'The moment I reached the top of the dovecote and sat down, I caught sight of him below me and saw his expression. It was full of jealousy and hate. *How* had I put up with him for so long, trying so hard to make *him* happy, when he was making me miserable – while spending all my money? When he looked at me, I think he knew that I was no longer going to put up with his nonsense. We were finished.

'I scrambled down, not as elegantly as I'd have liked, and was immediately surrounded by everyone cheering. It went to my head. Other guests had come outside to watch, including the owner of the house. I thought he would have me escorted off his property there and then, but he remembered me from all those years ago, and joked that he'd always known I'd turn out to be a terror.

'By then my arms and legs felt like jelly, and I had bloody scrapes over my elbows. Someone returned my bag and drink, and I drank that and then knocked back another before it dawned on me that it hadn't been Erik who'd given me my things.

'Then someone screamed and pointed to the dovecote. Erik had climbed the wisteria the same way as me, but slipped once he'd reached the sloping roof. Later, one of his friends said they'd heard him say, "It's easy, a kid of five could do it," but Erik hadn't understood that what might be easy for a small child was much more difficult for an adult.'

'He fell?'

'What I hadn't appreciated, either as a child or as an adult, was that the ground on the garden side was higher than the ground on the other side of the wall. Erik fell onto a tarmac cycle path that ran alongside the edge of the river and died instantly.'

Whit shook his head. 'You blame yourself, which is why you're telling me this story, but it was Erik's choice to climb that dovecote, nothing to do with you.'

It was what they'd said at the inquest.

Not her fault.

That she'd climbed the dovecote.

Escaped from the coffin.

Picked up the gun.

People *died* around her.

'It was *completely* my fault,' she said.

Like everything else.

'You're a good person, Iris.'

She was the very *opposite* of a good person.

Take last night. Wouldn't a 'good person' have called the police and admitted to killing a burglar?

'I'm *not* a good person, Whit. There's more. The other night, for example—'

He reached out, pushing a stray curl behind her ear. 'Maybe we should save that for date number two?' he said gently.

Did he think she was making this up? Attention-seeking in some way?

'Whit—'

'*Iris.* As you go through life, there'll always be stupid people doing stupid things, which you can't be held responsible for. Instead of torturing yourself with the "what ifs", maybe start thinking about yourself for a change? Stop trying to make others happy at the expense of *you.*' He took the plastic cup from her hand and helped her to her feet. 'Now, how about another dance?'

An excellent way to change the subject but, in a twisted

kind of way, he was right. She *was* a people pleaser and she needed to learn how to be selfish.

Except... hadn't it been thinking about herself that had got her into this mess in the first place?

And what would Whit do when he found out the *real* truth?

The Kinsella family had owned the house where the florist was now based for as long as anyone could remember. It was a flourishing business – everyone bought their flowers from Kinsella's. Yet the garden behind it had been neglected for decades. You could bury an entire regiment in that garden and no one would notice. And, like their own garden, it backed onto the forest...

'I'm going to need the shower curtain, duct tape and pliers,' he said. 'When I'm done, you're going to help me carry the body through the forest and into Eoin Kinsella's garden.'

He tensed, waiting for her usual tears and tantrums.

Instead, she appeared to be thinking it through. 'You're going to bury Aaron in Eoin's garden? I know it's overgrown but wouldn't the forest be easier?'

'At this time of year the ground will be too hard. If I bury it in Eoin's garden, I don't need to dig a deep grave and I can cover it with plants or loose bricks to stop the animals digging it up.'

She grimaced at this but didn't protest. She didn't say anything at all.

Would she coldly discuss the disposal of his body like this?

After she left to carry out his instructions, he stripped the corpse so that it couldn't be easily identified by the clothing. There wasn't much in the pockets: some loose change, a phone and some keys. He smashed the phone. He'd dispose of that later, with the clothes. He washed the body, cleaned beneath the fingernails and, when his wife returned with the pliars, he pulled out Aaron's teeth. It wasn't infallible but it should slow down identification. Once the body began to decompose, there would be no way of obtaining fingerprints. DNA would be the only way to confirm identification and, as it was unlikely Aaron had ever committed a crime, he wouldn't be on the National DNA Database.

His wife helped him wrap up the body and carry it into the forest. They followed the path, past two other houses, and entered Eoin's garden by clambering over a tumbledown wall, dragging the body after them. On the other side was a derelict greenhouse where plants still flourished, despite the broken glass.

He returned home for a shovel, dug up a plant, then buried the body and replaced the plant, tidying up any evidence he'd been there, and taking the shovel and shower curtain home with him.

As George March washed his hands in the bathroom he caught sight of himself in the mirror.

He looked the way he always looked. Tanned, fit, blond and clear-eyed – not, in any way, different.

But he was no longer the same man.

He was a murderer.

TWENTY-SEVEN

23rd December

Ben's black coffee – a takeaway from The Crooked Broomstick – was going slowly cold. He'd been stuck at his desk since the early-morning briefing, reading and re-reading reports and statements, wondering if it *was* physically possible to solve two murders in the two days before Christmas.

The person (or persons) responsible for the skeleton in the glasshouse was (were) probably long dead and therefore unlikely to strike again – unless there were other bodies buried in and around Raven's Edge that Ben didn't know about.

(He'd rather not think about that.)

Hunter's murder was likely to have been committed by a criminal friend he'd fallen out with, part of the kind of community which preferred to keep its business private, especially from the police. If so, his murder would never be solved.

That nagged at Ben's conscience. From the evidence his team had collected over the past few days, Hunter had come across as a deeply unpleasant man, but it didn't mean he wasn't entitled to justice.

Why *had* Hunter's body been left in that particular spot? If the murderer had wanted to make a point, why not leave the body in the middle of The Square for everyone to see? If they'd wanted to dispose of the body by shoving it out of a car, why not leave it on the dual carriageway between here and Norchester? If they'd timed it right, the body could have rolled into the forest never to be seen again, thus preventing an investigation by someone like him who never gave up, even though Christmas was only two days away.

Two days.

Damn, he needed that break.

He sipped at his now stone-cold coffee. Perfectionism was considered an excellent quality for a detective.

Other times, it was a pain in the arse.

He pulled up a map of the village. Apart from The Drop, there were only two houses on that stretch of road: Álfheimr (now renamed Raven's Hollow) and The Laurels. Iris Evergreen (novelist, new to the village) lived at Raven's Hollow. Anya March (Harriet's mother, owner of three boutiques) lived at The Laurels.

As far as his team had been able to discover, Iris had no connection to Dean Hunter.

However, Ben remembered how the snow on Iris's drive had been churned up, still visible beneath the layer that had fallen later. When he'd called round, the morning after, she'd been distinctly on edge. *Had* Iris murdered Hunter and dragged him down her drive to deposit him on the road? What would have been her motive? Why would Hunter have been at her house? Was he known to her? If Iris had killed him, wouldn't it have been easier for her to have shoved him off the cliff that bordered her property?

Anya, however, *had* been an 'acquaintance' of Hunter. Why had no one been sent to carry out a formal interview? If Anya and Hunter had had some kind of lovers' tiff, that would be a good motive for murder.

Had Hunter been walking to or from Anya's house on the night of his death?

It seemed likely.

Why had no one returned to interview Anya?

Because they were working flat out to solve two murders before Christmas?

Or because Anya was Harriet's mother?

Not a good enough reason.

No one should be above suspicion.

According to Harriet, Hunter had called on Anya the day before his body had been found, but he'd left her house after lunch and she hadn't seen him since.

Ben knew that Anya March was famous for her parties and social events, often held to raise money for charity. For a person like that, wasn't Raven's Edge a far too quiet place to live? Surely Anya would have been happier in an apartment somewhere livelier, like the centre of Norchester or beside Calahurst Marina?

Now *that* triggered something in his memory.

He opened his laptop, did a search and there it was: a statement from a Lisa Montague, who owned a beauty salon in Calahurst and an apartment in the same block as DCI Cameron, right on the edge of the marina. Dean Hunter had lived with her for a couple of months, but she soon realised she'd made a huge mistake and that he was only interested in her money.

Ben sped-read his way to the end of the statement.

Dean was going to dump me. I found that out at the gym. He'd lined up some rich woman, older than him, in Raven's Edge, and was moving in with her.

'Sam!' he called out to the main office. 'How many rich women do you know in Raven's Edge?'

Sam's face appeared in the doorway with a definite smirk. 'Personally or generally?'

'What do you think?' Ben grumbled, aware he sounded exactly like Cameron.

'OK... There's Brianna Graham, *Milla* Graham...' Sam paused, presumably to judge Ben's reaction to having his girl-friend namechecked.

Ben waved his hand dismissively.

'Um, Harriet's mum, I suppose. She lives in a big house with a swimming pool and owns three shops. Then there's that new woman who lives at Raven's Hollow. The writer. Someone told me she's made millions from those books of hers. I guess we're in the wrong job, eh sir?'

Ben waved his hand again, indicating that Sam should take his smartarse comments and leave, and stared down at the list he'd made in his notebook.

Brianna Graham: *Too old.*

Milla Graham: *Too young.*

Anya March: *Possibly?*

Iris Evergreen: *Was thirty 'old'?*

He hoped not. He'd turned thirty on his last birthday.

He flicked through the records, searching for Hunter's date of birth and doing the maths. Dean Hunter had been thirty-two when he'd died.

So, possibly not Iris Evergreen.

What did he know about Anya March?

Not much. She was the widow of Detective Superintendent George March – the famed 'hero' of Raven's Edge. Mrs March had married again, Ben remembered Harriet telling him that, to a wealthy antiques dealer who had died himself a few years later, leaving Anya with an income and a house – The Laurels – provided she didn't marry again.

It was curious that Harriet hardly mentioned Anya, whereas the rest of his team were always talking about their families – what they'd done, what they were going to do, funny things they'd said, birthday gifts they were going to buy.

Harriet only ever spoke about her brother Ryan and her grandmother.

Why had he never picked up on this before?

Perhaps it was fortunate Harriet had taken the day off, because Anya March and her 'acquaintance' with Dean Hunter required closer inspection.

Ben knew of Anya March and would have recognised her had he seen her in the street, but he'd never spoken directly to her. Again, this was unusual. Over the past year he'd met most of his team's various relations – one couldn't help it, living in such a small village.

Her housekeeper, Mrs Nore, was surprised and slightly anxious when he explained who he was and why he was there, but she showed him into some kind of drawing room at the back of the house. It was filled with ugly antiques, but nothing personal, such as photographs or holiday souvenirs, but perhaps it wasn't used that often?

The housekeeper brought him a tray with a cafetière and what appeared to be freshly baked chocolate chip cookies; after another ten minutes, Anya herself walked in, fully made-up and wearing a red knitted dress. Her hair was long, a paler blonde than Harriet's, styled straight with a middle parting. Her expression was surprisingly steely. She knew exactly why he was here.

'How may I help you, Detective Inspector? Is this about the body?'

The 'body'? Not, 'Dean's murder'?

Was her attempt at dissociation for his benefit or hers?

'I'm investigating the death of Dean Hunter,' he said, 'whose body was found on the pavement outside this property, on the morning of the sixteenth of December. While I appreciate DS March has already spoken to you about events on the day in question, I wanted to fill in a few blanks.'

'I'm happy to do whatever I can to help,' she said.

'I understand that you and Dean Hunter were...' – he refused to use the word 'acquaintance' – 'friends?'

Anya's gaze didn't waver. 'Yes, I met him at the gym. We got on very well. He'd often accompany me to events if I needed a partner, but we weren't in a relationship. We hardly knew each other.'

Lie.

'He was here at your house on the fourteenth of December?'

'Yes, he came to use the swimming pool. This is a big house, Detective Inspector, and I know how lucky I am to live here, so I allow my friends to use the pool whenever they wish.'

Lie.

'That's generous.' It also complicated things. How many other people had been in and out of the house on the day in question? 'How do these friends of yours gain access to the pool? Does it have its own entrance?'

'There's a garden door, but they usually call round the front and Mrs Nore, my housekeeper, lets them in.'

'Was Mr Hunter alone when he arrived?'

'Yes, it was lunchtime. Dean and I were eating when my daughter Harriet turned up. He went for a swim and left us alone to chat. He was always thoughtful like that.'

It was, more or less, what Harriet had put in her report. It sounded as though she didn't believe Anya's story either but had stopped short of putting it in writing.

He would need to have a word with her about *that.*

'Do you know how Mr Hunter intended spending the rest of the day?' Ben asked.

'He said he had a job to do but didn't elaborate further. It's quite tragic what happened to him, Detective Inspector. It goes to show that none of us are truly safe, even here in Raven's Edge. Poor, poor Dean.'

Her eyes remained remarkably dry as she said that and her voice was completely steady.

Ben was reminded of an old colleague, Detective Inspector Lydia Cavill; she'd been a good, hardworking, loyal officer, but he hadn't really liked her because she'd always given the impression she only cared about herself – an impression that later turned out to be wrong.

Was he now making the same mistake with Anya?

Did she know who Hunter's employers were? Did she realise how 'he said he had a job to do' could be construed? Was she implying that the 'job' had gone wrong? Did she know *exactly* how Hunter had died?

Even now he couldn't be sure.

And that bothered him.

He had a few more routine questions but there wasn't much to be gained by staying, so he made his excuses and left.

Was that relief he saw in her eyes?

Perhaps he should leave it a few days and then invite her to the station. It would be interesting to see how cool she remained then.

As he walked back to the MIT office, his phone rang.

It was DCI Cameron and, as usual, he came straight to the point. 'Benedict, that skeleton you found in the greenhouse?'

'Yes?'

'The forensic anthropologist was able to obtain a DNA sample from the remains and sent it off to the lab to be tested?'

'That's correct, but I've not heard anything since.'

It had only been a week. He could hardly have marked the request as 'urgent' when the victim must have been dead for a quarter of a century. Other cases would (and should) take priority.

'They sent the result to me,' Cameron said. 'There was no match with any profiles on the National DNA Database.'

Ben's fingers tightened on his phone. Why had the lab done that? *He* was the Senior Investigating Officer.

'However,' Cameron added, 'when we checked the personnel attending the crime scene, to exclude them from our own database, we found *two* matches.'

Oh, *great*.

'The DNA was compromised?' How had that happened? The sample would have been taken from a bone in the lab, not on site. They'd all been suited up, although Harriet hadn't been wearing a scene suit when Amelia had originally shown her the body. 'Was one of the matches DS Harriet March?'

'If you'd let me finish, Benedict? Your skeleton has been irrefutably identified as Detective Constable Aaron Cooper, a local officer who went missing twenty-five years ago. His profile was still on our system. Interestingly,' Cameron went on, 'the first profile that matched was, as you said, DS March. Not because the sample was contaminated, but it was flagged as a possible relative.'

'A relative?'

It wasn't surprising. Many of the village's residents were related by blood or marriage.

'A *close* relative,' Cameron said. 'Very close.'

Couldn't he speak plainly? 'That would mean—'

'I suggest DS March speaks with her mother,' Cameron said. 'In the meantime, I'll leave it to you to break the news to her. You have a good relationship, do you not?'

Oh, *hell*...

'Could there have been a mistake? Harriet lives on site; she was the first officer on the scene—'

'I have the results in front of me. I'll send you a copy. The professional opinion is that Cooper and March share a close family relationship.'

'Father and daughter?'

'As I said, that's a question DS March needs to raise with her mother. Insofar as your case goes, your skeleton is DC Aaron Cooper, and we now have a new line of investigation.'

Ben knew exactly what that meant.

A giant can of fat wriggling worms.

If Cooper was the murder victim, and Harriet was his biological daughter, the person with the biggest motive to kill Cooper would be the man he'd cuckolded.

Raven's Edge's very own hero.

Detective Superintendent George March.

TWENTY-EIGHT

Past Harriet had booked a day off after her mother's party because she'd assumed she'd stay out late having too much of a good thing and then need a lie-in the next morning to recover.

Present Harriet wondered why she'd bothered. She now had *another* whole day with nothing to do.

Maybe she did need a hobby.

Mid-morning, she walked the short distance to The Crooked Broomstick for cookies and cappuccino, even though she had a perfectly good coffee machine of her own. It was always fun to flirt with Misha, the handsome blond barista: quite the highlight of her day. Except this time, watching him flirt with every woman in the queue, regardless of age, turned out to be not so much fun after all.

Maybe she needed a new crush.

Or (and here was a revolutionary idea) a real-life boyfriend to restore her work/life balance, which was currently work/work/void.

Harriet was lying on her sofa covered in cookie crumbs, trying to read a book (but mostly feeling sorry for herself), when someone knocked hard on the door. Gabriel or Amelia would have knocked far more subtly. It must be Sam.

'Come on in,' she shouted, 'it's open,' resulting in the bizarre sight of Ben stooping to squeeze his six-foot frame through the low, narrow door, before almost banging his head on an overhead beam when he straightened up.

'I'm sorry,' she said. 'This used to be the servants' quarters. People must have been shorter in the old days.'

Or, more likely, no one had cared much about the comfort of servants.

'It's quaint,' he said, polite as ever. 'Cosy.'

There was an awkward moment when she remembered she was lying on her couch, liberally sprinkled with cookie crumbs, reading a spicy romantic fantasy, and her boss was standing in front of her.

She sat up, surreptitiously brushing herself down. 'Can I get you a coffee? I have a new machine.'

'Thank you, but I'd better not.'

His expression was more serious than usual.

'Has something happened?' she asked. 'To Sam or one of the others?'

'No, nothing like that.' He was still standing beside the door, giving every impression that he'd rather be somewhere else.

'Would you like to sit down?'

Because you're making me nervous...

'Um, thanks.' He sat in the only other available chair, unbuttoning his long coat but not taking it off. Just like all those times she'd visited her mother and refused to part with her own coat – to enable a quick getaway.

This wasn't good.

'We have a name for the skeleton Amelia Locke discovered in her glasshouse,' Ben said. 'The DNA sample enabled us to identify it as DC Aaron Cooper. He must have died around the time he was reported missing, killed by a blow to the head.'

What wasn't he telling her? There had to be a reason this couldn't have waited until tomorrow, when she was back at work.

'They were able to match the DNA to a profile?'

'By accident, really. We still had it on file, all these years after his disappearance.'

It was standard procedure to take the DNA of serving police officers, so any potential cross-contamination could be eliminated from crime scenes, but the DNA profiles were only held on the database for twelve months once an officer had left the Force.

'That *was* a stroke of luck,' she said.

'I expect he slipped through the net because he disappeared, rather than officially resigned.'

What on earth was the matter with him?

Get to the point.

'We also matched the sample with another profile on the same database.'

So *that* was what this was about.

What was it he'd said to her that day in the garden?

'Humour me, please? Put on a suit.'

Now here was the result.

'Me?' she said.

Although... that didn't make sense. The sample would have been taken in the laboratory, so there couldn't have been any cross-contamination. The only other explanation would be that Aaron was some kind of distant cousin.

'Yes,' he said.

She waited for him to say more, then realised she didn't have to. The answer was right there on his face.

Pity.

'You think the match is closer. That he could be my father. That's what you've come to tell me.'

He nodded.

'That *is* impossible. My father was Detective Superintendent George March.'

Everyone in Raven's Edge knew that. She was the daughter of a hero. It was a lot to live up to but she did her best. It was why she'd joined the police force. Was he telling her that her whole life had been a lie?

Ben didn't say anything. He didn't have to. It made no sense, but if a stranger in a laboratory had matched her DNA with Aaron Cooper's, it was a hard, cold, unassailable fact. It was *evidence*.

She remembered the shock on Mitchell Pavey's face when he'd first seen her. His words when she left: *'Your father? You look just like him. It's uncanny.'*

Mitchell had known the truth.

Aaron Cooper was her father.

Not George March.

And like that, she was cut adrift.

If she wasn't Harriet March, who did that make her? Harriet *Cooper*?

Ben was watching her. 'I can call someone to be with you?'

She'd almost forgotten he was there. 'No, thank you.'

'You *should* have someone with you. This is a lot to take in. It will take you a while to process it. You might need professional—'

A psychologist digging about in her head? No *thank* you!

'I'm good,' she said.

'No, Harriet, you're not. Shall I call Sam?'

What could *Sam* do? Hold her hand while she scoffed another bag of cookies?

'Harriet...' He moved to sit beside her and took her hand in his.

Belatedly she realised she wasn't reacting in the way she was 'supposed' to. Had he thought she'd collapse in floods of tears? What use would that be to anyone? Really, they'd worked together for a year. Didn't he know her by now?

It was odd though. She thought she'd feel *something*. Rage, bitterness, sorrow...

Right now, she didn't feel anything at all.

Was that... normal?

Who got to decide what was 'normal' anyway?

'I could call your brother?' Ben sounded increasingly desperate.

'Ryan?' Not that he was her brother anymore. 'He's in Italy.'

'Your grandmother?'

Who *also* wasn't her grandmother.

Well, that was awkward.

One click on a keyboard in some random laboratory and she'd lost her entire family.

Well, not her *entire* family. Not the one person she'd have been quite happy to discover she wasn't related to.

She pulled her hand away from his. 'I think I'll go and see my mum.'

'If you can wait a few moments, I'll fetch my car and drive you there.'

She wanted to tell him there was no need; that she could use the time it would take to walk over there to get her head straight. But Ben had that stubborn look about him, that she was well-acquainted with after working with him for a year, so she thanked him and agreed that it would be a good idea.

In truth, she wanted that conversation with her mother over and done with as soon as possible.

And then she could get on with the rest of her life.

George returned to his normal routine (the one that had brought him so much trouble in the first place), collapsing into bed at the end of each shift, utterly exhausted, and barely exchanging more than two words with his wife from one day to the next.

He was awarded the promotion Tia had craved. He didn't care about that either. It meant more meetings about massaging statistics and whittling down budgets, taking him away from the on-the-ground policing he'd always loved.

Ironically, everyone was pleased with him, especially Tia.

Starting the day with a shot of whisky went some way towards numbing his guilt but he knew he couldn't go on like this. He had to confess to what he'd done and face the consequences. Anything that happened after that – dismissal from the Force, prison, whatever – it would be better than suffering this living hell every day.

But in that ironic way that life has of throwing a curve ball at the most inconvenient moment, the same day he decided he had to see his boss and tell him everything was the same day Tia calmly told him she was pregnant.

He couldn't hide his disbelief. 'What do you mean?'

She rolled her eyes. 'Well, when a boy and a girl love each other very much—'

'Is the baby his?'

There was no need for him to explain who he meant. Her skin had already paled in shock.

'No!'

Did she genuinely believe that?

Unable to face having his hopes dashed, he tried to squash that tiny flicker of excitement.

A baby...

'How far are you gone?' he asked, slightly kinder this time.

'S... six weeks. It is your baby, George. I promise. There's not been anyone else since... since...'

Apparently she couldn't bring herself to say Aaron's name.

That made two of them. Every time he said it, it felt like ash on his tongue. How none of his colleagues had noticed, he'd never know.

As Tia's pregnancy progressed, George treated her like a particularly fragile princess, paying her lots of attention, which she loved. He delegated his work to younger colleagues, who had more enthusiasm and something to prove, while he spent his free time at home, listening to his baby's heartbeat and having fun arguing with Tia over names.

Tia gave up the gym and the tennis club, although she intended to return to her job at the flower shop after her maternity leave. George gave up alcohol – with slightly more difficulty. He solved a few big cases and got lots of good publicity for the Force. He was back to being good old George. Liked, respected, admired by everyone.

And then Tia went into labour.

Three months early.

TWENTY-NINE

Anya was lying on a recliner in the pool area. There was frost on the grass outside, yet the heating had been turned up to tropical and she was wearing a red one-piece swimsuit, a glass of champagne on the table beside her. She also had a wet cloth draped over her forehead. Did she have a hangover?

Ha! Once Harriet had said what she'd come here to say, a hangover would be the very least of it.

'Mrs Nore?' Anya bellowed, sliding the flannel from her face as she sat up. 'I think I need a new—' She broke off as she saw Harriet. 'Oh, it's *you*.'

Past Harriet would have been terribly hurt by that tone.

Present Harriet no longer gave a damn.

It was oddly liberating.

'Hello, Mum. Tell me about Aaron Cooper.'

If she hadn't been watching closely, she might have missed the way Anya tensed, before dropping the cloth into the ice bucket.

The housekeeper appeared in the doorway, slightly breathless. 'I'm sorry, ma'am. She forced her way—'

Anya waved a hand airily. 'No matter. Could you bring my daughter a cappuccino? She looks half-frozen.'

Normally Harriet might have been impressed that Anya had finally remembered the way she liked her coffee.

'Yes, ma'am.' The housekeeper all but curtseyed.

'The special brand, I think. Do we have any of those chocolate chip cookies left from earlier? Or did the DI eat them all?'

Although there should have been two, there was currently only one DI working in the King's Forest District.

'DI Taylor was here?'

'Didn't he tell you?' Anya patted the recliner and Caesar jumped up beside her. 'Perhaps he didn't think it was important.'

'OK, I'll bite. *Why* was DI Taylor here?'

Anya began to offer the dog savoury snacks from the hostess trolley, which he gobbled straight from her fingers. Nothing for Harriet, but then cookies were allegedly on their way.

'Something about Dean Hunter?' Anya sounded bored. 'I tell you, that man has been more of a nuisance to me dead than he ever was of use to me alive.'

Why would Ben want to talk to her mother about Dean? Harriet had already given him her informal report, and she'd expected Sam or Ash to call on Anya to follow it up, but Ben himself? He was the detective inspector. Did he believe Anya was in some way to blame for Dean's death? Knowing her mother was in a relationship with Dean, and that the body had been found on the roadside, close to her property, was something he couldn't ignore. But why visit himself? And why hadn't he mentioned it?

Mrs Nore arrived with an attractive silver tray containing a cappuccino and a small plate of cookies. Why was Anya being nice? She was up to something, Harriet was sure of it. Anya had already managed to successfully distract Harriet from her reason for coming here.

Harriet drank her cappuccino while she waited for the housekeeper to leave. It was surprisingly good.

'Enough about Dean Hunter,' she said, putting her cup back on the silver tray. 'You can get yourself out of that mess. I want to talk to you about Aaron Cooper.'

Anya poured herself another glass of champagne, apparently in no hurry.

'What would you like to know, darling?'

'Was he my father?'

Anya was watching her carefully over the top of the champagne glass, presumably wondering if it was worth spinning her usual web of lies.

As Harriet already knew Aaron's name, presumably not.

She shrugged. 'Does it matter?'

Three words – and the bottom dropped out of Harriet's world.

It was one thing to have a theory mooted by strangers, but when her mother confirmed it, as though it meant *nothing*...

'Uh, to me? Yes! Why would you do that? You were always telling me how George was the love of your life and how you could hardly bear to live without him. Now you're admitting to *cheating* on him?'

'Your father worked such long hours, I was bored. Aaron was someone I knew, someone I had fun with. I think he went to Europe shortly before you were born.'

'You're too late with that lie, Mum. Aaron Cooper is the skeleton Amelia Locke found in her glasshouse.'

'She always struck me as a very odd woman.'

'You must have *known* it was Aaron when we found the body – yet you said nothing?'

Anya shrugged again.

'That is not the action of an innocent woman. Do you have any idea how Aaron ended up in that glasshouse? Because I warn you, I bet DI Taylor has several theories already.'

'It wasn't anything to do with me, so you can stop shouting at—'

'DI Taylor won't see it that way.'

Anya's eyes narrowed. 'Why? What have you told him?'

'He knows about your relationship with Dean Hunter – yet all the time you were keeping *this* bombshell from me?'

'I don't understand what the problem is, darling. Does it matter if Aaron or George was your father? They're both dead.'

Harriet really, *really* wished Ryan was with her right now. Did Anya *intend* to say such cruel things or did she not care what came out of that perfectly shaped mouth?

'OK, Mum. Let *me* tell you about Aaron Cooper. He was a handsome lad, popular with his friends, much beloved by his family, particularly by his sister, Janie. He often helped with her catering business, even though they both knew he was terrible at it. He met a girl, probably at one of those same hospitality events, and fell head-over-heels in love. Except – shock, horror – she was married. I expect she promised to divorce her husband, because otherwise Aaron sounds like the kind of pragmatic man who would have moved on to someone more likely to commit. He was big on family.'

Anya's cheeks turned pale. 'How—'

'Except Aaron got tired of waiting for you to make your mind up, didn't he? What happened then, Mum? Did he threaten to tell your husband? *Did* he tell your husband?'

Despite the sweltering heat of the conservatory, Anya's face had turned pale.

Harriet knew she was on the right track.

The forensic anthropologist had confirmed that the victim died from a blow to the head.

Anything that could have identified the body had been removed. The kind of thing a professional killer would do – or a professional investigator.

Had *George* killed Aaron? If it had been anyone else investigating, George would have been an obvious suspect. Had George and Anya buried the body together?

Harriet felt distinctly queasy.

'What happened when George found out about your affair, Mum? Did he lose his temper? Did he punch Aaron? Did Aaron fall and hit his head on something? Is that how Aaron died?'

She should have taken Anya into the station for questioning – by Sam or even Ben – and under caution. This was not the way to go about accusing someone of murder.

'Tell me, Mum. Was that how Aaron died?'

'I don't *know* how Aaron died.'

Harriet didn't believe that for one minute. 'Did you help to dispose of the body? Was it your idea? Did Dad – I mean *George* – want to confess, but you begged and pleaded—'

'It *was* George!' Anya shouted back. 'Nothing to do with me! None of it! George killed Aaron all by himself.'

'*Everything* was to do with you! If you hadn't had an affair with Aaron, I would never have been born and George wouldn't have killed him.' Harriet shoved herself out of her chair and put her face close up to Anya's. '*Everything was your bloody fault!*'

'It was an *accident!*'

Did Anya still believe she could lie her way out of this?

'George came home early. He caught us together. He lost his temper. I'd never seen him like that before. He punched Aaron – just one punch! Aaron fell and hit his head on the nightstand. George was going to call for an ambulance but it was obvious Aaron was dead. There was no point in him confessing. He'd have gone to prison – and who would have looked after you and Ryan?'

Grandma Belle, Harriet thought, because that was precisely what *had* happened when George later died.

'It was *George* who dragged the body around to Eoin Kinsella's greenhouse,' Anya said.

On his own? Harriet doubted it. Dead bodies were usually far too heavy for one person to manage easily.

'It was *George* who buried the body in the greenhouse,' Anya said. 'None of this was anything to do with me. I'm innocent!'

There it was: a confession of sorts but completely inadmissible in court. Harriet would need to take Anya into the police station and do this properly, but there was a huge problem with that.

'I can't stand to look at you,' she told her mother as she turned away. 'You make me sick.'

Anya's voice rose hopefully. 'Is that it? You're going to... leave? You won't tell anyone?'

It was the last straw to realise her mother didn't know her at all.

'Yes, I'm leaving, but I'm phoning the station to arrange for someone to call and collect you for a formal interview, under caution.'

'A formal interview?'

'You will tell them exactly what you've told me. I suggest you contact your solicitor.' Harriet paused. 'You know, it would be better for you if you gave yourself up, admitted everything and showed some remorse.'

Anya was staring at her as though she were speaking a foreign language. 'You'd *betray* me? To the *police*? My own *daughter*?'

Harriet sighed, all the fight drained out of her. 'You were complicit in a murder, Mum. Surely you didn't think you'd get away with it?'

It was a relief to finally be outside in the cool air. That conservatory had been far too hot. Harriet's nausea had got worse and had been joined by a thumping headache and dizziness. Perhaps she was going down with a bug? Right before Christmas? *Wonderful.*

Hopefully a brisk walk to the police station would put her right.

She took out her phone to call Ben. While she waited for him to answer, she tried to imagine what Aaron had been like. Had he known Anya was pregnant before he died? Was he excited about becoming a father?

Had his sister, Janie Ware, known? She'd kept glancing at Harriet the day she'd been interviewed, but Harriet had assumed it was because George March had been in charge of the investigation into her brother's death.

So she'd gained an aunt... but Ryan and Grandma Belle weren't related to her at all?

That hurt most of all.

Harriet stumbled, her legs threatening to give way beneath her. Was it shock? Should she call Sam to come and collect her? The last thing she wanted was to faint here and be reliant on her mother for help.

Why wasn't Ben answering? His phone wasn't even going to voicemail.

She terminated the call and tried Sam instead, but the act of looking down at the phone made the ground lurch sideways. She lost her balance and then she was on her knees, swaying, the sharp stones of the drive digging into her palm as she tried to save herself from falling with her free hand.

What the... hell?

It was as though all her energy was being sucked out of her. She couldn't even stay upright. She slumped sideways, gravel scraping against the side of her cheek, yet quite unable to do anything about it.

Maybe she imagined it, but a tinny version of Sam's voice was saying 'Hello? Harriet? Is that you? Is everything OK?'

before someone took the phone from her hand and her world went blank.

THIRTY

Iris was working in the library, with Sparkle curled on the windowsill beside her, when she glanced up and saw someone with pale blond hair walking through the woods beyond the rowan trees.

Her trees. *Her* woods.

When had she become so possessive over a strip of land?

Right after she'd found poor Sparkle hiding in a tree – soaked, bedraggled and utterly terrified.

Iris had seen a blond-haired person in the woods that day too, although she'd later assumed she'd been mistaken and it had only been Sparkle.

What if she was wrong? What if someone was out there right now, dumping another helpless kitten?

Iris shoved back her chair, waking Sparkle (who hissed her displeasure), and ran out of the house, remembering to tug on her boots but not bothering with a coat.

Beyond the neat garden and the circle of rowans, the forest was dark and uninviting. Iris found a well-worn path curving between them, which followed (at a safe distance) the periphery of the gorge. She passed the fallen trunk of an old beech tree.

Behind it, the earth was flat and smooth, as though someone had been standing there not a moment before.

On the day Iris had moved into Raven's Hollow, she'd seen movement between the trees. Had someone been here, spying on her?

The same person now walking through the trees ahead of her?

No, she was making too much of this. It was her overly vivid 'writer's imagination'.

Yet what of the man who'd broken into her house with the intention of killing her? She hadn't imagined him!

As Iris slowed her pace, she saw the footpath was heavily scored with footprints and doggy paw prints. It was a regular thoroughfare, passing right beside her house, and she'd been completely oblivious.

She stopped as the path split in two.

Now which way?

Did it matter? She should go home. Her anger had evaporated, she was cold and damp...

Maybe one last try?

She closed her eyes to concentrate on her other senses. What could she hear? The River Thunor, crashing away in the distance. No animals, no birds – the forest around Raven's Edge was peculiar like that. No footsteps, no branches rustling as someone moved between—

Wait – there *was*... something.

A crunching, as though something – *someone* – had stepped off the path and was kicking through dead leaves.

She *wasn't* alone.

Iris held her breath. Listened harder. Was that a scraping – no, a *dragging* sound?

Like a body, being hauled—

Iris burst out laughing.

A body being dragged? Talk about a guilty conscience! Of

course there wasn't a *body*! If ever she needed a sign that she really ought to step away from her books and mix with real people, and talk to real people, not only the ones in her head, which had certainly skewed her decision-making processes the other night and—

Yip!

Iris glanced down.

A dog was sitting beside her foot, patiently awaiting her attention. A tiny little thing, white and improbably fluffy.

A *chihuahua*? How surreal.

It continued to regard her hopefully.

'Hello,' she said. 'Do you need rescuing?'

The dog turned its head to stare into the trees.

Sparkle liked to do that too.

Was there something out there?

Iris shivered. 'Do you believe in fairies?'

The dog didn't reply. Unlike Sparkle it was wearing a diamanté collar, so it must belong to someone. She crouched and held out her hand for the dog to sniff, which it did, and then licked her.

'What a dear little thing you are!' She felt around the collar for the tag. 'Let's see who you belong to.'

'Get your hands off my dog!'

'Anya?'

Her neighbour was in jeans, wellingtons and an anorak – far more sensible attire than what Iris was currently wearing – but her hair was all over the place, one cheek was streaked with mud and there was more on her hands and knees.

Iris was so surprised that instead of doing the British thing and talking about the weather, or even Anya's dog, she unfortunately said the first thing that came into her head.

'What are you doing in my garden?'

'*Your* garden.' Anya's laugh was brittle. 'This is the King's Forest. It's available for everyone to use. That's the point.'

Someone hadn't checked the boundaries when they'd bought their house.

This section of woodland *did* belong to Iris and she was quite happy to share it with anyone who wanted a relaxing walk, but not if they were dumping kittens – or whatever Anya was up to.

What *was* Anya up to? She looked as though she'd been burying a body!

'You know, Anya? I don't care what you're doing. It's your own business, whatever, but I'd like you to leave and I don't want to see you on my property again.'

'*Your* property?' Anya scoffed. 'Where were *you* when the local kids were playing loud music at all hours, spraying graffiti on the tree trunks and dumping rubbish? *I* was the one who had to pay for a security guard to scare them off. Now you're lording it over everyone else, because you're a famous writer—'

It was a bit hard to lord it over anyone when you hardly left the house.

'Shut up, Anya,' she said, surprising herself. (So much for people-pleasing.) 'I want you off my land or I'm calling the police.'

The police would be far too busy on more important things, but hopefully the threat of them would be enough to scare Anya off. Iris had had quite enough of this nasty, spiteful—

'You *stupid* woman.' Anya's disdainful gaze raked Iris. 'Who are *you* to threaten me? I've lived in Raven's Edge my whole life. My husband was a hero; my daughter's a police officer. You can't touch me.'

Wasn't *that* an invitation to punch the woman on her pert little nose, but Iris just shrugged. Hopefully Anya would find that more infuriating.

'I'm sure the police have to obey the same rules as everyone else,' Iris said.

Although, this was a very small, very *strange* village.

Maybe they *did* do things differently here?

'And you can stop spreading rumours about my husband,' Anya said, 'or I will sue you.'

Iris blinked. *That* was random.

Ignoring the voice in her head reminding her not to engage, she said, 'I've never met your husband.'

'You've been all around the village asking about the man in your precious photo, besmirching his good name, telling everyone he's your father.'

Oh, *him*. Yes, she *was* guilty of that.

Iris put on a bright smile. 'I have my mother's word, on her deathbed, that George March was my father, plus photographic evidence, which Harriet has also endorsed—'

It was completely the wrong thing to have said, because Anya clenched her fists and took a step forward. And even though Iris was nearly a foot taller, she found herself instinctively stepping back.

'You went behind my back?' Anya exploded. 'You spoke to my *daughter*? My George was *not* your father! How dare you suggest such a thing? He was a lovely man, a *hero*, everyone adored him.'

They were now standing so close Iris could feel the other woman's spittle on her cheek and she took another step back, bitterly aware she was moving further away from where she wanted to be.

'I'm sure he was. I'm sorry I never got to meet him.' Iris attempted to sidle around Anya, to return to the house, but the woman was effectively blocking the path – and likely to shove Iris into a bramble patch should she try it. 'Why don't we go back to my house and have a nice cup of tea?' she suggested, employing the bright smile again. As soon as she reached the door, she'd slam it in this witch's face and phone her daughter. Let Harriet sort her out.

'You did meet him,' Anya said. 'When he saved your life.'

'What?'

'Did your mother never tell you? My husband died because he jumped into the river to rescue you, your brother and your mother when your car crashed into the river. Perhaps that was why she had his photo?'

'*What?*'

'It came out at the inquest. Cressida Wainwright was driving to Raven's Edge for a reconciliation with your real father, when her car hit a stag.'

It was then that she saw the monster.

It flew out of the dark wood and ran alongside the car, its eyes glowing white fire.

'Cressida was knocked unconscious,' Anya was saying. 'The car veered off the road and rolled down the embankment.'

Mum slumped over the steering wheel. Without her to guide it, the car lurched off the road, tilted and began to roll. Over and over. Faster and faster.

'The car went straight into the river and began to sink.'

An explosion of white.

Her brother was screaming.

Her mother was silent.

'My darling George was driving behind her car, on his way back from police headquarters. He jumped into the water and saved the three of you single-handedly, but the strain caused his heart to shut down and he died, right there on the riverbank.'

Oh, *hell...*

Iris *did* remember the accident. She remembered the man in the suit who'd been driving behind them. She'd stuck her tongue out at him. He'd scrambled down the embankment and watched the car sink into the water, horrified. She'd thought he was going to let them drown but, with hindsight, he must have been in shock.

She'd had so many nightmares about the accident that her mother had taken her to see a child psychologist. In the end, the only thing that had worked was to convince herself it was just a bad dream.

George March had jumped into the river and saved them.

She'd never known that he'd died while doing so.

'He *was* a hero,' she said slowly. 'And I'll always be grateful—'

'He'd still be alive if it wasn't for you.'

Accurate, but if Anya held her responsible for what had happened to her husband all those years ago, why had she gone out of her way to be friendly to Iris, bringing cake and inviting Iris to her Christmas party? Why make a point of making friends with someone you'd always hated?

Unless...

'Did you send that man to my house to kill me?'

Anya smirked. 'I underestimated you, didn't I? Smart girl, despatching him like that and removing all the evidence. Still, one word from me and the police will arrest you for his murder.'

'I didn't kill him, it was an *accident*. He tripped over my cat.'

'So *you* say.'

'Why else would he have been inside my house?'

'Perhaps you invited him? You live on your own, you're lonely...'

'I hope you paid him in cash?' Iris said. 'Because anything else would be easily traced back to you.'

By the paleness of Anya's cheeks, that was something that hadn't occurred to her.

'Look,' Iris said, 'can't we start again? George's death was an accident, you said so yourself. A stag came out of the woods and hit the car. It was an *accident*,' she repeated, because there was a coldness in Anya's green eyes that was frightening. Iris took another step back. 'It couldn't have been helped.'

'An *accident*,' Anya mimicked, walking right into Iris's personal space. Now they were only centimetres apart. 'Funny thing, these "accidents". How they always seem to happen around *you*, Iris Hemsworth.'

How the *hell*...? Anya *knew*. Somehow, she knew everything that Iris had tried so hard to keep hidden.

'Anya,' she began. 'Please...'

Her feet slid on the loose stones.

What the—

Belatedly, she remembered where she was.

'Anya, we need to move away from the edge of the gorge.'

'Why?' The other woman's expression was pure triumph. 'You're exactly where I want you to be.'

And, far too late, Iris realised that every step Anya had taken forward had herded Iris towards the edge of the cliff.

Who was the 'smart' one now?

Iris tried to jump forward onto firmer ground but the shale slipped beneath her feet. She snatched into the air, hoping to grab onto something – anything – and caught the sleeve of Anya's anorak between her fingers.

This was the moment when Anya could have hauled them both to safety.

Instead she plucked at Iris's fingers, trying to force her to release her grip – and became caught herself in the momentum of the shifting stones.

Iris's feet slipped from under her, pulling Anya over too.

Iris hit the ground exactly as before, and they both began sliding down the slope towards the gorge.

Anya screamed and kicked out, pushing Iris closer to the edge, as though that would stop her own descent, as though the gorge were a creature that could be appeased with a single sacrifice.

Iris took a deep breath. She had seconds before she went over the side but she'd been here before. She knew what to do.

She flung out her arms.

One hand smacked a concrete post.

She hooked her arm around it.

Her shoulder wrenched as she skidded sideways and jerked to a stop, aware of something large rushing past in a shower of stones and dirt.

Then everything went quiet.

As before, it was a struggle for Iris to claw her way back onto firm ground, using the concrete post and the roots and slender branches of the overhanging trees.

Could Anya have survived the fall onto the rocks below?

Unlikely, but attempting to peer over the edge to find out what had happened was likely to result in her own death. Her best option would be to return home and call out the emergency services. In the meantime, Anya's dog was somewhere in the woods, the poor thing. She'd search for it on her return.

Iris ran back through the woods, past the ruins of those ancient cottages. But as she ran up that curious mound, the ground vanished beneath her feet and the earth swallowed her whole.

The drive to the hospital, with Tia screaming in pain in the passenger seat, was the most terrifying of George's life. Was he about to lose another wife and baby in childbirth? By his reckoning, their baby was at least three months premature. Why were the doctors dismissive, treating him like a nervous first-time father when he'd done this before? Why were they talking to him as though he were an idiot? Why wouldn't they let him into the delivery room?

Was it serious?

What weren't they telling him?

Reality hit when he finally held the baby in his arms.

A full-term, seven-pound baby girl, with a mass of blonde curls and enormous blue eyes.

'There must be a mistake,' he told the nurse, trying to hand the baby back. How could this be his daughter? She had hair! She was too big, too healthy, too loud. 'My daughter was premature. I think you'll find she'll be in an incubator somewhere.'

The nurse had laughed and placed the baby firmly into his arms. 'Mr March, you have a beautiful, healthy baby girl.'

He stared down at the little pink face, all scrunched and wrinkled.

The baby stared solemnly back.

'This isn't my child,' he told the doctor, when he came to check on Tia. 'She has blue eyes. Mine are brown, Tia's are green. There's been a mix-up.'

'It doesn't work quite like that,' the doctor told him gently. 'Does one of the grandparents have blue eyes?'

They did, but...

'All babies have blue eyes,' Tia told him, resting her head on his shoulder. 'In a few months she'll have beautiful brown eyes, just like you and Ryan.'

But Baby Harriet hadn't been home a week before George, drained and on edge, had snapped at Tia that he wanted a divorce. She must think him a mug for not guessing that Harriet was Aaron's daughter. The baby had inherited her rosebud mouth and pert nose from her mother but everything else was pure Aaron.

Tia flatly denied everything but told him to go ahead, petition for divorce, and good luck with it – because she'd tell everyone what had really happened to Detective Constable Aaron Cooper.

Would she? He wasn't entirely convinced but the suggestion was enough to give him pause. Telling the truth would implicate her as well, but Tia was ruthless enough to go through with it just to spite him.

What would happen if he were sent to prison for murder? Who would look after Ryan and Harriet? Certainly not Tia, who'd resumed her membership of the gym and the tennis club as soon as her doctor had allowed it.

George could almost understand. Being a parent was exhausting and Tia wasn't yet twenty-one years old. She'd never truly bonded with Ryan, who wasn't her child after all, but when he watched her reject little Harriet, who was so utterly adorable, he was devastated on her behalf.

He let it go.

Six months later, much to his surprise, George realised he was shattered but content. The happiest he'd been since his first wife had been alive. Harriet was a solemn but sweet-natured baby. She ate and slept on cue, and never made a fuss. She was happy to sit and quietly watch whatever was going on around her, taking everything in, although she hated to be parted from her big brother Ryan, whom she adored.

Maybe she wasn't his natural child but George was past caring.

He was Harriet's father and that was the only thing that mattered.

THIRTY-ONE

Iris opened her eyes and saw... nothing. Was she underground? Her cheek was pressed against cold, hard, compacted soil. She rolled onto her back, cataloguing the bruises she was likely to have tomorrow. How far had she dropped? She saw a ragged circle of light directly above her head, about a metre wide. Was that where she'd fallen through? She pushed herself up. Where the hell was she?

Slowly, her eyes became accustomed to the gloom. Wherever she was it was cold, condensation forming with every breath. She had no coat, no bag and no phone. No food or water. She'd better hope for rescue soon – but who would even notice she was gone? Her agent and editor perhaps, but only after a week or so, and then it would be too late.

Clamping down hard on the negative thoughts about to come tumbling after *that*, she staggered to her feet, feeling more twinges of pain, but nothing that would affect her mobility, thank goodness. She could have broken her leg or cracked her head from that fall, and if no one found her...

No, *no*. She mustn't think like that.

Happy thoughts, happy thoughts, happy thoughts.

First task: take stock of her surroundings. She'd landed in a large hole, maybe a cave? Was there an exit? She touched the nearest wall. Rock. It must be a cave... except... She took another step, her fingers trailing over the smooth, cold stone. A crack, perfectly straight, from top to bottom. More like a... seam? Could more than one slab have been deliberately placed together, to create a retaining wall or...

An awful idea popped into her head.

Squares of slabs lined up against a wall?

A line of... graves?

Could she be standing in an ancient, forgotten crypt?

In the middle of nowhere, with no trace of a church on top? That didn't make sense.

She tipped her head back. As far as she could see, the ceiling had been constructed from more enormous stones, which wasn't reassuring. What was keeping it up?

Taking a step back, she squinted into the dark. Were those columns stone pillars? Did that mean this was a man-made grotto? How long had it *been* here?

More pertinently, was it likely to collapse? With her *inside*?

Now her eyes had become used to the gloom, it was easier to see that the gap in the ceiling had been created when one of the stones had fallen. How long before someone else passed by and found the hole?

Except... she'd not taken the path.

In shock from what had happened with Anya, Iris had retraced her steps from her walk on the day she'd moved in, automatically heading towards the little lane that eventually became her driveway, rather than following the well-trodden path that had led her here from her garden.

How many people came *this* way?

That little flutter of panic was becoming increasingly hard to ignore.

She reached up. She was five foot ten, or thereabouts, but she still couldn't touch the roof.

Could she find something to stand on? Maybe that fallen stone?

Her eyes had adjusted enough for her to see the chamber she'd fallen into was small and piled with rubbish and dead leaves. No sign of a helpful lump of stone or anything else to climb onto. There appeared to be two little passages opposite each other, leading... somewhere. One had been deliberately closed off by another block of stone. The other tunnel, behind her, led away into the dark.

Maybe she'd wait a little longer before exploring *that*.

Surely *someone* would notice she was missing? Whit, for example? She'd thought they'd got on well. But he didn't have her number and they'd not made plans to meet up until tomorrow. Would he be likely to call on her before then? What would he think when she didn't answer her door?

Had she closed it when she'd run outside?

Would he think it odd she'd gone out and left the door wide open?

Or would he think she was 'just being Iris'?

It was tempting to collapse onto the floor and cry, but she forced herself to continue around the edge of the... chamber? Pit? Entrance to the Underworld? Her feet crunched over something she had a terrible feeling might be the skeletons of little woodland creatures that had also fallen through the hole and become trapped.

Happy thoughts, happy thoughts...

The stone slabs were cold and slightly bumpy to her touch, but there was nothing that felt like engravings. *Not* graves then. That was something!

A lump appeared out of the shadows, blocking her path. A fallen pillar? She took a step back, trying to work out the best place to stand for the light from above to reveal...

Oh, *great...*

A skeleton. A *human* skeleton! Sitting casually against the wall as if taking a nap.

She clapped a hand over her mouth. Not that anyone would hear her scream.

Happy thoughts.

Here was the last person to have fallen through the hole. Going by what was left of his formal suit and collection of antique camera equipment (that would once have been cutting-edge), he'd been here for decades and decades.

Was this what Phyllis Halfpenny had been trying to tell her?

'I'm definitely seeing a hill... and an old man in a suit. He seems frustrated about something... He's pacing... It's dark... He feels trapped.'

Clement Wainwright. It had to be him. It could hardly be anyone else.

He'd gone into the woods in search of his blessed fairies, fallen down here – and never been able to get out.

It was horrible, *horrible.* The poor man. As he was so famous, there must have been a huge search for him. What a terrible irony that he'd died within sight of his home.

Would that happen to her?

That little flicker of panic had grown to a persistent thump in her chest and was now crawling up her throat.

She *would* get out. She *would.* She'd seen the tracks on the path. Walkers, joggers, dog owners – they used that route all the time. Someone would find her.

Happy— Oh, bugger that!

'Help!' she yelled up at the hole in the roof. 'I'm down here! Please help me!'

Nothing, not even the bark of Anya's dog.

Surely if he arrived home without his mistress, the house-keeper would organise a search?

'Help me!'

A soft groan echoed around the chamber.

Iris flattened herself against the wall.

Was someone in here with her?

'Who... who's there?'

A very human moan was the only response.

Stepping *very* carefully around the skeleton, Iris picked her way through the debris to the other side of the chamber. As she moved past one of the stone pillars, the light from above revealed another small pile of leaves, which appeared to roll over and sit up, and then utter a string of impressive curses.

'Um, hello?' Iris said.

'What the *hell*?' said the pile of leaves, which obviously it wasn't.

Definitely female and... familiar?

'Hello,' Iris said again. 'My name is Iris Evergreen. Who are you?'

'Bloody hell, Iris! Where are we?'

'*Harriet?*'

'How did you get here?' they both said at the same time.

'I fell through the roof.' Iris pointed up before realising that Harriet, like herself earlier, probably couldn't see anything. 'The ground collapsed beneath me.'

'Where's "here"?'

'I've no idea. Somewhere in the woods behind my house. A cave or a secret chamber? I didn't know it was here. It's not on any of the plans.'

Harriet stood up and patted the wall behind her. 'Not a cave. This is stone, man-made, like...' She swore again. 'Do you think it's a crypt?'

'There's no church above us.'

Well, there wasn't one *now*. Iris remembered the little piles of stone in the woods. Who was to say there hadn't been one in the past?

'I meant older than that,' Harriet said. 'You know, like a burial mound?'

'I suppose so.' Iris patted the stone wall. 'I remember walking up a slope but it doesn't seem old enough for that.'

'Maybe it was rebuilt by a local landowner, to create a folly or a tourist attraction?'

How had they got on to the history of ancient tombs when surely the most pressing matter was to get out of the damn thing?

'Um... Harriet? How do you think we—'

'I wonder if there are any remains...?'

Iris sighed. 'Yes, actually.' She pointed to the wall behind her. 'Meet my great-great-grandfather, Clement Wainwright.'

'Oh... The one who went looking for fairies? He's been *here* all this time? Poor guy.'

Speaking of which, 'Harriet? How did you get here?'

There was silence and then, 'I... I'm not sure.'

Her voice sounded almost normal, apart from a slight slurring, but Iris knew she was lying. Harriet's tone lacked that breezy, blunt confidence Iris had come to associate with her.

But a fall like that would unnerve anyone, even a police officer.

'Harriet, have you hit your head? Your speech sounds a bit... slurred?'

'Does it?' Again, there was a delay before she continued. 'I don't know. Maybe?'

What should she say? Harriet had been unconscious, although she seemed all right now. But there had been that dragging sound and, shortly afterwards, Anya had appeared out of the undergrowth, uncharacteristically dishevelled.

Iris had a sudden thought so appalling, so utterly *horrific*, she hardly dared think it.

Had Anya...

No, Harriet was her *daughter*.

MURDER AT RAVEN'S HOLLOW   277

It was unthinkable.

In the meantime, 'Does your head hurt?' she asked.

'Y... yes.'

Either Harriet was confused or the world's worst liar, but why would she lie?

It was time for a practical change of subject.

'Do you have any ideas how we can get out of this hole?'

'None at all,' Harriet said, rather too cheerfully.

She'd definitely hit her head, which meant Iris was effectively on her own. Could she lift Harriet high enough to reach the hole in the roof? That might work – and it would be safer than trying to crawl down that narrow tunnel. Perhaps if Iris braced herself against one of the stone pillars...

Yes, and the wretched thing would fall over, and the whole roof cave in, and they'd be crushed by all that stone and die, probably lingeringly, and not be found for another hundred years, their skeletons ending up on display in a museum, in glass cases labelled: *See what happens when you leave the house!*

If they were lucky.

Thank *you*, writer's imagination.

Iris gave a heartfelt sigh. 'We're *never* getting out.'

'Sure we are.' Harriet laughed and pointed to the ceiling.

'*How?*' Iris's voice came out snappier than she'd intended. It was hardly Harriet's fault that she had concussion.

A man's voice echoed into the tomb. '*Harriet?* Are you down there?'

'Hi, Ben!' Harriet shouted back. 'Took you long enough! I've already missed lunch; I thought I was going to miss dinner too!' She turned her head and the dim light caught on her teeth as she grinned at Iris. 'Fortunately for us, I have a boss who never gives up.'

THIRTY-TWO

By the time Harriet and Iris were out of the tomb, the driveway to Raven's Hollow was packed with emergency vehicles, rounded off by a television crew, who weren't allowed closer than the road, thanks to Ash setting up a cordon.

The two women were checked over by a paramedic. Iris only had superficial bruises, but after shining a light into Harriet's dilated pupils, and hearing how she'd been unconscious and slurring her words, the paramedic recommended she went to hospital for a more thorough examination.

Harriet refused.

Ben insisted.

Harriet impolitely told him what she thought of that and promptly found herself bundled into a car by DC Sam King and driven off.

When Ben returned to the ambulance where he'd last seen Iris, he found it packing up ready to drive away. The paramedic pointed him in the direction of Raven's Hollow, so Ben walked up to the house. Before he could knock, Iris emerged with a tray of teas and coffees. Her big smile faltered at the sight of Ben.

'That's not your job,' he told her gently, taking the tray away and leaving it on the veranda. 'I need to talk to you about what happened today.'

'OK...' Her horrified expression should have sent up several red flags, but she'd recently undergone a horrible experience and would probably rather forget about it.

'Shall we go inside?' he suggested.

With one last, longing glance at the tea tray, Iris headed back into the house.

She led him into the sitting room, but he didn't miss the anxious glance she gave the library. Her poker face was worse than Harriet's, but maybe one murder inquiry at a time?

He ushered her towards one of the chairs set up around the unlit fire. The library must be where she spent most of her time.

'Now,' – he injected a note of amiability into his voice – 'how did you and Harriet end up inside a burial chamber?'

Iris slumped in her seat, twisting her hands. He was reminded of the day he'd interviewed Amelia – and she'd been hiding something too.

'I was working at my desk beside the library window,' Iris said, 'and I saw someone in the woods. I don't mind people walking there but I found Sparkle abandoned a few days ago and I wanted to make sure the same person wasn't doing it again.'

'Did you find this person?'

'No, but I found a cute little chihuahua, running around lost, trailing its lead. I stopped to talk to it but then Anya March appeared out of the bushes, covered in mud.'

He took out his notebook. 'Had Mrs March fallen over?'

'I didn't ask, but before I saw her, I'd heard this strange dragging sound, like someone...' Iris broke off, regarding him unhappily, as though she really didn't want to finish the sentence.

She didn't have to.

Ben remembered those terrifying moments, when he and

Sam had found Harriet's phone abandoned at the end of the driveway. Their frantic search for her had taken at least ten years off his life.

'Was Mrs March alone?' They still hadn't located the housekeeper.

'I didn't see or hear anyone else,' Iris said.

Yet Anya could not have acted alone.

'What happened then?' he asked.

'We had an argument.'

'About?'

'I came to Raven's Edge hoping to find my father. As you know, all I had was a photograph. I showed it to everyone in the village and they all denied they knew who it was – and then Harriet identified the photo as *her* father.'

'George March?' *This* he'd not been aware of.

'Anya was furious with me, telling me that her husband had been a hero and that I was ruining his good name. There was no way I could be his daughter...' Iris broke off, frowning. 'I remember now. Anya must have known who my real father was, because she said my mother had come to Raven's Edge twenty-five years ago for an attempt at reconciliation.'

Ben was about to get the interview back on track, when Iris added, 'It was so strange, the way Anya was obsessed by the idea that her husband was this great hero – and she blamed me for his death.'

'George March died twenty-five years ago. That would be impossible.'

'I know! I was only six years old. How could the accident have been my fault?'

'Accident?' What had he missed? 'What accident?'

'When my mother came to Raven's Edge, for this alleged "reconciliation" with my father, her car hit a stag and left the road, ending up in the river. George March rescued us. That's why Anya blamed me for his death.'

Ben sat back in the chair, staring at her in astonishment.

Everyone knew the story of Detective Superintendent George March. How he'd dived into the river to save two children, without any concern for himself. Ben had never heard of a car accident or that there'd been a third victim.

'You were one of the children he saved?'

'Yes – me, my brother Justin and my mother. I never knew any of this though. I'd always believed it was just a nightmare. My mother never mentioned any accident – and there was never any reconciliation with my father – but as soon as Anya began telling her story, it all came back.'

'Why did Mrs March blame you for her husband's death?'

'I don't know! It was very strange. She kept walking towards me, in a threatening way, and I know she's half my size, but I just wanted to get away from her. Later, I realised she was deliberately herding me towards the edge of the cliff.'

Did Iris realise how implausible this sounded?

'Yet Mrs March was the one who fell over?'

'We had a bit of a tussle. My feet slid on the loose gravel and I grabbed hold of her. She shoved me away but overbalanced herself. We both began sliding down towards the edge but I was able to grab hold of a concrete post and stop myself going over.'

'And Mrs March?'

'I assume she went over. I didn't actually see it, only heard it.'

He shut his notebook and stood up. 'Show me,' he said.

She hesitated.

He gave her a look that indicated the request wasn't optional.

As they left the house she pulled on a pair of boots and a thick winter coat – which she hadn't been wearing when she'd been pulled out of that tomb. It lined up with her story about rushing from the house – who'd go for a walk in the woods in this bitter cold without first putting on a coat? But what about the rest of her story? Why had Anya over-reacted?

And why had this all kicked off after Harriet went to talk to her mother?

Had Harriet accused Anya of Aaron's murder?

Iris led the way across the lawn and between the ring of rowan trees into the forest. He had to duck beneath the branches. There didn't appear to be a proper path. But then it opened out and followed the edge of the gorge – at a safe distance. He could hear the river on the rocks below and the faint voices of the emergency services, even glimpse the yellow of their hi-vis jackets between the trees.

Iris stopped and pointed to her feet. 'This was where I saw the little dog. And that' – she lifted her arm to indicate the hi-vis jackets – 'is where Anya came out of the bushes.'

Directly from the burial chamber.

It was a blow to his solar plexus.

If Ben and Sam hadn't found them...

No, he wouldn't think about it. It was too horrible.

He took a step forward, intending to retrace Anya's steps, or at least find the path to confirm his theory, but Iris abruptly yanked him back.

'Don't! It's too dangerous!' Carefully, she pulled back a branch of the nearest tree and he saw gashes in the muddy slope and the dizzying drop below – and a clump of pale blonde hair caught on one of the branches.

He didn't touch it, but took out his phone and took a photo.

It would be so easy to fall over the edge.

Why the hell wasn't there a fence?

The answer to this was the stubby concrete post Iris pointed out to him.

'I grabbed hold of that and pulled myself back up.'

There were posts at intervals along the edge. A fence, at one time, now completely disintegrated.

He turned away. No one could survive that fall.

So where was Anya's housekeeper? It would take two people to drag an unconscious body through the woods. Harriet would never have gone willingly – her silent call to Sam and the dropped phone was proof of that.

'Go back to the house,' he told Iris. 'I'll send someone around later to take a proper statement. I'd prefer it if you didn't tell anyone else what you've just told me – particularly the press – until we can investigate further.'

And track down that bloody housekeeper.

Iris appeared shocked that he'd even suggested it. 'Of course not!'

'Thank you for your time,' he said, walking back to the tomb, careful to go the long way round, through the garden and along the lane.

The CSIs were in the process of excavating the tomb with the help of Lucia Serrano (the forensic archaeologist) and the caving club. Two complete skeletons now lay topside. One wore the tattered fragments of a tweed suit and antique binoculars around his neck. Presumably this was the famous 'fairy hunter', Professor Clement Wainwright. The other skeleton was wearing a dark-blue uniform and had the remains of a mail bag with him: Rick Dyson, the unfortunate postman who'd gone missing the same time as Aaron.

As he watched Rick's remains being zipped into a body bag, Ben shuddered.

That could have been Harriet.

Leaving the experts to do their work, he walked back down the slope to where Ash was impatiently waiting for him.

Another body had been found.

Swallow's Creek was accessed via a bumpy lane which led west from Port Rell to a small car park already filled with forensic vehicles. From here, Ben and Ash had to walk along a sandy path to the long wooden jetty where the houseboats were moored.

Ben wondered which one had been Dean Hunter's.

The jetty was slippery with ice, despite the weak December sunshine, and had been blocked off with familiar barrier tape.

Ben suited up, signed the sheet and ducked beneath the tape.

Ash announced his intention to stay on this side to interview one of the lifeboat crew who'd discovered the body, and happily accepted a mug of coffee from one of the houseboat owners.

Ben shook his head in disbelief but left him to it. Due to squeamishness, Ash could sometimes be more of a hindrance than a help.

Caroline Warren, the Force forensic pathologist, was already in attendance. Ben summoned a polite smile but didn't ask his usual 'What have we got?' because there on the jetty, lying on a sheet of black tarpaulin, was Anya March. Her eyes were closed, her skin pale and mottled with bruising, her formerly immaculate white-blonde hair tangled and matted with mud, seaweed and bits of twigs.

Usually, Ben felt sympathy for the deceased.

Today he felt curiously stone-hearted.

'Hello Ben,' Caroline said. 'Is this the woman you were searching for?'

'Yes, this is Anya March.'

He was shocked by the anger that tore through him, because it turned out he *was* sorry Anya was dead. He'd been deprived of charging her with attempted murder and knowing she would rot in prison.

What kind of mother would try to kill their own child?

'*Tiana* March,' Caroline said. Even though they no longer bore any animosity towards each other, she still took pleasure in finding things to correct him about. 'We discovered a gym membership card in her pocket. I won't be able to confirm cause of death until the deceased is back in my lab, but she has various injuries consistent with a fall onto a hard surface – although she could have survived that and drowned. We won't know for sure until we run a post-mortem.'

'Accident or murder?'

Not that he cared.

'No idea.' Caroline frowned at his brusque tone. 'Isn't that *your* job?'

She was right, and he wasn't doing it.

If he could treat a career criminal like Dean Hunter as a victim deserving justice, why couldn't he do the same with Anya?

Because this time it was personal.

Ben dragged his thoughts back to the investigation and what he already knew.

Iris was hiding something, but her version of how Anya had fallen from the cliff sounded plausible. Perhaps that was one murder she *wasn't* guilty of?

Dean Hunter, however...

Abruptly, Ben turned and walked back down the jetty, tearing off his scene suit, so deep in thought he didn't notice Caroline had still been speaking to him and that Ash had to hastily hand back the coffee to catch up with him.

The murder of Dean Hunter was another matter.

But first, he needed evidence.

George's promotion meant he was now based in police headquarters at Norchester. He missed his former commute: stepping out his front door and walking the few metres down the road to the police station. Now he had to fight the rush-hour traffic, although, at this time of year, most people were headed towards Port Rell and the beach.

Today he'd left work slightly later and there was only one other car on the road, a battered red Ford Fiesta, driving at about five miles below the speed limit, and not worth overtaking.

The driver was a woman with a high ponytail that swung every time she turned her head to check on her two children on the back seat. There was a small one on a booster seat – George occasionally saw a chubby arm waving – and an older child drawing on the side window with her finger, until she was soundly told off.

He couldn't help smiling, although he did wish the mother would stop turning her head.

'Keep your eyes on the road,' he muttered, even though she couldn't hear him.

The older child, a girl, twisted around in her seat and saw him.

He gave a little wave.

In return, she stuck out her tongue and he laughed, feeling more light-hearted than he had done for months.

His friends were right. He had rushed into marriage. Tia had been too young to settle down, too immature, and he'd been carried away with the romance of it all. They were equally to blame. He could see that now. He'd increase her settlement, pay her whatever she wanted. She could keep the house and—

There was a blur of movement and something shot out of the forest. A stag? The car in front swerved and braked, forcing George into an emergency stop. He leant his head on the steering wheel, trying to catch his breath, his heart thudding irregularly in what was becoming a far too familiar way. Maybe he should see a doctor? But the doctor would tell him to cut back on the stress and—

Wait... He glanced up, remembering the stag and the other car, but the road was empty. How could that be? A car couldn't vanish...

George got out of his car. There were black skid marks on the tarmac in front of him, heading towards a steep embankment. Deep grooves scored through mud and fallen leaves, broken branches and saplings ripped from their roots...

He remembered the little girl drawing on the window – no, there had been two children, and he started half-sliding, half-falling down the embankment towards the river.

The red Fiesta was bobbing on the water like a child's toy.

Even then, he assumed he had plenty of time. He used his phone to dial the emergency services, taking care to tell them his rank, so they'd take him seriously, but when he looked back at the car, it was lower in the water. He couldn't see the driver, or the younger child, but the older girl was slamming her hand on the window, her lips moving.

'Help us!'

There wasn't time to wait for the emergency services. George abandoned his phone on the muddy bank, shrugged off his jacket and waded into the river. Soon he was out of his depth and had to swim. The water was halfway up the windows, which were tightly shut. The door wouldn't open either, due to the pressure. He mimed cranking open the window but the little girl shook her head, so he swam back to the shore, searching for a heavy rock with which to break the window.

By the time he got back, the girl – who must have thought he was abandoning them – was hysterical. He indicated for her to cover her eyes before slamming the rock into the window. The glass shattered immediately.

She reached through the window to grab him, heedless of the broken glass. 'Thank you! Thank you!'

Beside her, a small boy was slumped on a booster seat. The mother was unconscious in the front seat, bleeding from a head injury.

'What's your name, sweetheart?' he asked the girl, gently disentangling himself.

'Iris,' she said. 'Iris Hemsworth.'

George carefully removed the remaining shards of broken glass around the window frame.

'OK, Iris. I need you to be very brave and see if you can release your brother's and your mother's seatbelts?'

She did as she was told.

'Now, can you lift your brother over to me, so I can pull him through the window?'

'I think so.' She put both arms around her brother and dragged him onto her lap, enabling George to reach through the window and pick the boy up.

Iris watched stoically as he carried her brother to shore, before returning, slightly out of breath, to the car. 'Now you, sweetheart.'

'What about Mum?'

'Have you undone her seatbelt?'

'Yes.'

'Good girl. Let's get you out and then I'll return for your mother.'

By the time he'd carried Iris over to the bank, the car was underwater and there was no sign of the emergency services. With the unaccustomed exercise, his heart was beating fit to explode out of his chest.

He dived into the murky water, finding the car almost by accident, groping his way around to the driver's door. Now the car was completely filled with water, it was easy to yank open. He caught Iris's mother beneath her arms and dragged her out and up to the surface.

Someone splashed into the water beside him, taking her from him.

Someone else helped George back to the bank.

The emergency services had arrived.

'Bloody hell, mate!' said a man in a hi-vis jacket. 'You rescue this lot by yourself? You're a regular hero.'

George was so tired he couldn't answer. Was he really that unfit?

The other man frowned. 'Shall I get the paramedic to look at you too?'

George shook his head. 'I'll be fine once I've had a rest.' He lay back against the mud and closed his eyes, as his heart beat faster and faster. 'I'll be fine...'

THIRTY-THREE

Sam drove Harriet to Norchester General at his usual one mph below the speed limit.

'It would be quicker to walk,' she grumbled.

'Go ahead. It'll save me a trip.'

Harriet sulked for the rest of the journey.

Once in A&E she refused to queue-jump just because she was a police officer, which meant she and Sam spent several hours in the waiting room before she finally saw a consultant, who poked and prodded at her, announced, 'You'll live' and sent her home again.

The trip back to Raven's Edge took longer because of the rush-hour traffic, giving Sam far too much time to ask awkward questions.

'How did you *get* down there?' he asked, for about the hundredth time. 'Did you fall?'

'I don't remember.' Also said for about the hundredth time. It wasn't the easiest thing to tell your friends and colleagues that your mother had tried to kill you.

She must have been a spectacularly unlovable child.

Harriet rubbed her hand over her eyes and hoped it looked as though she had a headache.

The last thing she did remember was feeling faint on her mother's driveway and phoning Sam to come and collect her. After she'd collapsed on the gravel, someone had carefully taken the phone from her.

Her mother? Mrs Nore?

To phone the emergency services?

Not if she'd woken up a couple of hours later in an underground tomb.

Presumably, whoever had taken her phone had also dragged her through the woods and dropped her into that hole. Had they drugged her too? Is that why she'd felt as though all the energy was being sucked out of her?

'Could you bring my daughter a cappuccino? She looks half-frozen.'

'Yes, ma'am.' The housekeeper all but curtseyed.

'The special brand, I think.'

Harriet closed her eyes. Without a doubt, she was the world's biggest idiot. Had she honestly believed that rushing over to accuse her mother of murder wouldn't lead to consequences? Anya had kept Aaron Cooper's death secret for twenty-five years – to safeguard her husband's spotless 'hero' reputation, but also her own status in the village. When threatened, of course she was going to lash out. Being Anya's daughter had given Harriet no protection at all. She was lucky that whatever had been put into her coffee hadn't been a fatal dose.

Had it been intended to kill? To ensure Harriet never came out of that tomb, like poor deluded Professor Wainwright? Might *her* body not have been discovered for another hundred years?

Any remaining love she might have felt for Anya completely evaporated at that moment.

By now they'd reached the village but Harriet turned her

head away from her mum's house as they passed. If Sam noticed he didn't say anything, for which she was grateful.

When he pulled up outside Foxglove & Hemlock, and she released her seatbelt, he said, 'Wait.'

Harriet recognised the serious expression on his face. It was the same one she used when she had to break bad news to a recently bereaved relative.

'What's the matter?'

'Just before we left the hospital, I had a call from Ben. Some bad news, I'm afraid. Your mum...'

He didn't have to say the rest.

'Mum's dead?'

'Yes. I'm sorry, Harriet.'

He reached over to give her a clumsy sideways hug, but all Harriet felt was relief. One less thing for her to deal with.

'Your mother was walking through the woods with Caesar, the cliff crumbled and she went over the edge. It must have been the heavy snow we've had recently. It made the ground unstable when it thawed.'

Harriet thought there was probably more to it than that.

'Where's Caesar? With Mrs Nore?'

Sam grimaced. 'Mrs Nore took the opportunity to disappear, along with much of your mother's valuables, which she's already tried to dispose of in Norchester. They have her in custody. Ash volunteered to look after Caesar – which means his *mum* is looking after Caesar – but he'll bring the dog over to you when you're feeling better. It's already peed on his mum's carpet and she's not pleased.'

Harriet hid a grin. Ash, at twenty-six, still lived with his parents, who spoilt him rotten and treated him as though he were twelve. Mrs Chopra, however, was *extremely* house-proud.

'Tell Ash he can bring Caesar over whenever he likes.'

Sam considered her. 'You do look a little better. You have

some colour in your cheeks. You were quite out of it earlier. We were all worried about you.'

'I'm fine. Thank you all for rallying round, and thanks for the lift to the hospital.' She exited the car before Sam could jump out and open the door for her. 'It'll be a nice hot bath for me,' she added, to put him off following her inside, 'and I'll see you at work later.'

'Yeah, about that.' Sam looked shifty. 'The boss says he doesn't want to see you until the New Year.'

'Tough,' Harriet said, 'because as soon as I've had that bath, I'm heading right over. We have lots to catch up on.'

Too lazy to walk around to the back door, Harriet ran up the front steps – and straight into her grandmother, standing at the top with her arms folded.

'*Hello*, Harriet,' she said. 'I believe *we* have a lot to catch up on too. Such as, when, *exactly*, were you planning to tell me that you've spent the last few hours in A&E?'

Oh, she was in so much trouble...

Harriet switched on her coffee machine – anything to delay the moment when she'd be forced to explain to her grandmother the events of the past four hours. Grandma Belle had never cared much for cappuccinos and lattes, and would have been happier with a mug of the instant stuff, but that wasn't the point.

How was she going to tell Isabelle March that her only child was a murderer?

In the end, she didn't have to.

Once Harriet had presented her with a cappuccino, complete with chocolate sprinkles, and they were both sitting comfortably on the sofa, Grandma Belle blew Harriet's carefully thought-out speech right out of the water.

'DI Taylor came to see me earlier,' she said. 'He told me what had happened to you but that you were safe. I needed something stronger than coffee after *that* conversation, I can tell you.'

Harriet's heart began thudding in a way that couldn't be attributed to caffeine, seeing as she hadn't had the chance to drink any yet.

'What did he tell you?' she asked cautiously.

'That Anya – I refuse to call her "your mother" – tried to poison you and hide your body in some ancient burial chamber.'

Ben knew about the drugged coffee?

'How the hell—'

Her grandmother frowned at the curse. 'He *is* a detective. A very good one. You're always saying so yourself – slightly begrudgingly, admittedly.' She took a sip of coffee. 'This coffee isn't bad. How does the machine make it? With proper beans or those tricky little pods?'

'Proper beans,' Harriet lied. 'There's something else I have to tell you...'

Her grandmother sighed heavily. 'Ben also explained about that. He said the reason Anya tried to kill you was because you'd discovered the skeleton was her ex-lover – and your real father – and she wanted to prevent anyone else finding out that George was a murderer. Presumably because it would have reflected badly on her.'

What could Harriet say to *that*?

When her cup began rattling in its saucer, Harriet realised her hand was shaking.

Grandma Belle gently took the cup and saucer from her and placed them on the table.

Then she held out her arms and Harriet slumped into them and cried, and cried, and cried.

It must have been a good twenty minutes later, because it was growing dark outside, before she found the strength to raise her head.

'How are you, darling?' Her grandmother's concern was evident by her worried expression, but wasn't that Grandma Belle all over? Always putting others before herself?

'I should be comforting *you*,' Harriet muttered. 'It can't have been easy to hear...'

How much did her grandmother know? Exactly what *had* Ben told her?

And he didn't know the half of it.

At least, she didn't *think* he did.

'Why?' Grandma Belle asked. 'I'm the same person I was yesterday, whereas you've had a terrible shock.'

Wait? Did that mean...?

'You... *knew*? About Dad not being...'

She couldn't say it. She could *not* bring herself to say it out loud.

George March was not her father.

'Well, not all of it, obviously,' her grandmother said. 'Your mother married too young. She missed out on a lot of life experiences—'

Why did her grandmother always have to see the best in people?

'You're *defending* her?'

'I'm trying to make sense of it! We knew she was having an affair. We knew her mystery boyfriend was likely to be your real father, right from when you were born...'

Harriet narrowed her eyes. 'You keep saying "we".'

'Your grandfather and I,' Grandma Belle sighed. 'And George. He knew – he confirmed it – but he didn't care. As far as he was concerned, you were *his* daughter. He loved you exactly the same way he loved Ryan. It was clear to see by the way he behaved with you. It's important for you to know that.'

Her paternity wasn't the only issue here.

'But... he was a murderer.'

'*That*, I don't believe.' Grandma Belle raised her chin and her grey eyes took on a steely glint. 'To deliberately plan some-one's death? No. I know my son. Tell me, how did the boyfriend die? Did Anya tell you?'

Harriet thought back. 'When I went to confront her, Anya denied everything, but I knew she was lying so I kept pushing until she lost her temper and admitted that Dad – *George* – had killed Aaron.'

'But *how*? Was it a deliberate act?'

Her grandmother's expression was so stricken, Harriet didn't want to tell her the truth – but she could hardly lie either.

'I don't *think* so...'

From her grandmother's expression she knew that wasn't good enough.

Harriet closed her eyes, remembering Anya's face, hard and calculating, utterly outraged that she was being accused of something she hadn't done. She'd been so determined to save herself she'd happily blamed George for everything, denying that she'd been the catalyst for it all.

But what had Anya actually *said*?

George came home early. He caught us together. He lost his temper. I'd never seen him like that before. He punched Aaron – just one punch! Aaron fell and hit his head on the nightstand. George was going to call for an ambulance but it was obvious Aaron was dead. There was no point in him confessing. He'd have gone to prison – and who would have looked after you and Ryan?

'George punched him,' Harriet said slowly. 'He came home early, caught Aaron and Mum together, and lost his temper. Mum said he killed Aaron with a single punch.'

'I suspected it might have been something like that.' Grandma Belle sighed. 'It's why he had to give up boxing. He had such a talent. He could have been a professional. You've seen the trophies – I suspect you're the one keeping them polished – but he'd always had a short temper and he knew that if he ever lost control in the ring, it could be fatal for his opponent. That's why he gave it all up, took anger management classes and become a police officer. I asked him once if he regretted giving up boxing, but he said he'd made the right decision. George *loved* being a police officer. He wanted to help people – seek justice for those who could no longer do it themselves.'

How horribly ironic.

'It's why I joined the Force too,' Harriet said sadly.

'And now? Do you regret it?'

What did *that* mean?

Did Harriet feel cheated for following someone else's dream?

What else could she have done? She had no special interests, no hobbies, no other talents – apart from running, but she wasn't good enough to have taken it any further. She loved reading. Maybe she could have worked in a bookshop? She'd have enjoyed that.

Yeah – and would've been utterly bored after just one week.

'No,' she said firmly. 'I don't regret it.'

They sat in silence for a moment and then Harriet said, 'There was one other thing. I interviewed Aaron's friend Mitchell recently and he mentioned that Aaron received a blow to the head during a police operation on the night that he died. He refused to see a medic, so I'm not sure if...'

Grandma Belle placed her hand over Harriet's. 'We'll never know, so it's best not to torture yourself with the "what ifs".'

'Yes, but—'

'Do you know anything else about Aaron? His life, his character, his... family?'

'He was definitely my father and only twenty-five when he died. He and his family were close – like us.'

There, she'd said it. *Us.*

Grandma Belle nodded approvingly. 'We're still your family, Harriet. Ryan and I. Never doubt that. You'll want to make contact with your new family. I'm sure they'd love to meet you. But don't feel you have to choose one family at the expense of another. We'll always be here for you. There's no rule about how big a family can be. I'm sure you see Sam and Ben – and your other friends at the police station – as your family too?'

'Yes, but I'm having trouble getting my head round it. I'm not the person I thought I was. Am I Harriet March or Harriet Cooper?'

'You're the same person you've always been,' Grandma Belle said, in her usual no-nonsense manner – the manner Harriet had always assumed she'd inherited. 'You can be whoever you want to be – and call yourself whatever you like! Your mother changed her name from Tiana to Tia when she was a teenager, because she believed it was more glamorous, and then again to Anya when she opened her first clothing store.'

They were silent for a moment and then Harriet felt she had to say it.

'Dad – George – *Dad* would have been charged with manslaughter rather than murder, if the case had gone to court. He'd certainly have received a custodial sentence. Probably about five years.'

Her grandmother nodded. 'George had a split second to make a choice – and he made the wrong one.'

'He had so many chances to put it right. He was even put in charge of the investigation – and then made out Aaron was some work-shy womaniser who'd run off with his latest girlfriend.'

'That *was* unforgivable.'

'I wonder what was going through his head.'

'Probably that he didn't want to go to prison.'

'Anya said Dad was worried who would look after Ryan and me.'

'We shouldn't speculate.' Grandma Belle picked up the coffee cups and took them over to the sink. 'We'll never know the truth.'

That was easier for Grandma Belle to say than it was for Harriet to accept. 'I spent my whole life believing that Dad was a hero.'

Her grandmother snorted. 'That was Anya's doing. With hindsight, perhaps it was a reaction to her guilt about the part she played in Aaron's death. George wasn't a hero, he was *human*. A normal man who made a mistake – and made it worse by not owning up to it. He was also a man who helped two children in trouble. Although I hope anyone would have done the same in that situation. But doing the right thing doesn't make you a hero, it makes you a normal, decent human being. Heroes are for comic books.'

As Harriet lay in her bath sometime later, she reflected that Grandma Belle had certainly given her a lot to think about.

How hard *was* it to admit to making a mistake?

When you were faced with the loss of everything you held dear – family, career... even your liberty. Just how hard *was* it to do the right thing?

THIRTY-FOUR

Christmas Eve

The following morning Ben took a bouquet of flowers round to Harriet, listening with increasing horror as she detailed all the events leading up to her incarceration in that burial chamber. Then Ash turned up with a beautifully wrapped box of chocolates and Anya's dog Caesar, followed by Sam and Dakota with an enormous bag of cookies from The Crooked Broomstick.

Hadn't *anyone* gone into the office this morning?

Before leaving, Ben reiterated that he didn't want to see Harriet back at work until the New Year (at which she rolled her eyes), but her brother Ryan was flying back from Italy to spend a traditional Christmas with her and their grandmother, so she wasn't particularly bothered. And, maybe in January, she'd pluck up the courage to contact Janie Ware and reintroduce herself.

Before any of that, Harriet had one last job to do – repay her debt to Iris for helping to rescue her from that tomb, even if it had been by accident.

Which was why, two hours later, Harriet was standing

outside Raven's Hollow, knocking on the door. There was a brief moment when she thought Iris might be ignoring her – all she had to do was glance out of one of those windows and see Harriet standing there – but then she heard the echo of footsteps and the door creaked open.

'Hi,' Iris said carefully. 'Are you OK? Should you be out and about so soon?'

'Why not? There's nothing wrong with me.'

What else was she supposed to do? Lie in bed and feel sorry for herself? What would *that* achieve?

'Well,' Iris said awkwardly. 'You know…?'

Harriet did and she'd rather not talk about it, or even waste one more minute thinking about it, so instead she said, 'Your father? I've had an idea about how we can find out who he was.' That worked a treat because Iris's face positively lit up.

'*Really?* That would be lovely!'

'Can I come in?'

'Absolutely!'

As Harriet walked inside, even *she* picked up on the not-so-subtle hint that Iris would prefer they went into the room on the left. Again, she was struck by how empty the sitting room looked with so little furniture. The fire hadn't been lit either, although there were two old-fashioned radiators, one beneath each window.

'Would you like a cup of tea?' Iris asked.

'I'd love a coffee, but first I need you to fetch something for me. You see, last night I was thinking about…' – *fathers* – 'stuff, and I remembered your mother told you that everything you needed to know about your father was in a box in her study.'

'Gosh, you do have a good memory. Yes, that's right. When I opened the box I found her engagement ring, a photo album, some letters from her mother and various trinkets from her childhood. She called it her box of treasures.'

'Do you still have this box?'

'Oh yes.'

Was Iris being deliberately slow on the uptake?

'With all the contents still inside? You haven't thrown anything out?'

'Oh no. I'd never throw out anything that belonged to my mother. Would you like me to fetch it for you? This is so exciting!'

Iris *really* needed to get out more, Harriet thought. As she turned to stroke Iris's little white cat, who'd come to see who was visiting, she realised the photograph of George March was still propped up on the mantelpiece and picked it up, staring into his handsome face. Not *quite* the hero she'd grown up to believe him to be, but did that make him more relatable?

No. It would take time for her to adjust, but it was going to be hard to forgive him for not admitting his part in Aaron Cooper's death, whatever the circumstances.

Iris's footsteps echoed through the hall.

Harriet quickly put the photo back.

Iris returned carrying a large wooden box. Although quite plain, it looked old.

Iris carefully placed the box on the table in front of the sofa, unlocked it with a tiny key and stood back expectantly.

No pressure.

Harriet opened the box.

As Iris had said, on the very top was a photo album. Harriet took it out, leafing through the photos. They were neatly arranged in date order in fancy black corner mounts, and the same three people appeared regularly. Two young children and a woman who started off in her twenties but gradually aged.

She was the spitting image of Iris.

'Your mother?' Harriet pointed to her.

'Yes, that's me and the little boy is my brother Justin.'

Some of the photos were missing.

'Those were of my stepfather,' Iris said, reading her mind. 'I threw them away.'

'Oh, OK.' Hopefully *those* photos weren't relevant.

'Did you find the other photo amongst these?'

'Yes, but tucked into the back, which I thought was odd at the time. There's no space for it and it's a different shape to the others, even allowing for it being cut in half.'

Harriet set the album aside and took out the three letters, still in their envelopes. 'Have you read these?'

'Yes, they're from my grandmother, Beatrice Wainwright. I believe there must have been some sort of estrangement between my mother and her parents. The language in the letters is very stilted, and the writing's a little hard to read—'

'You didn't read them?'

'Not *every* word but I got the gist.'

Iris would make a *terrible* police detective.

Harriet held one up. 'May I?'

'Sure, if you like.' Then, after watching Harriet for a few minutes, Iris added, 'I'll make us some coffee.'

Harriet began reading. The dates of the letters were widely spaced out and they mainly detailed village gossip. Perhaps Beatrice Wainwright hadn't been much of a letter writer? Or were these the only ones Cressida wanted to keep? In which case, they must be important...

A mug of coffee appeared on the table next to her.

'Thanks, Iris. I think I've found something. Listen to this:

Do you remember George March, the husband of your old schoolfriend, Scarlett? He married for the second time today – photo attached. It was a strange affair. Hardly anyone turned up. I'm surprised you weren't invited, but then you were Scarlett's friend, not his.'

'Oh dear,' Iris said. 'That's quite conclusive, but now I'm completely confused. My mother sounded quite definite about what I'd find in the box.'

'Let's take a look.' Harriet laid the letters to one side, taking out the rest of the contents, one at a time. Stones with holes, concert tickets for bands she'd never heard of... and then her fingers closed over a little blue box. She held it up enquiringly.

'My mother's engagement ring,' Iris sighed, sipping her tea. 'Go on, open it. It's gorgeous.'

Harriet flicked open the box. Inside was a ring with a large violet-coloured stone surrounded by diamonds.

'Wow!'

'I know! I thought it was an amethyst but I took it to a jeweller and he told me it's a violet sapphire.'

Harriet turned the ring over in her hand, admiring the way the diamonds caught the light. 'I didn't know violet sapphires were a thing. Was this from your stepfather?'

Iris shuddered. 'No, he was stony-broke.'

Harriet put her hand back into the box but found only the newspaper lining it.

'You see,' Iris sighed. 'No clues.'

Was there though?

Using her fingernail, Harriet scraped up the newspaper.

The sheet had been folded into four but wasn't the right size to fit the box. She unfolded it carefully, spreading it out on the table. It was a single sheet, the front and back page of *The Calahurst Echo*, one of the local newspapers.

'This could be something?'

'It's dated 1997. I was born in 1994.'

The main story on the sports page was a local football team winning a prestigious cup. The headline on the front page mocked some political scandal, but below that was a colour photo of a society wedding. Harriet recognised the family immediately, even though they were thirty years younger. It would have been impossible not to. They were the most well-known family in Raven's Edge.

She turned the newspaper around to show Iris. '*This* is what your mother meant when she told you to look in the box.'

Iris read the headline out loud.

'*Patrick Graham married children's illustrator Rosemary McKenzie today at St Francis's Church...*'

'Patrick Graham? You think *he's* my father? You know, that's interesting because—'

Harriet rolled her eyes. 'Not *him*. You don't want to be related to *him*, trust me.' Harriet jabbed at the person standing next to Patrick: a tall, dark-haired man wearing an identical morning suit but swinging the top hat from his fingertips as though he'd rather be somewhere else – anywhere else. Harriet recognised that look. It was one she frequently wore herself. 'I'm talking about *this* guy.'

'How can you be so certain... *Oh!*'

'Oh?' That sounded encouraging. 'Do you know him?'

Mind you, pretty much everyone knew—

'I recognise him! I've met him! He was a friend of my mother! Oh my goodness! That's it. It's so obvious! I can't believe the answer was here all the time. Harriet, you're a *genius!*'

'I know,' Harriet said immodestly. She held up her hand for a congratulatory high five but Iris leant forward and threw her arms around her instead.

Yes, Iris Evergreen was a hugger.

THIRTY-FIVE

Ben's morning was spent completing the paperwork on the murder of Aaron Cooper, and the discovery of the remains of Clement Wainwright and Rick Dyson, as well as writing a report on the attempted murder of Harriet March and the accidental death of Anya March. After a short break for lunch, by the time he finally looked up it was dark and most of the MIT had left for a well-deserved two-day break, calling a cheery 'Merry Christmas' as they left.

Now there was only him and Dakota in the office.

As he packed up ready to leave, he told her, 'Don't work too late. It *is* Christmas.'

'I won't,' Dakota agreed, 'but I think I'm on to something. Iris Evergreen was born Iris Wainwright but for about ten years she was known as "Iris Hemsworth", so I'm checking that too.'

'Good work,' was his automatic response, but as he walked down the stairs a faint chill came over him.

Why did *that* name seem familiar?

. . .

Brianna Graham's annual Christmas Eve Ball at Hartfell, her family's modern glass and stone mansion, was considered *the* social event of the year in the King's Forest District, but this was the first time Ben had been invited. Fortunately, he was sharing a table with people he knew: the Merriweather sisters and the Reverend David Griffiths, but directly beside him was an empty seat and a place card that read 'Camilla Graham'.

Milla had found somewhere more interesting to be.

Typical.

They'd agreed, *weeks* ago, that her grandmother's party would be one of their non-date dates. It could have been fun – so why wasn't she here? He'd apologised after their row, and she'd laughed and forgiven him. Had something happened?

He tried phoning but it went straight to voicemail.

Meanwhile, on the next table, Iris was taking selfies of herself and Whit.

Were they a couple? When had *that* happened?

Iris saw him watching and leant across to say 'This is the first time I've been to a ball. Isn't it *wonderful?* I promised my brother Justin I'd send him the photos. He's an economics professor at a tiny little university in New York state. He'd think this was brilliant – utterly mad but totally British!'

An economics *professor?*

Perhaps Justin was a few years older than her?

In the centre of the dance floor was a massive Christmas tree. Feeling incredibly two-faced, Ben offered to take a photo of Iris and Whit in front of it. After thanking him profusely, the two of them went off to dance and Ben returned to his table, where his pocket vibrated with an incoming text from Milla:

> Sorry, sorry, sorry! We're stuck on the M3. Can you make my apologies to Granny Brianna? I'll pop over to your cottage later, M xxx

In that case he was definitely going home!

But before he could get up, his phone rang.

This time it was Dakota. He caught her saying 'Iris' but with the music from the band, he couldn't hear the rest of it. He left the table and went over to one of the sliding doors, stepping through and onto the decking that surrounded the house. Damn, it was cold!

'I'm sorry,' he said, 'can you say that again?'

'I've found out some very strange things about Iris Evergreen,' Dakota said, then muttered something beneath her breath that sounded like 'I hardly know where to begin.'

Was she still at work? He glanced at his watch. It was almost ten o'clock!

'Dakota, you really need to go home. I'm sure this can wait until the twenty-seventh.'

'I don't think it can, actually. Are you at the ball? I can hear music.'

She sounded wistful, which made him feel worse. 'You mentioned Iris?'

'Yes! A year ago, Iris's boyfriend, Erik Hansen – he was a famous thriller writer – died in a fall from a dovecote.'

'I remember.' He'd read some of Hansen's books, which he'd found formulaic, but he'd been sorry to hear about the man's death. 'I hadn't realised they were together. How sad.'

'It was at a party thrown by Graham Media, and Erik got it into his head to climb an old stone dovecote in the garden. He slipped and fell to his death. It was ruled an accident but do you think we should re-interview witnesses and investigate it more thoroughly?'

He could imagine DCI Cameron's reaction if he suggested *that*.

A *closed* case, that wasn't *their* case or even in their jurisdiction?

No chance.

'Dakota, the incident would have been thoroughly investigated at the time—'

'There's more,' she said.

He sighed. Of course there was. Dakota was very thorough.

'Dean Hunter was found at the end of Iris's driveway, also dead.'

'Yes, and our theory is that Hunter was a career criminal who'd upset the wrong person.'

'You don't see a pattern?'

'Not particularly.'

Iris Evergreen, romantic fantasy author and *serial killer*? Unlikely.

But how many 'accidents' could one person have?

'After we found Hunter's body, I visited Iris and spoke to her,' he said. 'There was no evidence to suggest she had anything to do with his death, but you're right. It does warrant further investigation.'

'OK... Death number three: Iris was present when Anya March fell into the river yesterday. Twenty-five years that woman has been walking a succession of little dogs through those woods, and she meets with a fatal accident the same month Iris moves into Raven's Hollow? Coincidence? I don't think so.'

Ben kept quiet. Everyone knew he didn't believe in coincidences, but where was Dakota going with this? Didn't she have a home to go to? Didn't she have a *life*?

'Now for the big one,' Dakota said. 'Fifteen years ago, Iris shot her stepfather.'

'*What?*'

For goodness' sake! Why hadn't Dakota *led* with that?

'Uh huh. It was in retaliation for killing her brother,' Dakota said. 'It was in all the newspapers. Quite a big thing at the time.'

No wonder 'Iris Hemsworth' had sounded so familiar!

Yet Iris had said her brother was alive and living in America.

Unless...

Did she have more than one brother?

'What was her brother's name?' Ben asked.

'Justin Hemsworth,' Dakota said. 'Even a simple search online will bring up all the details of the court case.'

Had he understood this correctly? 'Justin Hemsworth is *dead?*'

'Ye-es. He died at the age of twelve.'

Why would Iris lie about that? Had it hit her so hard when her brother had died that she'd pretended he was still alive?

What else had she lied about?

He remembered the churned-up snow leading away from her house and how it had bothered him at the time. *Had* Iris killed Dean Hunter in her house and dragged his body towards the road? With his height and weight it wouldn't have been easy for her, *but,* if it had snowed heavily and she had a sledge...?

But what about motive?

OK... What if Hunter had broken into her house, in search of money or valuables? Could she have killed him by accident? Hit him over the head with something heavy, like a vase or a candlestick – and then dropped it, causing that dent in the library floor? The obvious thing would have been for her to report the incident to the police. Anyone would – unless they had something to hide.

Or a complicated history with the police.

'Let me see if I've understood this correctly,' he said. 'Iris's stepfather killed Justin and, in retaliation, Iris shot him?'

'Yes. The stepfather – Paul Hemsworth – liked to drink, and then he'd become mean and would threaten Cressida and the children. One day he went too far. He was firing his gun aimlessly, trying to frighten them, and he accidentally shot little

Justin. Iris, as cool as you like, grabbed the gun and turned it on him.'

'That sounds like self-defence...'

'Iris was only fifteen,' Dakota said. 'The court agreed that she'd saved herself and her mother – but she spent nearly a year in a detention centre before being tried for murder as an adult.'

If the stepfather had been abusive, it would have been a perfect opportunity to get rid of him once and for all.

Dakota was still chatting away. 'The *really* interesting part is that Dermot Graham paid her legal costs and was able to get her cleared of all charges.'

'Why would he do that?'

There was a slight pause. 'Well... Dermot was the original owner of Iris's house in Primrose Hill, way back in the nineties. He transferred it to her mother just before Iris was born. My guess is that he's Iris's father and it was some kind of payoff.'

Bombshell.

'Um, sir? Are you still there? What would like me to do now?'

Go home, take a break, enjoy Christmas.

It would've been nice, but that wasn't how the job worked.

Christmas just got cancelled.

'Brilliant research, Dakota. Iris Evergreen is here at Brianna Graham's party. I'll ask her to come into the station for questioning,' – *and call out CSI to do a thorough check of that damned library* – 'but wait by the phone in case I need back-up.'

Back-up? To arrest a novelist?

The trick would be to separate Iris from Dermot Graham – a very wealthy, very powerful man who probably had the top legal team in the country permanently on standby.

And who was also Milla's father.

Which would make Iris Milla's half-sister.

Oh hell.

What if Iris hurt Milla?

Was he making a mistake? But why else would Iris lie about Hunter?

If Iris had been arrested and charged with murder as a fifteen-year-old, it would have been traumatising for her. She'd spent almost a year in custody and been tried as an adult in a Crown Court. It would be understandable if she didn't trust the police – *especially* if the death of her boyfriend had been badly managed too.

Ben searched for 'Iris Hemsworth' on his phone. It was much as Dakota had told him. Paul Hemsworth had terrified his family by drunkenly firing off a gun and had accidentally shot his son Justin. Iris had cold-bloodedly retaliated. *That* was the Crown Prosecution Service's version. Her defence team, meanwhile, maintained Iris had been protecting her mother.

The defence team paid for by Dermot Graham.

Through the window, Ben could see him waltzing with Iris.

Did she know he was her father? Was he telling her now?

And once Dermot's lawyers got involved...

Iris and Dermot had their heads close together in conversation.

What were they talking about?

Dakota was correct. When one added up all the deaths that had occurred in Iris's vicinity – Paul Hemsworth, Erik Hansen, Dean Hunter, Anya March – it looked incredibly suspicious. Yet could anyone look *less* like a murderer than friendly, smiling Iris...?

But then the cleverest ones never did.

He walked back into the ballroom, watching from the shadows as Iris twirled with Dermot, until they disappeared behind the Christmas tree.

Ben moved to intercept them from the other side but, as he stepped onto the dance floor, Fliss Merriweather caught his arm.

Despite her diminutive height, her grip was surprisingly strong. 'Would you like to dance, Detective Inspector?'

He liked Fliss and any other time he'd have happily obliged, but not now. He had too much on his mind and his sense of fun, as Milla would have said, had completely deserted him.

'I'm sorry, Fliss.' He untangled himself gently. 'There's something I have to do.'

Elvira appeared behind her sister, slightly out of breath. 'Watch out, DI Taylor, my sister is armed and dangerous.'

Fliss grinned unrepentantly, waving a small twig with green oval leaves. It took him a moment to realise it was mistletoe.

'You're very sweet,' he said, 'but I'm in the middle of something. Can you give me a few minutes?'

'Don't forget!' she called after him, but he could see her attention had already fixed on the Reverend David Griffiths.

'Shouldn't that mistletoe have berries on it?' he heard Elvira mutter, as they walked away.

Ben caught a glimpse of Iris's distinctive white and black ballgown through the branches of the Christmas tree and resumed his pursuit around the edge of the dance floor, squeezing between the exuberant dancing couples. He arrived exactly where he'd seen Iris with Dermot not a moment before.

They'd vanished.

THIRTY-SIX

Ten minutes earlier...

Iris was having one of the best nights of her life. Brianna Graham's Christmas Eve Ball was a 'proper' party, the kind she'd dreamed of as a teenager growing up in that draughty old house in Primrose Hill. Unlike the many publishing parties she'd been invited to since her books hit the bestseller charts, this time she actually *knew* people.

She'd been able to wear a beautiful ballgown (a big floofy white thing with a black zigzag pattern around the hem), they'd had a lovely dinner, and she'd danced with Whit several times, as well as the Reverend David Griffiths, who was now having an enthusiastic discussion with Whit and Brianna about the merits of cosy crime versus psychological thrillers. Preferring romance and fantasy, her attention had drifted back to the dancing, but she couldn't believe it when the very person she'd been so desperate to meet came over to their little group, nodded at Brianna and then asked Iris to dance.

As it turned out, the man knew who she was too.

'Hello, Iris. Do you remember me?'

'You're Dermot Graham,' she said. 'We met last year at your house, Riverside.'

How could she have forgotten him? The man who was big in publishing, the CEO of Graham Media, the billionaire head of a family who owned a publisher, a newspaper and magazines, a television production company...

The man who'd known her mother.

'You're my father.'

She hadn't meant to say it so bluntly.

'Yes... I am. You remind me of her so much, my dear. I was so sorry when I heard...' *When I heard she'd died.* He hesitated but Iris knew what was coming next. 'I should have told you before that, when I invited you to Riverside, but the accident...'

Erik's death...

'It wasn't the right time.' He sighed. 'When your mother was alive... Well, she refused to have anything to do with me after we quarrelled. Quite rightly. I treated her badly. I have no excuse. We'd planned a reconciliation when you were about six. The three of you were supposed to have come to Raven's Edge for a holiday and to meet my family, but there was the car accident, and after that...' He sighed. 'Again, the timing was terrible...'

So were his excuses, Iris found herself thinking. She'd expected more, she really had. This was *not* the reunion she'd dreamt of. She'd been so desperate to meet him and yet now...

Now she was disappointed.

Their dancing became slower, out of time. The other dancers were forced to step around them. Dermot tried to guide her to one side of the dance floor but she pulled away and stared at him.

'I am your father,' he said, as though she hadn't grasped the concept.

Had he expected her to throw herself into his arms?

Honestly, she was thirty years old. He'd had plenty of time to contact her and tell her the truth. Why now?

Yes...

'Why now?' she asked. If she hadn't confronted him, would he have been happy for her to continue in blithe ignorance, even though they now lived in the same village?

Or had something happened?

His smile turned wary and he glanced about. People were staring at them, scenting a scandal.

'Come with me.' He took hold of her hand and led her away from the dance floor.

Iris glanced back but couldn't see Whit or her table for the Christmas tree in the centre of the ballroom. Would he worry if she disappeared?

Should *she* worry?

Where was Dermot taking her?

The answer was along the corridor and past the staircase, almost to the main entrance, where Hodges, the butler, was lingering, talking to one of the catering staff. He glanced up, saw Dermot and nodded.

'In here,' Dermot said, opening a door and ushering her through.

Now she was alone with him.

It was an office, or perhaps a conference room. A long glass table stretched down the middle and there was an empty desk beside a window. The room didn't appear to be used much.

She turned to find him staring at her, checking her over, as though he could hardly believe she was real. His smile was encouraging but Iris was too busy cataloguing his features, trying to find the ones that were repeated on her own face. The slightly beaky nose unfortunately; maybe the wide mouth? She didn't recognise anything else. His hair was grey-streaked but jet-black like hers – but also like her mother's. His eyes were a curious shade of grey, like tarnished silver.

'I know everything,' he said, which didn't register at first, until he went on to explain that he'd paid for the legal team that had helped clear her of murdering her stepfather.

Her mouth fell open. 'You *knew*? About *that*?'

'Your mother wouldn't let me meet you; she refused to let me contact you, but I reached out when I saw the story on the news. I offered her my legal team. She accepted. She was... desperate.'

It felt as though the ground had dropped away beneath her. Those months spent in the detention centre she'd tried so hard to forget. The detention centre she'd sworn never to go back to.

Her hand found the back of a nearby chair, and she leant against it.

'The inquest into Erik's death,' she said, 'did you influence that too?'

He shook his head. 'That wasn't your fault, you know that. He chose to climb that dovecote. However, the man who was found dead outside your house? Dean Hunter?'

Her insides turned to ice.

'I suspect he died *in* your house?'

She said nothing.

'My private investigator believes that the night Hunter broke into your house, he'd been hired by someone who wanted you dead. Is that what happened? Did Dean try to kill you?'

'I have no idea what you're talking about.'

Her tone was too flat to sound authentic, but she'd never been any good at lying.

'Were you able to defend yourself?' Dermot asked. 'Did you drag him to the road, so his death wouldn't be blamed on you?'

This was the man who owned a newspaper famous for digging up dirt on celebrities. No way was she going to admit anything to *him*.

'My investigator suspects Hunter was hired by Anya March to protect her husband's reputation. You walked the length of the village, telling anyone who'd listen that you believed George March was your father.'

With hindsight, that had been a mistake.

'He also tells me that the Murder Investigation Team have been making inquiries about you. They know about your past. They know about your stepfather.'

'I wouldn't hurt... I didn't... I would never...' Her legs gave way and she dropped into the chair. 'It was an *accident. Everything* was an accident.'

'When Detective Inspector Taylor puts all the pieces of this puzzle together – Paul Hemsworth, Erik Hansen, Dean Hunter, Anya March – what do you think his conclusion will be?'

'I didn't kill any of them – well, apart from Hemsworth, but I was nowhere near Erik when *he* died. I didn't even see him climb the dovecote until he fell. Dean Hunter tripped over my cat and banged his head on my fireplace and yes, I did drag his body down to the road where I knew someone would find it, because if I'd called the police they'd have believed I'd killed him. I panicked. I wasn't thinking straight. If only I had the chance to do it differently... but I thought the police would send me back to prison and I couldn't bear it. I *can't* go through that again.'

'I know,' Dermot said, but his voice was gentle. 'I'm here to help. Tell me about Anya. How did she die?'

'Another accident. Anya was trying to push *me* off the cliff.'

'You see that's the problem. One person, yet so many "accidents"...'

She risked glancing up, but his face was expressionless.

'You have two choices,' he said. 'We can call DI Taylor in now and explain the whole story to him. Each event will have to be investigated properly. You'll be taken into custody...'

'The other choice?' she said quickly.

'We'll get you out of here; take you somewhere far away,

where you can stay for a few months while this is sorted out. I'll turn everything over to my legal team and let them control what happens and when. You'll need to meet with the police and give them your full cooperation. You may be taken into custody. You may be charged with either murder or manslaughter for the deaths of Dean and Anya. I can't prevent any of that from happening, but if this does go to trial, we'll be fully prepared.'

'I understand. I've accidentally killed someone. I have to pay for that... But is there a third choice?'

'We hide you and give you a new identity, but you can never come back.'

Is that what she wanted? Run away from justice? *Hide?*

'I have friends, a career...' *A life.* 'I like it here.'

'You can't come back,' he repeated, emphasising each word.

'You'd do that? You'd risk yourself, for me?'

'You're my daughter,' he said.

'In which case...' She closed her eyes and prayed that she was about to make the right decision. 'I'll take choice number two.'

THIRTY-SEVEN

Dermot took out his phone and sent a message, and then one of his staff quietly entered, closing the door behind him.

'Miss Evergreen,' Dermot said, 'may I introduce you to Gavin?'

Who the heck was Gavin?

The man didn't speak, merely inclined his head.

'Gavin will escort you to a more... private exit. It wouldn't be a good idea for you to leave via the front entrance.'

'OK...' Iris realised she was putting a lot of trust in this man, who *said* he was her father, but what did she *really* know about him?

Gavin opened the door and indicated that she should pass through.

Iris hesitated, wondering if Dermot might kiss her cheek or shake her hand, but he merely said, 'I'll be in touch.'

She took one last look at him as she stepped into the hall, but he'd already turned his attention to his phone.

Gavin took her through to a busy kitchen at the back of the house and asked her to wait in a small office.

After five minutes Hodges appeared, slightly out of breath.

'Hello, Miss Evergreen. I'm sorry to have kept you waiting. I was delayed by Detective Inspector Taylor. He was looking for you. A matter of some importance, I believe? Would you like to speak with him?'

Was this some kind of trick? Had Dermot led her here, only to betray her to the police?

'No! Please, I—'

'It's your decision, Miss Evergreen. If you wish to avoid him, I suggest we leave the house this way.' He winked before flourishing a bunch of keys and unlocking a white door on the far side of the office.

Beyond it was a descending flight of stone steps. Iris followed the butler to the bottom and ended up in an extensive wine cellar, which must have stretched a good way beneath the house.

This did not look like an exit. Had she misunderstood? Did Dermot intend for her to hide down here? For how long?

Before panic could set in, Hodges pushed gently at the nearest wooden rack. A soft 'click' and it swung back to reveal the entrance to a dark tunnel.

Iris regarded it dubiously. Did Hodges honestly expect her to go in there? She'd seen horror movies with less scary tunnels than that.

And let's not forget: Who the *hell* had their own secret passage?

Just who *was* Dermot Graham?

A small alcove was set into the tunnel wall, containing a shelf holding a couple of small torches and a pack of batteries.

Hodges handed her one of the torches. 'If you'll follow me, Miss Evergreen? We'll soon have you out of here and no one will be any the wiser.'

It was the 'no one will be any the wiser' part that worried her.

If she were to be locked in this tunnel, no one would ever find her.

Hodges picked up his own torch, switched it on and stepped into the tunnel.

When she didn't follow, he glanced back. 'Miss Evergreen?'

'Oh, bloody hell,' she muttered, and stepped into the tunnel.

The door immediately clicked shut behind her, as though on a timer or sensor. It was not reassuring. Neither was the pitch-black darkness that now surrounded her, apart from a little white light bobbing along the tunnel in front of her.

Was that Hodges? *Leaving* her here?

She gathered up the voluminous skirt of her ballgown, switched on the torch and hurried after him.

If Dermot was so rich, why hadn't he installed electricity down here?

'Electricity requires maintenance.' Hodges's voice echoed back to her, as though she'd spoken aloud. 'The only people who know about this tunnel are Mr Graham and myself, otherwise it would no longer be "secret".'

Perhaps she should have a tunnel installed at Raven's Hollow? Not that she'd be living there anymore – not unless Dermot could clear her name. Why was she running away? Wouldn't that make her seem more guilty?

Her conscience added a helpful montage of what had happened the last time she'd been arrested by the police. The horror of the many months spent in custody in that detention centre before her case had come to trial and she'd been exonerated of all charges. If Dermot hadn't come to her rescue then, would she have been sent to prison? Locked up and forgotten? It didn't bear thinking about.

It didn't help that she'd been unable to feel any guilt or remorse about killing Hemsworth. He'd shot at her mother and poor, darling Justin had died instead. *That* was the guilt she'd always felt. That she'd moved too slowly to save him. She deserved to be sent to prison for that. Not for killing that abusive pig of a stepfather, or for accidentally tripping up a burglar who would have been happy to see her suffocate, or even watching Anya March slide over that cliff – but for failing her family when they needed her most.

The tunnel was icy cold and damp. There were little frozen puddles on the concrete floor. They must be walking beneath the lake. Knowing the lake was man-made and only a metre or so deep did not make Iris feel any safer.

Her beautiful gown would be ruined. Her shoes were certainly wrecked.

How Justin would have laughed if he could see her now. All dressed up for a society ball – and sneaking away down a dark, narrow tunnel.

Even before Hemsworth's arrival in their family, her mother had teased Iris for living in her own make-believe world. When Justin had died, Iris had refused to accept it. Why should she? If she read a book and didn't like the ending, she'd create a new one in her head.

So she'd created an alternative universe, where Justin hadn't died but had gone to university and graduated with honours. He'd had his pick of a glittering career but, being Justin, had decided to take up a position in a little town in New York state. He had the job he'd always wanted, he'd met a girl, he'd fallen in love. Everything that had been stolen from him by Hemsworth had fallen back into place.

'We're here,' Hodges said, suddenly stopping. 'This is the tricky bit. I'll go up first and hold the hatch open.'

Hatch?

She shone the torch past him and saw more stone steps leading up to a square metal door in the ceiling, similar to a manhole cover. She was expected to scramble through *that*? In a *ballgown*?

Great.

'If you could extinguish your torch, Miss Evergreen?'

And be left in the dark?

She couldn't be bothered to argue. This was so surreal it was easier to go with the flow.

'I'll head up the steps first,' Hodges said.

Should he be doing all this clambering about at his age? She watched nervously as he reached the top of the steps, switched his own torch off and then pushed against the hatch.

Unlike regular manhole covers it was hinged, with a handle on this side enabling it to be lowered silently. Hodges continued up the steps and disappeared through the gap, surprisingly nifty for a man who must be in his seventies. Then his silhouette reappeared and he held out his hand towards her.

'Up you come, Miss Evergreen. There's no one about.'

Thank goodness for that! She followed him up the steps and, although there was one moment when she thought her dress might not fit, somehow she squeezed everything through the hatch and stepped onto the gravel surface of Hartfell's car park.

Hodges closed the hatch and locked it with one of his keys. It was half-hidden beneath some shrubs. No one would give it a second glance.

Genius!

(Although she'd still like to know why Dermot Graham felt the need to have his own secret exit.)

'All right, Miss Evergreen?'

'Yes, thank you.' How calm she sounded.

'Excellent. We have a car waiting to take you home. Mr Graham suggests one medium-sized suitcase, packed as quickly as possible, because if the police can't find you here, their next stop will be Raven's Hollow.'

As if she needed reminding!

He led her over to a black Range Rover lurking in a dark

corner of the car park and opened one of the back passenger doors.

'Sidney, Mr Graham's personal driver, will take you to Raven's Hollow,' he said cheerfully, before slamming the door.

'But—' She'd thought Hodges was going to take her home but she supposed it made sense that each member of Dermot's staff had their designated role.

A small voice at the back of her mind wondered why Dermot had felt the need to delegate at all. She was starting to feel like an unwanted parcel. Had this all been arranged so that she wouldn't cause him any embarrassment?

She fastened her seatbelt but slid down in the seat, hoping no one she knew had seen her leave. What an ignominious end to her evening.

Hi, I'm your long-lost daughter!

Great – but you need to leave the country as quickly as possible.

Sidney – was that his first name or his last? – drove away from Hartfell smoothly but extremely fast down the long tarmac drive. The wide, double gates opened on his approach, and he took a right turn towards the village.

'Um, where are you taking me?'

Hodges had said Sidney would take her home, but she had to be certain. The last thing she wanted was to be deposited in the middle of nowhere with only the clothes she had on.

'Your home, Raven's Hollow,' Sidney replied. 'You'll have twenty minutes to pack before we head off to the Southampton Airport FBO Terminal to catch your flight.'

'A *private plane?*'

'That's right, miss.'

What *had* she got herself into?

THIRTY-EIGHT

If she was going to be travelling in a private plane all to herself, Iris thought, she might as well stay in her ballgown. It would save time. She filled a (probably larger than Dermot would have liked) suitcase with more practical clothes, along with her favourite toiletries, and a couple of books she hadn't got around to reading, then left it by the front door. She found a thick wool coat that wasn't covered in mud, slung it over her ballgown and changed her high heels for a pair of boots. Her bag was in the sitting room. She checked she had everything she might need, including her laptop, tablet, phone, chargers and, most importantly of all, a passport, which luckily was new and therefore still in-date.

Then she found a cardboard box, lined it with a towel and put that in the hall.

'Sparkle! Where are you? We're going on a trip.'

It occurred to her that the cat hadn't come to greet her as she usually did when Iris returned. Had something happened to her?

The library was empty, including Sparkle's favourite windowsill above the radiator, as was the sitting room and kitchen. Iris eventually found the cat hiding amongst a forest of legs beneath the long table in the dining room, looking mutinous.

'Honestly, Sparkle! This is no time to play hide-and-seek.'

Sure enough, before she'd finished speaking, someone rapped hard on the front door.

'We've got to go!' Iris dropped to her knees and crawled beneath the dining table. But she'd forgotten about the wide ballgown and soon became stuck. 'Sparkle! Please! I can't leave you here.'

As she reached towards the cat, Sparkle flattened her ears and crouched back, hissing.

The knock came again, louder this time.

'Sparkle, you do pick your moments.' Iris went into reverse, shaking the skirts of the gown back into position, and returned to the hallway. Picking up the suitcase, she opened the door and threw it at the driver. 'Nearly done. I've just got to catch the cat.'

But instead of Sidney, a man in a dinner jacket staggered backwards under the weight of her suitcase, his russet hair flopping over his forehead.

'*Whit?*'

He put the suitcase down and pushed his black-rimmed glasses back up over the bridge of his nose, blinking a couple of times. 'You're leaving?'

Well, this wasn't awkward at all.

'Yes.' She could hardly lie, but how to explain? Maybe she shouldn't. 'Sorry.'

Sidney came up to the front door with a carefully blank expression and took the suitcase from beside Whit, who hardly seemed to notice.

'We have to go, Miss Evergreen.'

They had a plane to catch. She knew that. It didn't matter that it was a private plane, it still had an allocated slot. If she missed it the plane wouldn't be allowed to take off and all this would have been for nothing. She could have handed herself in to DI Taylor and saved everyone the trouble.

'You're running away,' Whit said.

Bother.

'Yes—'

'Don't say "sorry".'

Oh no... She'd been so caught up in her panic since DI Taylor had worked out the truth about Dean's death that she'd not stopped to consider the ramifications. She was leaving Raven's Edge – she might never see it again, especially if Dermot's intervention on her behalf failed. She'd never see *any* of the people again: Harriet, Ellie...

She'd never see Whit.

'Damn.'

Sparkle, typically, came to see what was going on, sitting on the mat and looking hopefully up at Whit.

'Oh, *now* you've decided you want to come along,' Iris muttered.

'You're running away but you're taking the cat?' Whit said.

She said nothing but handed over her bag when Sidney returned. If he thought it beneath him to carry a woman's handbag, he said nothing, returning with it to the car.

'Can you at least tell me why?'

She shook her head, not at all confident that her voice would come out without a wobble.

'Why not?' His tone was gentler this time. 'You're heading off to the airport in one of Dermot Graham's cars, wearing a ballgown. I'm not an idiot, Iris. I can tell when something is up.'

'I don't want you to think badly of me.'

On the far side of Whit, Sidney had returned. His expression was impassive, as ever, but his arms were folded and he was tapping one finger against his bicep.

'Could you give us a minute?' Whit asked him. 'Please?'

'One minute,' he said, abruptly turning away, 'and that cat has to have its own passport and be microchipped.'

'I'm not going without the cat!' Iris had another go at picking her up, but Sparkle sidestepped and hid behind Whit's legs.

'Iris,' Whit said firmly, 'tell me what's going on.'

She glanced over at Sidney, now leaning back against the car. He was out of earshot but as soon as he saw her glance in his direction, he raised his arm and pointed to his watch.

'I had a break-in,' Iris said quickly, 'a few days ago. The man tried to suffocate me by locking me in my glass coffin but he tripped over Sparkle and hit his head on the dragon's snout on the fireplace in the library. He was killed.'

Whit said nothing, his face as blank as Sidney's as he waited for her to continue.

'I don't understand,' he said, when she didn't speak. 'Why do you need to run away? Are you worried about the press finding out?'

The press were the least of her problems. Iris found she couldn't look him in the eye and stared at his white bow tie instead.

'I didn't report the death to anyone. I didn't call an ambulance – it was obvious he was dead – and I didn't call the police.' She swallowed. Her behaviour sounded so appalling, so cold-hearted and selfish now she was explaining it (excusing herself?) to someone else. 'On top of that, I dragged the body out onto the pavement and left it there, hoping that when it was found, everyone would assume he'd been the victim of a hit-and-run.'

He blinked again. 'Did you panic?'

'Quite the opposite. It was very odd. I felt calm, as though all my emotions had been switched off.'

'That sounds like shock. Why do you think you did that?'

'It wasn't the first time someone had died in front of me. I remembered what happened last time and I assumed the police would behave the same way. And that once the police found out about the other deaths, they'd immediately believe I killed this man deliberately. Last time, I was locked up until the case got to court. I didn't want to go through all that again. I *couldn't*. At the time, it made perfect sense to me.'

'Other... deaths?'

She tried to grimace but her mouth wouldn't work the way she wanted it to.

'You mentioned the ex-boyfriend, Erik Hansen,' Whit said. 'There was another?'

She glanced towards Sidney, but he was leaning against the car, talking on his phone. Hopefully not to Dermot, who'd be asking why they weren't already on their way to the airport.

'I was fifteen years old,' she said, 'and living with my mother, stepfather and younger brother in Primrose Hill. With hindsight, perhaps my stepfather thought my mother was rich because she lived in a nice house. I expect she was given it by my father, as compensation for him abandoning her when she was pregnant. I only remember that my stepfather gradually became more resentful when he realised we were broke and Mum refused to sell the house. He drowned his sorrows in alcohol and then one day he began shooting off his gun in the sitting room – a "joke", he called it. He took sadistic pleasure, firing the bullets closer and closer to my mother. He was a good shot. Perhaps he was trying to intimidate her, but we didn't know that. We were too terrified to move. Then my younger brother ran in front of her, to protect her, and was killed instead. He was twelve years old. My stepfather was horrified. He threw down the gun and collapsed in hysterics, but I was so angry at all the years we'd put up with him bullying us, I picked it up and shot him.

'When the case came to Court I was found not guilty. It helped that Dermot Graham – although I didn't know this at the time – paid for the best lawyers, who claimed I'd acted in self-defence. But it was a lie. I killed him deliberately.'

Whit was silent. She knew he'd walk away, something she deserved completely.

Instead, he said, 'If you hadn't killed your stepfather, he'd have got drunk again the next week, and the same thing would have happened.'

'That's what my mother said. She blamed herself for not kicking him out as soon as she realised what he was like.'

'It wasn't your fault,' he said softly.

'I'm a murderer...'

'No, you're not.' He reached out for her, as though to soothe her, but she stepped abruptly back.

'I'm dangerous. People die around me.'

He shrugged. 'I've only known you a few days but you seem like a kind person.'

'Seem?' she repeated bitterly.

'You *are* a kind person. OK, you're slightly eccentric but isn't everyone?'

'*Whit!*'

He grinned and somehow she knew what he was going to say next – and beat him to it. '*Please* don't say "nobody's perfect".'

'That line's been taken,' – his smile was rueful – 'but Iris, to me you *are* perfect.'

She burst into tears.

'Excuse me?' Sidney was standing beside them, and they hadn't even noticed. 'Miss Evergreen, you have a plane to catch. If you miss it, it's not just a case of catching the next one to come along. The police will stop you leaving the country and there's nothing Mr Graham will be able to do about it. He's good but he's not a miracle worker. DI Taylor knows you've left the party and is probably on his way here right now.' He gave

Whit a scathing look. 'Neither of you have time for...' – he gestured exasperatedly – 'whatever *this* is.'

'He's right,' Whit said. 'You'd better go. When this is sorted out, I'll still be here. We can continue this conversation then.'

'I'll call you,' Iris said.

'You'd better not. The police will be able to work out where you are from the call. I've seen it on TV.'

Sidney shook his head as though they were both idiots. 'I'll be in the car, waiting.' He pointed to Sparkle. 'If that cat isn't in a box, it isn't coming.'

Whit bent to pick Sparkle up with no trouble at all. 'Aren't you a cutie,' he said. The cat purred.

Iris knew how she felt. 'Can you look after Sparkle for me, Whit? I'm not sure when I'll be coming back.'

'Sure,' he said. 'What about the house?'

She glanced back into the hall. All the lights were on, the heating was on, the door was wide open – and she was about to walk out and leave it like that?

'Do you think you could look after that too? I'm sure Dermot will sort something out, but in the meantime?'

Sidney began revving the engine.

'I've got to go,' she sighed.

'I know.' Whit leant forward and kissed her.

Sidney blasted the horn three times.

Whit broke off to rest his forehead on hers.

'We'll be here when you get back,' he said. 'Both me and Sparkle.'

Whit didn't watch the car drive away. Instead, he went into the house and carefully made sure everything was securely locked up and that the lights were switched off. He even turned the boiler down to minimum. He collected a few things for Sparkle and found a box to carry her in. He thought she might make a fuss about being put into it, but once he'd found one of Iris's cardigans on the back of a chair in the library and put it in the bottom of the box, Sparkle got into it quite happily.

Everything was going really well – a little too well, because as he exited the house and locked the door behind him, someone came up behind him.

He turned slowly, recognising the tall blond man standing in front of him, also wearing formal attire.

'She's gone,' Whit said. 'You're too late.'

'So I gathered,' DI Taylor replied. 'Where's she gone? To the airport?'

'I couldn't tell you.'

'Can't or won't?' the DI said, his pleasant voice belying his words.

'Whatever you like.'

The DI sighed heavily. 'Honestly, Whit? Come on, you know me – you hardly know her. If you don't tell me where she's gone, you're aiding and abetting.'

'Yes.' Whit lifted his chin. 'I am.'

The DI rolled his eyes. 'Are you *trying* to get arrested?'

Whit shrugged, but when he stepped around the DI, the other man made no move to stop him, or even follow him to his car.

It turned out to be tricky to open the car door while holding a box with a cat in it. Whit didn't want to put the box down, in case Sparkle got it into her head to leap out and explore the forest, but then an arm appeared and opened the door for him.

Whit slid the box onto the passenger seat, loosely dropped the flaps over Sparkle's head and tied a seatbelt around the box to keep it from sliding off. Was that secure enough? What if Sparkle decided to jump out? Was it even legal? He glanced up at the DI, who shook his head pityingly.

'Better not let a police officer catch you,' he said, before putting his hands into his pockets and returning to his own car.

Whit drove home.

Very carefully and very slowly.

THIRTY-NINE

Christmas Day

Whit parked in his usual space, around the back of the bookshop. He lived above the store, in what had once been the attic. His flat was small – he preferred 'snug' – and he was forever banging his head on either the supporting beams or the sloping roof, but it was his home and he loved it. He owned the entire building as well as the shop – thanks to a loan from an uncle who'd known it had been his ambition to work in a bookshop ever since he was a child. When Whit had admitted this during a careers talk as a teenager, his fellow students had laughed themselves sick. *They'd* wanted to be football players or pop stars but, fifteen years later, how many of *them* could say they'd achieved their dream?

Sparkle was surprisingly docile as he carried her inside, cuddled inside his tailcoat to keep her warm. He was slightly nervous about doing this, because he knew cats could turn on you for no reason – happy to play one moment, attempting to disembowel you the next – but Sparkle seemed supremely unbothered. He could even feel the vibration of her purr.

The back door led to the same kitchen where he'd given Iris a pile of his stock to sign. It seemed like a lifetime ago.

He paused by the table, remembering her sitting there, black hair tumbling over her shoulders. He'd been struck by how friendly she was. Would he ever see—

'Ow!'

Sparkle had ruined the moment by sticking her claws through his shirt.

Apparently Her Highness wanted to be put on the ground.

'Enough with the claws,' he admonished her, unhooking them from his shirt and placing her gently on the floor, 'or we'll no longer be friends.' While she sniffed around the cabinets, swishing her tail – presumably unhappy with her new home – he poured her some water into a bowl, which she ignored with a disgusted expression and pranced into the bookshop instead.

The possibilities for this all to go horribly wrong were endless. He bit his lip as he watched her weave in and out of the mounds of books. This was the test. What would she do when presented with the perfect cat playground?

But she stepped carefully around the stacks and didn't try to knock them over or climb any of them, or even jump onto a bookshelf, any of which would end in disaster.

Although, when he went to double-check the front door was secure, he did catch her having a sneaky play with the fake ivy trailing from the display table – the same table which Iris had walked into the first day she came into the shop.

He swallowed what felt like a lump in his throat.

'Oh, Iris...'

Once they went upstairs, Whit thought Sparkle might make herself at home on the sofa, or even his bed. But no, Sparkle had chosen her own happy place – jumping onto the windowsill above the radiator so she could gaze down onto the street.

And wait for Iris to come back to Raven's Edge?

'You and me both, Sparkle,' he sighed, staring out the window at the deserted street. 'You and me both.'

As he turned away, a light caught his eye.

A smart black Range Rover driving slowly down the high street.

It couldn't be...

'Iris?'

He was hallucinating. Why would Iris come back to Raven's Edge? She'd be arrested! And OK, she hadn't deliberately killed anyone but she'd still have to prove that, perhaps in court. She might have to spend time on remand, which was why she'd wanted to leave in the first place.

Beside him, on the windowsill, Sparkle was pacing up and down, her tail swishing.

The car stopped.

Whit held his breath.

A woman in a white ballgown got out.

'Iris!' He banged on the window and waved, but she didn't hear him; she was too intent on running up to his front door.

Sidney deposited a suitcase and a handbag on the pavement, gave Whit a sarcastic salute and drove off.

'Oh, bloody hell!' Whit said, running downstairs, and then again when he accidentally set off the alarm by opening the front door.

'I came back,' Iris said, throwing herself into his arms, while Sparkle fussed around them both. 'I'm going to give myself up to the police and confess everything.'

Everything?

'Excellent idea,' Whit said cautiously, 'but maybe seek some legal advice first?'

'Won't everything be shut until the twenty-seventh?'

As this was England, more likely the 2nd of January.

'I'm sure we can sort something out,' he said.

'I'll put the kettle on,' Iris said, heading in the direction of the kitchen. 'I'd kill for a cup of tea.'

Whit stepped out onto the street to pick up Iris's suitcase, which weighed a ton, along with her handbag, and also retrieve the cat, which had decided now would be a good idea to explore the neighbourhood.

'Some cats,' he muttered to a protesting Sparkle, as he tucked her beneath his arm, 'would *love* to live in a bookshop.'

Ben went home, changed into more comfortable clothes and switched on the television to watch Alastair Sim in *Scrooge*. He tried phoning Milla again, but she didn't reply.

He'd just got to the part where Scrooge was asking Mrs Dilber what day it was, when he thought he heard a knock. Binx began fussing around the door, so Ben felt obliged to get off the sofa and see who was there.

He really hoped it wasn't carol singers.

He glanced at his watch. Ten past midnight?

Could it be a member of his team? Had they caught Iris? Not that she was exactly public enemy number one.

Cautiously, he opened the door and found Milla on the other side, wrapped up in a short scarlet coat worn over black jeans and boots, a wary smile on her face.

Did she believe he'd shut the door on her?

'Hi...' she began, as though she was still working on what to say next.

He noticed her black woolly hat had a cat face on it, complete with ears. It looked like Binx. He couldn't help but smile.

She grinned in response.

'You could have used your key,' he said. 'Don't you still have it?'

'You didn't change the locks after we split up?'

'Why would I do that?'

'Because I'm irritating, annoying, interfering—'

'Yes, but then you wouldn't be *you* – and that's why I love you.'

'That's so sweet! I love you too!'

'I know.' He opened the door so she could come inside.

She stepped into the hall and he held out his arms, expecting her to step into them, but she thrust her bag at him instead, kneeling on the floor to pet Binx.

Was it possible to be jealous of a cat?

Binx rose up on his hind legs, placing his front paws on Milla's forearm.

'Go on then,' she said, and the cat sprang up her arm and onto her shoulder, before draping himself around her neck. Milla laughed and stood up. 'Wow, Binx! Not fat-shaming or anything, but I think you've overdone the treats.'

Ben stared. He'd never seen Binx do that before.

'He likes you.'

Milla rolled her eyes. 'Of course he likes me. I feed him.'

'There's an automatic dispenser...' He broke off. Was she side-eyeing him – to the *cat*?

'It's adorable that he thinks you use that thing,' she told the cat. 'Ooh, I've just remembered. I've got you something for Christmas.'

Presumably she meant the cat.

Milla took Binx from her shoulders and placed him gently on the floor.

'Is it OK if Binx has his Christmas present now?'

'It's not as though he knows what day it is.'

'Of course he knows what day it is! Don't you, Binxy? You're a very smart cat.'

With all the fuss she was making over him, Binx certainly knew something was up, but he appeared slightly disappointed when Milla took out what looked like a tiny fishing rod with a soft toy mouse on the end.

'Look at this, Binx,' she said, dangling it in front of the cat. 'Isn't this the best thing ever?'

The cat eyed it dubiously.

'Binx, you're hurting my feelings. Can't you *pretend* to like it?'

'Maybe move the mouse a little slower?' Ben said. 'Binx is supposed to think it's prey.'

'He's not going to think it's prey, he's far too smart for that, but I thought he might like to play with it.'

Binx began washing himself.

'Oh well.' She grinned up at Ben. 'Would you like to see *your* present?'

'You've got me a present?'

'Well, duh!' She regarded him sharply. 'Don't you have one for me?'

It was entertaining to see her pout in exactly the same way that his daughter Sophie might have done.

He grinned. 'You'll have to wait a few more hours yet.'

'When I was a child, Grandma McKenzie used to allow me to open one present on Christmas Eve...'

'You've missed that opportunity. It's already Christmas Day.'

'Is it?' She grabbed his wrist and turned it so she could see his watch. 'So it is! Happy Christmas!' She threw her arms around his neck and kissed him.

He froze, unsure what he was supposed to do. Did this mean their relationship was back on?

She opened her eyes and stared into his. 'You know, you can kiss me back?'

'Is this a Christmas kiss or a "more than just good friends" kiss?'

'It can be any kind of kiss you like!'

'So we're back to being "more than just good friends"?'

'Yes – I thought we discussed that?'

Not that he remembered. 'No more non-date dates?'

'What idiot thought *that* up?'

'That would be you.'

'And *that* would be most ungentlemanly of you to say so.'

'Do you *want* me to be gentlemanly?'

'Hell, no!' Milla pulled him down to her level so that she could kiss him more comfortably.

To save getting a crick in the neck (that was *his* excuse) he scooped her into his arms – and then wasn't quite sure what to do with her.

'Upstairs,' Milla waved regally in that direction. 'We don't want to embarrass Binx.' Then she shrieked as Ben tossed her over his shoulder to make it easier for him to climb the stairs.

Binx, meanwhile, took the stuffed mouse in his mouth and, dragging the little stick behind him, jumped up onto the windowsill before settling down to happily tear the mouse into shreds.

A LETTER FROM THE AUTHOR

Dear reader,

Thank you so much for reading *Murder at Raven's Hollow*! I do hope you've enjoyed it. I have lots more mysteries planned for Ben, Harriet and their team to solve. If you'd like to be the first to hear about new releases and bonus content, you can click on the link below to sign up. Don't miss out!

www.stormpublishing.co/louise-marley

If you've enjoyed this book and could spare a few moments to leave a review that would be hugely appreciated. Even a short review can make all the difference in encouraging a reader to discover my books for the first time. Thank you so much!

As with all my books, lots of different kinds of inspiration came together to create this story.

My grandfather was a fireman, killed during the Sheffield Blitz when my mother was three years old. Like Harriet, she often talked about her sadness that she couldn't remember him and her guilt that she hadn't really missed him until she was an adult and realised she'd never get the chance to meet him. She had to rely on other people's memories to build up an idea of what his character had been like.

My grandmother never really recovered from his death, so there were no photos of him in her flat. It was only after she died that we found an album, begun when he'd been a teenager, filled with photos of people and places we didn't know. Like Iris, I went back to where my grandparents had lived and tried to follow in their footsteps, matching up the photos to the places. It was a very emotional experience.

If you've read my previous books, you'll know how much I love fairy tales! I've always thought it unfair that the stepmother is usually cast as the villain, so my story has a twist. Another idea I wanted to explore was that people are flawed; they can be both good *and* bad, and that everyone makes stupid mistakes.

The buildings and places in my stories are made-up, but often inspired by somewhere real. The idea of a café entirely covered in Virginia creeper (The Witch's Brew), was suggested by Tu Hwnt I'r Bont Tea Rooms in Llanrwst, close to where I used to live. Whit's bookstore (The Secret Grimoire) owes its slightly chaotic feel to the wonderful Shakespeare and Company in Paris. For a bookworm like me, the idea of a store so completely crammed with books that they won't all fit onto the shelves is absolute bliss.

Finally, I've always been fascinated by ancient burial mounds and the legends that surround them, so one was bound to find its way into one of my books sooner or later. The chamber in my story is loosely based on one that was practically next door when I lived on Anglesey. Bryn Celli Ddu (the Mound in the Dark Grove) is a neolithic tomb where bones, arrowheads and carved stones have been found.

I had such fun bringing everything together for this story. I do hope you've enjoyed reading it!

Thank you for being part of this journey with me. Would you like to know what happens next in Raven's Edge? Are there any other buried bodies/secrets waiting for Ben and the Murder Investigation Team to discover? Will Milla keep working for Drake? Can Harriet and Mal ever learn to get along? Do stay in touch. I have so many new stories planned!

KEEP IN TOUCH WITH THE AUTHOR

You can contact me at louise@louisemarley.co.uk. I'd love to hear from you!

You can also find me here:

Website: www.louisemarley.co.uk
Raven's Edge: ravens-edge.co.uk

 facebook.com/LouiseMarleyAuthor
 x.com/LouiseMarley
instagram.com/louisemarleywrites

ACKNOWLEDGEMENTS

Huge thanks to Kathryn Taussig for picking *Murder at Raven's Edge* off the slush pile two years ago and asking if I'd ever thought of turning it into a series. Cue panic: but look where we are now! Her invaluable advice and insight have helped me keep my characters in line and breathe life into the village of Raven's Edge. Also, a big thank-you to Oliver Rhodes, Kate Smith, Alexandra Holmes and the fabulous team at Storm for all the hard work that goes on behind the scenes – without whom you wouldn't be reading this book!

There were times while writing this story when I thought *I'd* been cursed by fairies, after catching one virus after another. Thank you to my wonderful family for taking over all the cooking and the chores, and for continuing with them even after I got better. Um, I did tell you I'd got better, didn't I...?

Thank you to Novelistas Ink for the writerly chat and pep talks. We always have the *best* fun at our book launches. Special thanks to Lottie Cardew for her encouragement and the trips to Gladstone's Library for coffee and cake!

Finally, a big hug to my lovely readers for the support, the kind-hearted messages and the wonderful reviews. You are all brilliant!

Printed in Great Britain
by Amazon

54873676R00199